MW00890345

Steamsworn

Books by Eric R. Asher

The Steamborn Series

Steamborn

Steamforged

Steamsworn

Vesik, The Series:

(Recommended for Ages 17+)

Days Gone Bad

Wolves and the River of Stone

Winter's Demon

This Broken World

Destroyer Rising

STEAMSWORN

THE STEAMBORN SERIES, BOOK THREE

By

ERIC R. ASHER

Copyright © 2016 by Eric R. Asher
Print Edition

All rights reserved. This book or any portion thereof may not be reproduced or used in any manner whatsoever without the express written permission of the publisher except for the use of brief quotations in a book review.

This is a work of fiction. Names, characters, businesses, places, events and incidents are either the products of the author's imagination or used in a fictitious manner. Any resemblance to actual persons, living or dead, or actual events is purely coincidental.

Produced by ReAnimus Press
http://www.ReAnimus.com

Edited by Indie Solutions by Murphy Rae
Cover typography by Indie Solutions by Murphy Rae
Cover artwork by Enggar Adirasa

The end shows only a path to a new beginning.

CHAPTER ONE

J ACOB WATCHED THE desert sands drift by as the crawler's treads pulled them over dunes and rocks alike. The grains of sand in the gusts of hot wind stung his face, but the ride was far smoother than that of a Walker. Here, on the northwest edge of the Burning Forest, the cacti towered higher than any he'd seen before.

A halo of fire erupted from the stone trees in the distance. It looked like the world burned, and the cacti shimmered and danced in the waves of heat. The place bore an apt name.

"Do you really think stopping the army in Dauschen will be enough?" Jacob asked, his thoughts trailing from the fiery landscape to the flames of war.

Charles scratched his wide gray beard. "I know what Archibald said, and he's not entirely wrong, but strapping all of his forces down to protect Bollwerk is a fool's gambit. We don't have the manpower to attack Fel directly. Destroying their army—not just stopping it, but destroying it in Dauschen—should be enough to force a retreat."

Jacob nodded. He wished Smith had traveled with them, but Jacob knew Mary needed the tinker more. Smith had helped build the bombs, and that was more than most anyone could do.

Jacob was going to miss Alice, too. She'd stayed behind with Gladys and George to train, so if something like Rana's abduction happened again, they'd be ready. The royal guard from Midstream had signed on with Archibald to help prepare the city for the worst. Jacob thought it was probably unnecessary, with the two giant warships docked in Bollwerk, but he knew enough to know he didn't know much about preparing for war. If all went well, it wouldn't be long until he saw her again. Until then, he at least had the memory of her lips on his cheek and the warmth of their parting hugs.

Jacob frowned and studied his hands for a moment.

"I've seen that look on a dozen soldiers," Samuel said, shifting in the front seat of the crawler to look back at Jacob.

"What?" Jacob said as his brain registered that Samuel had been speaking to him.

"You're either sick about not getting Cocoa Crunch until this little campaign is over, or you miss her."

"No," Jacob said. He gave Samuel a half frown. "That's not ..." Jacob sighed and rubbed his head. "Yeah, I miss her. It's dumb, I guess, but I didn't really realize it until Rana. After she killed him? I just wanted to take it away."

"Take what away?" Charles asked.

Jacob glanced at Charles and Samuel in turn. Drakkar stayed silent behind the levers of the crawler. Jacob took a deep breath and a small crease deepened between his eyebrows. "I didn't want her to have that memory."

Charles wore a gentle smile as he turned back to the landscape. "You're a good man, Jacob. You don't need to worry about Alice. She has a fire in her that will weather any storm."

Samuel propped his arm up on the back of his seat. The crawler jerked and bounced over a small, nearly dry creek, and the Spider Knight grinned at Jacob before turning around. The mountains soared into the sky beyond the Burning Forest. Beyond them lay the meadows, and then Dauschen.

It was there, below the streets of that fallen place, they would launch the first counterstrike.

✦　✦　✦

"This is a hell of a lot nicer when the Tail Swords aren't trying to kill you," Samuel said.

Drakkar let out a slow laugh. "It is a good rule to find shelter when the rains come to the desert, and not to be slow about it."

"It doesn't hurt to be driving around in a giant metal beast, either."

"No," Drakkar said as he pulled one of the brass levers and adjusted their angle into the mountain pass. "It does not."

The metal treads of the crawler slammed into the stone foothills with a squeal before they gained enough traction to lift the bulk of the crawler at a forty-five-degree angle. Jacob threw his arms out against the seat as he feared getting tossed out the top of the open cabin.

"No need to worry," Charles said. "There's a gyro that detects an overbalance. It can fail if you hit something too quickly, of course, but it's designed to release the gears and reverse automatically."

"What if you really needed it to try anyway?" Jacob asked. "Like if you're getting chased by an army of Tail Swords and your only hope is to crawl up a steeper wall?"

"There's an override," Charles said.

"Yes," Drakkar said as he pointed to a plunger with a ruby top. "Although, if it was only Tail Swords, and you were in a crawler of this size, run them down. They are not the smartest creatures in the desert. They will strike the metal of the crawler instead of its passengers."

"Why the hell didn't we take crawlers last time?" Samuel muttered.

"Things turned out alright," Charles said.

"Tell that to the dead people," Samuel said. "I didn't exactly have a fun time getting poisoned by Stone Dogs either."

"You lived," Drakkar said. "Be thankful for that life, and do the best you can with it."

"I get what you're saying, Drakkar, but I kind of feel like I lived just to die somewhere else."

"We all live to die somewhere else. We die when there is nowhere else for us to be. You, Spider Knight, you still have somewhere to be."

"Or he's just a stubborn bastard," Charles said.

Jacob laughed at the cutting look Samuel threw in Charles's direction.

"You're one to talk, old man," Samuel said. "I've already broken my oaths to the city and the Spider Knights. It seems a bit daft to put my life on the line for them now."

"It's not for them though," Jacob said. "We're doing this for our family, and our friends, and the people who aren't strong enough to do it for themselves. Like my dad. I mean, if he could, he'd be out here fighting with us. I know it. But he can't, so we have to."

"Kid's right," Charles said.

"I'm not a kid."

"He did have sake," Drakkar said.

Jacob's mouth twisted at the memory of the awful drink they'd had at The Fish Head. He didn't think he'd ever want to taste something that terrible again.

Charles patted Jacob's shoulder. "It's an acquired taste, boy."

"Why bother acquiring it?" Jacob asked.

"You will change your mind when you're older and have less sense," Drakkar said, shifting the steering levers to swerve around a boulder.

"I thought I was supposed to get *more* sense as I got older. At least my mom seemed to hope so."

"Jacob," Charles said as he set his arm on the edge of the crawler's door. "If men gained more sense as they got older, I would be a damn genius by now."

"You kind of are," Jacob said.

Samuel snorted and turned in his seat again. "Now I know why you needed Jacob on this trip, old man. Pad the ego a bit, eh?"

Charles gave the Spider Knight a knowing smile, but Jacob knew why Charles really had him along, and that burden came crashing back into his mind. They were on their way to Dauschen to lay waste to the military base on the southwest cliff face. Jacob's actions would kill men, and women, and whatever else was standing inside.

Jacob looked back at the Burning Forest before it vanished beyond the mountain pass. Those old stones had burned as long as history could remember, and they'd be burning long after he'd been lost to time. It was hard to reconcile that such a thing as war could seem trivial to a future generation. Now, at this moment, there was nothing more important to Jacob than freeing Ancora from the war it didn't know was coming.

The darkness of the pass closed over them, and the Burning Forest slipped into a shadowed oblivion.

CHAPTER TWO

"**A**RE YOU DONE, Smith?" Mary's tinny voice crackled through the horn above his workbench.

Smith glared at the blasted thing and seriously considered not answering. Nothing got under Mary's skin more than a lack of communication.

"Smith!"

He sighed and cranked down on the bolt above his head. Smith's body wasn't made to be wedged into tight spaces, and he was practically bent in half to reach the back of the manifold. Mary did not seem to care. She only wanted things done yesterday, so *now* was never good enough.

"Yes, Captain!" he shouted, hoping the sound would carry around the thick mesh of brass and copper pipes.

"What?"

It didn't.

Smith cursed and squeezed his left hand up toward his right shoulder. His fingertips found the switch for his biomechanics, and he cranked the tension up in his arm. With a higher output, the bolt twisted home and clinked against the washer. He might have to cut it out if he ever needed to drop the manifold again, but that was a problem for another time.

He powered his biomechanics down again and wiggled his way back out of the crawlspace between the pipes and support beams.

"What the hell are you doing down here?"

This time the voice was close, and it made him jump, cracking his head against the iron box that encased the crawlspace. "Dammit, Mary, I told you it would take a while."

"Archibald wants us down at the Council Hall."

"For what? We have more work to do."

Mary shrugged. "Something to do with Gladys, so I'm thinking we should get our asses moving instead of just floating half a mile from the docks!"

Smith sighed and wiped his hands on a towel as he stood up. It was no fault of his the old anchor had snapped off when the thrusters malfunctioned. He had warned Mary about cheap parts. Between the loss of the engine and the anchor, they had been drifting for a good three hours. Smith thought it was good luck it had happened so close to home. Mary was just pissed.

"Well?" she asked.

"Should be done. We can go."

"Good work. Let's go see what the hell Archibald wants us to get ourselves into this time."

Smith nodded, but it was not Archibald's missions that came to his mind; it was memories of their last bit of trouble—the warlord Rana, when he took Gladys. Smith could still remember the recoil of the chaingun bouncing in his hands as it roared, cutting through the warlord's men like so much wheat, and the awful sound of Alice killing Rana with a nail glove.

"Why don't you come topside? Help me dock."

Smith nodded. It was good to have things to do with his hands. Sometimes it was all he could ask, just to forget the sight of what his own hands had done. The chaingun Jacob had helped him rebuild. Charles had told Smith the boy had a mind for machines, but it almost seemed an understatement. Jacob had the potential to build the greatest wonders humanity would ever see, or its most horrifying weapons. Smith had never been fond of thin lines, but he knew he walked one now.

"What's with you?" Mary asked. "You've been quiet since Gareth Cave."

He had known Mary for quite a long time now, and her ability to pluck unsaid things from his mind grew no less disturbing with time.

Smith blew a breath out through his nose as he grabbed the ladder that lead to the deck. "I should not have rebuilt that gun, or let Jacob help me with it."

Mary paused at the hatch and glanced down at him. "Smith, if you hadn't, we'd all be dead. We'd be deader than dead, and Alice and Gladys would probably be enslaved in Rana's harem in some godforsaken hole of a city.

"Why don't you think about that instead of this ridiculous guilt trip you're running yourself through, hmm? You've killed more men than that before." She hopped up the last rung and swung out onto the deck.

Mary was right, and he knew it. He had never killed anyone who did not need killing. To keep Gladys out of the hands of a warlord, he would do it again. The memory of that devil's hands on her filled him with a rage like he had never felt. He had *reveled* in it, in the blood and bone and death, and part of him knew that was very wrong. Vengeance could be a powerful thing, and he had dealt it with abandon.

Smith ground his teeth as he reached the top of the ladder, pulled on the handrail, and stepped onto the deck.

Mary vanished into the cabin and Smith followed. If there was one thing he was sure of, he was glad to have Mary with him. If there were two things he was sure of, things were going to get a lot worse before they had a chance to get better.

✧　✧　✧

"THANKS FOR COMING with me," Gladys said. She led the way into the stables.

"Happy to," Alice said. "Plus, training with George? Sounds fun." She paused just inside the door and dug through the top layer of dead Sweet-Flies. There were a couple juicy ones, almost bigger than her hand. She stacked them up in the crook of her left arm.

"What are you doing?" Gladys asked as she turned around.

"Getting a snack for George."

"George won't eat those."

"Not that George, Drakkar's Walker George." Alice headed over to the far stable. It stretched to the ceiling, completely enclosing the Walker in its steel cage. "Hi George!"

The coiled beast's legs rolled in a hypnotizing cadence, thumping against the floor. His antennae shot straight up.

"Open the gate for me, would you?"

Gladys eyed Alice like she might be out of her mind, but she slid the stable door open anyway.

George shot across the wide stable and reared up in front of Alice, his antennae pounding her shoulders and probing the Sweet-Flies. Alice held up one of the bugs and George speared it with one of his barb-like forelegs. She knew they held enough venom to kill a person in one strike, but Alice felt comfortable around George.

The Walker shuffled closer and started digging the flies out of Alice's grasp while she patted him between his two enormous faceted eyes.

"Oh gods, is he eating you?" Gladys squeaked from outside the stable.

Alice laughed and let out a stuttered, "No," as George smashed his face into her chest, probably trying to find more Sweet-Flies. When his quest failed, he retreated to the opposite corner of the stable, tossing sand and hay into the air before he coiled up once more. Alice brushed her denim skirt off, stepped outside, and slid the gate closed.

"Is everything okay?" the other George asked as he stepped up behind Gladys, hand on his sword.

"Oh, it's great," Gladys said. "I thought I was watching my friend get eaten by a giant venomous Walker. You know, just like any other day."

"What?"

"She went in the stable and fed it *by hand!*"

"It's a him," Alice said, "and his name is George."

"So I've been told," George said with a laugh. "Gladys tells me you're interested in training a bit, yes?"

Alice nodded.

"Gladys is probably more advanced than you. She can at least use you as target practice. This could work well."

"Thanks for the vote of confidence there, Royal George."

"What?"

"I don't want you to think I'm talking to the Walker. Royal George it is."

"She calls you that when you're not around," Gladys said with a grin. "It has a nice ring to it."

George rubbed his forehead. "It's going to be a trying day."

"Please," Alice said. "I'm one of the best Waltz dancers ever to come out of Ancora. I finished a dance with *Jacob* without my feet getting stepped on *once.*"

"And so modest," George said as he drew his sword. "But tell me, do you know how to disarm a—"

George almost squealed as Alice lunged at him, hooked her foot behind the larger man's ankle, and pushed. She watched with a great deal of satisfaction as he tried to catch his balance and then flopped onto one of the dried haystacks.

"Well, that's one way," George said. "I still could have done tremendous damage with this sword as I fell."

"Not likely," Alice said. "You were too surprised that you were falling. Any strike would've been sloppy and easily avoided."

"You know how to fight?" Gladys said. "I mean, I knew you did after Rana, to some degree anyway, but …"

Alice didn't like remembering Rana. She'd do it again if she had to, but that sound … that sound of his skull shattering beneath something *she* had done. Alice shivered.

"Sorry, I didn't mean to bring that up," Gladys said.

"It's okay."

"Well," George said, "clearly you know some basics. Let's try teaching you some more advanced self-defense skills. They may become very important in a very short time."

✧　✧　✧

ALICE WASN'T SURE how long they stayed there, sparring and falling and cursing. Gladys could give as good as she got, giving George a run for his money and even landing some painful kicks in the process.

George was the best kind of teacher. Quick to praise a well-executed move, but even quicker to explain how being sloppy could get you killed. He always wore a smile, whether you'd just landed a kick to his ribs, or he'd just slammed you onto a haystack for the tenth time.

"You're fast, Alice," George said, releasing his grip from around her neck, "but not so fast I can't catch you."

Alice wasn't entirely sure what had happened. She'd dodge a blow from George's sheathed sword, there was a pressure on her neck, and then she was upside down before she crashed onto a haystack. She blinked at the upside-down world.

"Gladys, strike."

Alice twisted around on the loose straws of hay and watched. She could stare for hours at the deadly grace that was Gladys. Where George was quick, efficient, and brutal, Gladys flowed from one move to the next. A high, arcing kick followed a jab and a sweep until the momentum carried her into a stiff mid-kick.

Alice didn't think Gladys moved faster than her, but Gladys always had another move ready, another defense, another trick.

George reached out and grabbed a slow punch from Gladys, and then he cursed as he realized his mistake. Gladys wrapped her own hand around George's wrist and launched herself into his arm. Her legs wrapped around the royal guard's neck as she bent his arm backwards.

A choking gasp filled the stable as Gladys tightened her grip, immobilizing the arm and cutting off George's air in one vicious attack. He tapped rapidly on her arm and she released him.

He took three deep, rattled breaths as he rubbed at his throat. "One wonders if there's any position you *can't* choke me from."

Gladys grinned as she walked toward Alice and flopped onto the haystack beside her.

"Why didn't you do that when … you know?" Alice asked.

"Because she is a smart girl," George said, lowering himself onto the edge of a barrel. "If she had attacked Rana, even killed Rana, her fate could have been a thousand times worse."

Gladys stared at her hands. "I should have killed him." She glanced at Alice. "Then you wouldn't have had to."

"It's okay," Alice said. "I'm just glad you're safe and we're all alive."

"I wish I could have seen it," George said. "Did you know Rana's family once kept fiery slaves? People with hair as bright as the sun, that's what they called them. It could have been your ancestors. It's a crazy thing to think about, and then you kill him. There is irony in that, Alice. A great and wonderful irony."

Alice was … well, she wouldn't say she was happy, but she was glad George derived some kind of pleasure from that awful day.

"We'll continue tomorrow morning. I would like to focus more on weapons training. It's best not to get into close quarters if you do not need to." Something crackled and squawked, and George fumbled at his collar.

"Say again?"

"Come to the Council Hall. I'd like to speak with you and Gladys."

"Alice is with us."

"Perfect! Bring her too, please, and make it quick. We have urgent business to discuss."

"Was that Archibald?" Gladys asked as she narrowed her eyes at George. "What happened to shunning the "pale-skinned monkey's mechanical abominations?"

"I ... umm ... never ... well ... I ..." George rubbed his hands together and offered Alice a weak smile. "I meant no offense, my friend. Please, take no offense. It was only a joke."

"Please," Alice said as she waved her hand. "I've heard worse from school kids. Besides, I never imagined I'd get to see you flustered."

"It's an art form," Gladys said with a sage nod of her head.

"You don't think he meant George the Walker, do you?" Alice asked, pointing at the infinite nest of legs in the corner. George the Walker popped up his antennae, twitched them a few times, and then returned to sleep. Alice had promised Drakkar she'd come and visit the Walker while the Cave Guardian was away with Jacob, and now she felt she'd done her job quite thoroughly.

George—the Royal George, as Alice had come to think of him— folded his collar back down and sighed. "I make one oath to my king, never realizing I'd doomed myself to a life of babysitting."

"We better get moving," Gladys said. "Archibald sounded pretty firm about getting there fast."

George nodded and locked the stable behind him. "We'll take one of the crawlers."

"There's one here now," one of the stable boys said, apparently having overhead George.

"Thank you," George said as he followed Gladys out the wide sliding doors.

Alice trailed behind them. When the stable boy looked up and met her eyes, she said, "Get some better Sweet-Flies. George likes the big fat ones."

The boy looked after the Royal Guard before his head jerked back to Alice. "Oh, you mean the Walker."

Alice grinned and left the stable boy to ponder her meaning. She was pretty sure he'd get better Sweet-Flies for the occupants of the stables either way.

CHAPTER THREE

ARCHIBALD WAITED. HE'D made the calls, and he knew his people would come as fast as they could. It was strange to think of some of them as 'his people.' They weren't, really. They were from Midstream and Ancora and far older places he could scarcely recall the name of. Common goals brought people together better than anything.

He'd always been good at waiting, but now impatience had him drumming his fingers and shuffling the papers laid upon the bench. Charles's plan was bold, vicious, and everything he expected from the old tinker. It was exactly what they needed, no matter how much Archibald didn't like the risk.

The tall metal door to the Hall creaked open, and Archibald's impatience turned to something approaching excitement. It was a feeling he hated, the anticipation before the storm. The calm before the trial that would tell him how many people his commands had sent to their graves.

Archibald took a deep breath and composed himself as Smith and Mary stepped into the Hall. Archibald listened to the footsteps, the heavy thud of the tinker and the quiet click of the pilot's boots echoing around him.

"Welcome," he said as the two stopped before the bench.

Mary leaned forward and crossed her arms before laying her head on the bench. "What are we doing here, Archibald? I'm exhausted."

Archibald said the words that filled him with anxiety and anticipation all at once. "I want you to prepare the warships."

There was no sound in the Hall as Mary snapped her head up and stared at him. Her eyes were a light brown, and they reminded Archibald so much of her mother.

Smith crossed his arms and took a deep breath. "Prepare them for what?"

"Anything," Archibald said. "The defense of Bollwerk is always the priority, but if Charles fails in Dauschen, we have to be ready."

"Those ships are best prepared for air-to-air combat," Smith said. "How do you want us to adapt them for air-to-ground?"

"Install the underbelly cannons."

Smith blew out a deep breath and ran a hand through his hair. "We have not tested them thoroughly enough for that. I am still concerned we could buckle the frame."

"It'll work," Mary said.

"Mary ..." Smith said.

She glanced up at him, and something flickered across her face that Archibald couldn't place.

"We've done enough testing. I don't think the frames are in danger."

Smith squeezed his eyes shut and sighed. "It was never my intention to build an assault ship. Those cannons were meant for the defense of Bollwerk. Nothing more."

"That's what they'll be used for," Archibald said. "Even with the cannons, I'm afraid those ships are vulnerable outside the wall."

"They are heavily armored," Smith said. "There is little we have to fear from Dauschen, or Fel. Their ballistae should not be able to penetrate the armor."

"We need something else to cover the ground forces," Archibald said. "I want you to mount a chaingun on each gun pod."

Mary cursed.

"I have no desire for death on such a scale," Smith said. He lowered his eyes.

"Understand what is happening," Archibald said, hoping the tinker didn't take offense to the cutting words. "If they aren't stopped in Dauschen, Ancora falls. If Ancora falls, Cave will fall. Once Fel rules the North with the Butcher a king in all but name, they *will* come for the Deadlands. They'll come for our steel and our gunpowder, and if they control the trade of everything from medicine to candy, we'll have little choice but to fight.

"We'll have *no* choice," Mary said. "Those bastards would put us to death. You've heard what they did in Dauschen. You want to see that here, Smith? You want to see Gladys gutted and hanging from the walls? Alice?"

It took everything Archibald had not to back away from the bench when Smith growled.

"I will need assistance," Smith said. "Jacob and the old man are in Dauschen. I cannot build four chainguns with my own hands in a short amount of time."

"George has two of the tinkers from Midstream who have already offered to help."

Smith looked up, unable to hide the surprise on his face. "Midstream?"

Archibald nodded.

"I know of no tinkers from Midstream. They are luddites, though I mean no disrespect by that. They have no love for steam or biomechanics."

Archibald squeezed his hands together and flexed his thumbs. "That's not entirely accurate. Since Rana and the other warlords brought violence into the province and destroyed the remnants of Midstream, another side of the desert folk has shown itself. George tells me their blacksmiths have been working on weapons for nearly half a decade."

Smith frowned and nodded. "Well, if they have experience with fire-arms, they may be able to help."

"They have experience with a great many things," Archibald said. "Do not discount them so quickly.

"Where did they learn the trade?" Smith asked.

"Belldorn," Archibald said as he met Mary's gaze.

"Wh … what?" Mary asked. "What could you possibly need with my old hometown? And what do you mean some backwards Midstreamers are learning from Belldorn?"

"Belldorn saw this war coming long before the rest of us were willing to believe it."

"How can you even know that?" Mary asked. "My ancestral home is isolated, cut off from the rest of the continent on the other side of the wastes."

"You're not wrong," Archibald said. "Their isolation gains them a great deal of freedom, but also a different perspective—an outsider's perspective—on the conflicts all around them."

Mary frowned slightly but didn't interrupt. She leaned forward, hanging on Archibald's words.

"What I am telling you does not leave this room. It wasn't ten years after the Deadlands War before Belldorn approached me. Bollwerk was their last attempt after Ancora turned them away. They came to offer a silent partnership. In exchange for information from my spies, they would help build our warships."

"Why?" Smith asked. "What do they gain by arming a potential ene-my?"

"Wait for the others," Archibald said. "I don't want to repeat this story."

"What others?" Mary asked.

"George, and Gladys, and Alice."

"Not the kids," Smith said. "We already had to build a leg for Jacob. What else do you intend to risk?"

"Everything."

✧   ✧   ✧

ALICE HEARD RAISED voices on the other side of the door. She exchanged a glance with George. He shrugged and then knocked on the tall bronze door at the top of the lift. The shouting receded. Someone distinctly said, "Come."

George pushed the levered handle down until it clicked. He pushed the heavy slab of metal to the side. Alice's ever-widening view eventually showed her Archibald, Mary, and Smith at the bench on the far side of the Hall. Papers and glasses were strewn about, and it was obvious that some of them had been thrown onto the floor.

"This looks friendly," Alice said as she stepped in behind Gladys.

"Stay with me, Gladys," George whispered.

Alice thought he sounded paranoid. It was three of their friends, not a pack of warlords. Then she remembered how George had been hurt because he'd tried to fight off Rana and his men. George was a protector. Alice chastised herself for the thoughts she hadn't spoken aloud.

"They are here now," Smith said. He glanced from Alice to Archibald. "Tell us of the secret pact with Belldorn."

"What?" George asked.

"They've kept their word," Archibald said, "if even you are unaware, George. I've told Smith and Mary some of what I'm about to tell you. Do not repeat this outside of our circle."

"Not even to Jacob?" Alice asked.

Archibald nodded. "Jacob and your friends can know."

"George knows the story," Archibald said. "Long before the Dead-lands War, Belldorn was attacked by the desert natives. It was a terrible, bloody war with no decisive victor. In the end, the tribes forged an uneasy alliance. Eventually, they settled what would eventually be known as Bollwerk.

"The same war sent Belldorn spiraling into isolation. They filled in the mountain passes that granted access to their trade routes, and eventually the entire city faded from the political landscape, obscured by the civil wars waged in Bollwerk.

"What few immigrants came here told us they were from a small village near the sea. Only a few of us knew the truth," Archibald said as he glanced at Alice. His eyes lingered on her for a while before returning to the others.

Archibald tapped his fingers on the bench. "It is now Bollwerk that has an uneasy alliance with Belldorn. It is us, and some of our spies in that alliance, more specifically. Not ten years after the Deadlands War, Belldorn approached me. Our alliance depends on the exchange of information from my spies."

"Exchange for what?" George asked. He frowned and removed his hand from Gladys's shoulder.

"They helped build the warships," Smith said.

George cursed and closed his eyes as he ran his hands over his hair. "Why, in all that burns upon the desert, would they do *that?*"

"They gain warning against an invasion from someone other than Ballern," Archibald said. Before anyone could say more in the confused silence that followed, Archibald continued. "Belldorn has been defending itself against Ballern for almost two centuries. When Ballern struck at Fel, it was only after one of Belldorn's spies was captured during an air raid. Ballern didn't know of the other cities here. They'd only ever attacked Belldorn."

"My mentor, Targrove?" Smith asked.

"Targrove was from Belldorn," Archibald said with a nod. "It's why you could never place his accent."

Smith frowned and glanced at Mary. "He told me he spent time in several cities."

"It wasn't a lie," Archibald said, "but it wasn't the entire truth."

Smith dismissed the thought with a flick of his hand.

"Why are you telling us all this now?" Alice asked, breaking her silence. "You've kept this to yourself for years."

"I'm telling you this because we need their help. They helped us design the warships, and we've never raised arms against them. I need Mary to go back there and speak with the Council of Stone."

Mary took a deep breath and squeezed her forehead. "They won't listen to a woman who isn't even part of their bloodline, Archibald. Those people are so disconnected from the modern world, they didn't let women choose their own brides until a few years ago."

"That's why you should take Alice."

Mary stared at Archibald and blinked. "So she can be married off?"

"What?" he said as he almost choked on the word. "No! Because of her blood, for the sake of the gods, not to marry her off. She has hair like the old blood of Ballern."

"Fine, I grew up in Belldorn, but how do you know they won't just kill us for showing up on their doorstep? They *blew up a mountain*, Archibald, just to stop that kind of thing from happening."

"You risk our lives, sending us into Belldorn," Smith said.

"You don't have to go," Archibald said. "Mary, Alice, and the royal guard are more than capable."

"Where Mary goes, I go. The Skysworn does not fly without me."

Archibald nodded. "Do as you wish, Smith. Gods know you've earned it. Get Alice in front of the priests. They'll recognize the bloodline soon enough. Rally them behind us. It's no guarantee that Bollwerk's destruction would lead to an invasion of Belldorn, but it's likely. You'll need leverage. Exaggerate the threat if you must. The Midstream refugees will recognize George and Gladys's status. Be sure to wear the bracelet."

George nodded. "I don't want to put Gladys at risk, Archibald, but I understand why you want to do this."

"Will you still make the journey?" Archibald asked.

"If the princess wishes it, I will."

Gladys nodded. "Our people should know that the royal line still lives. Even if it doesn't thrive, it still lives on in the desert outside the wastes."

George smiled. "We will make the journey."

"What bloodline?" Alice asked, dragging everyone back to Archibald's earlier words.

Archibald didn't answer immediately, so Mary did.

"People from Belldorn all used to have hair like yours," she said quietly. "It's likely your grandparents, or your great grandparents, were from Belldorn. It's the only other place I've seen hair like yours."

Alice's fingers threaded through her curls without her really thinking about it. "And that means they'll listen to me?"

Mary gave a half shrug. "There's a better chance they'll listen to us if you're with us than if you're not. It's not but a day's journey in the Skysworn with the wind at our back."

"A day?" Smith said. "If you ran the thrusters the entire time, perhaps."

"What's the matter, Smith? Don't think your engines are up to the task?"

"My engines are not the question here," Smith said.

"That's okay. If you don't think your equipment is up to the task, we can take it slow."

The tinker absently slapped the surface of the table and glared at Mary. "I know your game, but it will not change my intentions."

"Maybe one day someone can invent a better engine," Mary said, letting her voice rise into a higher register.

Smith almost growled at her.

"I suspect," Archibald said as he glanced between the two, "you won't be able to anger Smith enough to prevent the trip."

Mary huffed out a deep breath and cursed. "Fine, *fine*, I'm overdue for a family reunion anyway. How soon do we need to be there?"

"Three days' time."

"That's when Jacob is supposed to get to Dauschen," Alice said.

Archibald turned his attention to her. "It's actually when Charles plans to detonate the bomb, assuming they're able to get everything put in place ahead of time."

"We should try to be back in Bollwerk by then," Mary said.

"I agree," Smith said. "If they need us, we should be ready." He made a frustrated huff and said, "I will prepare the thrusters as best I can. How in the world can I get the warships re-armed *and* get the Skysworn to Belldorn in three days?"

Archibald tapped the end of an engraved copper pen on the bench. "Have the dock tinkers install the cannons while you're away. Worry about the chainguns once you're back. I'd rather have the power to take down large targets in Dauschen than pick off infantry with a chaingun."

Alice watched, caught between horror, relief, and fascination, as those men and women—people she considered friends—plotted the potential death of an entire city.

CHAPTER FOUR

T HEY'D REACHED A flat, straight stretch in the mountain pass, and Drakkar had the crawler speeding between the sheer rock walls. Jacob held his hand outside the crawler, shifting it to catch the wind as it sped by.

"Almost out," Samuel said. The sun cut through the shadows ahead. "Why is this pass so much longer than the Bull's Horns?"

"It runs through the mountain itself," Drakkar said. "We are traveling through the Broken Peak, not a pass between two mountains."

The treads roared as the crawler ramped through a dip in the pass and briefly left the ground. The entire machine slammed into the earth, and Jacob felt like a giant had placed its hand on his back, smashing him into the seat.

"Sorry, my friends," Drakkar said as he slowed the crawler. "We are nearing the Meadow."

Jacob was about to ask if they'd broken the crawler. Instead, he stared at the stretch of green grass as it unfolded before him. A few trees towered so high into the sky he could scarcely comprehend it, but most of the vista was tall grass, waving gently in the breeze.

Something roared beside them, and Jacob turned to find a waterfall cascading out of the stony gray mountainside. It met up with a web of smaller streams, eventually crashing into a river and trailing off into the distance. Something large and black and round surfaced briefly, and then vanished as quickly as it had appeared.

"Let us refill our canteens here," Drakkar said as he slowed the crawler down beside a stream. "I could stand to stretch my legs for a time. The water comes from within the stone, so it is safe to drink."

"Usually safe to drink," Charles said. He popped the door open when Drakkar stopped the crawler. "I've still had a bad experience or two from groundwater, best to boil it."

"Do as you will." Drakkar stepped onto the riverbank. "I prefer my water cold."

Jacob hopped out beside Samuel and stretched his back until his vision swam with shadows and stars. "Ugh."

"Shouldn't stretch that much after you've been sitting down for so long," the Spider Knight said. "You don't want to black out right before an ambush."

"What man in his right mind would plan an ambush here?" Charles asked, pulling two extra canteens out of a saddlebag. The leather satchel was near the two massive trunks in the back of the crawler. They were a stark reminder of what was to come, as they carried the bombs. "Maybe an ambush in the pass itself, but the Meadow is wide open. Not to mention it's a death trap."

"Why would you say that?" Jacob asked as he took one of the leather-wrapped canteens from Charles. It was square, mostly, except where the corners had been dented in. Some of the leather was cracked and even missing along the strap. Jacob suspected the canteen had seen more years than Charles.

"Those grasses hide a great deal of nasty things."

"Emerald Needles are all you really need worry about here," Drakkar said.

Jacob recoiled at the name. "*Here?* But they ... they ..."

"Paralyze you and lay their eggs inside you?" Samuel said with a terribly casual tone.

"Then eat you from the inside out!"

"That is why I would advise you to keep an eye out," Drakkar said. "They are not so aggressive as Sky Needles, and this is not the time of day they hunt."

"Just don't step on one," Charles said.

Jacob spent the rest of the hike up to the waterfall staring at his feet. He knew the Emerald Needles would be obvious if he saw them. Miss Penny had told them stories of the beasts. Smaller than a Sky Needle, but infinitely more terrifying in what they could do. At least a Sky Needle would just kill you.

"Relax, Jacob," Charles said. "Emerald Needles aren't out much past noon. Most of them will be underground at this time anyway."

"Underground like where we have to go in Dauschen?" Jacob asked.

Samuel burst into laughter.

"No," Charles said with a smile and a shake of his head. "It's too cold for them up there. They stay in the Meadow and the lowest of the foothills."

The thought made Jacob feel a little better as he thrust his canteen into the smaller stream of water running off the cliff face. The water was ice cold. The ringing of droplets splashing against the exposed metal grew deeper as his fingers grew numb. After what seemed like an hour, water splashed out the top of the last canteen and Jacob screwed the cap back on.

He slid the canteen's strap over his shoulder and shivered, exhaling into his cupped palms in an effort to warm himself up.

Charles closed the lid on his second canteen after Drakkar and Samuel had finished, and they started back for the crawler. "Let's get this over with. We're only an hour or so away from Dauschen. Once we're through the gates, we can set up with the refugees."

"We're not going to the last safe house?" Samuel asked. "I don't want to sleep in a damn tent."

"Not at first," Charles said. "Second or third night, we can convincingly appear to be fast friends with some of the other spies and assess the situation."

They walked in silence for a while until they climbed back into the crawler. Drakkar threw a lever that released the engine's flywheel, and steam once more billowed out the back of the contraption.

"Do we start on the bombs tonight?" Jacob asked.

Charles took a deep breath. The crawler lurched forward and splashed through a ford in the river. "Some preliminary assembly would go unnoticed. I think we can start with that. I don't want to assemble any of the detonators until the day we go underground. It's not safe, for one," Charles said, answering the question Jacob hadn't asked, "and it's more likely to be recognized by someone who knows a little about explosives."

There it was, Jacob thought as the crawler zipped through the Meadow, leaving a trail of crushed grass behind it. The time for doubt and fear was past; now it was time to put their plan in motion. He took a deep breath and hoped Alice was having a better time of it in Bollwerk.

THE NEXT MORNING on the docks, Alice rolled her shoulders and winced at the soreness training had left behind. She stared up at the massive warship. Alice could scarcely comprehend the size from the ground, and now that she was close enough to touch it, it seemed even more impossible.

One of the dockhands walked up beside Smith and said, "She's all locked in, sir. You should be able to mount the cannons in the gun pods."

Smith nodded. "Thank you. Can you tell the other towers to begin?"

"Sir," the man said before marching off to the glass cabin at the end of the dock.

"Why all at once?" Mary asked as she flopped onto the bench beside Alice.

"We are anchored," Smith said. He ran his hand across the massive barrel propped up along a series of sawhorses. "I want to keep the weight even. The Midstream tinkers do not think it will be an issue, but I would rather not take chances with the frame."

"You think adding *more* weight at the same time will help the frame?"

"It should, yes." He smeared a semi-translucent glob of gel along the end of the barrel.

"I guess that's why I pay you and I just steer."

Smith flashed Mary a smile and threw a series of levers on his biomechanics. They clicked and hummed, and then his arms began to shake with their newfound power. Alice stared as the tinker lifted the twelve-foot length of steel by himself.

"Smith, what the hell are you doing?" Mary asked. "You need a hoist!"

"It is threaded. Watch."

Mary and Alice both leaned forward, staring at Smith as he fed the barrel in through the gun pod and bumped it up against the mount. It almost looked effortless when he began twisting it, causing the threaded post to slowly disappear into the barrel. After a minute of turning the massive barrel, it clanged home.

Smith powered down his biomechanics and took a deep breath. "I need to do a little welding, but that should do it."

"Are you kidding?" Mary asked. "You just installed the goddamned cannon in five minutes?"

"No," Smith said as he frowned and shook his head. "I spent most of the night with the Midstream tinkers. We got the firing mechanism, breach, and the catch for spent ammo mounted last night."

Mary folded her arms and narrowed her eyes. "There is no way—*no way*—you built those mounts last night."

"You are right," Smith said. "Those mounts have been built for months. Archibald asked for them quite some time ago. I did not realize what his intentions were at the time. I honestly suspected a weaponized crawler, but it was not long before he asked for the barrels."

"What do those shoot?" Alice asked. She stood up and walked over to the barrel. Alice could easily stick her arm down the dark metal tube. Rough ridges spiraled up the inside of the barrel.

"Very large things," Smith said. "George and Gladys are teaching some of the soldiers how to build them. The Midstream folks are the best there are with gunpowder.

"Alice, I need to see how easily this can be targeted. Will you climb into the gun pod for me?"

She nodded, trying to hide her excitement. Smith reached through a gap in the pod and slid a bolt to the side. It released a section of the glass, and Alice climbed in behind the massive cannon. The roar of the wind around the docks died off when she stuck her head into the heavy glass-and-steel pod. Smith closed the hatch and cut off the outside world. The tap of Alice's shoe echoed above Smith's voice until he leaned in and spoke louder.

"Turn the vertical crank to adjust the altitude, and sweep with the flat wheel."

Alice jerked in surprise when she moved the flat wheel, and the entire gun pod swiveled. She caught the grin on Smith's face as he dodged the end of the barrel. She glanced at her feet and almost felt like the floor was dropping out beneath her. She could see people far below, moving around like so many ants.

"Try the other!" he shouted over a gust of wind.

Alice continued moving the pod until the barrel hung over the gap in the platform. She cranked forward on the vertical mechanism, and the barrel swung down. She reversed the movement, and it slowly rose again. At all times she could see the crosshairs mounted to a mirror. It was like a scope she'd seen at Festival once that would let you see around corners.

"Come on out," Smith said. "It still needs to be test fired, but that is not for today. The Midstream folks are going to check the welds and bolts before then."

Alice climbed out. "That's quite a view."

"I half expected a scream, or something, when you realized the floor was glass too," Smith said.

"Please," Mary said, "that girl's not all panicky like you tinkers. Be reasonable."

Smith laughed slowly as he closed the hatch and threw the bolt. "Alright, alright, let me check in with the Midstreamers, and then we can hit the skies."

CHAPTER FIVE

T HE CRAWLER ROLLED into a large stable on the outskirts of Dausch-
en. The guards had been somewhat suspicious, but apparently
they'd had "defectors" from Bollwerk join their cause over the past
weeks, given shelter in exchange for intel. Jacob was surprised at how fast
they were waved through the gates.

Jacob figured the other defectors had been the spies, which made him
wonder just how many spies were out there. Not only from Bollwerk, but
how many spies came from Ancora or even Belldorn? Using Archibald's
network as a gauge, the potential was insane. It was little wonder most
cities put spies to death.

"Keep your leg hidden," Charles said as he glanced back at Jacob. "I
won't say it's impossible for a Biomech to defect from Bollwerk, but it's
unlikely. There were some in the last group, so let's not risk drawing
attention to it."

Jacob nodded and checked the thick socks beneath his denim pants.
They were plenty high to conceal the leg, even when he was sitting down.
"It's kind of annoying not being able to tell when your socks are falling
down."

Charles smiled and pulled one of the trunks to the edge of the crawler. "You'll get used to it. Everyone does."

"I need those clips to hold them up, like my dad used to wear."

"Sock garters?" Samuel asked as he snapped a saddlebag closed and
tossed it over his shoulder.

"Don't laugh," Jacob said. "That's not very nice."

Samuel chuckled and shook his head. "No disrespect, kid. I've only ever seen old men like Charles with them."

"Are they not part of your uniform?" Drakkar asked. "I am quite certain the Spider Knights all wear them beneath their greaves."

"He's got you there," Charles said. "You're looking older by the minute."

"That's different."

"I'm quite sure it's not," Charles said as he cracked open one of the trunks. "Jacob, grab the *rope*, would you?"

Cedar filled his nose, wafting from the trunk with the carefully folded leathers. Jacob nodded. He slid two of the thin coils over his shoulder. It wasn't rope at all, he knew, it was a fuse they'd use to synchronize the bombs. Charles thought they could work on it a bit without raising suspicions. It was easy to hide the canisters in a saddlebag, and the coil looked like a thin rope from a distance. The blasting powder would be harder to explain away if anyone searched Drakkar's saddlebag.

"Is it safe to leave the crawler here?" Jacob asked.

Drakkar held up a thick brass cog and smiled. "It will not move without this transfer. I doubt it will be scavenged for parts. I suspect thieves will be put to death without delay in the current climate."

Jacob made a mental note not to try pickpocketing anyone. If he was going to get killed, it was going to be for a better reason than that.

"Let's move," Charles said, and they all followed him toward the back of the building, past the Walkers curled up in the far corner of the stables and out into a field of tents.

"They're huge," Jacob said. He eyed the house-sized tents. Massive cables stretched across the field, leaving only a narrow road between the canvas shelters. At a glance, it looked to be four rows, each six tents deep. "You could fit the entire Square in one of those."

"Not quite," Samuel said, "but they *are* big."

"There," Charles said as they passed the second row. Jacob adjusted his backpack and the coils on his shoulder while he followed the old man.

"It stinks," Jacob said.

"Probably the latrines," Charles said. "They won't have plumbing in the camp. You'll get used to it."

Jacob frowned at the sharp, pungent odor and couldn't imagine how anyone could get used to that.

"Where are we heading?" Samuel asked.

"The far tent," Drakkar said. "Look at the red flag."

Jacob found it flapping above the soiled tan canvas amid a sea of flags. A black octagon framed in red snapped and rippled in the wind. "What is it?"

Drakkar leaned in close to Jacob and whispered, "Steamsworn. It is an old flag, a very old flag, before the fist."

"It's the first flag of Bollwerk, as a matter of fact," Charles said. "From the times of the alliance. The defectors come from a wide range of tribes and cities, all with their own flags. I doubt that old flag will raise suspicions when it's all but lost among so many others."

It wasn't long before they arrived at the edge of the tent flap, and Samuel smiled at the giant of a man who pulled it open.

"Welcome, brothers," the man said.

"Clark, was it?" Charles asked.

"Yes, it's good to see you after so many years."

Jacob didn't think it had really been years. In fact, he was pretty sure he recognized the Biomech from Bollwerk.

"It's safe here," Clark said, letting the tent flap fall closed. "We have men in the three surrounding tents and an alternating lookout."

"Good," Charles said. "Do you have a dry place to hold our saddle-bags?"

"Anywhere you'd like. We patched what few leaks the tent had. The only opening now is for the fire."

Charles frowned. "We'll need to stay away from that too."

Clark raised an eyebrow but said nothing. "The last patrol came by only ten minutes ago. You probably have an hour if you want to get some work done."

Charles nodded and pointed to the far corner of the tent, past the rows of cots, somewhat shadowed behind a large bundle of shelves. Jacob followed the old tinker and sighed when the weight of the coils and his backpack lifted from his shoulders.

✦   ✦   ✦

"How is this any different from gunpowder?" Jacob asked. He tapped the funnel to clear it of the stray grains. He handed the metal canister off to Samuel and started measuring the next batch of white powder.

"The blast wave is almost twice as fast," Charles said. "I knew a man who tried to craft a cartridge out of it for a small handgun."

"I suspect 'knew' is the operative word there," Drakkar said as he glanced back from his post by the shelves.

"You aren't wrong," Charles said. "Idiot was holding the gun for the first test fire. It took half his …" He trailed off and looked up at Jacob. "It killed him."

"Must have been bad if you're not telling us the rest," Samuel said.

"It was. It was very bad."

Charles ran a clear gel around a gray metal cap and handed it to Jacob. He affixed it to the canister, leaving a curved stretch of blasting cord exposed that made the entire assembly look like a mug more than a bomb.

"So, what could one of these things do?" Samuel asked. He leaned forward and slid the bomb into a satchel of completed canisters.

"They're shaped," Charles said, "so the blast is concentrated. Whatever's beneath it—iron, stone, or steel—won't be there afterwards. Four of them would be enough to cut down a watchtower."

Samuel's deft movements suddenly slowed to a very great degree. He turned his head and stared at the middle of the tent. Jacob turned to follow his gaze. The fire was larger in tent's center, giving them heat but also providing them an ignition that was frighteningly close to the bombs.

"It's fine," Charles said.

Jacob saw Samuel shiver out of the corner of his eye before the Spider Knight turned back to Charles and said, "I hope you're right, old man."

IT WAS CLARK who woke them the next morning. "First patrol is past. If you hurry, we can be out of here by the time the second comes."

Jacob blinked and looked at the man crouched down, whispering to Charles.

"Good," Charles said. "Samuel, up!"

He slapped Samuel on the chest and the Spider Knight bolted up, reaching for a sword he didn't have at his waist. Samuel looked wide awake until he finished taking in his surroundings. Then he looked dead tired again. "I hate sleeping on cots."

Jacob agreed. His back ached when he sat up and put his feet on the floor.

"Get dressed," Charles said. "We're leaving in ten minutes."

Samuel groaned and dragged his light leather armor out from under the cot. He'd left the heavier armor of the Spider Knights hidden in the crawler.

Jacob pulled out his vest and slid it on. He was still wearing the same denim pants from the day before. "I'm glad we packed everything up last night."

Charles nodded.

"Where's Drakkar?"

The Cave Guardian stepped out from behind the shelves at the edge of the tent, a saddlebag over either shoulder. "I am here. Everything is ready, Charles."

"Good, good. Let's get out of here."

✧   ✧   ✧

CLARK HAD TOLD them the safe house wasn't far, but Charles was surprised when they were walking into a modest two-story home after a brief ten-minute walk. Charles recognized the two Steamsworn inside from their first trip to Dauschen.

"No issues since you arrived?" Charles asked.

The short, black-haired woman shook her head. "Not a one." Her name slipped his mind, but after fumbling after it for a bit, he remembered it was Lottie.

"Unless you count that awful latrine," the man said as he took the saddlebags from Drakkar.

"It *was* pretty rank," Samuel said. He took a deep breath. "Not like here. What's that smell?"

"Cookies," Lottie said with a smile.

"You baked cookies?" Samuel asked.

She shook her head. "What? I'm the woman, so I do the cooking? Gods, you must be from Ancora."

Samuel stared at her and blinked, clearly at a loss for words.

"Lottie, leave the poor kid alone," the man said. He extended his hand to Samuel. He wasn't as dark-skinned as Drakkar, but he was certainly not as pale as most Ancorans. "I'm Morgan."

Lottie let out a low laugh and brushed a lock of hair over her shoulder. She looked like the kind of woman who spent too much time in the bars, and not the friendly establishments either. She was the kind of woman Charles liked to have on his side in a brawl.

"It's good to see you both again," Charles said. "I'm sorry we didn't get a chance to talk much on the road here."

"Think nothing of it," Lottie said. "We're spies. Too much communication could compromise us. The Tail Swords were … unfortunate."

Charles nodded and glanced back at the door. It was closed, and Clark leaned against it. "Did you all serve together?"

"We took the vow together," Clark said. "Smith worked on our bio-mechanics. We're as close to family as you can be without blood."

Lottie and Morgan didn't protest the claim. They didn't even blink at it. If what Clark said wasn't true, they were screwed anyway, so Charles just came out with it.

"What has Archibald told you?"

The three echoed it like they'd been practicing for days. "Support the Caddiswing in whatever mad scheme he brings."

"The Caddiswing?" Jacob asked.

Charles released a low laugh. "My codename in the Deadlands War. Some things don't stay in the past. They come back and find you when you least expect it. Did he tell you of my scheme?"

"Are these the bombs?" Lottie asked. She patted one of the saddle-bags.

"Some of them. We need to get the trunks out of the stables. They're on the back of a crawler."

"If one of you can go with me," Clark said, "we should have no problems getting them here."

"We have flares," Morgan said. "They should burn hot enough to ignite the blasting cord."

"Good," Charles said. "It's always good to have a backup. Drakkar, go with Clark, please." The Cave Guardian nodded. "Jacob, Samuel, help me go over the plans with Lottie and Morgan."

"When do we start?" Lottie asked.

A dark smile lifted the corners of the old tinker's mouth.

"Tonight."

CHAPTER SIX

EXHAUSTION PULLED AT Alice's eyelids. She hadn't slept well, her mind warring between excitement and anxiety. Belldorn was more of a myth than anything else, briefly mentioned in some of her history lessons with Miss Penny. It was an ancient city that had been all but lost in the Deadlands War. Now she was going there. They'd be there in a matter of hours!

"You look like you just ate a pound of Cocoa Crunch and slammed a gallon of coffee," Mary said as she glanced over her shoulder. The roar of the thrusters made Mary a little hard to understand, but Alice picked up enough of it.

"I'm just excited," she shouted back.

"Me too," Mary said with a smile. "I haven't been home in years. I wonder what's left."

"What do you mean?"

"Back when I lived there, the edge of the city was falling into the ocean. The government was trying all sorts of half-insane plans to save the rest of those old towers."

Alice glanced to the side, briefly studying the knots and whorls on the floor while contemplating what kind of towers could be waiting in Belldorn. "Like the skeleton?"

Mary shot her a sideways smile. "Just wait, girl. Just wait."

It wouldn't be long now, but Alice didn't want to wait. "I wish Gladys was here, and Jacob."

"I wouldn't mind having George along either," Mary said. "That man is wickedly good at killing things. I've never known a deadlier fighter."

The thought that Mary had never known a better fighter than George, and George had been beaten so easily at The Fish Head, made her shiver. All it took was an attack you didn't see coming, and it was all over.

That awful thought stayed with her while she watched the sparsely green desert fade into the barren sands of the waste.

✧ ✧ ✧

THE SKYSWORN LURCHED when Smith cut off the thrusters. He was ready for it, but the sudden swing in inertia still slammed him into the side of the workbench below the brass levers. Smith cursed and rubbed his side.

"Just use the damn harness next time, idiot," he muttered to himself.

The gauges looked good. He released a valve, sending a cloud of steam rushing through a secondary temperature gauge. Smith smiled when it barely tapped into the red. He half expected the thrusters to be burned up after that run, but things were looking good. Smith opened the rest of the valves to gradually cool down the larger turbines. If they cooled too fast, they could crack, but at these temperatures he was more worried about a fire.

Smith looked over the gauges one last time, nodded to himself, and climbed the ladder that would take him to the deck and then to the cabin.

✧ ✧ ✧

"HOW'S SHE HOLDING up?" Mary asked when Smith opened the hatch and stepped into the cabin.

"As long as they do not lock up when they cool off, I would say very well. Temperature is normal and pressures are well within the Skysworn's thresholds."

"You're good, Smith. Nobody can argue that." Mary leaned forward, over the steering column, and cursed. "Do you see them?"

Alice jumped in her seat like something might be terribly wrong. She realized that wasn't the case when Mary flashed her a smile and pointed off the bow of the ship.

"It has been a long time," Smith said. He walked closer to the windscreen.

The sky was almost filled with diving, buzzing forms longer than Smith was tall. Huge faceted eyes crowned the end of narrow, jewel-like bodies. Their wings flashed in the light but moved too fast to be seen clearly.

Smith smiled when Alice sidled up beside him and leaned into the windscreen.

"Are those … Dragonwings?" Alice asked.

"Yes," Mary said. "See how they're clustered around the mountains? They nest above the walls that separate Belldorn from the Deadlands. We'll probably see some of the larger ones when we cross the pass. They're docile creatures, despite the fact they could take your arm off in one bite."

"They're beautiful," Alice said.

Smith turned his attention back to the chaos in the sky ahead of them. He'd seen Dragonwings all along the coasts across the entire continent, from Fel to Ancora and back to Belldorn. There was no other place with such an enormous concentration of them, though.

"Would you like to feed them?" Smith asked.

"I don't know if we should slow down that much …" Mary checked her pocket watch and frowned slightly. "I suppose we're a bit ahead of schedule."

"Alice?"

Alice looked up, drawing her gaze away from the Dragonwings. "Yes!"

Mary brought the throttle down a gear, and the howling of the wind past the cabin receded a bit. "You're just a big kid sometimes, Smith."

"This way," Smith said with a laugh.

Alice almost flew out of the hatch to the cabin when he cracked it open. The wind was still intense out on the deck, but not so much it felt like it would knock you over. Smith brushed his hair out of his eyes, but the black mass was immediately thrown back across his face.

"We keep a trunk of bait bugs, just in case we are in need of a distraction."

"From what?" Alice asked.

Smith shrugged as he made his way toward the aft deck. "Sky Needles, usually, but you run into some stranger things every now and then in the skies." Smith cracked open one of the large wicker trunks, revealing dozens of Sweet-Flies. He handed Alice four of them and then let the trunk slide closed.

Alice looked up at the fabric-covered gas chambers above them and followed the edge until it dipped in a bit, leaving the railing exposed from above. She adjusted the Sweet-Flies and walked over to her chosen spot.

"You have a good eye," Smith said.

Alice sat three of the bugs at her feet and held the last between her hands. They were close enough now that she could hear the buzz of wings and the blast of air when one of the Dragonwings got curious.

She leaned over the railing and looked down at the wasteland below. "It's all dead."

Smith joined her at the railing and peered over the edge. "It only looks dead. It may not be as active as Ancora's lands, or even Bollwerk's, but there is far more life in those sands than you would suspect."

One of the Dragonwings slammed onto the railing beside Alice. Smith hesitated to call it a landing, because he could feel the bone-rattling impact through the wood. "Keep your fingers clear."

"I know," Alice said. "I used to feed the Spider Knights, you know."

"Samuel does not seem so likely to bite your hand off."

Alice turned slightly and gave him a put-upon look before turning her attention back to the Dragonwing. Their visitor had a deep-blue body with four prismatic wings that caught the light and shattered it into a million colors. Where the wings met the back, the Dragonwing was almost furry, but it was always the eyes that grabbed Smith's attention. Enormous, faceted, and oblong, the eyes were mesmerizing. They met in the middle of the Dragonwing's forehead and seemed to change colors when the creature tilted its head back and forth.

Alice raised the Sweet-Fly, and the Dragonwing took two quick steps forward. It nosed the Sweet-Fly, and then its mouth opened like a vertical hatch, snatching the Sweet-Fly off Alice's hand as its front legs closed around its snack. Alice rubbed her hands together and grinned.

"His face is all scratchy, like he has stubble."

"If you are slow, and careful, you can pet him below the wings. Do not make sudden movements. Docile as they are, if they feel threatened, you are not likely to survive."

Alice didn't even hesitate as she took a slow step closer to the Dragonwing. It cocked its head a bit but didn't move when Alice reached out and rubbed the furry spots below its wings.

"It's soft."

"The Midstreamers used to weave the hides together to build mattresses. Not the most comfortable, mind you, but not terrible."

The Dragonwing finished its Sweet-Fly and shifted to face Alice. It perched on the railing, all six of its legs close together and its tail sticking out in the wind. Alice bent down and grabbed another Sweet-Fly. The Dragonwing snatched it up with its forelegs, stuffed it into its mouth, and launched into the air.

"They're amazing."

"They are some of the most efficient killers I have ever seen." Smith picked up the last two Sweet-Flies and said, "Watch."

He threw the two bugs off the side of the Skysworn. They didn't drop more than fifty feet before two Dragonwings swooped up from below and grabbed them.

"Did you see how they approached? Always from behind and below when they can. It is a blind spot for most creatures. Dragonwings terrify me sometimes. A bug should not be so smart."

Alice smiled and looked up at him. "Amazing. They're just amazing."

Smith let out a slow laugh. "You have issues, girl. That is all I will say on it."

He stayed there with Alice as the Skysworn cut into the mountain pass. Dragonwings dove and streaked and hovered all around them. It was a beautiful sight, and that was a fact with which Smith would not argue.

✧   ✧   ✧

BY THE TIME they reached the wall in the center of the mountain pass, Alice was back in the cabin with Mary. She'd always liked Smith and Mary, but she'd seen a side of Smith she hadn't really expected. He seemed to have deep appreciation for the Dragonwings—the kind she only expected he had for biomechanics. It may have been her old Ancoran prejudices, or maybe the fact she'd heard Smith talk about them more than anything else, but she had clearly misjudged him.

"I thought Smith only cared about the Skysworn," Alice said before she could convince herself she shouldn't say it.

Mary laughed. "I can see where you'd get that impression. It's definitely his passion—and the biomechanics. He has a soft spot for nature too. Even the deadlier parts of it."

"That's … it's nice."

"I know all about Ancora and what they call Mechs," Mary said. "I'm surprised you didn't run screaming the first time you saw all the work on Smith's chest and arms."

"He saved Jacob."

"He's saved a lot of people, Alice. He's a benevolent soul, trapped in a violent era. It happens."

"A violent era?" Alice asked. "But we've had peace for almost fifty years."

Mary let out a sigh before she glanced at Alice. "Not everyone has had peace. You've been safely locked away behind your walls. Until the Fall. There's always evil in the world, kid. Be glad for the times you don't have to face it."

Alice understood what Mary was saying, but it seemed like a sad outlook. Almost as though Mary was saying the horrible things in the world were inevitable, and there was nothing that could be done to change them. Alice didn't believe that. Her mother raised her to believe that one person could change the world, for better or for worse.

"There it is," Mary said. She pointed beyond the windscreen.

Alice was blinded by a glare on something below, but another minute of traveling through the pass changed everything. She gasped when the ancient city came into focus. Stone and brick towers higher than the Skeleton in the wastelands seemed to scrape the clouds.

"That's ... impossible."

"No, it's not. We may have forgotten how to build them so high, but those monsters were made by human hands. They've stood for thousands of years. Most of them, anyway."

"Thousands?" Alice asked. "We don't have history books that go back that far. How can anyone be sure?"

Mary shot her a sideways glance. "There is more history in Belldorn than most places. They have records mapping the evolution of bugs into the giants they are today. You know some spiders used to be the size of your hand? Like a young Jumper? That was as big as they got."

"How can they know that?"

"Books from the Old World."

Like Archibald's book? Alice wondered if that was the case, and then she wondered just how old Mary meant. Every thought left her mind when the clouds opened up and she saw the ocean for the first time.

Endless, crystal-blue waters surged and pulsed at the shoreline. She could see people out in the water as the Skysworn descended. The unfathomable stretch of blue, background to the towering city of Belldorn, brought only one word to Alice's mind.

Impossible.

CHAPTER SEVEN

NIGHT CAME BARRELING forward at a breakneck pace. Jacob watched Charles as the old tinker stood up and stared out the window. A man lit the lanterns along the street with a long, sparking pole.

"What are you working on now?" Charles asked as he slid the last bomb into a backpack.

Jacob looked up from the pile of gears and springs he'd been assembling. "It's a bolt gun, like the Steamsworn were using."

Charles leaned down and looked it over. "Looks a bit different." He pointed to a cluster of gears and said, "These aren't the usual balance for a bolt gun. You have some heavier springs than they would normally use too.

Jacob nodded as he closed the gearbox and ratcheted the assembly closed. He spun the barrels and listened to the springs clicking and locking inside. Jacob slid a belt of crossbow bolts into the breach and turned the barrels two clicks to the right, and then two clicks to the left.

"Have you tried firing it yet?" Charles asked.

Jacob shook his head and slid some of the tools back into the leather pack Smith had given him.

"Here," the old tinker said. He dragged an old half-rotted chair across the room. "Try it on this."

"You're going to fire that in here?" Samuel asked, scooting away from Jacob.

"No sense in testing it outside," Charles said. "The patrols are skittish enough knowing there are soldiers from Bollwerk within their walls who have supposedly defected. Give it a shot, Jacob."

Jacob snapped his arm out and smiled when the counterweights shifted and primed the springs. It was a deep, healthy click. He flexed his fingers slightly and then angled his hand downward before curling it into a fist.

The barrels around his wrist spun up faster than he expected, but the result was beautiful. A series of twelve clicks, nearly silent in the dimly lit room, followed by thunks of steel on wood when the bolts found their target. Jacob snapped his arm forward again, and the braided ammo belt fell from the breach.

"I'd say you almost double the rate of fire," Charles said. "Could be useful, could be a disaster if you run out of ammo too fast."

"I was thinking it could be a secondary weapon," Jacob said. "A backup, in case you need it in an emergency." He knew Charles had heard the story of what happened at the entrance to Gareth cave. Jacob half expected Charles to say more about it, or argue, but the old tinker only nodded.

"It's time," Charles said.

Jacob knew what he meant. It was time to start planting bombs. Clark had gotten them the trunks without issue before returning to the refugee encampment. They'd spent the rest of the day building bombs.

Jacob and Charles grabbed their backpacks, and they each took a lantern off the little oak shelf by the door. It looked a lot like the lanterns the miners used in Ancora, but Lottie swore the fuel wouldn't smell as strongly.

"We're only planting a few tonight," Charles said. "If I can't get the transmitter working as an igniter, we're going to have to go back and attach blasting coils to everything anyway, and I don't think we have enough to join them together."

"It worked from close by," Samuel said.

"Unless you plan on blowing yourself into a million pieces, that doesn't do much good." Charles adjusted his backpack, waited a moment, and then nodded. "Right then, let's get this done."

"No one else knows about this passage," Morgan said. He led them down the hall of the safe house. The leather duster he wore was newly tanned and filled the small space with a thick, pungent aroma. Morgan stopped before he reached the study at the end of the hall. He leaned over and pried at a loose board. It clattered to the floor when he tossed it aside, and then he pulled at the edge of the hole, revealing a set of narrow stairs descending into the dark.

Morgan clicked the button on the torch in his hand and a small flame sprang to life. The reflector at the end of the tube-like light cast a narrow but effective beam. They all followed him down the stairs as he said, "This is just a cellar, like any other, but there's no external entrance. The old man we bought the place from was quite a paranoid bastard, so we're guessing he's the one who built the false wall down here.

Morgan reached his hand into a dark square on the wall and fumbled at something. After a short time, there was a click and the sound of a bolt sliding across stone. "There's a handle on the other side."

"Thank you," Charles said as he reached out and shook Morgan's hand.

"Good luck."

Morgan, Lottie, and Drakkar stayed behind. Jacob couldn't be sure, but he thought Drakkar may have remained because Charles didn't fully trust Morgan and Lottie. They seemed like good people to Jacob, but he'd seen good people do terrible things. He clenched his fist, remembering how someone in Dauschen had leaked information about Archibald's spies. It had cost several lives.

Charles lit his lantern when Morgan climbed back up the stairs and disappeared into the dim light above. "No sense delaying this further. We make for the intersection on the map. If everything lines up, we'll split up and plant our bombs along the two western supports."

"I still think we should do the closest supports first," Samuel said.

Charles shook his head. "We go to the far side tonight. You won't fit in the nearby smaller passages. We've been over this. It will give us a good idea of travel time and let us map out any potential hazards along the way. It's the best strategy at this point."

"It's your show," Samuel said.

Charles nodded. "Follow me for now. We'll make the decision when we reach the northwestern support."

"Good luck, Atlier."

Charles turned his head up to Morgan's voice, echoing from the chamber above, and nodded.

Jacob watched as the silhouette disappeared and the hatch closed behind them. The only light came from the brass lanterns clipped to each of their vests.

"Let's get this done," Charles said as he pushed ahead, into the darkness of the passage.

✧　　✧　　✧

JACOB WASN'T SURE how long they'd been walking, but he knew it had been a good while. It was Samuel who finally broke the silence.

"Can we trust Lottie and Morgan?"

"They are Steamsworn," Charles said as his boots scraped against a rise in the stone pathway.

Samuel adjusted the lantern hooked on his vest. "I know."

It was odd to see the Spider Knight without his armor, even if it was the smart thing to do to stay hidden. Jacob didn't see how they could stay much more hidden than being underground, but Charles insisted that

Samuel stay out of the armor. The Spider Knight clearly wasn't happy about it.

"I don't even have a halberd," Samuel muttered.

"A halberd?" Charles said, his voice rising. "What in the hell are you going to do with a halberd in close quarters? A knife or a gun in close quarters, always."

"I'm better with a halberd, that's all."

Jacob tripped on the same elevated stone he'd heard Charles's boots scrape on.

"Careful," Charles said.

Jacob thought about arguing, but then he remembered the multitude of explosives strapped to his back. There wasn't anything he should be but careful, and dry.

The darkness, as close as it had been with the rough walls, dropped away from them into a seemingly infinite pool.

"We're here," Charles said as he unclipped the lantern from his vest and raised it toward the ceiling. "Gods but that's huge."

The light glinted on the steel supports that ran underneath the cliff base of Dauschen. It was their target, though Jacob couldn't see how they could possible reach it.

"It's higher than I expected," Charles said before he cursed. "I'm not sure we can even reach that from here."

Charles swept the lantern to his left and then his right. A path led out in both directions. To the left, the path descended while the steel seemed to rise ever higher. "Come on. Let's try following the right path deeper into the cave."

Jacob adjusted his heavy backpack and followed Charles. Samuel brought up the rear.

The humidity made the ever-narrowing tunnel even more claustrophobic than the space itself should have been. Jacob had never considered himself frightened of small spaces, but by the time Charles had to squeeze sideways through the narrower parts of the tunnel, he was ready for wide-open spaces.

Jacob's right hand clenched his backpack as he sidestepped down the corridor beside Charles. His left held up his lantern, for all the good it did.

It was only a few more minutes in the tighter sections of the corridor before it opened into a wider cavern and Charles leaned over, taking a deep breath.

"I may be getting too old for this," Charles said with a weak laugh.

Samuel grunted as he slid out of the narrows. "Yes you are." He ruffled Jacob's hair and winked.

Charles raised his lantern and squinted at the wide steel cylinder. "That'll do. We need more charges at each location," he said as he patted the steel. "I want to be damn sure this goes down in one blast."

Something squeaked in the shadows, and the sound echoed all around them.

Samuel swung his lantern around the small cave. "Let's plant the charges and get out."

"You'd never make it as a miner," Charles said.

"A miner? I'm much too pretty for that."

Charles snorted. "Just an observation." He lowered his backpack to the ground. He ducked around the steel supports and stretched his arms around them. "I think five charges would probably cut them, but let's play it safe."

"What's safe?" Jacob asked.

"Damn good question there," Samuel muttered.

Jacob caught a smile beneath the glint of lantern light on Charles's glasses. "Six should be fine. Tie them down with a length of blasting coil. With the transmitter attached to the igniter, we should be able to detonate these remotely."

"Should," Samuel said. "We better be sure."

Charles nodded and pulled a copper trigger out of his vest. He stared at it for a moment and then pulled the trigger, held it, and slowly released it. "We'll know soon enough. There's a lot of rock between here and there, but I'm optimistic. Smith claims the advances they've made over the past decade give the transmitters an expansive range."

"Well, they reach Bollwerk from here," Samuel said, "but that's not with thirty feet of stone in between."

Charles nodded. "I know. Let's get these charges set." He slid a brass bar through the copper trigger, tested it to make sure it couldn't move, and then nodded to himself.

"What's that?" Samuel asked.

"It's a safety, so we don't accidentally blow your pretty face off while we're underground."

"Oh," Samuel said with a frown. "I may not have thought this adventure all the way through."

Charles dragged his backpack over to the nearest support and held up his lantern.

Jacob walked over to the cave wall. "This used to be a copper mine, but it looks strange."

"Yes," Charles said. "There's a webwork of copper running all through these caves. I've never seen anything else like it, personally, but copper will stop a signal from just about anything."

Jacob frowned and followed the line of Charles's lantern. "How's the remote trigger going to work?"

"We'll know when we get back to the safe house. There's no sense worrying about it until then."

Jacob knew Charles was right, but the thought of the remote trigger not working made him shiver. That would mean someone would have to light a fuse by hand. He knew enough about mining to know there were a thousand little things that could go wrong with that.

Worrying wouldn't fix it. Jacob opened his backpack and pulled out a length of blasting coil. Even if they had to light a fuse, they'd still need the coils in place.

✧   ✧   ✧

CHARLES EYED THE ring of explosives. It was the third ring they'd set up and mounted with a receiver and blasting coil.

"We used six bombs on each," Samuel said. "We're going to need more charges."

Charles nodded. "You aren't wrong. We're going to have to drop onto the outer supports from up top."

Samuel blew out a breath and turned to Charles. "Are you insane? How can we possibly drop in from somewhere else, loaded down with explosives, without getting detected."

"It's more than that," Charles said. He rubbed his hands together. "I don't know if we'll all fit. The crawlspaces around the cross supports are going to be short and tight."

"What are you saying?"

"I'm saying it should just be me and Jacob. Don't even start. I know you don't like it, and neither do I, but he's the only one here I trust with these triggers."

Jacob swelled with pride at the old man's words, but he knew he didn't know as much as Charles.

"I know," Samuel said. "I know. Let's just get it over with."

"We'll finish the last ring and then head for the safe house. Once we know if the trigger will work, we'll make our plans from there."

"And if it didn't work?" Samuel asked.

"Then things get interesting."

CHAPTER EIGHT

"GEORGE!" GLADYS SAID for the third time, ever more irritated with the royal guard's ability to ignore her.

"Yes … Princess?"

"How many more of these things do we need to make?" She looked at the workbenches full of shells and bullets and gunpowder. Having so much of the explosive in one place, and indoors no less, seemed like a terrible idea. She still remembered when the old factory in Midstream had gone up like the Burning Forest. It had been beautiful but tragic. Many people lost their lives.

George ran his finger along the top row, counting the massive cannon shells. They'd been assembling them for two days now with help from some of the other Midstream tinkers, though it felt like years. It was unbelievably boring. Gladys wished she were with Alice, exploring the lost city of Belldorn, but she knew the tasks from Archibald were important.

"Twenty rows deep," Gladys said when George started counting down.

George nodded. "Twenty deep, almost fifty across. We are close to one thousand rounds."

"No wonder I'm bored," Gladys muttered. "How many more could they possibly need?"

"You never know, until you run out."

"Sometimes I hate you, George."

George smiled. "There is something your father used to say to me, and to your mother, when we would complain of our boring lives. 'Be thankful for the calm, for the storm will take everything away.' I will take those words to my grave, Princess, for they are some of the truest I have ever heard spoken."

"Now I'm bored *and* depressed."

If Gladys was being honest, she wasn't as bored as she had been when the other two tinkers were still in the room. She'd felt like she needed to conduct herself in the ways of the Midstream Court, and that certainly didn't involve heckling George.

"Are we going to take these to the warships soon?" Gladys asked.

"We will let the other tinkers take them, as not everyone in Bollwerk even knows who they are."

"Safer?" Gladys asked.

"I think it will be, yes."

She sighed and set another brass shell on the scale. The counter-weight sat flush with the workbench's surface until the tiny grains of gunpowder began to clink and shift as she poured them through a funnel. Slowly the counterweight rose until the scale balanced. Once done, she set one of the massive gray metal bullets in the neck of the brass and slid the entire assembly into a press.

Gladys pulled the lever down. She grunted and put all her weight on it. The cylinder rose into the shaped die above it, and when she lowered the press, the bullet was seated, ready for firing. Fully assembled, the monsters weighed almost a pound each. Gladys knew she was building death dealers as she set the assembled cartridge onto the workbench and lined it up with the others.

These shells wouldn't light up the night sky in a blinding array of beauty. These were made to destroy, and she had no illusions about what they'd wrought.

"They are necessary," George said. "You have that look on your face."

Gladys smiled. "I don't like killing, George."

"That is not a bad thing, but sometimes war is necessary. With war comes death. It is the way of things."

"I still don't have to like it."

"No sane person does, Princess." George shifted a shell to start another row on the workbench. It would be the last row they could fit on the wide bench. "If it is a choice between death and survival, take up arms. Defend your people and your country, but do not go looking for death. That is a fool's errand."

"We're breaking almost half a century of peace, George."

George turned away from the assembled cartridges and faced Gladys. "Our people still suffer in that peace, Princess. Our lands taken by warlords, our families forced to depend on the generosity of this city. If your friends had not killed Rana and his men, you may be dead. You are the last of the royal line. If there is any glimmer of hope for our people, it lies within you."

Gladys took a deep breath and opened another crate of empty shells. The wood cracked and splintered when she levered it over the nails. "I may not be alive if Alice hadn't killed Rana, and we both might be dead if Smith hadn't gunned the rest of them down."

"There are times for killing," George said, his voice soft as he squeezed Gladys's shoulder.

She stared at the brass and the bullets, sighed, and returned to her task.

ALICE LEANED ON the deck railing as the Skysworn drifted into the docks. She glanced at the escort hovering beside them. It was unlike anything she'd seen before, with a clear glass windscreen, curved like the section of sphere with a long wooden tail. The pilot sat behind it, just below what seemed to be a fan of some sort that was moving too fast to be seen.

The pilot made a series of hand gestures and then pointed down. Mary gave them a thumbs up from the cabin, and the Skysworn tilted to the left before following the escort down to a lower dock. Alice watched as the contraption landed on a circular pad and the pilot hopped out. There was a loud metallic thump when Smith released the landing lines and threw them overboard.

Below, the pilot scrambled to feed the lines through some kind of spool-looking anchors on the dock.

"Oh wow," Alice said when the spools began to turn. The Skysworn lurched slightly as it was dragged toward the dock, finally stopping when it gently met the bumpers.

"What was that?" Alice asked when Smith started extending the gangplank.

"The copter? It is a death trap, if you ask me. Leaving your life in the hands of a few spinning blades and a pile of wood?" Smith shook his head. "No thank you."

"They aren't *that* bad," the pilot said as they walked up to the edge of the gangplank. Alice gasped when the pilot removed her helmet, revealing skin as pale as Alice's and hair almost as red. "A lot safer than one of these gasbags."

Mary stepped out of the Skysworn's cabin and started down the gangplank. "Eva," she said as she opened her arms.

Eva laughed and then threw herself against Mary, hugging her like a long-lost love. "I didn't know you were coming back!"

"I didn't either," Mary said.

"Ma'am," Smith said with a nod.

"Ma'am?" Eva said with a grimace. "Let's not ever call me that again, okay?"

Smith smiled and crossed his arms.

"You've met Smith," Mary said, "and this is Alice."

Eva turned her bright blue eyes onto Alice. "You're of the old blood."

"I told you they'd recognize the bloodlines," Mary said, with more than a bit of satisfaction threading through her words.

"I still see your parents almost every week," Eva said as she pulled Mary toward the docks. "They still eat at that awful fish place you liked so much."

"The one with the fried Sweet Bread?"

Eva frowned. "You're going to make us eat there, aren't you? Bittersweet reunion indeed."

"Stop whining. We aren't fifteen anymore."

Eva's face fell a little. "No, Mary. No, we're not. I missed you."

"I missed you too."

"So why are you really back?"

"We need to speak with the House. There is grave news from Archibald's spies, and more from Archibald himself."

Eva didn't ask any more questions; she only gave a brief nod and pulled Mary forward toward one of the lifts set at either end of the docks.

Alice started after them, with Smith trailing behind her. Before she reached the pair on the lift, Alice overheard Mary tell Eva, "The Skysworn is mine. We can go anywhere now."

Anywhere, Alice thought. She looked out toward the city with its towering brick-and-copper spires. A clocktower rose close to the city center, covered in gargoyles and lightning rods and a thousand wrought iron windows. *Why would you want to be anywhere else?*

Smith stepped into the lift behind Alice and slid the grate closed. Eva threw a lever, and the lift started down without so much as a hesitation. Mary kept Eva's hand wrapped in her own and the pair seemed to do nothing but stare at each other.

"Who is the House Speaker?" Mary asked.

Eva stepped away slightly and straightened her jacket. "The Lady Katherine has been for the past seven years."

"She's still in power?"

"Yes. She's pushed Belldorn to be more progressive. It's caused some hostilities in the House among the older Ladies. There have even been marriages that were not arranged."

"Truly?" Mary asked.

Alice yawned and popped her ears. The pressure seemed high as the lift reached the bottom. "How low are we? My head feels like it's getting crushed."

"We're at sea level," Eva said. "It is quite a bit lower even than Boll-werk." Eva glanced at the sky. "I've been ordered to take you to an audience with Lady Katherine. Let's hurry."

Mary eyed Smith and then Alice in turn. "Stay close to me. I don't want either of you wandering off until we speak to Lady Katherine. Or at least until one of her underlings approves your presence."

Alice nodded, wondering just how strict Belldorn was about visitors.

Smith slid the gate open, and Alice stepped out into the city. Something about it reminded her of Ancora, with all the brick and stone construction, but it was infinitely larger, taller, and more imposing. Alice imagined it would be a long ride to the House. She followed Eva across the busy street, crowded with citizens wearing tight-fitted leather jackets and utilitarian pants. A few ladies wore skirts, but they were long and narrow, and Alice could scarcely imagine trying to move her legs in something so restrictive.

The noise of the street increased as they reached a wide, ornately carved door. Eva pulled it open and ushered them all inside. Alice caught a glimpse of Dragonwings and huge ships that sailed on the sea etched into the door.

"It's nice that they built the docks so close to the Hall," Mary said.

"What?" Alice asked as she took in the room. The ceilings weren't as high as the Council Hall in Bollwerk, but they had a gradual arch to them with a polished copper ceiling that made it seem taller than it was. "We're already there? Here? We're already here?"

"It is a more convenient layout than Bollwerk," Smith said. "There is no doubt of that."

A few passersby slowed and stared at their group when Smith mentioned Bollwerk.

Eva shot an annoyed look over her shoulder. "You want to say that a little louder? It'll still take a good two or three minutes for the entire city to know we have visitors."

"Sorry," Smith said.

"He's not one for subtlety," Mary said. "Intricate gadgets and perfectly tuned engines, yes, but not so subtle when it comes to words." She paused and then added, "Or common sense."

Eva let out a short laugh and flashed a smile at the group. She led them between a pair of bronze statues, halberds held high to create the entrance to another hall. The wide stones of the entrance hall gave way to an impossibly detailed mosaic of tiny square tiles. They'd walked halfway down the hall before Alice saw the name Bollwerk laid out in the squares, and eventually they came to Ancora.

She glanced behind them, taking in what she now realized was a map of their continent, all green and tan and surrounded by a wide blue ocean. It was enormous and beautiful, and she could have stared at it for an hour, but Smith hurried her along to catch up with Mary and Eva.

The presence of guards, armed with swords and guns, grew heavy the farther into the Hall they walked. They entered a rotunda, lined with more guards, and Eva led them to one of the many doors off to the northwest.

"Lady," one of the guards said with a nod to Eva.

Beyond the doors was a room made of wood and brass. Alice had never seen anything like it. A gear of polished metal sat embedded in the floor, some twenty feet in diameter. Chairs built of different metals sat on each tooth on the outside of the wheel. Alice wondered if the floor moved. It looked like it might, as there were more gears on the outside of the largest.

Above it all sat a throne. Upon that throne was a tired-looking woman, but she still summoned a smile beneath her bulbous, jeweled crown. "Welcome, Eva."

"Lady Katherine," Eva said. "These are travelers from Bollwerk. They have news from Archibald, Speaker of Bollwerk."

"Alice," Eva said as she gestured for her.

Alice stepped out from behind Mary and took two short steps to stand beside Eva.

Lady Katherine leaned forward and narrowed her eyes. Those bright eyes were set in a face almost as pale as Alice's. "Child ... I did not realize the bloodline had survived outside of Belldorn. And you are a child of this city, there can be no doubt of that."

"What bloodline?" Alice asked. "Eva mentioned it, and Mary, but what is it?"

Lady Katherine lifted the jewel-encrusted crown off her head, letting wide curls fall to her shoulders. Hints of gray wove through those curls, but the rest was unmistakably red. "The founders of our fair city, child, for no one else has hair of fire and skin of light."

Goosebumps ran down Alice's arms. She'd never heard of her hair, or her paleness, referred to like that. She liked it.

"Archibald is a wise man to send you." Lady Katherine rapped her fingernails on the arm of the throne. The metallic clicking filled her pause. "You have grown up, Mary."

Mary gave a little bow. "My Lady."

Lady Katherine smiled. "This must be an odd thing for you, having known me when I was but a baker."

Mary looked up. "My favorite baker. I still remember the soft Iced Bread you used to make."

Lady Katherine sighed and her smile waned. "What brings you back to our city? And with news from Archibald?"

"We …" Mary started before she glanced at Alice.

Alice nodded, and she let it all spill out. From the end of the trade routes, the Fall of Ancora that was fast becoming legend, to Charles's discovery of the transmitters in the invaders, the kidnapping of Gladys, and the death of Rana. It wasn't until she reached the tale of Mordair, the Butcher's brother's rule in Fel, the collapse of Dauschen, and Newton Burns—the Butcher's—influence of Parliament in Ancora that Lady Katherine's indifference turned to something far, far darker.

"So …" Lady Katherine said. "The Butcher is showing his hand."

"Dauschen and Ancora are in his grasp now," Mary said. "An attack on Bollwerk seems imminent. And if Bollwerk falls …" Mary shrugged.

"He rules three of the largest cities in the Northlands and commands their armies." Lady Katherine squeezed her forehead. "That is why Archibald sent you. They will take Cave, and the small villages in the western deserts, and then they will come for Bollwerk."

"My Lady," Smith said as he stepped forward.

She looked up. "Archibald hopes we will support Bollwerk with our airships."

Smith hesitated. "Only as a last resort. Archibald does not wish to force you into a war."

"Clearly he does," Lady Katherine said. "It is his way, Biomech."

"He …" Smith took a hesitant step backwards. "We need help."

"My lady," Alice said, stepping up beside Eva. "If Archibald moves one of the warships away, half the city will be unguarded."

"Why would he move one of the warships away?"

Alice didn't think, she spoke. She told the Lady Katherine of the plan to cut out the invasion force in Dauschen. Charles's mad plan to collapse the base and send it off the cliff. She told her of Samuel and Drakkar and Jacob.

"It is a bold plan," Lady Katherine said once Alice finished speaking. "I can tell you have feelings for these people, but that does not justify our city entering a war, old blood though you are."

"What? No, I don't—I mean I do, but I didn't mean that's why you should help us!" Someone squeezed her shoulder, and she looked back to find Mary.

"We fear there may be an alliance with Ballern," Mary said, her voice just loud enough for Lady Katherine to hear. "If Archibald's spies are right—and they're rarely wrong—Fel could have the support of Ballern's warships. If the attack fails in Dauschen, it could bring forces against us by land and air. If it succeeds, it could trigger a response from Ballern that we can't foresee."

Lady Katherine was silent. Her posture stiffened and her hands squeezed the ends of her armrests. "If either of those scenarios come to pass, Bollwerk will fall."

"Yes."

"I know you wish for decisive action, but I must think on this." Lady Katherine looked at each of them in turn. "We have been an isolated, defense-oriented nation for almost a century. Archibald is asking us to openly enter a war. It is not a decision to be made lightly. I have heard your plea. I will have your answer by daybreak."

CHAPTER NINE

J ACOB SPENT THE rest of the night on a flimsy cot on the first floor of the safe house. It wasn't much, but at least no one else was in the room for him to disturb. *The Dead Scourge* was open, propped up on a loosely piled blanket. The book felt more real somehow, now that he'd met Archibald.

He slid the photo of Alice and the Jumper out of the back cover and stared at it for a moment. Some part of him wished he could go back to that inn. Jacob sighed as he slid the photograph into a pocket on his vest. He wished he had one of his parents. Some days it felt like he was on a grand adventure with Charles and Alice and would see his parents at the end of the day. Other times he remembered the dead and prayed his parents weren't part of them.

"Still up?"

Jacob looked toward the gruff, sleep-laden voice. Charles stood in the doorway, barely lit by the lamp Jacob was using.

"She's safe with Smith and Mary. Don't worry about that."

Jacob's eyes flashed to his vest and then up to Charles.

"I saw you looking at the picture again," Charles said with a small smile. "You miss her. It's natural."

Jacob frowned and then fumbled with *The Dead Scourge*. "I'm worried about my parents too."

Charles nodded. "I'm worried about most everyone who's still back in Ancora with that madman pulling Parliament's strings."

"I feel like we're not helping anything by being outside Ancora. Like every time I smile or enjoy myself, or try a new food, I'm rubbing it in their faces."

"Whose faces?" Charles asked as he stepped closer and crouched down beside the cot.

"Everyone trapped in Ancora."

Charles offered a kind smile and shook his head. "What you're doing here is more than most people could ever hope, Jacob. The people left in Dauschen are trapped under the heel of an oppressor they can't fight on their own."

"What if it doesn't work?"

Charles settled himself onto the floor. "What if we fail?"

Jacob nodded.

"Then we will rest easy, knowing we did all we can, and that is a thing anyone could be proud of." Charles squeezed Jacob's shoulder and stood up. "Get some sleep, kid. We make for the upper supports tomorrow."

Charles walked back into the shadowed hallway. Jacob clicked the lantern off and laid back on the cot in the darkness. They were doing everything they could. That was definitely something he could be proud of.

✧   ✧   ✧

"WHAT REASON DO you have to be here, outsiders?"

Alice thought the hostess at the restaurant was being rather rude, and Alice spoke before she really thought about what she was saying. "I've been called an outsider more in the past months than in my entire life. If we only ever call each other outsiders, how can we be friends?"

"*You* are not an outsider here, child."

Alice frowned slightly. "I'm not a child, either."

The woman opened her hands slightly and bowed her head.

"They're my friends," Alice said. "I trust them with my life."

Mary stepped up beside Alice. "I grew up here, lady. Why don't you drop the attitude and show us to our seats? We've traveled a long way to get here, and it starts all over again sooner than I'd like."

The hostess eyed Smith. "Bollwerk is a distant journey."

"I'm from Ancora," Alice said.

The woman's eyebrows rose slightly, the first sign of surprise Alice had seen. "That is a distant journey indeed."

Alice couldn't quite place what was bothering her about the woman's attitude. They were on their way to a booth in the back before she realized the woman reminded her of one of the Highborns in Ancora.

Eva slid in beside Mary, and Alice sat down next to Smith.

"Menus?" Smith said. "Fancy place."

"It would certainly explain that bitch of a hostess," Eva muttered when the woman walked away.

"Don't worry about it," Mary said. "Let's get some fried bread and maybe a beer." She ran her fingers through her hair and flipped her menu over. "I need to relax before we head back to Bollwerk."

"So soon?" Eva asked.

Mary nodded. "We have to be there. It's … it's not just a debt anymore, Eva. Jacob and Charles and their friends need us. Bollwerk's been good to me, and I'll be damned if I let the Butcher march into that city unchallenged."

Eva frowned and rubbed the back of her hand. "How long can you stay?"

"We'll at least be here through the night. We have to wait for Lady Katherine's decision. Do you think she'll help?"

Eva shook her head slowly. Alice didn't think she meant it as a no. She was fairly certain Eva meant she had no idea what Lady Katherine would say. Eva shrugged. "She's turned down many pleas from the wasteland villages for assistance. Their requests are almost always due to some infighting between the tribes. I don't know."

They ordered and waited in relative silence until Smith began drumming his fork on the wooden table.

"Stop that," Mary said.

"What?" Smith asked as his tempo increased.

"It's rude and you're drawing attention to us."

Smith sighed and let the fork fall from his hands, clattering onto the bare wood as the server dropped off three pewter steins, filled with a dark ale, and one glass of milk.

"Milk?" Alice asked. "Ugh, I thought you were joking."

"Just try it," Eva said. "It's not bug milk, if that's what you're worried about."

"She's not worried about that," Smith said. "The girl drinks Sweetwing tea like it's water."

Alice slid the glass closer and said, "I'm feeling a bit outnumbered here." She took a tentative sip and jerked her head away from the straw, smacking her lips when the taste of cocoa and sugar hit her tongue. "What?"

"White Cocoa Milk," Eva said. "It's a lot better than the regular stuff."

Alice took another deep drink. "Yeah it is. Wow."

Smith started drumming his fork on the table again.

"Oh, *gods!*" Mary said. "Smith! Stop it. Drumming that fork into submission isn't going to change anything about you meeting with the tinkers."

Eva glanced between Mary and Smith and kept her voice low. "The tinkers here aren't fond of Biomechs."

"I know," Smith said.

"So why do you want to talk to them?"

Smith set his fork down and sighed. He spun his stein of ale around, took a large drink, and let it thump down on the wood. "It is better that they hear the state of things from me."

"Why?"

Smith and Mary locked gazes for a moment before Mary nodded.

He turned his gaze to Eva and said, "I am Targrove's last apprentice."

"Targrove?" Eva asked, and she looked like Smith had just declared himself the king of the entire world. "Targrove didn't take any apprentices after the Deadlands War."

"He designed the early skeleton of the technology I used in my arm, Eva. He taught me most of what I knew when I first became a tinker. Proving that to the tinkers here could be the difference between their support or their continued fear of Biomechs."

The table fell silent when the server returned with two steaming plates, heaped with fried breads and salted pork. She brought another round of drinks, but no one touched them. Eva stared at Smith while everyone else watched Eva.

"That's not possible," Eva said. "Targrove wouldn't have touched biomechanics if his life depended on it."

"His did," Smith said quietly. "And I would not be alive if he had not become proficient in them. Targrove's pilgrimage to Bollwerk was not without its tragedies. The other men traveling with him died when they were swarmed by Tail Swords. Targrove found shelter in an ancient ironwood, only to lose his arm to a Tree Killer."

"Like Jacob?" Alice asked.

"Yes, but closer to Bollwerk. One of our patrols found him and brought him into the city. Archibald rebuilt Targrove's arm with a rudimentary biomech valve. I do not know the entire story, but at the end of it Targrove became a revolutionary. He built things you cannot imagine."

"He built you?" Eva asked.

Smith let out a slow chuckle. "Parts of me, yes. It is not an inaccurate statement."

Eva took a deep drink of her beer and then drank some more. She gasped when she finished the stein and set it onto the table. "Smith, you intend to tell the other tinkers about this?"

"Yes."

"Why?"

"We need their help. For one, we don't have enough biomech tinkers to repair our soldiers and tend to our city at the same time."

Eva cursed and grabbed Mary's stein. "I'm going to need about ten more of these."

Mary took it back and smiled at Eva.

"You can't," Eva said. "They could kill you for even suggesting it. Biomechanics are forbidden in Belldorn."

Smith nodded. "If that were entirely true, I suspect the Lady Katherine would have killed me during our audience. She knew what I was. She knows what Archibald builds. Do you really think she does not know what Targrove did in Bollwerk? Look at the world with an unbiased eye, and its secrets will fall away."

Eva froze. Alice was a little afraid the girl had just died at the table she'd become so immobile.

"That's … that's the mantra of the Skyriders."

"Yes," Smith said as he tapped his stein with his index finger.

"No one knows that outside of Belldorn. It's their code."

"Targrove knew. Targrove wrote it. Our early biomechanics were based on the weapons and gliders of the Skyriders."

"What if they won't go with you?" Eva asked.

Smith shrugged. "That is secondary, honestly. If we can get them to understand that Targrove changed his opinions of Biomechs before he passed away, they will be more likely to support our initial request."

Eva slumped back onto the padded bench. "That's brilliant."

Mary grabbed a piece of the fried Sweet Bread off the platter and chewed it up. She pushed the plate toward Alice before turning back to Eva. "Don't tell him that. I'll never hear the end of it."

"End of what?" Smith asked. "That your girlfriend thinks I am brilliant?"

Eva started in her seat. "Did you tell him?" she asked as she fidgeted.

Mary shook her head.

"You two weren't exactly subtle about it in the elevator," Alice said as she snatched up a chunk of fried Sweet Bread.

Mary laughed and crossed her arms. "Shut up, kid."

Alice grinned. "These are so good! I haven't had cinnamon since I won a cake at Festival last year. We ate off it for a week."

"It is good Sweet Bread," Smith said. "I admit, I was a bit concerned Mary meant 'sweetbreads.' She likes those disgusting things too."

"You're not upset?" Eva said as she looked at Smith.

"Upset? Why?"

"I thought … I thought we'd be frowned on by people from Bollwerk."

Smith shook his head. "I would say those times died with the last Bishop, though some remnants may exist. People do enjoy their hatred. And really, Mary …" He turned his gaze to her. "Did you think I believed your stories about our scouting expeditions in the wastes? Every damn time we went, we ran into a Skyrider patrol. The *same* Skyrider patrol."

"I didn't want to make you uncomfortable," Mary said.

"Sometimes you should not worry about what people think, and you should only worry about living the life you want."

"That's why I needed the Skysworn."

Smith popped a Sweet Bread into his mouth and smiled. "I know."

CHAPTER TEN

S MITH MADE HIS way from Mary's favorite restaurant to the tinker guild's workshop. It was not hard to find, being that Targrove had told him a thousand stories about it. It had been rather annoying when he was a young man, but now he was thankful for it. Mary had decided to visit her family that night with Eva and Alice. He hoped very much that it would be a happy reunion.

The ocean grew louder as he neared the workshop. The tower was close to the older parts of the city, much of which had been lost to the seas. He stopped before the iron-barred door. It looked heavy, and immovable, and Smith's lips quirked into a half smile when he saw the subtle pattern of a Steamsworn fist etched into the rusted iron. His eyes followed the door up to its peak, and the peak to the windows far above that stretched into the brick and vanished into the night sky. He thought about Targrove standing here, admiring his handiwork, and there was a twinge in his heart, an echo that rode between happiness and loss.

Smith reached out and knocked on the old door.

The peephole slid open after a moment and a small, frail voice said, "Yes?"

"May I speak with the tinkers of Belldorn? I have information you need."

The old voice on the other side of the door quieted as the peephole slid closed. A series of clacks and squeaks echoed around the door before it cracked open. "Come in and tell us what truly brings you here."

Smith stepped inside, and he *knew* it had been Targrove's home. Everything inside spoke to what he knew of the man. From the tall brass-emblazoned fireplace to the immaculate stone workbenches.

"Why did you let him in here?" one of the three men inside asked. They were all pale, with flaming hair, and it reminded Smith very much of his old mentor.

"I am Targrove's apprentice, come to warn his homeland."

Smith's words silenced the room.

An aged, crackling voice spoke from the shadows. "None of Targrove's apprentices still live." Her voice was frail, and her body looked even more so as her wheelchair puttered into the light of the fireplace. "Do not lie to us."

Smith couldn't hide the broad smile that split his face. Targrove had described his lady as a vibrant goddess, and how could this beautiful old woman be anyone else? "Theodosia."

She narrowed her eyes. "What did you say?"

"Theodosia, Targrove's only regret for leaving Belldorn, you are her."

He knows her true name.

No one knows that name.

It's not possible.

But how else …

Smith let the whispers continue and watched as Theodosia shifted a lever on her wheelchair. A tiny puff of smoke rose from the back, forming a perfect ring.

Theodosia's voice rose as she leaned forward. "It cannot be."

"I am Smith, the last of Targrove's apprentices." Smith unbuttoned his vest and began to remove it as he spoke. "Targrove studied biomechanics with Archibald in Bollwerk. He became one of our greatest tinkers, a biomechanic unlike any other." Smith let his shirt fall to the floor. "He gave me the knowledge to one day build this."

"Sacrilege!" One of the men shouted. "Targrove would never defile his hands with biomechanics." He made for the front door. "I won't listen to you drag our patron's name through the dirt."

"Stop!" Theodosia snapped.

The man froze mid stride.

"We will not insult our guest further. Sit down."

Smith did not often take his shirt off in front of people, even people he knew well. A handful of Steamsworn, and Mary, had been the only ones who had truly had a chance to study the masterpiece he'd built on Targrove's foundation.

"By the gods …" Theodosia's finger traced the pattern of the brass chest plate that covered the right half of Smith's upper body. "What happened to you?"

"A cannon shot took my arm. It would have been my life if not for Targrove."

"You're too young to have been in the war, son."

Smith unlatched the layered metal plates running down his upper arm and set the construct on one of the workbenches. He rubbed his hands together, such a simple motion that sent a hundred different gears and pistons to turning and pumping along his arm. "I was one of Archibald's spies, sent to watch over Ballern."

"Ballern?" Theodosia said as her eyes widened. "That is a mighty journey for one from Bollwerk."

Smith nodded. "We were caught by one of their scout ships off the coast. They boarded us and interrogated the crew. Everything seemed okay, as we showed them our damaged navigation console—our excuse for being there—but before we could fully retreat, they opened fire. Most of the crew died. Targrove had been on the airship to make an appraisal of Ballern's battlements. If he had not been, I would have died.

One of the tinkers, the shortest of the three, stepped closer and looked at Smith's shoulder. "You're made of metal. How is that pivot joint anchored?"

"It is in the bone," Smith said.

The man shivered, his cold blue eyes meeting Smith's. "That must have hurt something fierce. Gods, look at that." He leaned in closer and reached out, before pausing and glancing up at Smith. "May I?"

Smith nodded.

"The core here, look how the top of the piston is braided. Only man I ever saw do that was Targrove. Too much damn work if you ask me."

"I hope you will listen to the rest of the story I have to share. Dark times are coming for every city from Ancora to Belldorn, and we need your help."

"How are you not mad?" The man who'd almost stormed out asked. "How are you not a Berserker?"

"It is the metal," Smith said. "Targrove used a different alloy on me. One he had used on himself as it was stronger. It was not long before I discovered some metals would drive men insane, while others are harmless."

The tinker cocked his head to the side and glanced at the others in the room. "What do you think, Theo?"

A broad smile raised the woman's wrinkled cheeks. "Let him speak, Frederick. It is the least we can do for the last apprentice of Targrove."

Theo extended her hand and clasped Smith's forearm. "Welcome home, Smith."

✧   ✧   ✧

ALICE LOOKED UP at the small brick one-story house. She'd never seen a home quite that short. It seemed like a terrible waste of living space to only have one floor.

"Are you ready?" Eva asked.

Mary nodded, raised her fist, and hesitated just above the wood. She took a deep breath and then knocked three times.

"Coming!" A voice said from behind the door. There was one quiet click before the door started to open.

One click? Alice could scarcely imagine a home with only one lock. How could you ever feel safe with that?

The door opened fully to reveal a wide-eyed woman who could have been Mary's sister if it weren't for the perfectly white hair pulled back into a bun. "I ... Mary? Mallory, get in here! You won't ... you won't believe ..." And then her voice fractured as she took two quick steps forward and threw her arms around Mary.

Heavy boots fell against thick wooden tiles before Mallory appeared at the door. Her gray hair lifted slightly in the breeze. "What is it, Maxine?"

Maxine stepped away, tears running down her blushed cheeks as she ushered Mary forward.

Something flashed across the woman's face. Alice couldn't quite place it, but she'd seen her own father look at her like that when she was top of her class one year. That was it, she was proud, but there was a deeper sadness there. Alice could almost feel her loss.

"Mary ..." Mallory's voice was barely a whisper. "Oh, we missed you so much."

Mary choked on a sob and squeezed her mother even harder. "I got the Skysworn. It's mine. I miss you both so much."

"Come in," Maxine said. "Bring your friends. We have food and drinks, and you're welcome to stay as long as you like. All of you."

Maxine reminded Alice of her mother, and it made her homesick and happy all at once. Alice followed the rest of the group through a modest hallway covered in paintings of airships and oceans so filled with detail she couldn't believe they weren't photographs.

Eva slid into a chair in the next room, beside a small brick fireplace. There were two framed photos on the mantle. One was a much younger Maxine and Mallory, beaming with a bundle of blankets in their arm. The other was Mary with pilot's goggles and some sort of scroll held in her hand. It took a moment for Alice to realize it was a diploma.

She felt a little more comfortable in the small house once the tearful reunion of Mary and her parents had subsided. From what Alice knew, the family hadn't seen each other in years. Alice couldn't imagine going that long without seeing her parents. The time she'd gone already without seeing them felt like an eternity.

"Here, honey, have something to eat," Mary's mom said as she sat a platter of cheese and flatbread on the wrought iron coffee table. She bustled out of the room and returned in short order, carrying what looked like a plate of homemade candies.

Alice thought she might explode if she took another bite of anything, but she did it anyway. She was beginning to regret eating so much at the restaurant, and cheese wasn't going to help. The flatbread was firm enough to support the cheese, but it didn't break like a cracker. It was soft and chewy, and Alice knew right then she was going to stuff her face.

"I see you've already found Eva," Mallory said as she settled into the leather chair across the coffee table.

Mary sat down beside Alice on the couch, and she scooted closer to the armrest when Maxine came to join them with three drinks balanced in her hands. Mary reached out toward Eva and squeezed her hand. "I didn't mean to find her first. She just happened to be working the docks."

Eva fidgeted a bit and blushed.

"She might have mentioned something about a message on one of those transmitters you brought home last time," Mallory said as she sipped the steaming drink Maxine had brought.

"You weren't supposed to tell them," Mary said under her breath.

Eva gave her a sideways grin. "They were the only other people who would be as excited as I was. I told them I wasn't really sure you were coming, even though I figured you were."

"We certainly didn't expect you to be knocking at our door tonight," Maxine said as she patted Mary's knee. "Who's your new friend?"

"Oh, I'm so sorry!" Mary said. "This is Alice. She's from Ancora."

"Well, she may live there now," Mallory said, "but someone in her family is from here. You have beautiful hair, Alice."

"Thank you," Alice said. "And thank you for your hospitality."

Mallory sipped her drink and smiled. "You're quite well spoken for a … an Ancoran."

That familiar feeling of being judged crawled up Alice's back. It was like walking into the Highlands. Everyone stared and made a snap judgment because your clothes weren't the right style, or your haircut, or the lack of whatever ridiculous trend was sweeping through the Highlanders. She leaned over and picked up one of the warm mugs.

"Mum," Mary hissed. "That was rude."

"I don't think I was rude," Mallory said. "I was just impressed that she was well spoken."

"Rude," Mary said.

"I'm sorry if you took offense," Mallory said.

Alice took a drink of the tea—it was rich with a hint of sweetness—and smacked her lips. "It's fine. So you're Mallory, Maxine, and Mary?"

"The three M's of Ocean Street," Maxine said with a smile.

Mary sighed. "There's a name I never thought I'd live down. Thankfully no one outside of Belldorn knows it." Her eyes flashed to Alice. "Except you."

"Blackmail," Alice said with a slow nod of her head.

"That is *not* what I meant."

"I'm sure Smith would love to hear that story," Alice said as she turned to Maxine and leaned forward. "Tell me more."

"Oh, I like her," Maxine said.

Mary groaned and flopped back into her seat.

As irritated as Alice had been with Mallory's thoughtless words, the rest of the evening was nice. It was much like spending time with her own family, lots of teasing and laughter. It seemed like everything here was made to remind her of home.

There was nothing left on the tray but crumbs and a few wedges of cheese by the time there was a knock at the door. It was late, Alice knew, but she wasn't sure how late.

"Who would be knocking at this hour?" Mallory asked.

Mary jumped off the couch and ran down the hall. Alice heard muted voices before the door closed again. A tall, bulky shadow followed Mary back into the living room.

"Smith!" Alice said. "Back already?"

"Already?" Smith asked. "I had to buy a round of whiskey for the tinkers." He frowned. "It was not unlike an engine degreaser, but I have a strange craving for more."

"They take you to the Sand Bar?" Mallory asked.

Smith nodded.

"Nice place."

"Oh, I'm sorry. Mom, Mum, this is Smith. Sometimes I forget you three haven't met in person."

"Did it hurt having all that metal jammed into your body?" Mallory asked.

Smith leveled his gaze at Mallory. "No, it was like the feather-soft touch of a sledgehammer."

Alice smiled as Smith's comment seemed to shut Mallory up. It wasn't that she didn't like the woman, but she really didn't like her. She'd already been rude to her *and* Smith, and she was just waiting for her to be a jerk to Eva.

"Did you want to head back to the Skysworn tonight?" Smith asked. There was a small hint of something in his voice, and Alice thought it might be hope.

"Oh, no," Maxine said. "You're all staying here. We have plenty of space."

"That is … so kind of you," Smith said.

Eva stood up and stretched her back. "It's getting late. Why don't we call it a night?"

"Might as well," Mary said. "I need some rest before we see Lady Katherine again."

"Will you show our guests to their rooms?" Maxine asked. "I need to speak with your Mum about *manners*."

Mallory frowned at her wife.

"Come on," Mary said. She led the group through a doorway by the couch. It opened up into a long hallway with hardwood floors and a dizzying black and white pattern painted on the walls. "Ignore the walls if you can. They're awful, I know. Third door down is the bathroom. Smith, the largest guest bed is at that end of the hall."

He nodded and headed that way.

"Alice, you can have the room next to him. Eva and I will split my old bedroom. Goodnight, everyone."

Alice hesitated and then hugged Mary. "See you in the morning."

"Sleep well, kid."

Alice smiled as she ducked into her bedroom for the night. She wasn't sure how long it would take to fall asleep. She was worried about her family, and Jacob, and the others. The room was a disgusting green color, but the bed was soft and warm, and she was asleep far faster than she thought possible.

Alice's last thoughts were of Lady Katherine and what her decision could mean for her friends.

CHAPTER ELEVEN

TWO LOUD KNOCKS echoed through the small home in Belldorn. Alice looked up from the dishes she was rinsing off in the sink.

"I'll get it," Mary said as she dried her hands.

Alice turned the water off, dried her own hands, and followed Mary into the hallway. It seemed strangely early for someone to be calling. They'd gotten up with the sunrise and eaten Mallory's tower of pancakes drizzled in cocoa syrup. Alice thought it had sounded odd, but she never wanted regular pancakes again.

Mary unlocked the deadbolt and froze when she opened the door.

"Oh, heavens," Maxine said behind her. "It's Lady Katherine. I wish Mallory hadn't left for work already, she'd …"

Alice smiled when Smith walked up behind her and patted her shoulder. Eva hung back by the doorway to the kitchen.

"I've come to give you my decision," Lady Katherine said when Mary did nothing but stare at the casually garbed woman at their door. "May I come in?"

Mary nodded slowly and opened the door as wide as it would go.

"I've spoken to the tinkers and the Skyriders alike." Lady Katherine led the way down the hall until they were all standing in the living room. "It would seem you have had a busy night." Lady Katherine frowned and crossed her arms. "I've been informed that if I *don't* help you, some of my tinkers may abandon Belldorn and head for Bollwerk themselves."

"My apologies, Lady Katherine," Smith said with a slight bow.

"I intended to offer my help regardless, Smith. I admit, I thought of having you thrown from the tower when I heard of your ... assistance."

"I am sorry, my lady. Ballern and the Butcher could be the end of us all. I had to take the risk."

"That is why we are not checking to see if you have wings built into your biomechanics, Smith." The lady paused and rubbed her shoulder. "It is because you are right that you live. Do not take our compliance for weakness. We have turned Ballern away at every strike. They try new tactics every few months, from sea and by air, but they always fail."

"It speaks volumes of your leadership, my lady."

Lady Katherine snorted. "Cut the shit, Smith. It does not fit you."

A smile lifted the corners of Smith's mouth. The crack in the lady's façade made her more human, and Alice liked it.

"Regardless of my ... level of appreciation," Lady Katherine said, "I am glad to have another of Targrove's ilk on our side. I hope your skills are as deft as your tongue.

"Two Porcupine class airships left this morning, each carrying a tinker. You'll have Frederick and his younger apprentice, Tobias. The two ships are not our largest, but they will serve you well. I am not willing to send more as it could compromise our defenses too severely. By sending ships to Bollwerk—and they should arrive in a few days—we leave ourselves more vulnerable than we have been in a very long time. Do not forget that. Do not forget *us*."

Lady Katherine turned to leave but paused at the door. "Return here after the war, and we will celebrate the Empire's victory, or plan our revenge."

The door cracked shut behind Lady Katherine, echoing for a short time.

"What's a Porcupine class ship?" Alice asked.

"It is a warship of terrible power," Smith said, his eyes still on the front door. "Its bristles are mortars and cannons, and it is more deadly than you can imagine." He frowned and looked at Mary. "Targrove used to say they carried so much iron they should not be able to float an inch off the ground."

Mary rubbed her face and cursed. "Did that just happen? Lady Katherine, and the warships? Did that seriously just happen?"

"What did she mean by *don't forget us*?" Eva asked. She stepped out from the doorway and leaned against the fireplace's mantle.

"That was fancy talk for don't fuck up," Alice said.

"Bah!" Smith said before he burst into laughter. "You have clearly been around bad influences, girl."

"And what Empire?" Alice asked.

"I'll get you a book from the city's library," Mary said.

"Can I come with you?" Alice asked. "I'd like to see that, and learn about the evolution of the bugs."

"They consider that information too valuable to allow the public inside. I've never gotten access before." She paused. "At least not that they know of."

Alice raised her eyebrows.

Mary smiled. "The Old Empire of Belldorn was full of people like you, pale skin and hair like a bonfire. There are old stories here that basically say you're good luck."

"Good luck?" Alice said. "People tend to chop things up and make jewelry out of stuff that's good luck."

Maxine took a deep breath and focused on Mary. "Do you have to leave? I can see it in your face. You're anxious already."

Mary nodded. "We have to." She stepped closer to Maxine and hugged her. "I'll be home soon. I promise."

"We'll be waiting," Eva said.

Mary pulled away from her mother and looked to Eva. "You could come with us."

Eva shook her head. "With the warships away at Bollwerk, they'll need as much help here as they can get."

Mary's forehead wrinkled. "I know you're right, but I miss you."

Eva laughed. "I doubt the Lady Katherine will consider that an acceptable reason for abandoning my post."

"I'll be back as soon as it's over."

"You better be," Eva said. She embraced Mary.

✧   ✧   ✧

JACOB HELD HIS breath while the patrol walked by, a tiny knot of dread unraveling in his gut when they vanished around the corner. He looked down at the old man sitting on the bench next to him.

"Breathe," Charles said. "I thought you were good a stealing things? The look on your face is just screaming for someone to notice you."

Jacob took two deep breaths. "This is different, and you know it."

Charles smiled and elbowed him in the ribs. "I'm just giving you trouble, boy."

Jacob shifted the straps on his backpack so they weren't cutting into the same spots on his shoulders. They'd brought more bombs today, and the packs were a lot heavier than he'd expected.

"Now, let's move." The old tinker grunted as he picked himself up off the bench.

"How much farther?"

Charles glanced over his shoulder. "We're about six blocks past the safe house, so we need to go left at the next street. Should be able to see the base by then."

"And we're supposed to find the abandoned storefront where Morgan will be waiting for us?"

"That's the plan."

"Why do you think it was abandoned?" Jacob asked. He took a few quick steps to catch up to Charles's pace.

"You'll see."

Jacob pondered what Charles meant as they made their way onto the next cobblestone street and continued on a few blocks. There were a lot of people in the shopping district, carrying canvas bags and wheeling carts with handfuls of essential foods while they bickered and bartered.

"Are they safe here?" Jacob asked.

Charles nodded. "Should be. The breakaway point is just inside the base's walls. If it's not a clean break, there's almost a city block between the base and the shopping district."

Jacob flinched and wrinkled his nose when a terrible stench almost choked him. "What's that smell? It's awful."

"You don't want to know, kid."

Jacob felt a little better about the explosives, but he'd also seen how bad things could go when someone made the wrong calculation. City walls could collapse, buildings could fall, and people would die.

"There it is," Charles said. He pointed to a two-story building with a gray wooden façade. Charles led the way through a cluster of pedestrians, dodging foul-tempered men and women until they eventually reached the front door. It seemed to be nailed shut.

Jacob looked around and didn't see any patrols. "Looks clear." The base wall in the distance caught his eye, and his entire body shivered. "Charles …" The dead hung in masses from the walls. Several had been there long enough for scavengers to tear them apart, leaving bits and gore piled along the base of the wall. Clouds of fat flies crawled everywhere, and Jacob had his answer about the smell.

"I know." Charles paused and looked at the man sitting near the door. When the huddled figure nodded, Charles pulled on the board hammered across the door, opening it with a quiet squeak.

Jacob grabbed the door after Charles slipped through. The gray paint warmed his fingers in the morning sun, and then they were inside. Jacob blinked, trying to make out shapes and people in the sudden darkness of the boarded-up shop, and trying to rid himself of that awful vision of the dead. He wondered about the Carrion Worms that would inevitably show up, but then he remembered the city sat on solid rock. The worms couldn't burrow through stone.

"You made it." Jacob recognized Morgan's voice, but he couldn't quite make out his face.

"Of course we did," Charles said. "What are Steamsworn if not reliable?"

"Crazy, in my experience."

"That too, that too," Charles said as he rubbed his beard. "Your lookout is somewhat obvious outside. Are you not concerned about him bringing attention?"

"No," Morgan said. "He's disciplined and smells rancid. Most soldiers assume he's a drunk."

Charles nodded slowly. "Let's not waste any more time. Where's the tunnel?"

"Follow me," Morgan said.

It took Jacob a few more seconds of shuffling his feet in the dim light before he could make out their surroundings. He gasped when he saw the small piles of shredded and discarded bindings. There had to be hundreds of them … *thousands*.

"This is the legacy Fel and the Butcher want to leave behind." A man moved in the corner, slowly stepping into a sliver of dusty light. "We have to stop them."

"Clark?" Jacob asked. He recognized the man who had greeted them at the tents when they first arrived at Dauschen. There was a rage boiling within Clark that Jacob could scarcely believe was there. The man was soft-spoken, and deliberate in everything Jacob had seen him do. Now he looked ready to kill.

Clark almost growled. "They built pyres behind the building too. They burned the most 'vile' writings before they boarded up the library. Everything here about Bollwerk and the Steamsworn is gone. Every page about Midstream and the genocide of their people is burned and buried. They took it all."

Jacob turned to Charles. Charles adjusted his glasses and said, "Yes, I knew, and yes, it's terrible."

"We have to stop them," Jacob said.

"That's why we're here. Don't forget it."

Jacob nodded and pulled at his pant leg. He hadn't thought about his leg much, but if the invaders were burning books about the Steamsworn, what the hell would they do if they saw someone with a biomech leg?

"Drakkar is at the safe house?" Charles said.

"Yes," Morgan said. "He'll keep the transmitter guarded."

Morgan lifted a false panel in the back of one of the tallest bookcases. His hand vanished into the darkness before a metallic snap echoed through the room. The bookcase swung forward as easily as a hinged door. Morgan clicked the igniter on a lantern hanging within.

Darkness became shadowed stairs, dancing in the light of the dusty lantern. Jacob stepped closer and leaned over the top landing. "How far down does that go?"

"Very far," Morgan said, "but you two need to go left at the second landing. That will drop you onto the supports. From there, you'll have an escape hatch every block or so."

"Escape hatch?"

"Remember the access points to the underground in Ancora?" Charles asked.

Jacob nodded.

"Same kind of thing.

Morgan held out a small brass box. It had a speaker on it, much like the one Mary had on the Skysworn, and a button on the side. "You'll be shallow, just below the street. We should be able to reach you if there's an emergency."

Charles took it and slid it into a pocket high on his vest. "I'll be lucky if my knees don't give out on these damn stairs with all these damn bombs." He stepped into the stairwell. "But this is a blow I want to strike myself."

"You're a legend to the Steamsworn, Charles von Atlier."

Jacob wasn't sure who was speaking as the bookcase door closed behind them. It was a trio of voices that said, "Fist in hand, we strike together."

Jacob shivered at the quiet chant.

Charles sighed, pulled the lantern off the wall, and started down the stone stairway.

"It's … it's inspiring," Jacob said. "It makes you not want to let them down. I mean, I didn't want to let them down anyway."

"That's the biggest trick when it comes to war. Keeping people motivated and willing to die for a cause that they probably don't need to die for. I hate war, kid."

Jacob wanted to say something about how he thought Charles was great at it, and everyone they met seemed to respect Charles's thoughts and strategies, but the old tinker's words stayed with him. Charles hated war. How could you be so good at something you hated? Why would you be so good at it?

"To keep my friends and family safe."

"Did I say all that out loud?" Jacob asked.

Charles let out a quiet chuckle as they hit the second landing. "Enough for me to hear your questions, yes." He swung the lantern to the left and nodded.

"It's musty," Jacob said. "And … and something's moving."

"That's the smaller river," Charles said. "Not nearly so large as the river below Ancora, or even the main river below Dauschen, but far deadlier. This one travels through miles of stone before resurfacing. If you fall in, you're dead. Simple as that.

"We're not going near it though, right?" Jacob couldn't keep his voice steady.

Charles didn't answer.

The back of Jacob's hand brushed the rough stone wall and came away damp. There was either a concentration of groundwater here, or they were closing in on the river.

Charles fumbled at his vest pocket and pulled out the little brass box. He clicked the button. "Water beetle, over."

"Received."

"Water beetle?" Jacob asked, remembering that horrifying creature that almost smashed the life out of him beneath Ancora. "Are those things here too?"

"Never seen one here before," Charles said. "I'd never seen one in Ancora before either, so take that as you will. Good news is, the signal reaches us here. The detonators should both be in range from the library or the safe house. We can decide which route is better once we finish with the explosives."

Charles slid his backpack off and pulled something out. It looked more like a Sky Pirate's grappling gun from one of the stories he'd read when he was a kid than anything they'd use here.

"What is that?"

"Grappling gun, of course."

"Are you serious?" Jacob asked, half annoyed and half giddy. "What do we need that for?"

"Step up here and take a look."

Jacob did, and then he froze as Charles raised the lantern. The only word that came to his mind was *chasm*. It was deep—so deep the lantern's light couldn't reach the bottom. A few thin beams of sunlight pierced the top of the cavern, but that was it. Everything else was darkness, and shadows, and the menacing sound of a rushing river.

When Jacob's brain managed to start working again, he cursed. "I won't have to worry about drowning if I fall into that river."

"No, I reckon you won't," Charles said. He offered Jacob a grin. "You'll either have a heart attack before you reach the bottom, or you'll break apart like a fine china bowl on those rocks. See where the lamplight breaks on the stone up there?"

Jacob nodded.

"Those are the supports we need to wire with the charges."

"Gods, tell me you're joking. Could we have dropped onto them from above?"

Charles shook his head. "Perhaps in one or two spots, but they would likely be locked. Underground is our best option. When we get closer, you'll see the branching supports that bear the extra load from the base. Some hatches have a ladder leading to the surface. If we have an emergency, that's where you go. You get out and head for the safe house or the library. I don't care what's happening, you understand me?" Charles turned to Jacob and put a hand on his shoulder. His voice was darker, almost menacing. "You get out. This *is* war now, and these people won't hesitate to kill us. You have to remember that. Them or us, that's your mantra in war. *It's them or us.* It has to be, or you die.

"Now then," Charles said, changing the tone of his voice so fast it made Jacob's head spin. "This is one of my favorite inventions, but it has about as many uses as a strainer. By that, I mean it has one use, and it's worthless for everything else."

Jacob had heard what the old tinker said, but all that was really going through his mind at that point was, *It's them or us.*

CHAPTER TWELVE

"WHAT?" DRAKKAR ASKED, unwilling to believe the words Lottie had spoken.

"We have a mole. Someone leaked our plans. We have to leave *now*. Morgan and the others should be at the old library."

"How do you know this?"

"We can find them there. I have the rations in the base. I …"

Drakkar blew out a breath and let Lottie ramble. She was gone, locked into the routine her training had taught her, gathering weapons, gathering food. Whether the threat was real or imagined, Drakkar could not risk himself and Samuel by staying in the safe house. He looked up and met the Spider Knight's eyes. Samuel nodded and buckled his greaves before tightening his chest plate.

"We have to warn Archibald," Drakkar said. "If we have been compromised, his communications may have been overheard as well."

Drakkar opened the closet door, revealing the hidden radio with its tower of glass tubes and brass fittings. He had seen enough people use it now to understand the simplicity of the thing, even if he did not understand exactly *how* one's voice could travel so far.

He picked up the transmitter and clicked the copper button. "Water Beetle to Nest, Water Beetle to Nest."

Archibald's response was almost instantaneous. "Nest."

"Water Beetle compromised. Mission underway. This is our last transmission."

There was a brief moment of silence before Archibald said, "Understood."

"What now?" Samuel asked.

"We make for the library."

✧　✧　✧

THE REST OF the morning had been a blur. Alice remembered packing her things and making the short walk back to the docks, but it was almost like the details were missing from her head. She wasn't focused, and she knew it.

No, it wasn't that she wasn't focused. Her mind was sharp, and she felt jittery because of it. She was focused on other things, like the Porcupines from Belldorn. Smith had shown her a picture and called them madness given life. Each Porcupine was a floating mass of cannons, and they were headed for Bollwerk.

What if the Lady Katherine wasn't really on their side? What if she was secretly aligned with Ballern? What if this was the perfect excuse to take down Bollwerk? Alice shivered as the questions cycled through her head over and over again.

"You okay?"

Alice looked up to find Mary with her back turned to the windscreen.

"I'm fine."

"You look like you're about to gnaw your own hand off."

Alice offered a weak smile. "I was just wondering what Lady Katherine gains from helping Archibald."

"Ah, politics. I've found it best to keep my head out of politics."

"Didn't you get this ship from Archibald because of some kind of politics? Or he owed you something, or … something?"

Mary hung her head and laughed. She glanced back up at Alice before spinning her chair back around. "Well, that's not the entire story, but it had a lot to do with politics. Might be why I hate them so much."

"What happened?"

"More than I'm going to tell you here. You don't need to be worrying about Archibald's more questionable tactics of the last ten years right now. You already know he has spies in every city on the continent. That should be unsettling enough."

"I thought that was all to help keep Bollwerk informed. From possible threats, right?"

"Good intentions, Alice. People end up doing a lot of bad things, even when they start with good intentions." Mary glanced at a cluster of gauges before she said, "*Especially* when they start with good intentions."

One of the horns rattled beside Mary. "Thrusters are at maximum."

"Thanks, Smith."

"We have been in the sky for a few hours. Keep an eye out. You should be seeing those warships soon. I would not want Alice to miss that."

"I'm more worried about running into them in the literal sense," Mary said.

"Yes, that would also be bad."

Mary turned and smiled at Alice. "You're in for a sight. That'll be a story you can make Jacob jealous with. You know that's how Belldorn dealt with pirates?"

"They have pirates in Belldorn?"

"Not anymore. They blew them out of the sky. Truth be told, that may have been heavy-handed of the Lady Katherine. We could have turned some of them into allies."

"Was that the political issue you had with Archibald?"

Mary turned in her seat and stared at Alice. "How in the ..." She laughed and spun back around. "That's a long story for another day. Let's just say I used to have more in common with Jacob's pickpocketing than

I did with the Steamsworn."

"Look!" Mary said as she popped open one of the horns. "They're on the horizon, Smith. You coming up?"

"Not at these speeds," Smith said. "I will check the porthole."

"Take off your harness. It won't do you any good at these speeds anyway."

With that reassuring thought, Alice unfastened herself and stepped up beside Mary.

At first, she didn't see what Mary was talking about, but then the sun glinted on a shadow in the distance. It grew faster than she could believe, reminding her of just how impossibly fast the Skysworn traveled.

"Don't blink," Mary said. She gave Alice a sideways smile.

It felt like no more than a heartbeat from the time she caught the glint of light to the time the monstrosity filled the windscreen, and then it was gone. The vision of what Alice had seen wasn't gone, though. It was a floating city of cannons. That was the only description that made sense. Some of the cannons had been so large she'd thought they were smoke-stacks, others were angled down and back, covering the terrain behind the massive warship. It didn't matter where an attacker would come from … It would be in the crosshairs.

Smith howled into the horn. "Did you see that, Mary! Damn! Tell me the kid saw it!"

"Where … where were the gas chambers?" Alice asked. "It was all metal."

Smith's tinny voice laughed in the horn. "Oh yes, she saw it."

"They're inside of it," Mary said. "It has more thrusters across the bottom to add lift and propulsion. It's a mad weapon."

"It is utter insanity," Smith said. "And they are sending *two* toward Bollwerk? Archibald is a genius, Mary. Tell me he is not."

"He is," Mary said, "and it terrifies me."

"He is much like a Berserker when pushed," Smith said. "Be glad he is on your side, and do not concern yourself with the collateral."

"Sometimes the collateral is our friends," Mary said.

Smith cursed, and his voice was much more reserved when he came back over the horn. "I know, but keep your chin up. You have the Skysworn now, and there is nothing we cannot do. Nothing."

Mary gently closed the cover to the horn. "I hope you're right, Smith. Gods but I hope you're right."

They spent the rest of the trip in relative silence. Alice fastened herself back into her harness. Smith's voice popped onto the horn a few times while he complained about some level or some pressure being too high for the ship, but after a terse word from Mary he'd usually find a way to fix it.

It reminded Alice of Jacob, and that made her smile before it made her worry. Charles had taken Jacob into Dauschen. They were on the front line of this disaster. Alice supposed they had been already, after what happened in Ancora. Those guards would have killed Jacob, or at least would have taken him to be killed, if Charles hadn't stopped them. And what about her parents? Or Reggie, or Bobby, or Miss Penny?

She took a deep breath and tried to clear her mind while she watched the blue sky streak by around them. At some point she nodded off, only to awaken when the Skysworn lurched forward.

"Guess it's a good thing I put my harness back on," Alice said with an edge to her voice.

Mary laughed and glanced back at her. "You're awake, good. And I made sure you were buckled in. Don't worry about that."

The door to the cabin opened and Smith stepped through. "Everything still looks good. After I swapped out that last gauge, I have not seen another bad pressure reading."

"You've done some amazing work on her," Mary said, patting the dashboard.

"I think I'm going to go out on deck for a bit," Alice said. She unbuckled her harness.

Smith stopped before he closed the door. "By all means."

Alice was almost to the door when the radio crackled to life. There were no codes or hidden messages, only Archibald's voice, fast and clipped.

"Something's happened in Dauschen. We've lost contact with the safe house and Charles. I have information that the bombs have gone off and the base is in ruins, but it's not from one of my regular spies, and I don't know if I can trust him. One of the others is saying the Steamsworn have been captured and the mission is compromised. I don't know who to trust. The last message from Drakkar was they'd been compromised."

The world closed in around Alice like someone had wrapped her in an icy blanket. "What about Jacob?"

"Get there as fast as you can, Mary. I'm … I'm releasing one of the warships. We're taking Dauschen."

We've lost contact with the safe house and Charles.

Mary was speechless, staring out the windscreen. "Smith …" Her voice was quiet, barely above a whisper.

We've lost contact with the safe house and Charles.

"It does not matter," Smith said as he ushered Alice back into her seat. "Buckle yourself in. I am going to jump the thrusters, and it is going to be rough as hell."

We've lost contact with the safe house and Charles.

Mary clicked the transmitter. "We're on our way."

Mary said something else before Smith vanished out the door. There was a cold, merciless thing that took root in Alice's gut. If someone had hurt her friends, they'd pay. She'd killed once, and she could do it again. She was sure of it. She'd barely known Gladys, and this was Jacob. *Jacob.*

Mary was screaming something when the force of the Skysworn's thrusters slammed her into the back of her seat, but all Alice heard was the echo of Archibald's words.

We've lost contact with the safe house and Charles.

CHAPTER THIRTEEN

J ACOB FELT THE weight of the grappling gun in his hand and aimed it as best he could. It was awkward with the weighted hooks on either end. Jacob thought that would make it balanced, but it felt more like it just wanted to tilt even more than Charles's unwieldy air cannon.

"Remember to keep it over your shoulder," Charles said. "I'm not going to drag you out of here if you fire a hook through your head. I've seen smarter men do stupider things."

Jacob smiled and slowly depressed the trigger. The brass gun jumped in his hands as the thin cables screamed out in either direction. The one firing behind him thunked into the stone much faster than the hook that had to bridge the chasm. It was still only a couple seconds before they heard the chink of the second hook anchoring into the wall.

"Flip the second safety," Charles said.

Jacob did. This was the third time they'd had to use the grappling gun to traverse the massive steel supports beneath the city. Each time they laid explosives, their packs grew lighter, and Jacob thought there was a better chance he wouldn't be dying in the chasm.

"You first," Charles said as he tugged on the line and nodded.

Jacob took a deep breath and stared into the pit in front of him. "This is crazy."

"Some of the best plans are."

"Right," Jacob said with a laugh. He double-checked the safety line buckled to the harness of his backpack and jumped. Jacob kept one hand on top of the grappling gun and pulled the trigger with the other. The wheels engaged and propelled him toward the far wall at a fairly alarming rate.

"Slow down!" Charles shouted.

Jacob eased up on the trigger, and the wheels slowed immediately. He pumped the trigger a few times, like Charles had shown him, and it set a much more reasonable pace across the chasm. It was almost as exhilarating as it was terrifying, hanging over that infinite darkness.

He released the trigger when the steel supports filled the void beneath him in the dim lantern light. Jacob smiled to himself as he set his foot down. It was almost at a perfect height for him. That might make it a bit of a drop for Charles, but he didn't feel too bad after the old man had run Jacob's shins directly into the last support.

Jacob tapped his boot to check his foothold before detaching his safety line from the gun. He flipped the reverse switch and watched the brass contraption zip back toward Charles. Grappling became more difficult the farther in they went. There were huge stone columns here they had to avoid that seemed to help support some of the city's weight. Jacob worried they'd support it so well that the base wouldn't break, but Charles didn't seem concerned at all.

Jacob couldn't see Charles very well until he turned around. The old tinker had his lantern clipped to the front of his vest. The only way he could tell Charles was moving at all was the sudden blossoming of the lantern light as he closed in.

Charles dangled above the support and looked down at his feet. "My knees aren't made for this." He grumbled some more and then dropped onto the steel beam with a thump.

"It beats ramming your shins though, doesn't it?"

Charles laughed quietly. "Maybe, boy. Maybe."

Jacob unclipped his own lantern and swung it around the support.

"Looks like another crossbeam here." He pointed to the intersection of the support they were standing on and then a massive girder that stretched from one side of the chasm to the other.

Jacob pulled a loop of explosives out of his backpack and began tying it down to the joint with blasting cord.

Charles slapped the wall beside him. "Hmm, more stone. All the way up, it would appear, and it's thicker. Let's anchor this receiver a little higher." Charles took a few steps up the ladder that led to one of the access grates overhead. He held a small metal bracket out and punched the stone with his right hand. The heavy nail glove shot an anchoring bolt into the wall. Tiny bits of broken rock pinged off the ladder rungs.

Jacob finished positioning the charges at the crossbeam, attached the blasting cord to the receiver, hopped up a few steps, and handed the assembly up to Charles.

"That should do it," the old tinker said as he started back down the ladder. "One more and we're done. Set the grapple again. It's a narrow angle back to the other side, but I'm sure you can hit it."

Jacob held his lantern out, aiming it across the chasm. He couldn't see the other side very clearly, but at just the right angle, the steel supports glinted in the light. Charles hadn't been exaggerating when he said it was a narrow angle. They'd have maybe two feet on either side of the cable, and that was if Jacob could shoot straight.

He took his time, lining up the shot and slowly depressing the trigger. The sound of the anchor cracking into the wall behind him was almost familiar now, followed by the distant thunk of the forward bolt. Jacob threw the switch on the grappling gun, and the lines tightened. It wasn't perfectly centered in the narrow pass, but they'd make it.

"Alright, it's set."

The world seemed to slow when the grate overhead squealed and the dim light around it brightened as someone pried the hinges open.

Charles swung the air cannon off his back and pointed it at the rectangular hole of light. The silhouette of a head appeared above them, and then there were shouts and the head vanished.

"What was that?" Jacob asked.

Charles shook his head. "I don't know. We need to take a look."

Jacob didn't question Charles's statement. He swung up onto the ladder on one side of the support while Charles began climbing the opposite. They both slowed near the top when a series of explosions and screams echoed down into the chasm.

"Keep your head low," Charles whispered. "Angle your neck back, keep as low a profile as you can."

Jacob heard Charles speaking, but he didn't acknowledge the old man. There were more sounds, like the crack of gunfire, and more screams. Jacob tried to take a deep breath, but all his pounding heart did was speed up. He watched Charles as the old man poked his head just above the edge of the grate.

Charles ducked back down and leaned his forehead on the wall.

Jacob slowly raised his head enough that his eyes breached street level, and he almost screamed. Lottie, Morgan, and Clark were sprawled across the cobblestones just outside the wall to the base. Jacob could only assume the third body was Clark, because the face was ruined. He'd been hit by something large, and there was very little left but blood and gore.

City guards from Fel lay dead and wounded all around them. They'd killed at least three men for every one of their own, but that still left three dead Steamsworn on the streets of Dauschen. More soldiers arrived by the minute, marching out of the gate, and as Jacob turned to look behind him, he saw more rushing out of the city proper.

Charles joined him again at street level, only to yank Jacob back into the shadows when one of the squads began walking toward their hiding place. "We have to move," Charles said. "We finish planting the bombs and we set them off today. *That* is our mission now."

Shouts sounded above them and Charles cursed.

"I swear I saw something in that grate!" The words that echoed into the chasm sent a tremor of ice down Jacob's back.

"They're onto us," Charles said as he hurried down the ladder. "Take the last of the bombs. You *have* to get them mounted at the last cross-beam. I don't care what you hear, or what you see. You don't turn back for anything, you understand?" He handed the air cannon to Jacob. "If you need to, use it. Get yourself out of here."

"But you—"

"I'm not defenseless, boy. Now go!"

There was a shuffling sound above them, and Charles pushed Jacob away before a beam of light lanced down from above.

"You there! Halt!"

Charles raised his hands and glanced at Jacob. He tilted his head down slightly and whispered, "Go. Now."

Jacob wedged the air cannon beneath the strap of his backpack. He glanced at Charles, wrapped his hands around the grappling gun, and zipped off across the chasm. The panic and adrenaline broke his concentration. He held on to the trigger too long, and it slammed him into the far wall. Jacob knew he was bleeding. He could taste the blood where his teeth had sliced open his cheek.

He turned back toward the shaft of light surrounding Charles. It seemed so far away now, like a play he was watching in the Square. Jacob couldn't hear what was being said. The voices were muffled at that distance, empty echoes in a vast darkness. The meaning was clear enough.

Charles reached out, grabbed the ladder, and slowly started to climb. Jacob watched each step the old tinker took. It felt like his hope was disappearing along with Charles, and then the old man vanished through the distant square of light.

Jacob's breath came fast. It felt like his ribs were crushed and his heart fluttered. The room spun, and Jacob dropped to a knee. This was no place to get dizzy. He had a job to do. Charles was counting on him. Thousands were counting on him, but that was too big to think about. He focused on Charles and Alice and his parents. Jacob took a deep breath and stood up, turning up the light on his lantern before jogging down the supports to the crossbeam.

The walls closed in on him in the dim light as he shuffled closer to his target. His backpack brushed the stone behind him when he turned sideways to squeeze past a small collapse. At the path's narrowest point, Jacob had to remove the pack altogether. He dragged it behind him, tied to his ankle, as he forced himself through the gap with his elbows. Charles had been right. Samuel would not have fit after all.

You don't turn back for anything, you understand?

Charles's words played over and over in Jacob's head. He knew this was important, maybe the most important thing he'd ever do, and he wasn't going to let Charles down.

The passage finally widened. Jacob pulled himself to his feet and shined his lantern around. Part of the stone wall had sheared off and now leaned against the crossbeam. That had created the passage he'd had to crawl through. He shivered, looking at that seemingly unstable path.

The lantern light flashed on a series of steel bars. It took a moment for Jacob to realize it was another ladder leading to a poorly lit hatch. There hadn't been one at every crossbeam like they had expected. A small measure of relief worked at the knot in his stomach.

He unbuttoned his backpack and went to work. There was a lot of extra blasting cord. Jacob was glad to see that. He wanted to elevate the receiver, and even though he didn't have a heavy nail glove to anchor it, he thought tying it to a high rung on the ladder would work just as well.

Jacob positioned and repositioned the charges. He snapped the clips onto the blasting cord, checked the knots, and then went over it all again. Charles wasn't there to tell him the angles were right this time. If he had it wrong, it might not go off, or might not cut the beam, but it was as good as he was going to get it.

Jacob dumped his backpack out, snatching up the trigger and tucking it into a pocket. He started up the ladder but froze when he saw the edge of the glider pack resting on ground. He just couldn't leave it. Jacob hooked the air cannon to his belt and strapped the glider pack on. He grabbed the cold metal rungs and resumed his climb up the ladder, trailing the coil of blasting cord. He could still see light coming through the hatch, but not nearly so much as the one where Charles had vanished.

He looped the blasting cord around two rungs and tied off the receiver. Jacob checked the switch three times to be sure it was turned on before moving his attention to the light above him. Jacob fumbled with the release and breathed a sigh of relief when the hatch swung open in almost complete silence. Fresh air flowed around him, dry and clean and nothing like the musty darkness of the chasm.

The base wall rose into the sky beside him, and a row of homes stood off to his right. The street was empty. No guards, no citizens, it was a perfect escape route. He heard shouts rising around the corner. Jacob crept out of the hatch before lowering it slowly back into the street.

It was only then that he realized he was below the corpses strung from the wall. The stench was mild, and the bodies looked far fresher than he'd expected. They weren't long dead, which meant the soldiers had been killing more people. Would they hang Lottie and Morgan and Clark up there? Did they mean to hang Charles?

When Jacob got closer to the corner of the wall, the words he heard froze his heart.

"It's Atlier, I'm telling you! We need to take him to the king."

Jacob edged his way to the corner of the wall. He shivered when he brushed the foot of a corpse with his shoulder, but he had to see. He *had* to.

Charles's head slowly turned and the old tinker locked eyes with Jacob. Jacob started, and Charles gave only a small shake of his head.

It was then that the crumpled forms caught Jacob's eye: two dead soldiers, one with an anchor sticking out of his chest. That's why they'd tied up Charles; he'd already attacked them. Why? Why would he do that?

One of the soldiers grabbed the old tinker's hair and sneered in his face. "We'll be rich. The reward on your head is—"

Charles headbutted the man's nose. Blood sprayed across his face and the old man laughed. "I've had a good, long life. That's more than I can say for your friends." He spat on the nearest corpse.

The soldier pulled a handgun out of the holster on his thigh. It gleamed in the sun while the man cursed and dripped blood across the ground. "Those are fine last words you old bastard."

Charles stared at Jacob.

Jacob's hand wrapped around the trigger of the air cannon, but Charles held his gaze. He gave a sharp, quick shake of his head. There was an awful look on the old man's face. Jacob had seen the same look on his father's face when he learned he'd likely die from miner's lung.

The gunshot stole whatever hope Jacob had left for the world.

Charles slumped forward, and the cry that left the old man's lips was a dagger in Jacob's chest. Charles lifted his heaving chest with his arms tied behind his back, blood streaming from his stomach.

Jacob barely recognized Charles's voice as it rose and fractured, and his words echoed louder than the cries of the citizens. He almost missed the flash of copper twisting in the old tinker's hands.

"This is my Steamsworn grave!"

"*Charles!*" Jacob screamed.

A tremendous blast sounded, and then there was only silence. Charles hadn't planted all of the bombs. He'd kept the last belted inside his vest. There was nothing left of Charles or his murderers. Jacob stared at the streak of gore, staggering at the heavy sense of loss and the cold blade of satisfaction.

Charles was gone. There was only Samuel now, and Drakkar, and …

"Alice."

"There!" someone shouted. "At the wall!"

Tears rolled down Jacob's face as he ran from the guards sprinting towards him. He'd barely taken ten steps when a shot fired over his head and the guard shouted, "Stop!"

Jacob froze, staring at the cold copper trigger grasped tightly in his hand. He turned slowly to face the guards. They wore Fel's colors. He could still see the small patch of earth where Charles had died. Jacob snarled and his fingers crushed the trigger. A massive shockwave sent him and the guards to their knees.

The blast of the underground charges was unlike anything Jacob had felt before, like his guts had been liquefied as he wobbled back to his feet. Jacob pulled the release and the glider snapped out, unfolding from the backpack as smoothly as Charles had designed it.

The world tilted, and soldiers and citizens began shouting. Jacob ignored them all as they tried to scramble out of the base. He pulled the trigger again, and another blast rocked the earth. This time the ground beneath them fell away. Time slowed, and Jacob stared at the expression of disbelief and terror on the guards' faces. They screamed and reached out to him for aid as his wings caught in the sudden, violent updraft. The guards vanished into the darkness. Jacob cursed as the dust and debris shot him higher into the air.

The wings caught the sky, jarring and jerking him through the air until the levelers clicked and shifted, carrying him away from that nightmare.

The rumble grew louder and more frantic. Jacob looked back and watched a waterfall of carnage—filled with men and buildings and the base walls—slide off the side of the cliff. The massive supports fell out of the mountain like teeth, collapsing stone and rerouting the river as it failed.

Somewhere in the dwindling cloud of smoke and dust was Charles. Jacob let the vision burn into his mind, the death of a battalion. The old tinker's murderers and most of the invading force stationed at the base might be dead, but the men who caused the war were still alive. Jacob's fists tightened around the straps of his harness as the reality of it all throttled him. There was no stopping the tears, or the unholy rage in his chest.

This was war.

CHAPTER FOURTEEN

A N OFFICER'S RECEIVER crackled to life beside Gladys and George. "Water Beetle, compromised."

The wide-eyed officer fumbled for his transmitter before speaking into his collar. "Received, initiating offensive." The man ran for one of the cabins before Gladys could so much as ask a question.

Noise erupted all around them, and the ship burst into panicked life. Men and women ran to their posts and began detaching the landing lines, securing barrels and hatches, while the droning alarm bleated a steady, horrible rhythm.

George reached out and grabbed another officer as he ran by. "What is happening?"

The officer glanced at George's hand on his arm but offered no harsh words for the breach in protocol. "They're sending us to Dauschen."

"For what purpose?"

"We're taking the city."

George thanked the officer as the man sprinted away.

"Jacob and Charles?"

"I can only guess, Princess."

"I don't want to leave them alone."

As if summoned by George's words, the announcements began, made cold and lifeless by the tinny loudspeakers above them.

"Citizens, please disembark Warship One. We are deploying to Dauschen. Citizens, please disembark for your own safety. Warship One is set to engage Dauschen. Citizens ..." The announcements began to repeat, but no one left the ship.

Gladys shivered. The warships had never been sent away from Bollwerk outside of a training exercise. Everyone knew that.

"What can they do?" Gladys whispered as she looked up to George. "What can we do?"

"We can stay and help the tinkers assemble more belts for the chainguns," George said.

Gladys nodded.

"Good," George said. "Get to the third deck. This old ship isn't fast, but she's carrying enough firepower to level a city. Should be enough cartridges to fill a dozen more belts, and enough gunpowder to build a thousand more rounds."

"We don't have the time for that," Gladys said.

"Well, we better get to work then. Now move!"

George took off at a run, and Gladys followed. She'd worn a long gray skirt today, and she scowled at it as she tried to keep up with George. Gladys cursed and ran a hand down either side of her dress, guiding a knife from her thigh to the hem. Free to move again, she caught George in a matter of moments. Gladys already felt better, moving with a purpose. They wouldn't leave her people behind, and they wouldn't abandon their new friends to whatever fate had befallen them in Dauschen.

✧   ✧   ✧

"CHARLES! NO!"

Drakkar held Samuel back yet again when the Spider Knight tried to rush out the door. They'd watched their ally, one of Samuel's mentors, cut down a block away. Drakkar had seen enough of war to know if Samuel went after those men now, he would not come back alive.

Samuel cried out and tried to push the guardian away again.

The crackling agony in the Spider Knight's voice cut Drakkar worse than he had expected. Drakkar himself felt a hollowness at the loss of Charles von Atlier, and a grave concern for Jacob.

Drakkar levered an iron grip on Samuel's shoulders and shouted. "Listen! We have to go, brother, now! The city is shaking itself apart. We can leave now and no one will be the wiser. We leave. We find Jacob."

"We have to kill them," Samuel said as he finally stopped struggling and squeezed Drakkar's shoulders instead. "They killed Charles!"

Drakkar slammed Samuel against the nearest bookshelf. "We do not know what Archibald's response will be. It's done. We look after the living now. Once we find Jacob, we can make for Cave or Bollwerk. It is not safe here. Come, let us leave before the chaos recedes, or this old building falls down on our heads."

Samuel nodded and followed Drakkar away from that terrible vision.

They both froze on the doorsteps, choking on a cloud of debris. What had been the base was only a cloud of dust and dirt and fire now. Drakkar had only heard the stories of Midstream and how the towering Mechs had flattened the city of the oasis. The choking clouds and invisible screams brought those stories to awful life.

A shadow wavered and creaked before stones and timbers crashed to the earth. The sudden chiming of bells that trailed into the distance told them it was a clocktower. Only death stood where there had once been a base, a trading post, and a home for a thousand soldiers.

Samuel stumbled backwards when Drakkar pulled on his arm, drawing his attention to the path away from the last stand of Charles von Atlier. Drakkar felt there should be satisfaction in the mad tinker's death. The creator of Midstream's destruction had fallen into the abyss, but the hollowness in Drakkar's chest persisted, a sadness he could not explain.

Charles had been a good man. A man who had made terrible mistakes, but he had also been a good man. "He deserved a better end."

Samuel glanced back at Drakkar. The Cave Guardian could not read the Spider Knight's expression, but he suspected there were many words left to speak of their lost friend.

Friend.

He had been a friend.

A coughing, gasping form stumbled out of the dust before them, almost close enough to touch. Cold fury swelled in Drakkar's limbs when he saw one of the uniforms of Fel's soldiers beneath the dirt. Drakkar's hand moved without thought, the blade of his sword unfolding, clicking out in stages. The soldier turned in time to see the guardian's eyes.

Drakkar stepped into the attack, pivoting his hips as he swung his blade in a simple, practiced arc. The strike sent a spray of blood across the cobblestones. The soldier grabbed at his neck, trying to staunch the stream of blood. Drakkar repositioned himself for the next strike.

"No," Samuel said, pulling on the guardian's shoulder. The Spider Knight clipped the soldier in the temple with his boot. "Let him bleed. We have to find Jacob."

Drakkar took two deep, shaky breaths before he wiped off his sword, slid the release forward, and let the blade collapse unto itself. The earth moved again, sending the world sideways. They stumbled away from that mad place.

Drakkar's cloak snapped in the wind as they rounded an intersection and started down a hill. It was not long before the city gates came into view. Impaled upon them were the remains of two Fel guards. Drakkar paused at the gate, looking at the carnage strewn across the earth.

"Look!" Samuel said, pointing into the distance.

Drakkar squinted against a gust of wind, but there it was, gliding like a bird above the carnage. "Jacob?"

"It has to be. Let's go!"

Drakkar didn't argue.

They ran.

✧   ✧   ✧

ALICE STARED AT the clouds of roiling black and white smoke. Flames licked at the edges of the fallen city but stayed mostly contained in a gaping wound in the mountainside.

Mary lifted the lid to one of the horns. "Smith. Get up here now."

"Cooling the turbines and then I will join you."

Alice wasn't sure how long it had been since Mary made the call and Smith opened the hatch to the cabin. She couldn't take her eyes away from billowing clouds of ash.

"By the gods!" Smith shouted as he slammed his palms onto the dashboard and leaned into the windscreen. "They did it. Raise Archibald, Mary. Raise him now!"

"I ... Yes, I should have done that already." Mary pulled down the transmitter with a shaking hand and clicked the button on the side. "Archibald, this is Mary." She waited almost a minute. "Archibald, this is Mary."

Smith looked at her and a line of creases appeared across his forehead. "We shouldn't just wait here. We should look for Jacob and Charles and the others."

An explosion sent debris hurtling into the air on a fireball.

Mary's radio crackled to life. "Skysworn, this is Archibald. Message received."

"Where the hell have you been?" Mary snapped.

"Busy with the Council, Mary. The base is gone?"

Mary blew out a breath and snarled before she clicked the transmitter again. "Yes, it's gone. Do you have any clue where we should look for the others?"

"All I know is that Jacob and Charles were setting the bombs. If they went off today, then what plans there were are gone. The safe house was compromised, so no one will be there. Watch the entrances. Check the grounds closer to the collapse. The soldiers from Fel that are left won't be guarding either. If they are, they're fools. If they have a mind for survival, they'll be regrouping somewhere inside the city. I have to return to the Council. They understand the need for our movements against Fel, but there are rising hostilities from the desert clans."

"Remind them of the Porcupines, Archibald. Those things are death given form."

"I know. Be safe. Look for the Steamsworn if it goes sideways."

"It's already ten ways from sideways, Archibald. It looks like a bloody war down there."

"It is a war, Mary. Don't forget it."

Mary cursed and hung her transmitter back on its clip. "So it is."

Smith started to speak. It was old words. Alice knew them from Archibald's book. It was part of the Steamsworn oath.

> *Through the black we ride once more*
> *Within the flames our fortune's told*
> *The gates of Hell lie broken wide*
> *Within the steam, no hold abides*

"I hate that damned oath," Mary spat. "Glory and honor to the dead." She ratcheted one of the levers down and spun the wheel to her left. The Skysworn lurched to the east and swooped toward the earth. "Once you're dead, you're dead. Glory be damned."

"To die for a cause is an honor denied to many."

A terrible, seething fear clawed at Alice's spine. She remembered the last line of that oath, and it seemed more terrible now, before that ruin of a city, than it ever had before. She whispered it.

> *Find me in that Steamsworn grave*

CHAPTER FIFTEEN

Jacob's tears had lessened by the time the soft sands of the dried riverbank sprayed out beneath his feet. He stumbled as he landed, keeping the glider held high so he wouldn't break it. Charles wouldn't be happy if … if …

Jacob shook and fell to a knee. The awful snap of the gunshot played over and over in his head, and Charles's slumped form was a frozen vision. A glance over his shoulder showed him the remains of Dauschen. The base was a smoky, ruined scar, and it was the only thing that brought some measure of comfort to Jacob at that moment.

They'd struck a terrible blow to the Fel army stationed at Dauschen. How many were left? How many were stationed in Ancora? Did the Butcher have as many spies as Archibald did? He closed his eyes and turned away from the burning city.

Were the others okay? That was the thought driving him back to his feet. He needed to find Samuel and Drakkar. He slid the glider off and grimaced as the straps released the air cannon from his side, dropping it onto the sand. He had no doubt of the bruising he was in for. The glider folded neatly back into its housing. It looked like nothing more than a leather pack by the time it was secured.

He needed to regroup with his people and plan their next attack. They needed to strike Fel while the city still roiled in chaos. That thinking jarred him, and he took a hesitant step before his mind followed that line of thought through to its end. There wasn't another choice.

They'd either drive away the Butcher and his army, or die trying. Die like Charles.

Jacob pulled the air cannon out of the sand and shook the grains from it. He racked the slide three times and slid it through one of the ties on his backpack. A shadow moved across him, blocking the sun. He thought it was the clouds of smoke at first, but the sun was on the other side of the sky.

A ship hovered up above. It looked familiar, but he didn't trust anything at that moment. A landing line slammed into the sand thirty feet away and Jacob slid the air cannon into his hands once more.

Someone yelled from above. "Jacob! Jacob!" The voice was deep, booming. A dark shadow slid down the landing line on a belayer. Jacob could only stare when Smith's boots slammed into the earth beside him.

"Smith?" Jacob said. Something felt warm inside him. It took him a moment to realize he was happy to see a friendly face, having been so focused on wanting to kill more soldiers.

"Gods, kid. You are bleeding."

Jacob frowned. "I am?"

Smith slid his fingers beneath his collar and said, "Mary, it is Jacob. He is battered, but it would appear he will live." The tinker leaned down and pulled Jacob's pant leg up. "Looks like it's just a leak." Smith pulled a knob out and twisted it to the side. The trickle of blood stopped. "Your leg is going to start locking up in about an hour. I can fix it once we return to the ship."

A crackly voice came over the copper speaker at Smith's neck. "Alice is on her way down."

"Alice?" Jacob asked. If he was being honest, he wanted to see her more than anyone else, but this was no place for her. This was an unbiased land of soldiers and murderers and death. She didn't need to see that. No one did.

"Jacob!"

That voice. Her voice. And then she was there. Her arms wrapped around him and it felt like she'd brought him home. Something shattered inside his chest and stabbed at his eyes, and Jacob fell to his knees. He squeezed her so tightly he knew it had to be hurting, but he couldn't soften his grip. She leeched the poison from him.

He felt Alice pulling at his arms, but he just pulled her closer and buried his face in her stomach. Her fingers ran through his hair, catching in the knots and tangles as she whispered to him. She hadn't done that since his pet Fire Lizard was taken away once his parents realized what it was, some seven years gone.

Jacob let out an agonized cry as everything he'd lost since Ancora came crashing down around him. His parents. His friends. His leg. His world.

His voice was tiny against the roar of the fires in the distance and the scream of the wind overhead. "Charles is gone."

"What?"

"He's dead, Alice." All he could taste was ash, the words filling him with poison once more. "They killed him, right in front of me. I should have done ... I should have done *something*."

"No," Alice said after a pause. "This is ... We all knew this could happen. You're still here. We're still here. We can still fight."

Jacob opened his eyes and looked up at her face. Lit by the sun, her silhouette was harsh, and the rage in her eyes was matched only by the hatred he felt burning beneath his anguish. He relaxed his arms and Alice pulled him to his feet.

"We're still here, Jacob. I'm not going anywhere. We can carry on for Charles."

"We need to find the others," Smith said.

Jacob nodded and took a deep, shaky breath. "I don't know who's left."

"I am sorry you had to witness this." Smith gestured to the burning hole of Dauschen. "All of this."

"I didn't witness it," Jacob said as he put his arm around Alice and grabbed the landing line. "I pulled the trigger."

He could feel Smith's eyes on his back as Alice hooked a belayer onto the landing line and slammed a Burner into the engine. They both kept a hand on the belayer and an arm around each other as it took them to the Skysworn.

The joy of the wind whipping through his hair may have been gone, but Alice was a welcome presence in what had become a very dark place.

✧   ✧   ✧

"YOU KNOW WHAT scares me?" Alice asked as she watched Smith crack open Jacob's leg. She winced when the blood that had pooled inside leaked out onto the table and dripped to the floor.

"What?" Smith asked. He reached into the leg and tightened a clamp on an interior hose.

"If they'd taken over Dauschen, what have they done in Ancora?"

"They already did it," Jacob said. "We were there when it happened."

The pieces slammed together in Alice's mind. "The Fall? They did all of that."

"The Butcher is orchestrating this entire ordeal." Smith shined a light into Jacob's leg and cursed.

"Bad?" Alice asked.

"One of the anchors is cracked." He exhaled and stood up straight. "I need to break it off and insert a new anchor. Jacob, it is going to hurt."

"Fine," he said. "Just get it over with."

Alice reached out and grabbed Jacob's hand. She wasn't sure if he would want her to or not, but when he squeezed her fingers, she had no intention of letting go.

"I would normally not do this on a conscious person," Smith said.

"I get that a lot," Jacob said with a small smile.

Smith arranged his tools, pointed at each in turn, and mumbled to himself. Alice watched the tinker. He was much younger than Charles, but he seemed almost as knowledgeable. She'd seen him save Jacob's life and seen him kill a dozen men in a few seconds. It was hard to reconcile what his true face was.

Alice slowly smiled.

"What?" Jacob asked, staring at her and obviously keeping his eyes averted from the menacing tools Smith was about to implement.

"His true face. I was just thinking that's a phrase my mom likes to use."

"That is a very old saying," Smith said as he glanced up at her. "My people, before we became Bollwerk, told stories that every man and woman had two faces. You could live with someone for a decade without meeting their true face, but when both sides of those people met for the first time, that was the true test of a marriage."

"Sounds stupid," Jacob said.

"Most stupid sayings are true on some level. Brace yourself."

Alice gasped when Jacob's hand spasmed and crushed her own. She didn't scream at the pain of her fingers being smashed together, she squeezed back. She held on to Jacob until his breath fell short, and the pain pushed him over the edge into unconsciousness.

"He's out," she said.

"Probably for the best." Smith twisted something in the leg and a horrible crack echoed around the small lab. He squinted at a bloody screw that was missing its head. "I do not understand how that happened. Hell of a place to get a faulty screw."

Alice squeezed Jacob's hand again before stepping closer to Smith.

She grimaced at the mass of scar tissue around the plates bolted to Jacob's leg. "Will it hold?"

"Yes, it will hold this time. I am reinforcing the anchoring with a back plate. The screw will be deeper, and he will be in pain when he wakes up, but it will not have to come off again." He scraped a flint striker across a small silver nozzle. A blue flame burst into brilliant life, and Smith ran the new screw and plate through the fire.

Alice watched the man bind flesh to metal. The sheer scale of pistons and gears inside that leg was madness. She watched him cap the tubing and replace the connection. It was a strange thing, seeing blood flow through a machine like that.

"It's like it's not a machine."

"It is not," Smith said. "It is Jacob, through and through. It will live as long as he does and no more." The tinker began tightening everything down before he moved Jacob's leg. Alice watched the mechanisms inside shift and flex and move.

"It's amazing, Smith."

He gave her a small smile as he wiped out the last of the blood and began closing Jacob's leg once more. "Can you tell Mary we are almost ready to move?"

Alice slid behind Smith and popped the cover off the largest brass horn. "Mary, we're almost ready to move."

"Glad to hear it," Mary said, her voice made tinny by the horn. "Come topside when you're ready."

Alice leaned over and kissed Jacob's forehead.

Smith cocked an eyebrow.

She gave him a flat look. "What?"

He smiled and snapped Jacob's leg closed.

CHAPTER SIXTEEN

DRAKKAR DID NOT look back at Dauschen. He had no need to look upon that burning mass of flesh and wood and ruin.

"Did you hear that?" Samuel asked.

Drakkar looked back at him and narrowed his eyes. "More falling stone?"

Samuel shook his head. "That's a train, Drakkar. I know it. It sounds like … hell, it sounds like the engine on the personnel carrier we used in training."

"There are no tracks here."

"There are," Samuel said, "but I can't imagine the old station survived the collapse."

Drakkar pointed to a ship in the sky, moving in a slow circle not far from where they'd last seen the glider drifting through the clouds of debris. "Look."

"Is that the Skysworn?"

"I … think it may be," Drakkar said, disbelief warring with hope as he watched the slowly drifting vessel. "We need to get their attention."

"Use the reflector of the lantern. Three quick bursts, three long bursts, three—"

"I know the signal," Drakkar said as he pulled the lantern off his belt and snapped the reflector off.

"Good, go."

Drakkar started toward the ship so he could locate a better angle for the windscreen. It wasn't long before he realized Samuel wasn't following him. "What are you doing?"

"There's a second station," Samuel said. He was on his knees close to the preliminary guardhouse. "I have to find it. Have them wait. I'll be back as quick as I can. It has to be close."

Drakkar thought to argue with the Spider Knight, but what if Samuel was right? What if there was a train beneath their very feet. That kind of knowledge could turn the tide of a war.

"Hurry."

He didn't watch Samuel leave. Instead he concentrated on the reflector. The sun was high enough to cast a bright light. At the right angle, he could see the thin beam bounce from the reflector onto the windscreen above. The ship hovered in a small circle, though Drakkar couldn't imagine why.

Minutes passed, and the Cave Guardian began to lose hope for Samuel's idea. Then the pattern changed. The ship wasn't moving in a wide circle anymore, it drifted closer to him. At first he feared it could be his imagination, but then a landing line crashed to the ground not thirty feet away.

There was a shout, and then he heard Mary's voice. "Drakkar!"

✧   ✧   ✧

WHAT THE HELL *are you doing, Samuel?*

At some level he knew he was right, but he didn't want to leave Drakkar behind. He couldn't stay and try to flag down the airship and still be sure he'd find the train. If it left while he was hunting, and the sound died away, that would be it. They'd never really know what he'd heard.

At the forward guardhouse the rumble grew louder. A muffled whistle sounded nearby, and any doubt he'd had was erased. They had a train.

Samuel jogged to the next guardhouse and the rumble was even louder. This was it. He had no doubt. How else would Archibald's spies not have known? He tried the door, but it only rattled in its frame. Another whistle blew. It was going to leave.

The Spider Knight snarled and kicked at the old wooden door with the flat of his boot. Something cracked, but the door held. He took a step back and landed another forward kick beside the frame where the bolts should be. A larger crack, and the door began to move.

"Come on!"

He leaned into the last kick, and it was enough to tear the bolt through the frame. The door cracked open, only to be caught by a thin chain. Samuel rammed through it with his shoulder, opening the door the rest of the way.

A dirty ancient rug sat piled in the corner. There was a hatch exposed in the floor. Samuel grabbed the round iron handle and threw it open without thinking. Below waited lights and noise, and the sounds of a massive steam engine pumping away.

He'd expected to find a flimsy ladder at best, but a stone staircase spiraled down at his feet. Now the question was a matter of guards. Would they be at the bottom of the staircase, or would the attack on the base have been enough to break whatever protocol they had set? Or were they overconfident enough to not even have protocol?

"Screw it," Samuel said under his breath. The leather boots he had on were quiet on the stone—much quieter than his armored ones would have been. He followed the smooth stone walls around several times before he could see an end to the stairs. The lower he got, the louder the steam engines and shouts were. He didn't think it would have mattered if he'd walked in playing a drum at that point.

Chaos reigned on the platform below, but in that chaos Samuel saw everything he needed to know. Most of the men were soldiers, dressed in the colors of Fel. They scrambled off and on the train like a swarm of angry Sky Needles, hauling crates and pushing barrels filled with gods know what up the loading ramps.

No guards stood at the base of the stairs, but armed soldiers stood farther in, watching the tracks for some reason Samuel did not know. With the cargo sealed, it didn't matter if he got closer, there was no telling what was in those crates.

He knew where the tracks led, and there was no way the engines came from there.

Those tracks led to Ancora. Fel was moving on Ancora.

Samuel cursed and ran back up the staircase.

JACOB AWOKE TO shouts echoing through the horns beside his bed. "Horns?" he muttered to himself while his brain slowly pieced his world back together. He was on the Skysworn. Alice was here, and from the sound of it, there were more people in the cabin.

He grunted and unfastened the harness holding him in the bed. He found his boots tucked into the tight space below, and he slid them on before making his way to the ladder. His leg hurt like hell, but at least he wasn't dripping blood everywhere he went.

Jacob twisted the iron handle and pushed on the hatch at the top of the ladder. It felt heavier than it should, but he saw nothing on top of it once he managed to climb out onto the wooden surface of the deck.

He sat for a moment, taking three deep breaths before pushing himself to his feet. The doorway into the cabin wasn't far, but it felt like a mile with his newly repaired leg. The Skysworn coasted in a wide circle, and before he made it to the cabin, the towers of smoke that used to be the base at Dauschen swept into view.

Memories of Charles and the dead guards and the bodies strung along the walls came screaming into his mind. Jacob pushed the thoughts away with a grimace as he made his way into the pilot's cabin. A sharp pain in his side caused him to clutch at his ribs.

"Jacob?"

He looked up as the twinge of pain subsided. Drakkar stared at him.

"Hey," was the extent of Jacob's words.

"I am so sorry, my friend. Charles was a loss to us all."

Jacob nodded and lowered himself onto one of the retractable flight chairs beside Alice. "Thank you."

"How are you feeling?" Smith asked as he took two steps away from Mary and crouched beside Jacob. He pulled up the cuff on Jacob's pants and started prodding his biomechanics.

"Like I blew up half a city and jumped off a mountain."

Alice reached over and squeezed his thigh before wrapping her fingers between his own. She felt warm, almost feverish.

Jacob looked over at her and offered a weak smile. "Are you feeling okay? You feel hot, like you're sick."

"I'm fine."

"It is likely the blood loss, Jacob," Smith said before he pulled Jacob's pant cuff back down over his boot. "You lost a lot, and that will make anyone cold. We will get you a good meal and water. The chill will not last too long."

"And sake," Jacob said quietly.

Smith hesitated. "I am not sure if that—"

Jacob looked him in the eye. "I'm older and I need less sense."

Smith glanced at Mary and then nodded.

"Glad to see you up and about, kid," Mary said. She pulled two floor levers beside the Skysworn's dashboard. "We're waiting on Samuel, and then we're getting the hell out of here."

"You've heard from him?" He glanced at Smith and then turned to

Drakkar. "You both made it out?" Then he paused and *really* looked at Drakkar. "And how did *you* get up here?"

Drakkar flashed him a wide smile. "One of Samuel's better ideas, in fact. I used the reflector of my lantern to signal Mary."

"So he's okay?"

Drakkar nodded. "Last I saw him. He headed below ground to check a noise he heard."

"He wasn't just hearing things, was he?" Alice asked. "I could see him doing that."

Drakkar spread his cloak and tucked it behind him. "No, I heard it as well."

"I think I've got something," Mary said, leaning in toward the windscreen. "Yes, we've got a flash. Hold on."

The Skysworn lurched out of its holding pattern and drifted onto whatever path Mary set.

"Smith, drop a short line. I'm taking us in."

"Yes, Captain." Smith jogged out the hatch and headed for the coiled landing lines.

Jacob's ears popped when Mary dropped the Skysworn's altitude. He yawned and they cleared with a crackling sound.

"Samuel!" Smith shouted from the edge of the railing.

It was only another minute before Samuel, half his clothes covered in dust, appeared at the edge of the deck. Smith offered him a hand and pulled him over.

"Did you find Jacob?" Samuel asked.

Smith gestured to the cabin and Samuel's eyes followed.

"Thank the gods." Samuel darted into the cabin and crushed Jacob in a hug. "Well done, kid. Well done."

"You too."

"Me too?" he said with a laugh. "I didn't do shit. I watched Charles …

I …"

"There was nothing we could have done," Jacob said, and something in his heart knew it was the truth.

"That doesn't make it hurt any less," the Spider Knight said as he flopped onto the floor beside Alice's chair.

"I know."

"He was a friend to many," Drakkar said, "and a friend I did not expect to make."

"I rather thought you would have tried to kill the old tinker at some point," Smith said.

Drakkar let out a humorless laugh. "I may have dreamed of it as a child, but the reality of things changes when you meet an enemy face to face. They are no different from us, or you."

"Some of them are," Mary said. Her gaze stayed locked on the windscreen as she raised the Skysworn into the clouds. "The Butcher is a monster, and his time has come. What did you find?"

Samuel blinked. "Oh gods, right."

"Was it an engine?" Drakkar asked.

Samuel nodded and cursed. "It was two massive engines, two personnel carriers on the tracks. Soldiers were loading crates and barrels and gods know what else."

"What do they intend?" Smith asked.

"Ancora. It's the only place those tracks go, unless they ride them all the way through the city."

Drakkar shook his head. "The underground tunnels are long collapsed close to Cave. Ancora is their only option."

"They're supposed to be working with the Butcher, right?" Samuel asked. He didn't wait for anyone to answer. Everyone already knew the answer.

"We don't know how long the station has been running," Alice said.

"They could have moved soldiers into Ancora already."

Samuel cursed. "There may be more going on in Ancora than we know of. Has Archibald heard anything?"

Mary shook her head without looking back. "He's lost touch with most of his spies."

"Unsettling," Drakkar said.

"So what do we do about the station?" Smith asked. "And the soldiers?"

Mary let out a short breath. "Nothing. What can we do? Ram the trestle and sink the Skysworn?"

"We may be able to take the tracks out with the cannons," Smith said. "Though we are not well stocked on cartridges."

Samuel ran his fingers through his hair and banged the back of his head on the wall. "They're likely gone already, or will be shortly. All we can do is take out their route to Dauschen."

"Charles didn't die so we could be stupid," Alice said quietly. "Report what we found. We may need to follow the threat to Ancora."

Samuel stared at her, slack-jawed.

"I like her," Mary said as she turned and winked at Alice. "Kid speaks wisdom of someone twice her age. Or more. We make for Bollwerk. We can inform Archibald on the way and stock up on cartridges for the cannons."

"We have bombs in Smith's workshop," Jacob said. "Charles and I were building them."

"What?" Smith said with a sharp edge to his voice.

"They're compound bombs. They won't work until the components are mixed."

"And then?" Smith asked.

"Then you run."

Mary laughed and pushed the throttle forward. "Grab your seats. We're riding the thrusters back to Bollwerk."

CHAPTER SEVENTEEN

"THAT WAS THE Skysworn!" Gladys said. She watched the dull bronzed ship glide past and disappear into a cloud bank.

George laid the ammunition belt he was assembling onto the bench and grabbed Gladys's arm. "Let us find a transmitter. We must speak with Archibald. One of the officers will know where to locate one."

Gladys didn't hesitate. She jumped up from her seat and followed George's quick strides out of the powder room and into the hall. The ship was a well-controlled chaos now, nothing like the mad scramble when the alarms had first sounded.

George slid to a stop in front of a steel door. He raised his arm to knock, paused, and threw the door open instead. Two women and a man looked up. They wore the sharp tan armor of Bollwerk officers.

"Yes?"

Gladys was surprised that the officers hadn't verbally torn George in half for barging in like that.

"Our friend is the warrior known as Skysworn Mary. Her ship just passed us, fleeing Dauschen. I need to speak with Archibald immediately on behalf of her Royal Highness."

"What? Me?" Gladys inched her way behind George. She hadn't realized she was going to be the leverage.

The officers straightened. "Princess, it is an honor to have you with us."

Gladys tried not to blush and hid behind George when the three bowed slightly.

"The nearest communications tower is on the other side of this wall," one of the women said as she patted the far wall. "Tell them Major Wilks has granted you full and immediate access. If they give you any lip, come get me."

"Thank you, Major." George ushered Gladys back out the door.

They didn't wait for the door to fall closed behind them. George sprinted around the corner, Gladys close behind. The deck changed from wood to textured steel and then back to wood. Gladys wondered why there was a wide stretch of steel in the center of the ship, but a moment later George stopped and pounded on an iron-bound door.

"State your purpose!" a voice shouted from behind the door.

"Major Wilks has granted us full access."

The door flew open, almost before George had finished speaking. The young communications officer looked more and more terrified as George relayed the story and introduced Gladys. The next thing she knew, George was flipping the dials and switches on the transmitter, perched on a wooden stool.

"What signal is that?" the officer asked.

George stared at him, clicked the button, and said, "Speaker of Bollwerk, Archibald, come in. This is the Royal Guard requesting communication."

The officer looked like he might faint. Gladys smiled when the man stepped outside and closed the door behind him.

"This is Archibald."

"We saw the Skysworn fleeing opposite us. Do you have a channel we can reach them on?"

The line was silent for a moment. "Some of our people survived Dauschen then."

"Have you heard anything more?" George asked.

"Pieces and rumors, nothing more. I expect to hear from Mary at any moment."

"Nothing else?"

"Look to Dauschen and the sands of the old riverbed. You'll see for yourself soon enough." Something crackled in the background before the line went dead. Gladys watched George. He seemed calm for a while, but then he began to fidget.

"Is everything okay?" Gladys asked.

He glanced at her and took a deep breath. "Archibald? Are you there? Archibald, come in."

The speaker crackled back to life. "Yes, sorry. I've raised Mary on another channel. I ..." Archibald cursed, and something loud and thick sounded like it splintered. "We lost Charles."

Something heavy took hold in Gladys's chest, a kind of terrible weight that tried to steal the breath from her lungs. "No ..." She heard George and Archibald speaking more words, but they were lost to her. The kind, generous tinker was gone. How?

Gladys grabbed George's arm. "What about Alice? Jacob? Are the others okay?"

"Is that Gladys?"

"Yes."

"The condition of our remaining spies is mostly unknown," Archibald said, giving the issue of Gladys's audience no more attention. "Mary, Smith, Drakkar, Jacob, Samuel, and Alice are heading back to Bollwerk. Charles's plan was a success. Fel incurred a serious loss in Dauschen, and the survivors are in a state of disarray. Samuel discovered an additional threat below the city."

"Below it?" George said.

"Yes. The old tracks that lead to Ancora. Tell Major Wilks to secure the station. We have to remove Dauschen from Fel's list of assets. I fear

Ancora is facing the same fate as Dauschen. If Major Wilks has any questions, you have her raise me on this channel. I'll keep it open for the next hour. After that, the Porcupines will be in Bollwerk. Watch yourself out there."

The speaker went dead, and this time Gladys knew he wasn't saying more.

"Why isn't Archibald giving the orders himself?" Gladys asked.

"Why indeed." George hung the transmitter back on its clip. "Well, back to see the major, it would appear."

The young officer was waiting outside when they stepped out. He saluted George and Gladys in turn.

"You do not need to salute," George said.

"Thank you, sir."

George smiled and hid a laugh as he ushered Gladys around the corner.

"Charles is gone."

George sighed and looked at Gladys. "I know. I rather liked the old rogue."

"Me too."

"Well, we can tell stories of the Atlier *we* knew and help fix how people remember him after our work is done. If Midstream's princess liked him, he could not be all bad."

Gladys smiled as George knocked on the officer's door on the other side of the ship.

"Come!"

The door opened to reveal Major Wilks leaning over a desk, poring over a map and making small tick marks around a gray area. She glanced up when the door closed again.

"You two? Did you have problems with our communications officer?"

George shook his head. "He was most agreeable. The mention of your esteemed rank and name had quite the effect."

"Ha, as well it should. What can I help you with now?"

"I spoke with Archibald."

Major Wilks sat down in her chair and gave George her full attention. George relayed Archibald's words, and the expression on the Major's face grew darker with every sentence.

"So be it," Major Wilks said. "I'll inform the infantry. The chainguns and cannons will remain manned during the operation. If anything goes sideways, we'll have to level the city and remove the threat."

"You can't do that," Gladys said. "There are people down there who have nothing to do with this fight."

Major Wilks crossed her arms. "Princess, the infantry will evacuate as many as they can, but our priority is to protect Bollwerk."

The door to the office cracked open.

The major glanced up but didn't otherwise acknowledge the newcomers. "And if Archibald thinks that mission is served by leveling the city and turning it into a smoking crater, that's what we'll do."

"You may be a little late for that," one of the newcomers said. "You better take a look."

Wilks didn't say anything else. She tossed her chair out of the way, slamming it against a thin metal cabinet. The nearest soldier, a young man, cringed at the bang of the wood on metal.

Gladys followed Wilks out of the office without even thinking to ask George if they should. Wilks froze a few steps outside the door. "What happened here? Archibald didn't ... He said there was an operation, but ..."

Gladys gasped when she saw the billowing clouds of smoke and the ruined face of Dauschen. The meadows broke against the dry, sandy riverbanks that led up to the mountain, crowned by a broken city skyline.

Brick and metal and flame marred the mountainside.

"What happened?" Wilks leaned on the railing at the edge of the deck.

George joined her. "The last great plan of a great man."

"What?"

"Charles von Atlier, destroyer and savior of Midstream. Conquerer of Gareth Cave. Adversary of the Butcher. A man I am proud to say was my friend."

Wilks was quiet for a moment. "I'd heard Archibald tell stories of the man when he'd had a few too many drinks at the pub, but …" She paused and turned away from the carnage before them. "What do you mean the 'last great plan'?"

"He died down there. Somewhere in that rubble is our friend."

Gladys curled her hands around George's forearm and leaned against him. "He was one of the great Steamsworn tinkers."

"I heard he lived in Ancora," Major Wilks said. "What was he doing there?"

"Trying to save it from the Butcher," George said.

Gladys let go of George's arm and leaned against the railing beside Wilks. "He saved Jacob and Alice, and Samuel."

"I don't know who any of those people are."

"They're my friends," Gladys said. "Some of them were down there with Charles."

"If they helped make that mess, I wouldn't mind adding them to Bollwerk's Skyriders."

Gladys watched the smoke curl and rise, surging past the mountaintops, only to be caught and flattened by the higher windstreams. It was a funeral pyre unlike any she'd ever seen, for in her heart she knew what it was.

"Rest well, Charles, in your Steamsworn grave."

They watched in silence as the warship closed on Dauschen. Charles had meant a great deal to her new friends, and that made him important to her too. There were still men like Rana left in the world, and who would fight them if not the people who had the means?

Her fists tightened on the brass railing as the sharp stench of the burning city filled her nostrils. She had the means and the influence. There might not be a great many of her people left, but Midstream would not fade quietly into the night.

CHAPTER EIGHTEEN

JACOB STARED AT the monster docked beside one of Bollwerk's warships.

"I told you," Alice said.

He leaned forward and wrapped his fingers around the railing before shaking his head. "I know … but … it's a lot different when you actually see it."

The ship wore cannons like a bird wore feathers. It wouldn't have to aim to hit its targets. It would only need to fire the right cannon, and it must have had a hundred to choose from. Some were long and lean like a rifle, and others looked wide enough to fit a person.

"I thought the big ones were smokestacks the first time I saw it," Alice said.

"The one that looks like it could fire a full-grown Pilly?"

She laughed. "Yeah."

"Targrove used to call the Porcupines 'Madness given life,'" Smith said from behind them. "Of course, he died before they ever finished building them."

Smith went below deck with Samuel and Drakkar when something started whistling, which was never a good sign around high-pressure engines. Jacob and Alice stayed at the railing while Mary guided the Skysworn into the docks. They helped drop the landing lines to the workers below when a man in a royal-blue jacket caught his eye.

"Is that Archibald?"

Alice squinted at the dock below while the gears slowly pulled the landing lines in, securing the Skysworn to the moorings.

"Mary!" Jacob shouted.

"I see him." Her voice echoed out of the pilot's cabin. "Drop the gangplank, would you?"

Jacob did. The railing dropped into the deck while the plank extended out to the docks. It didn't seem as magical now, how the gears worked to move all the metal around. It seemed slow, like it was keeping him from where he needed to be.

Finally it locked into place, and Archibald started across. Mary came out of the pilot's cabin to meet him.

"Where are Smith and the others?" the Speaker asked.

"Below deck. One of the turbines overheated. Drakkar and Samuel are helping replace two of the valves.

Archibald nodded. "Let's go to them. We don't need to talk about this in the open. I have no wish to cause a panic."

"Why don't you ever visit when you have *good* news."

Archibald smiled and patted Mary's back. "Good news is in short supply these days, but the Porcupines are here to help us, and that is the best sort of news."

Mary led the way to the ladder and held the hatch for Archibald. She glanced at Alice and met Jacob's eyes briefly. "Go on. Let's get this over with."

Jacob followed Alice into the yellow light of Smith's realm.

There was a string of cursing followed by metal slamming against metal repeatedly. Footsteps echoed in the silence that followed.

They turned a corner and found Smith and the others gathered beside a wide copper pipe. Smith shook a smaller pipe beside it, tapped on a gauge, and said, "Huh, it would appear that fixed it."

"Sometimes you just need to hit things," Samuel said.

"Is it any wonder how the Spider Knights received their reputation?" Archibald asked.

The trio glanced up, and Samuel snapped to attention beside Smith. "Sir, I didn't realize you were there."

"Thank you for your service, Samuel" Archibald said with a short nod. "I am sorry for the loss of Charles. He was a good friend." Archibald took a deep breath. "We have news from the West. Ballern's destroyers have been spotted in Fel."

"They attacked?" Mary asked.

"No, no they didn't."

Archibald's words hung in the air. If they hadn't attacked, then they were welcome there. If they were welcome there, they were allied to some extent with Fel.

It was Alice that broke the silence. "Then Ballern really did ally with Fel. Who are they attacking?"

Archibald nodded at Alice. "Correct. Their combined fleet is already on its way. If not for the spies there, we would have been blindsided by their attack. If their course holds true, they'll be close enough to strike late tomorrow morning.

"Ballern has spies in Belldorn. Two of Lady Katherine's guards vanished after your audience there. I don't believe it's a coincidence that Ballern's fleet is moving against us now."

"Why now?" Smith asked. "The city is better protected than it's ever been with two Porcupines to watch over the walls."

Archibald rubbed his forehead and took a deep breath. "They aren't moving against Bollwerk directly. According to the spies, they're coming for the Porcupines."

"Because the Porcupines don't have the rest of the fleet as support this far from Belldorn," Alice said.

Archibald frowned. "I think that's exactly it. There are twelve destroyers headed our way. We can't get our second warship back from Dauschen before they arrive, so I'm leaving it to engage the remnants of Fel's army there. The Porcupine captains are the best Belldorn has to offer. They can hold their ground, even outnumbered as they are.

"Mary, I want you to take the Skysworn and get back to Dauschen."

"What?" Mary snapped. "I'm not abandoning Bollwerk."

"No, you're going to go back to Dauschen and help Gladys and George."

Alice's eyes flickered between Mary and Archibald. "Gladys is in Dauschen?"

"On the warship," Archibald said with a nod.

"Damn it all!" Mary shouted as she slammed her hand onto one of the metal benches.

"Our infantry is going to evacuate the civilians and remove the remains of Fel's army," Archibald said. "If it comes to it, the warship will commence bombing the city. We have to stop Fel from hollowing out Ancora like they did Dauschen."

"We need to go to the lab first," Jacob said. "We have weapons we may need."

"The tinkers already cleaned out everything from the lab that could be used as a weapon," Archibald said.

"No, they didn't."

Archibald eyed Jacob and then Smith. "Fine, but make it fast. I can't imagine they missed anything down there. I want you and the Skysworn out of here by tomorrow."

Mary crossed her arms and nodded. "Of course."

Archibald hesitated and then turned back to the ladder. "I know I can't force you to leave, but I do hope you'll listen just this once."

Mary watched him go. He was out the hatch and onto the deck before she said, "I've listened to you many times, Archibald, but I don't think I can this time."

"Are we not leaving?" Smith asked.

A savage grin crawled across Mary's face. "We're leaving, but not before we take a shot at Ballern's fleet."

"We can't match them in this," Samuel said as he gestured to the mass of pipes and gauges at the center of the Skysworn.

Mary nodded. "Let's get back to Smith's lab."

✧   ✧   ✧

THEY RODE A crawler back to Council Hall, the treads beating a rhythmic tune across the cobblestones of some back road Jacob didn't recall seeing. The driver swore there was too much traffic on the major roads, and when they swung out of an alley and onto the main street running through the center of the city, Jacob knew he was right.

Alice leaned into Jacob, trying to get a better view of the mess on the roads. Jacob put his arm around her and leaned into the edge of the seat.

"Look at them all," Alice said, and the awe in her voice was plain.

Women and children and men all carried sacks or crates, or pushed trolleys across the sidewalks and streets. Leafy greens peeked out of one crate, and a small box of rambunctious rabbits kept a small boy juggling the crate while he tried to keep them in place.

"Rabbits?" Jacob asked. "I haven't seen a rabbit in years."

"They aren't too uncommon here," the driver said.

"They're rare in Ancora," Samuel said.

"It's so loud," Alice said. "No one's yelling, but it's like a thunderstorm. It's … weird."

Drakkar looked out across the mass of people. "It is a wall of flesh and chaos."

The crawler slowed to a stop outside the Hall. "Our Speaker declared a state of emergency," the driver said. "Everyone has a job to do, and so they're doing it."

"Preparing for war," Samuel said.

The driver nodded. "We have drills every now and then. Some folks think this one is a drill too, but it feels different."

"Feels like a great storm is closing in," Drakkar said. "Can you wait for us?"

The driver frowned and then shook his head. "I'll send another crawler for you, but Archibald gave me other orders."

"That will be fine," Drakkar said. "I doubt we need more than an hour."

"Make it two," Smith said.

The driver nodded as everyone climbed out and headed for the Hall.

"Be quick," Smith said. "Two hours does not give us much time."

The entire group followed the tinker through the front doors and into the rotunda of the Council Hall.

CHAPTER NINETEEN

INSIDE THE LAB, Jacob headed straight for the largest bench. It was the same bench he'd worked at with Charles, building Burners and Bangers and bombs. Jacob kneeled down beside one of the legs, opened a small panel, and threw the switch inside. One of the large flat stones popped up nearby and slowly rose on a pair of pistons.

"How did you know about that?" Smith asked.

Jacob smiled. "Charles hid the junk you had in there inside the vault by all the wires you keep."

"Of course he did. Of course he did." Smith crouched down and helped Jacob lift the top wooden crate up and out of the bolt-hole.

"There's another one too."

"Looks heavy," Alice said. She tugged on the first crate. "Wow, it *is* heavy." She pried the latch open and lifted the wooden lid. "Gods …"

The second crate thumped down beside the first and Jacob grinned.

"How many are there?" Alice ran her hand through the top of the mountain of metal orbs.

"A lot," Jacob said. "That's not the best part though. Can you get the lid off, Smith?"

There wasn't a latch on the second crate. Smith took off his gloves and slowly worked the metallic tips of his fingers into the narrow wooden gap. The outer slat cracked and pulled away. Once Smith could get his hand inside, the rest of the lid popped off easily.

Inside were dozens of iron shells, hinged in the middle.

"Jacob …" Smith said. "I am torn between being furious you helped Charles hide these in my lab, and being extremely grateful you did. If anything had gone wrong …" Smith shuddered.

"What are they?" Mary asked. "Looks like some overgrown Burners."

"These are Firebombs," Jacob said as he held up one of the orbs riddled with tiny holes. "Imagine a bomb with the power to fill the entire Council Hall with flames in the blink of an eye, and enough heat to melt lead." He slid the locking mechanism to the side on one of the Firebombs and started to pull it open.

"What are you doing!" Drakkar shouted.

"It's fine," Jacob said. "It's fine. It needs a Burner to detonate."

"Thankfully those are at least three inches away," Samuel grumbled, hopping up on one of the benches. "You're as nuts as the old man, kid."

Jacob smiled at Samuel. He knew the Spider Knight hadn't exactly meant it as a compliment, but that's how Jacob took it. "You ignite a Burner and lock it down. Charles used to say you better have a really good arm, or a really good head start."

"You could fire them with an air cannon," Smith said. He picked up one of the other solid gray spheres and studied it. "What are these? Without the holes?"

"Grenades," Jacob said. "Same principal as a Banger, but scaled up. You can ignite it with a Burner or a Banger."

"What?" Samuel asked. "How?"

"It is an impact fuse," Smith said as he stared at the open half of one shell. "How sensitive is this, Jacob?"

Jacob picked one up and dropped it on the stone floor.

Half the room shouted and raised their arms, like that would help.

Jacob laughed and picked the grenade up. "Not very. It needs a heavy hit from the interior, like a Banger failing. You get a more violent explosion if you use a Banger inside the grenade, but Burners are a lot more consistent with timing."

"Let's get this loaded on the Skysworn," Mary said.

"Not yet," Smith said. He looked up at Mary and let a slow smile pull his lips up. "Not quite yet.

Smith stood up, grunted, and walked over to the far wall. He slid one of the panels open, revealing his stash of wires and tubes that Archibald's men must not have thought much of. "No one knows …" Smith pushed two of the metal racks up "… about …" and then two more went down before he lifted the edge of a workbench and pressed a button "… this."

Something in the wall hissed, and the stone itself slowly vanished into the floor in silence.

Jacob stared at the mass of armor, blades, and the Steamsworn fist that stood tall at the back of the room.

Samuel stepped inside behind Smith and looked around. "Gods."

"These are what I wanted," Smith said. "They are much like a crossbow, but you can lock anything into the chamber and launch it at speed." He pulled the long gray tube of metal off the wall and handed it to Jacob.

It wasn't nearly as heavy as Jacob expected. "It's not an air cannon?"

Smith shook his head. "The resistance is self-contained. It is geared so a grandmother could load it and cock it, but it has the force to launch a four-inch lead ball almost two hundred yards.

With that kind of force behind them, they could hit targets much farther than Jacob had hoped. "Maybe not for the impact fuses."

"Indeed." Smith pulled a metal vest off a stand on the wall. He ran his fingers over the interlocking plates and said, "Mary." He tossed it to her and she caught it.

"What is it?" Mary asked.

"Light armor. It will not slow you down, but it can stop a bullet or a sword. I know you have an aversion to armor, so I have been working on that for the past month."

"Why?"

"Because we always find trouble, and you are my friend, and some-times you can be an idiot."

Mary grinned and shrugged the vest over her shoulders. She didn't touch it further, but it snapped together across her chest with a clank. "What was that?"

Smith gave her a small smile. "Magnets. One of Targrove's designs."

Mary pulled at the seam. "I can't get it off."

"It is a good design."

"Smith," Mary said, her voice flat.

He laughed and pulled her collar up. "Here, press this to shield the magnets." As soon as he did, the seam fell open. "They will stay shielded for about ten seconds before the mechanism resets. Then it will close again."

Smith eyed the rest of the group, glanced at the wall, and nodded. "We're going to need a crate." He started counting the weapons and armor left along the wall.

Jacob shuffled past Smith to the corner. Two square brass trunks sat stacked on top of each other. He opened the lid to the first and found it empty except for a coil of rope and a thin black blanket. He pulled everything out and slid it to Smith. "Here's one."

The tinker blinked and looked at the trunk. "I forgot those were in here."

"Good sign you have too much crap," Mary said.

"Indeed," Smith said as he began laying the armor into the trunk.

"Can I have this?" Jacob asked, holding up the rope.

"Is that a fuse?" Smith asked. "Was it in the trunk?"

Jacob nodded. "I have an idea."

"So be it. I have no use for it. Be warned, it is thick and tends to be noisy."

"Perfect." Jacob laid it on the workbench and slowly sliced off several wafer thin sections. "I'd like to line the grenades with it."

Smith stood beside him for a moment before he resumed packing. It only took a few minutes to fit most everything from the room into the two trunks. They may have been light before, but now they were more like anchors. What they couldn't fit, they threw over their shoulders or stuffed into their packs. Only a few items stayed behind.

Samuel lifted the first trunk about an inch off the ground before letting it slam back to the ground, brass ringing against stone. "How much does that weigh?"

"I'll get it." Smith slid a lever on his arm, waited a beat, and then picked the trunk up like it was no heavier than a Cork ball.

"I can't even imagine what a Berserker must have been like in the Deadlands War," Samuel said, watching Smith set one trunk on top of the other and carrying them both to the door.

"Terrifying for everyone," Smith said. "Just ... be glad you do not know. Grab the crates with the bombs, would you?"

"Let's get everything back to the Skysworn," Mary said. "We can head back to Dauschen tomorrow. I need food and sleep." She looked at Drakkar. "There's a small Cave eatery close to the docks. If anyone would like to join me."

Drakkar nodded. "I would welcome the chance to treat you all to some of my native dishes."

"Free food," Samuel said. "I'm in."

"Do you know what is more terrifying than a Berserker, Drakkar?" Smith asked.

The guardian shook his head.

"A free-loading Spider Knight."

"Hey!" Samuel protested with a laugh.

"Come on," Mary said. She adjusted her vest. "Let's get back to the

Skysworn before Smith blows a gasket, and I don't mean that metaphorically."

Jacob frowned at the thought. If Smith's biomechanics were like his own, a blown gasket would be …

"Messy," Alice said as she grimaced at Jacob.

✧   ✧   ✧

A DIFFERENT CRAWLER waited for them when they made their way outside. Apparently the last driver had been good on his word. The streets were no less busy, but this new driver was no less savvy when it came to avoiding the crowds. He dropped them at the docks in no time.

"Are you okay?" Jacob asked.

Smith set the trunks down inside the elevator. The tinker's arms trembled and shook. Smith nodded, but he didn't speak.

"Yeah, that's a no," Mary said. "Why don't you power down?"

"Soon."

Mary sighed. "Who's the idiot?"

Smith summoned a small smile, but he still looked pained. The doors slid open. Smith scooped up the trunks and hurried over to the Skysworn, crossing the gangplank well before anyone else.

Jacob hooked his fingers into one side of the lighter bomb crate, and Alice carried the other side. She shuffled backwards across the gangplank, leading Jacob. A breeze brought the stench of burning rubber. Something had overheated nearby. The wind came from behind them, so Jacob didn't think it was the Skysworn.

"Watch your step," he said.

Alice glanced over her shoulder and stepped down, onto the surface of the deck.

"Here," Mary said as she opened one of the wide storage benches along the side of the pilot's cabin. "Set them in here."

"So close to the cabin?" Alice asked.

"If those things go off, I don't much think it will matter where they are." Mary took Jacob's side of the crate and helped Alice lower it in.

"You want this one in there too?" Samuel asked.

"Yes, please."

The Spider Knight dropped the crate in beside the first before Mary closed the bench and locked it.

"Smith?" Mary said. "Smith, where are you? If you die, so help me, I'll kill you."

A shaky—but living—Smith rounded the corner by the pilot's cabin. "I am alive. I just need rest, and food."

"And food you shall have," Drakkar said.

"I'll catch up," Jacob said. "I want to try repacking some of those grenades."

Mary eyed him for a moment. "Just don't blow up my ship."

✧   ✧   ✧

IT WASN'T LONG before Jacob joined the others. He took a deep breath over the steaming bowl of rice and beans and mystery meat. It smelled as amazing as it tasted, permeated by thyme and sage and another dozen scents he couldn't identify. He sighed and let his chopsticks clatter onto the side of the bowl.

"Still upset I will not tell you what the mystery meat is?" Drakkar asked before taking another bite from his bowl.

Jacob smiled and shook his head. "I know what it is. It's a Pilly. I could tell by the look on Alice's face as soon as she took a bite."

"Yeah?" Alice said around a mouthful of food. "I'm still eating it, aren't I?"

Drakkar grinned and set his chopsticks down. "What troubles you, Jacob?"

Jacob looked around the table at his friends. Everyone was enjoying the food and the company and the drinks. "We're just *sitting* here. Our friends could be out there dying. Gladys and George could be doing gods know what, and what about our families back in Ancora? And we're just sitting here *eating*." He slammed his palm onto the table and nearly growled.

Drakkar reached out and placed his hand on Jacob's shoulder. "No matter what is happening in the world, you must rest, and you must eat. Do not dismiss these quiet times as a waste. These are the times you savor, the times that will keep you moving when the darkest hours come crashing down upon your head."

"I will drink to that," Smith said, raising his pewter stein. "And to Jacob. Do not lose that fire, kid. It is the fire that will lead us into victory."

The entire table cracked their steins together.

"For Charles," Jacob said, taking a deep swig of ale. He frowned and brushed his tongue over his teeth. Drakkar's drink wasn't as harsh as the sake had been, but it was potent enough to calm his nerves.

"We'll be on our way tomorrow," Mary said. "And Drakkar's right. We need our rest. You get sluggish without rest, and then you get dead. I'd prefer not to be dead when I just got a ship of my own."

Alice squeezed Jacob's thigh. "We'll be back home soon. We can find our families and Reggie and Bobby."

Jacob nodded and stared at her face, partially shadowed by the dim light inside the eatery, and said, "Then we take back the Lowlands."

CHAPTER TWENTY

"**W**E SHOULD STAY here and rest," George said.

Major Wilks could see the pang of guilt cross Gladys's face, but she kept her expression in place.

"We can help," Gladys said, "and we will help. We're going to ground with the infantry. I'm not going to sit here and listen to Major Wilks tell us all the terrible things they've found. It's our *duty* to help those people."

"She's a leader," Major Wilks said from the corner of her office.

George sighed and rubbed his face.

"These people aren't like Rana," Gladys said. "They aren't trained to kill and maim like Rana was. We are stronger than their soldiers, and we can do more to help than those people can do for themselves. We're going."

Of all the assumptions Wilks had ever made about princesses, Gladys shattered them all. She was well spoken, but she didn't shy away from battle. She practically dragged her guard into the front lines, and that made Wilks smile.

Something boomed nearby, and the floor of the warship shook. It wasn't a minute before a soldier slammed open the door to the office.

"Major Wilks, we're taking fire!"

Wilks blew out a breath and snarled. "I can see that, you fool. *Fire back.*"

Gladys and George vanished out the door without so much as a goodbye.

The gunnery sergeant began speaking into the transmitter on his collar as he left the major's office. Wilks watched him go, wondering why in the hell he needed her approval to return fire. The bureaucracy Archibald had established on the warships was unnecessary and infuriating. If someone was shooting at you, you shot back. Simple.

Her heart leapt when the warship rocked. Someone had fired the main cannon. Wilks spread her fingers out across the map on her desk. The main cannons were probably overkill for such a small engagement. She clicked the transmitter on her collar. "Gunny, try the chainguns. We don't want to level the city unless we have to."

"Aye, Captain. Er, Major."

Wilks sighed and turned her attention back to the maps. If the Mid-streamers were right—and with the resistance they were seeing now, it seemed likely—Archibald had been right to send the warship. An underground railroad that led to Ancora?

The door to her cabin swung open again and slammed against the wall. The princess wore an expression that could flay a man alive.

"Major," George said, and there was a fury in his voice. "That cannon just destroyed residential homes. Those are *not* military targets."

"*Shit*," Wilks said. "I asked them to switch to chainguns."

"We need to go in on foot. Send infantry, unless you plan to destroy the entire city."

"We'll lose men."

"Those were Archibald's orders, and you will lose allies if you destroy Dauschen. These people will fight against the Butcher. They have *nothing* to lose. Send us in. I know the city well, and I can help you reach the resistance."

"Archibald's safe houses? They were already compromised."

"There are survivors. There are always survivors. They will be in the refugee camps. It is their rally point."

"Watch yourselves on the ground," Wilks said with a nod.

"Thank you," George said.

GEORGE LEAD GLADYS out of the office with a determined, if resigned, swagger. When they were clear of the major's office and headed to the landing lines, George spoke again. "If you get me killed, I want you to feel very, very guilty about it."

"Stop it," Gladys said with a laugh.

"The tragic death of the royal guard. Think of the stories … and the guilt."

"And what if you let *me* die?"

"Oh," George said, "then I will take a long overdue vacation. I believe you may have frightened the major with that glare of yours."

Gladys punched him in the arm.

A few minutes later they stood at the edge of the warship. The inferno of the old base had died down, but something still blazed in the heart of the pit.

"It's weird," Gladys said. "If you look to the east, it's like any other city."

"Do not get comfortable with that thought. Those are the thoughts that lower your guard and get you killed. Though I would enjoy a vacation …" George pulled two sets of Wheels off the rack beside them and handed one to Gladys.

"You have everything you need?" she asked as she took the belayer from him.

He patted himself down. "Armor, blades," he said, pulling his tight-fitting cloak back to reveal the rows of throwing knives tucked around his waist. George gestured at his thighs and said, "Guns, ammunition, yes."

Gladys patted the cargo belt at her waist. "I got snacks too, just in case."

George nodded and frowned slightly. "I suppose you are more prepared than I, Princess."

Gladys slapped her belayer onto the rope and leapt over the side of the warship. She cursed when she realized just how high they were. The trip down took fifteen seconds. Even with the belayer slowing her descent, Gladys knew that was a long, long fall.

She slipped the belayer off and into one of the pouches on her side. George landed beside her a moment later. The belayer vanished from his hand, only to be replaced with the wavy blade of a dagger.

"What is that?" Gladys asked.

"The vibrations?"

She nodded.

"The underground is likely settling still. I would not be surprised if the area experiences a great deal of earthquakes over the coming weeks."

Gladys hadn't considered that. They were going to be around and inside buildings set upon a shaking mountain. Maybe George's hesitation wasn't so misplaced after all. Gladys strode forward, leading George diagonally away from the smoking ruin of the old base.

He stayed right beside her, the dagger concealed just beneath his cloak. "Stay behind the buildings here. The refugee camp should be a straight line down this street and a little south."

"How do you know that?"

George smiled. "I am a nosy man, Gladys. Sometimes that provides a wealth of information, and sometimes a wealth of trouble."

Gladys pondered that as they walked in the shadows of the old brick buildings. Something roared above them, like a thousand angry bees. Her gaze snapped over her shoulder and watched the conical flames spitting from the base of one of the gun pods.

"Chaingun," George said. "At least the major listened to reason. We should not need to worry about getting blown apart by cannon fire."

"Right, we only have to worry about getting cut in half by a chaingun."

George let out a humorless laugh and stepped around a fire pit dug into the ground. He stepped out ahead of Gladys when voices echoed down the narrow alley that led to the street.

"I'm telling you, the three of us can take out that entire force. Those fools are disorganized and unfit to fight. Imagine the rewards the Butcher will lay at our feet if we remove the last of the resistance in Dauschen!"

The man's excited whispers had betrayed him. George's dagger was joined by a throwing knife in his opposite hand.

Gladys wrapped her fingers around two of the jagged throwing knives at her waist. They were terrible weapons, shaped and cut to inflict as much damage as possible in a single strike, a hallmark of the warriors from Midstream. Here she followed George.

Killing soldiers was something Gladys was intimately familiar with. Before her parents died, they'd changed the traditions of the Midstream survivors. Where their culture had been pacifist for a century, they learned to defend themselves, and kill when necessary, within a single generation.

George struck with the dagger first, slashing through vocal cords and arteries in one vicious slice. He pulled the man backwards by his coat so his comrades wouldn't see him fall.

Killing in the shadows was better. You couldn't see the blood. Gladys had killed her first man at nine years old. She flicked her arm forward, snapping the throwing knife through the air. The impact had enough force to crack the soldier's skull, and he went down like he'd been dropped from one of the nearby roofs.

Gladys didn't know what number he was. She wondered sometimes, but fighting the warlord's armies in the deserts made it easy to forget. In the end, she supposed it didn't matter. She dragged a second blade across the soldier's throat. Threat eliminated, Gladys retrieved her knives.

George allowed himself to make a sound with the last soldier. A deep, primal grunt as he twisted the man's neck until it snapped. The soldier had to be dead with his neck at such a severe angle, but George slit the man's throat to remove any possible error.

"Nicely done, Princess."

Gladys nodded as she re-sheathed her blades. "Should we hide the bodies?"

George shook his head. "Let them be found. They will assume the danger is nearby, as men are wont to do."

Gladys didn't question him. She'd known the royal guard long enough to realize he knew much more than she did when it came to war. Still, it was an odd thing to turn the next corner, only to nod and smile at passersby. Those people had no idea of what Gladys and George had done. It's why Gladys was not one to make fast friends. She was always alert, always suspicious, except with Alice.

At the next street, they slipped back into the shadowed alleys behind the old brick homes. Every sound drew a sharp look from George and a sharp blade in either of their hands. Despite the tremors in the earth and larger creatures scuttling through the night, there were no more soldiers between them and the small sea of white tents. Gladys almost longed for another encounter. It was the waiting, and the terrible suspense within, that could fray one's nerves to nothing.

Screams went up from within the tent city. George and Gladys exchanged looks and then ran into the neat rows of giant tents. One of the tents fluttered in the wind, shredded and bloodied and filled with things that may once have been men.

"Carrion Worms!" George yelled as he sheathed his dagger and unholstered two guns. He tossed one to Gladys, and she caught it mid-flight by the grip.

The white, maggoty flesh of the nearest monster reared up at the scent of fresh meat. The bright blue-and-orange rings around its segments meant it was a venomous worm, one of the few creatures that made Gladys's skin crawl. She raised the pistol and shivered when the thing's face split into three wide, triangular masses of flesh and teeth.

"Go for the eyes!" she said, though she knew she didn't need to tell George a thing.

The nearest worm lunged and George shouted, narrowly avoiding a strip of venom-laced teeth. The worms didn't growl so much as they roared. As silent as the awful things could be, they were loud as hell in an open fight.

Gladys took a deep breath and exhaled slowly, lining up her sights as best she could in the dim light. She slowly squeezed the trigger as the dying sun glinted on the Carrion Worm's eyes, and the first shot found its home.

The worm reared back and released a horrific squeal. Gladys heard George's gun fire, and the squeal seemed to intensify a hundredfold. Two of the limbs that formed that wretched mouth flopped down, dragging the earth. The entire body stilled.

Gladys had fought enough Carrion Worms to know what it was doing. The worms played dead when wounded.

"Behind you!" a voice shouted from somewhere beyond George, on the other side of the worm.

Another tent collapsed when two Carrion Worms burst through the fabric, jaws wide and trained on George. The wounded worm struck, lashing out with its last functioning appendage.

"George!" Gladys screamed.

The guard was calm, cold. He threw himself into the dirt in the ruins of the first tent. The newcomers sailed past, smashing into the first worm and crushing its wounded head into the earth.

Gladys aimed and fired. One of the worms went down, limp and dying. It was a lucky shot, and she knew it, but she didn't have a shot on the worm closing in on George.

"Shoot it!"

She couldn't understand why he hadn't fired, and then she caught a glimpse of him trying to pry something out of the gun's action. Dread crawled up from her toes to her head. George's gun was jammed.

Gladys unloaded the remaining rounds into the back of the Carrion Worm. It curled one of its mouth parts toward her, enough to curve a pitch black eye in her direction, and then its attention returned to George.

George cursed as one of the tent's ropes caught his ankle, and he went down hard. He threw two knives at the worm, and one managed to clip an eye. It wasn't nearly enough to chase the creature away. The worm rose up for a killing blow, spreading its mouth wide. Its venom glistened in the dying, burning sun—venom that would melt flesh and bone alike.

Gladys charged the worm. She didn't know what she was going to do, but she had to try.

There was a boom like a cannon shot, and the worm's head exploded into gory ribbons.

George stripped out of his cloak as he scrambled to his feet. Drops of venom had reached him and were already dissolving the fabric in gouts of hissing smoke.

Gladys ran around the other worms, tripping through the felled tent to get to George faster. "Are you okay?"

He nodded, and the knot of terror she'd been suppressing unwound itself in her gut.

"What are you two doing here?"

Gladys looked toward the voice. He was an average man, with an average face, and an average build. He was forgettable in every way, which made Gladys's hackles rise. "Who are you?"

"Peace, Princess. He's one of Archibald's."

"Bold claim in Dauschen right now, but you're not wrong."

"I am the Royal Guard of Midstream, and this—"

"Is Princess Gladys," the man finished. He studied them both for a moment and then nodded. "I'm Cage, captain in the resistance here. Come with me. It's not safe for us, much less a princess."

George released a humorless laugh. "It is safer for the princess than it is for most men. Of that, I am quite sure."

Cage glanced back at Gladys. She slid her cloak back, revealing the rows of throwing knives across her waist.

"We're glad to have you," Cage said. "Things are worse than you know."

CHAPTER TWENTY-ONE

T HE WALLS FELL all around him, and Jacob screamed. He ran from the mass of glowing red eyes that streamed out of the darkness and devoured the streets around him. He saw his mom and dad overrun and taken by the horde of Red Death.

Charles! They needed the bike, and so it was. The cobblestones rattled the frame as he and Charles rocketed through the bloody streets of Ancora. The eyes rose up ahead of them. There was no way through.

"Stop!" he cried. Charles turned to look at him, his face purple and swollen. Jacob screamed when the old tinker opened his mouth and his jaw unhinged, revealing an infinite blackness filled with glowing eyes.

Jacob fell from the bike and crashed into the cobblestones. Alice, he could still get to Alice. It wasn't much farther up the hill, but he couldn't catch his breath. If he slowed at all, they'd be on him. He'd be dead, and Alice would be gone.

Something sounded in the distance, someone yelled his name. Jacob's gaze shot to the side when a metallic voice filled the shadows. His hand reached beneath the soft feathers at his back, wrapping around a blade before he struck out at the darkness, screaming. The blade slammed into something hard and sank far enough that he couldn't budge it.

A shadow moved, and the metallic voice grew louder.

"Jacob! It's me!"

He lunged at the sound. They wouldn't hurt Alice. He wouldn't let them. Something caught him in the ribs. Fiery pain lanced through his side and he hit the floor. A warm weight dropped on top of him a moment later and screamed.

"Stop!"

The voice …

"Jacob, stop!"

"Alice?"

The shadows receded as he came back to his senses, caught between the horror of the dream and the horror of who he'd just attacked. "Gods, Alice! Are you okay?" He started pawing at the white shift she wore. It looked gray in the lantern light, but he didn't see any blood.

"I'm okay," she said as she pushed herself away and flopped onto his bunk. "Gods, you scared me."

He stared at her and then back down at his trembling hands. "Bad dream."

She reached out and squeezed his hand. They stayed there for a minute while Jacob's tremors gradually calmed.

He rocketed to his feet when someone began barking over the horn. Jacob managed to crack his forehead on a low-hanging pipe and stub his toe at the same time. He groaned and held his throbbing head. Drakkar's insistence on raising a drink to Charles the night before seemed like a bad idea now. Alice let out a small laugh. He turned to watch her on his bunk. She wore a sideways, bleary-eyed smile.

What was left of her good humor died when the voice continued over the horn. It was Mary.

"I repeat, Ballern's destroyers are already closing in on Bollwerk. Archibald has ordered us to leave for Dauschen, but I'll be damned if we don't strike first. Get dressed. Get to the cabin. Now."

Alice rolled out of the bunk. She dropped to her feet beside Jacob, which was about the time he realized she was wearing nothing but that white shift.

"You're uh …" Jacob started, unsure of what to say.

"Not decent?" Alice said as she turned around. "Are you just going to stare, or are we going to get to the cabin?"

Jacob averted his eyes and reached for his shirt. Alice's nightgown was thinner than he would have thought, and her skin seemed to glow against the pale fabric. He couldn't banish the image from his mind. It was silly. He'd danced with her and grown up with her, but now he felt uncomfortable.

He cleared his throat—as his dad liked to do when he didn't have anything to say—and threw his vest on over his shirt before fastening the buckles. It took a little wiggling and a few yanks to retrieve his knife from the bedframe.

"You don't look too bad yourself," Alice said from behind him.

Jacob could feel the blush crawling up his face as he stood up. He cleared his throat again, tried to think of something to say, and just sat down to tie his boots instead.

"Ready?"

He glanced up as he finished tying his laces and nodded. It was Alice. Just Alice. One of his best friends, if not the best friend he'd ever had. He watched her for a moment while she adjusted the belt at her waist.

Jacob pulled the brass lever down on the hatch to their quarters and pulled it open. He squinted at the early sunlight that cut into the shadows of the small cabin.

Alice groaned. "We're going to talk about that dream later."

Jacob nodded. "Let's go."

They'd gotten dressed in moments. Jacob didn't think his mom would have recognized her own son as someone who could move that fast.

He rubbed his forehead and they jogged slowly across the deck, their boots echoing out through the nearly empty docks and back again.

"How's the head?" Alice asked.

"Not too bad. At least it wasn't sharp."

"It's never been sharp."

It took Jacob a moment to register what Alice had said. "Hey now ..."

She slapped his shoulder and sped up, reaching the hatch to the pilot's cabin a few steps before him. Drakkar and Samuel waited inside, and the heavy footfalls behind them turned out to be Smith.

The tinker rubbed his face and yawned.

"Wake the hell up," Mary said. "Are the cannons ready to fire?"

Smith shrugged. "I would assume so, though I have not checked them today."

"Get to checking them," Mary said. "What about the chaingun?"

Smith nodded. "Mounted in the first gun pod."

"Two seats in the pod?"

"Yes ..." Smith said, drawing out the word. "Why?"

"We're going after the Ballern ships."

Mary's words were greeted with silence.

"We don't have the firepower for that," Samuel said. "You're talking about *destroyers*. They're heavily armored and we don't have a cannon large enough to break through."

"This is what you meant by striking first?" Drakkar asked. "I admit, I had not considered that as a possibility."

"I can't abandon Bollwerk," Mary said. "Not when we can gather intel and look for weaknesses."

"Those are *destroyers*," Samuel said as he spread his arms. "What do you think we can do with a couple cannons and a chaingun? We're not talking about infantry and armor on the ground, Mary."

"I know," she said, "I have a plan. It's what we have to do. We'll take out as many as we can and then head for Dauschen."

"Take them out?" Samuel said, his jaw hanging open at the words.

"We'll be lucky to survive a flyby! We can't engage them, Mary. We *can't*."

Mary turned to the windscreen. "If you want out, get out now."

"*Fine*, I'm gone. Jacob, grab your pack, we're getting off this death ship."

"No," Alice said, her voice quiet beside Samuel's heated words.

The Spider Knight turned slowly to face Alice. "What?"

"The Skysworn is the only ship fast enough to get us back to Dauschen before sunset."

"Kid, the Skysworn is about to get smashed into tiny bits by destroyers thanks to her idiot captain."

Smith stepped toward Samuel and loomed above him. "You may disagree with Mary's decisions, but I will not let you insult her in her own house."

"You going to back that threat up, Mech?" Samuel spat as he stepped closer to Smith, almost close enough to touch.

"You do not want that to happen."

"*Enough!*" Drakkar shouted as he pushed Samuel away from Smith and laid a hand on the tinker's chest. "Enough from both of you. I agree with Alice. We stay with the Skysworn. I already know Alice's vote. Jacob?"

Jacob met the guardian's stone gaze. "We fight with the Skysworn, and if we must, we die with her."

"Fucking hell, kid. You sound like Charles." Samuel squeezed his forehead and then slammed his palm against a wooden panel at the back of the cabin.

"If the decision's made, take a seat." Mary didn't turn back to look at anyone. "Smith, pull up the anchor. Are we ready to make the jump with the thrusters?"

"Yes, Captain."

"Go help Smith with the landing lines, Samuel."

The Spider Knight didn't speak. He followed Smith out of the hatch.

"You made the right call, Alice," Mary said. "We're the only ship that can get back to Dauschen. We're also the only ship crazy enough to fly through Ballern's fleet. Consider it a bonus."

"It's not ideal," Alice said as she pulled out one of the jump seats and snapped it into place.

"Samuel could be right," Jacob said. "I don't think there's really a way for us to know, but he could be right."

Mary glanced back at him as the ship lurched to one side. "I know."

The Skysworn evened out as the last of the landing lines released. Once Samuel and Smith had returned to the cabin, Mary steered the ship away from the docks. She glanced at Smith. "We do what damage we can, and then make for Dauschen."

"I'll have the thrusters ready for another jump," Smith said.

Mary nodded. She pulled one of the floor levers down and threw it to the side. The turbines outside roared to life. Mary didn't bother with a countdown this time. She slammed the throttle forward and the Skysworn screamed through the skies.

THERE WAS A story Jacob's mom read to him when he was a child. It was the story of a knight who faced impossible odds, and the thoughts that ravaged his mind as he watched death march upon the field before him.

Lo' I shall find the rider who falls upon his sword and lives to walk tomorrow. For upon his steed lie the dogs of war, and within his grasp is the end of all I know. I am but a man, and he, he is death.

Jacob had never understood those words so well as when Ballern's fleet appeared through the Skysworn's bronze scope. They flew in a V formation. Each ship was not so well armed as a Porcupine, but the cannons loomed large across the bows of the massive ships. Each destroyer had two banks of cannons strafing the skies. One of the massive guns swung past them, and Jacob froze in his seat.

"Hold on!" Mary said. She pulled on two levers, and the Skysworn swooped to a higher altitude, shaking as the thrusters fought against inertia. They broke through a cloud bank and Mary disengaged the turbines.

"That was … that was …" Alice didn't finish the thought.

"Those are twice as large as the Porcupines," Drakkar said. "What can two Porcupines do against ten of those destroyers? They will fail."

"More than we can do," Smith said. "Orders?"

The wisps of clouds gave way to an intense blue sky. The sun shone down as it would on any other day, but today was different. He felt his life balanced on the edge of a dagger, and all someone needed to do was give him the slightest push to die upon the blade. The rage and fire he'd felt at the death of Charles was smothered in the terror of staring down those cannons.

"Where do we hit them?" Mary asked, turning to face Smith. "We have two cannons and a chaingun."

"Can we hit the cockpits?" Alice asked. "Or is the armor too thick?"

"Depends on the class of destroyer," Mary said.

"Then the gas chambers," Alice said. "Take them out of the sky."

"They'll be heavily armored," Smith said.

"We have bombs," Jacob said, forcing his nagging doubt back down into the furthest reaches of his mind. "Charles's bombs." He said it with venom, wrapping his heart around that righteous fury and holding onto it with everything he had. "We can blow them out of the sky until they return the favor." He heard the words come out of his mouth, and they sounded like someone else. They sounded hateful, and fierce, and wronged, and furious.

Mary was silent for a moment. She looked down at the levers and controls around the wheel. "You scare me, kid."

Jacob took two deep breaths before he asked, "Why?"

"Because that little speech made me want to follow you into the gates of hell, and I've never wanted to follow anyone."

Jacob didn't know how to respond to that. It felt good, knowing Mary placed some level of confidence in him, but what did you say to that? Smith saved him from trying to come up with an answer.

"I will get the shoulder cannons," Smith said. "Maybe they can launch the bombs against the wind."

"Not at this velocity," Mary said. "You'll barely be able to stand on the deck, and we can't slow down without becoming an easy target."

Smith stopped fumbling with his harness when the buckles released. He let the metal clatter against the wooden floor. "We can try. Samuel, Drakkar, come with me. I will show you the gun pods. Leave the bombs and grenades to Jacob and Alice. They know more about them than any of us." Smith took two quick steps and opened the hatch. The wind roared around them as he disappeared into the rising sun.

Samuel and Drakkar followed.

"What do we do?" Alice asked once the others were gone.

Mary stood up at the wheel and squinted out the windscreen. Another cloud bank rolled by, and then the shadows of the Ballern fleet soiled the skies ahead. "We're close. Very close." She reached out and flipped one of the brass horns open. "Smith, you there?"

A rattle sounded over the horn. "Yes, we just arrived at the first gun pod."

Mary took a deep breath and nodded as she sat down. "I see more cannons in the front on those destroyers. We're going in between. Strafe them from above, and we can see how the armor looks from there. If they stay in that formation it will limit their angle of fire."

"Let me show Samuel and Drakkar the cannons and the chaingun, and I will be right there."

"We'll get the shoulder cannons out," Mary said. "They're in the locker by the hatch." Mary glanced back at Alice and Jacob as she closed the horn. "Jacob, you're heavier, and you should have less trouble with the wind. Grab the shoulder cannons out of the locker at the back of the cabin."

Jacob threw off his harness and started for the hatch.

"Clip yourself into the safety line. I'll never hear the end of it if you get blown overboard."

Mary winked at Alice. Jacob reached around the corner and grabbed the safety line. A simple spring-loaded clip fastened onto his vest, and then he stepped into the maelstrom of wind and cold.

The locker waited only a dozen steps from the hatch, but it felt like a mile as the cold howling winds tried to push him away, and down, and slammed him into the exterior cabin walls. Jacob leaned into the wind and struggled to put one foot in front of the other until finally he fell to his knees before the locker.

He pushed the lid back to reveal the two cannons Smith had stashed there. Jacob wrapped his fingers around the icy barrels and shivered as he pulled them free of the padded locker. One of the explosive crates was beside the cannons, and he pulled out four of the larger shells and a pocketful of Burners.

The instant he stopped leaning into the lid, the wind slammed it closed, nearly taking his fingertips with it. Jacob hugged the cannons to his chest and struggled to his feet, only to be propelled into a stumbling sprint back to the hatch. He smacked his shoulder on the doorframe, shouted, and fell onto the wooden floor of the pilot's cabin.

"Jacob!" Alice threw her harness off and kneeled next to him.

"I'm okay. It's just ... windy."

She gave him a small smile and picked up one of the cannons.

"How's the weather?" Mary shouted.

Jacob couldn't stop a small laugh. "Brisk."

"Why don't you take your safety line off so Smith can close the hatch?"

Jacob glanced over his shoulder and found Smith braced in the doorway, a hand on either side. Jacob slid the clip off his vest and handed it to the tinker. Smith nodded and hooked the clip back into the spool outside the hatch.

Jacob held up one of the cannons when Smith closed the door. "How do you prime it?"

Smith took the long, dark metal cannon into his hands. "It is not much different from Charles's air cannon. Rack the slide here ..." He pointed to a brass peg along the right side of the cannon's barrel. "Pull it back repeatedly until it clicks."

Alice followed his instructions, pulling the slide back with an underhanded grip three times, and the click was hard to miss. It was more like a ca-chunk. "That's it?"

Smith nodded. "Anything that is in the barrel will get shot out like a crossbow bolt. Mind you, if it is not made to fly straight, it will not."

"How well are these going to fly?" Jacob asked as he pulled out one of the bombs.

"I suppose we are about to find out." Smith took the bomb from Jacob and frowned. "It is too large to fit in the standard barrel. "We will need to unfold them in order to launch the bombs."

"Unfold what?" Alice asked. "The cannon?"

"Only the barrel," Smith said, as though that made any more sense. "Here." He placed his thumb on a ribbed catch near the muzzle. "And here." When he squeezed the two catches, the barrel folded down into a narrow imperfect U-shape, leaving space for a larger projectile.

With the launch mechanism exposed, Smith slid the bomb down the channel, squinted at its placement, and nodded. "It is not a bad fit. Not as ideal as an enclosed chamber, but good nonetheless.

Alice grunted, squeezed her barrel, and then fumbled the cannon when the barrel opened with a snap.

"I'll slow down," Mary said. "Keep us away from the sun so you can fire a test shot."

"We could fly into them from the sun," Smith said. "They would be blind to the attack."

"We're not going after them with the cannons and chainguns yet. I want you to fire a test shot without any hint of where we are. Samuel and Drakkar need to be ready to fire if things go bad." Mary reached up and tapped on the horn. "You two hear that."

"Aye, Captain," came the synchronized response.

Jacob leaned forward when Mary pulled one of the floor levers. The Skysworn slowed and leaned to the left, circling the fleet of warships below.

"Come up from behind," Smith said. "We will try the left of the V. Jacob, Alice, come with me."

"Where?" Alice asked.

"We are going out onto the deck to see if these cannons have enough range."

Jacob stared at one of the bombs in his hands. The thought of attacking one of those airborne monstrosities with such a small weapon seemed futile, if not downright insane. He crammed the thought into the back of his mind and remembered the devastation one bomb had caused during the Fall of Ancora. The bombs would work.

They had to.

CHAPTER TWENTY-TWO

T HE CANNON JUMPED as the tensioners were freed and the cables shot forward, sending the bomb whistling into the void between the Skysworn and the nearest of Ballern's warships.

Smith cursed when the bomb didn't travel so much as half the distance. "That is why I did not prime the bomb, Jacob."

Jacob watched the orb fall, vanishing into the green and brown patterns etched across the desert below. "But what if it had been a good shot?"

"Then I would have been very happy. If it had missed, as it did?"

Alice leaned on the railing, tugging on her safety line. "It would have detonated too far off the ship to do any damage. Then they'd know we were above them."

"Yes," Smith said. "It is still only a matter of time before they spot us. We are mostly hidden here, from the nearest ships, but there are platforms all around the gas chambers, and the warships on the far side of the V will notice us soon enough."

Jacob looked out across the mass of destroyers and shivered. The largest cannons were at least as long as the Skysworn itself. If the Porcupines shouldn't have been able to fly, what did that say about Ballern's destroyers? What did it say about the mind that built them?

It was then that Jacob realized they were keeping pace with the destroyers, and the Skysworn barely felt like it was moving. Mary could position them almost anywhere without the ships being able to respond quickly with the larger cannons. "We can drop the bombs onto the ships."

"What?" Smith asked, glancing at Jacob.

"Yes!" Alice said. "Get higher." She pointed toward the clouds gathering above them.

Smith rapidly tapped his palm on the Skysworn's railing and then nodded. "Cabin, now."

It was a quick jog back to the pilot's cabin. Smith stopped only to grab the crate of explosives before he pushed the door open and they all stepped inside.

Mary was talking into the horn. "Keep the cannon focused on the second destroyer from the apex. Clip the front of the gas chambers if you have to. Its position will cause the most confusion." She glanced up when the hatch slammed closed.

"Get above them and slightly ahead," Smith said as he began gathering up bombs.

"They could see our shadow in that position," Mary said.

Smith nodded. "It is possible, but not before we rain fire upon them."

Mary's eyes widened. She stared at the tinker as he stuffed his pockets full of bombs that contained enough power to level a city block. "You can't hit the decks from there, but the gas chambers …"

"We can make them target practice for the Porcupines, and then we can get the hell out of here."

"Hold on." Mary pulled back on two levers, and Jacob had learned enough by now to lean against the back wall. The Skysworn titled at a forty-five degree angle and drifted ahead of the rear ship. "Did you catch that Samuel? Drakkar?"

"We're bombing them from above?" Samuel asked.

"Yes," Mary said. "Same strategy. While Smith and the kids hit the rear of the V, I want you to focus on the second ship's gas chambers."

"It will be done." Drakkar's voice was calm and focused, and it reminded Jacob just how much he liked the guardian.

Jacob stuffed his vest with six of the compound bombs. The cold steel felt good against his fingers, like he was carrying Charles into battle with him one last time.

They were silent as they made their way to the stern. Jacob followed Alice. She had the cannon resting on her shoulder as she ducked past one of the angled supports that held the gas chambers in place.

Jacob gazed down at the massive destroyer when they reached the edge. It was different from this angle. The wide stretches of plating covering the gas chambers glinted in the sunlight. The cannons mounted above seemed impossible, though the Porcupines were no more conventional.

Ballern's ships flew flags to either side.

"Is that a Ballern flag?" Jacob asked.

"Signal flags," Smith said. "If you watch them after we drop the first bombs, they will change, either in color or pattern of motion."

Alice hefted the cannon onto the edge of the railing and tried aiming at the warship. "We're too close. The bomb is going to roll off the end."

Smith clicked the button on his collar. "Speed up a little, Mary. We need a better angle."

"You're all static, Smith," Mary said, her voice small and tinny on the receiver. "I heard you, but once we're moving faster, I'm not going to be able to understand you. You'll have to get back to the cabin."

He clicked the transmitter and said, "Understood."

Jacob felt the Skysworn lurch slightly beneath his feet. It forced him against the railing on the stern as the ship accelerated. He reached down and threw two switches on his leg. A jolt shot through his thigh when a plate slid out either side of his foot, giving him better balance on the moving airship.

Alice tracked the destroyer with her cannon until it was at a milder angle. "Should work."

Smith took a deep breath. "We are in range of their rear cannons, or very nearly so. We need speed and accuracy, and I truly hope these bombs are as effective as you claim."

"Charles taught us how to shoot," Jacob said. He cracked open one of the larger bombs he'd modified with the fuse, clicked the igniter on a Banger, and locked it inside the larger orb before sliding it onto Alice's cannon. "Ready!"

Smith cursed and loaded his own cannon. About the time he leveled it to aim, Alice pulled the trigger on her own cannon. It jumped in her hands, the release of tension silent in the rushing air on the Skysworn's deck. The orb sailed in a smooth arc, dropping toward the warship as she pumped the cannon to prime it again.

"Load," Alice said.

Jacob clicked the igniter on a Burner and locked into one of the larger Firebombs.

Smith launched his first volley. "How long is the fuse? I would have thought—"

The first round detonated as Alice fired her second. The explosion blossomed far below, just to the side of one of the massive cannons. Jacob gaped, his eyes wide at the sheer destruction as the blast tore away armor and ripped a hole into one of the gas chambers that would have been large enough for the Skysworn to dock in.

The shockwave reached them a moment later, a sound that sent Jacob's mind reeling back to the Fall of Ancora, back to the escape with Charles and the bomb that shattered a wall of Red Death. It was a thunder given deadly purpose.

Smith's shot mimicked Alice's, tearing through a watchtower on the port side of the warship. Alice's Firebomb detonated somewhere inside the hole her first shot had created. A burst of flame as large as the Council Hall tore through the sides of Ballern's battleship, and it began to list.

"Yes!" Jacob shouted. "I didn't think it would do *that!*"

"Reload!" Alice shouted back, a grim smile etched across her face. She fired again. The shot arced through the hole in the side of the destroyer.

"Nice shot!" Jacob said. "Your aim is—"

The grenade detonated, and a secondary explosion sent one of the destroyer's cannons spiraling off in a fiery descent.

Alice laughed and smacked his arm. "Nice work on those bombs!"

The flags across two of the battleships retracted, and bright red flags replaced them, moving in intricate patterns through the air.

"Shit," Smith said as he slammed the cannon into Jacob's hands. "It is already primed. Keep firing. I have to get to Mary." With that, he was gone.

Jacob shuffled up beside Alice, dragging the crate of grenades with him. "Here!" He held out a handful of Burners.

She squeezed his hand and then scooped up the small pile of metal orbs. "All the flags are red now. The cannons!"

Jacob leaned forward to see what she was talking about, and a rush of terror flowed through his limbs. One of the far destroyers was shifting its cannons. They were on a slow arc that would soon find the Skysworn's path.

"Take out as many as you can," Alice screamed as she slid another bomb home, aimed, and fired it over the stern.

Jacob did the same. The first destroyer still flew, but it was much lower than the others and falling out of formation. Jacob swung his sights to the next closest warship and fired. The Skysworn lurched, and something like a flaming cannonball streaked past them, a trail of burning ash behind it and a burst of heat that washed over the Skysworn's deck.

The boom of the destroyer's cannon echoed through the cloudy sky. Alice lined up another shot and fired. Some part of Jacob's mind realized how close they'd come to being blown out of the sky, and it sent him scampering for more bombs.

Rhythmic vibrations rattled Jacob's legs, and Alice froze. She looked up at him and back down at the deck. He waited for the Skysworn to fall out of the clouds, but it didn't happen.

Alice slid closer to him. "What is that?"

Tiny balls of fiery orange light streaked across the sky toward the furthest ship from beneath the Skysworn.

"It's the cannons!" Jacob said, his fear of their imminent death abating.

"Keep firing!" Alice shouted back.

SMITH PULLED THE harness over his shoulders and strapped himself into the jump seat. "Those bombs did more damage than I would have thought possible."

Mary did not answer. She turned the wheel and pulled two levers in a complicated maneuver that caused the Skysworn to stutter and drift to the port side. Cannon fire streaked past them and the report rocked the ship. Smith knew if they had not moved, they would be rubble on the ground. They passed the second warship and settled over the third, forcing their enemy to recalibrate their cannons yet again.

Mary threw open the horn and shouted "Focus on the far destroyer and *fire!*"

Samuel and Drakkar brought the cannons to life. Smith dropped his harness to the floor and stepped to the porthole. He could feel the vibrations in the Skysworn's skeleton, and he smiled as the rounds ripped into the starboard side of the destroyer.

Samuel or Drakkar had gotten off a lucky shot, and it blew a watchtower off the side of the warship. They would need about a hundred more lucky shots to bring down one of those beasts.

"They are breaking formation," Smith said.

The receiver above Mary crackled to life. The voices were faint beside the rattle of gunfire and bombs. "… Skysworn, come in. This is George. I have urgent news. Skysworn …"

Smith stepped up beside Mary and snatched the transmitter off its hook. "This is Smith. We hear you."

"Thank the gods," George said. "I am with the leader of the resistance in Dauschen, and you need to know what he knows. Cage, take it."

Another man's voice—Smith assumed it was the man George called Cage—sounded over the tinny speakers. "The Butcher plans to burn Dauschen to the ground."

"Why?" Smith asked. "There are resources there he could use."

"I mean he intends to kill every citizen and take over the city."

"Why would he do that?" Smith asked.

"The man has promised Belldorn to Ballern for their help in destroying Bollwerk."

"Gods," Mary said, "so he means to divide the Northlands between Ballern and Fel?"

"Yes," Cage said, his voice flat.

"How do you know all this?" Smith asked.

"The Butcher may not take prisoners, but we did. We have some of his officers in custody. Many of his forces serve him under duress. He has their families and children held hostage, promising to kill them should they desert … or fail."

Smith frowned, glanced at Mary, and then stared at the speaker with

Cage's voice. "What about Ancora and Dauschen? The other towns they have captured?"

"You haven't heard?" Cage asked. "They're putting their prisoners to death, declaring them traitors and spies and warmongers. They executed ten kids in Ancora this week." Cage's voice rose and sparked with rage, fracturing his calm demeanor. "Not more than ten years old. Ten-year-old spies?"

The Skysworn lurched to the side, slamming Smith into the wall as another volley of cannon fire streaked past the bow.

"Message received," Smith said as he rubbed his forehead. "We are heading to Dauschen."

George's voice came back over the speaker. "The resistance is willing to invade Ancora, my friend. They will march on the Butcher with us. We will need your help to succeed."

Smith looked down at Mary. She glanced up at him and nodded.

He clicked the transmitter and said, "You will have it."

CHAPTER TWENTY-THREE

"THEY'RE BREAKING FORMATION!" Jacob watched two of the destroyers as the slow-moving airships drifted apart.

"The first one's back," Alice said, pointing off the stern, toward the starboard side.

The overwhelming sense of hope he'd felt when they'd damaged that destroyer left him. Seeing the monstrosity closing in on them—even from a distance, with that smoking crater in the top of the gas chambers—was disheartening at best.

"We knew we couldn't bring them down," Alice said. "We were only trying to damage what we could. Keep firing!"

She was right, of course, and he knew it. Jacob slid another Firebomb into his cannon, aimed, and fired. He cursed when the arc curved more than he expected, threatening to send it off into the void, but it caught the very front of the ship, shooting a cloud of fire and soot out all along the bow.

Alice's next shot followed Jacob's down and blew a hole into the structure by the largest cannon. The cannon had been moving in a steady arc, but now it stopped dead, the gun no longer tracking them.

Jacob reached out and squeezed her arm. "I don't know if we broke the mechanism or killed the gunners, but that's where we need to aim!" He pulled the slide back until the now-familiar ka-chunk sounded in the screaming wind. The sharp stench of burning rubber and superheated metal wafted up with the gusts.

The Skysworn dipped down until it flew nearly parallel with the destroyer. Small guns fired from the gaping, smoky ruin of the pilot's cabin. Jacob grabbed Alice and pulled her to the deck as bullets pinged and ricocheted off the metal around them.

"What the hell is Mary doing!" Alice screamed. She wrapped her arms around Jacob and buried her head in his neck. Something else came to life, like the buzz of a swarm of Dragonwings. The high-pitched whine of bullets ricocheting off steel and brass continued, but now it was farther away.

Jacob and Alice scooted up beside the solid railing and barely poked their eyes over it. Jacob stared at the carnage as some invisible force cut through the men and women in the pilot's cabin. Holes appeared in the destroyer's glass, and the wooden floors, and the people, before Jacob realized what was happening.

"Someone's on the chaingun!"

Alice pointed up. Jacob followed her gaze and cursed. One of the destroyers had risen above them and was swinging its lower cannons into position. They must not have been the only ones who noticed, because the Skysworn dove and slowed, drifting beneath the damaged destroyer.

"Mary's going to do something crazy, isn't she?" Alice asked.

"Probably," Jacob said as he opened his arms. Alice wrapped herself around him and the railing an instant before the Skysworn zipped to one side, rocking the deck enough to send the bombs sliding away. Alice caught them with her foot, and then the deck angled back toward the stern as Mary punched the Skysworn into the clouds again.

The Skysworn shook as she leveled out and her cannons began firing again. Alice scrambled up to the railing and aimed her own cannon. Jacob prepped another Firebomb and slid it into the launcher. Alice fired.

Jacob squinted, trying to follow the path of the bomb, but it vanished by the smokestacks. His eyes snapped to Alice's. "Did that just hit what I think it hit?"

She smiled.

The explosion below sent arcs of shrapnel out like the wilting branches of an ironwood tree.

Alice shouted and whooped as the destroyer's gas chambers began collapsing, sending the warship into a limping spiral. The Skysworn pulled away, up into the cloud bank, as another destroyer opened fire. A hatch slammed against the wooden deck behind them and Samuel's head popped up.

"Nice shot, kid!"

"It was me," Alice said with a mad grin.

"Keep it up! The Porcupines are on the horizon. As soon as they engage the destroyers, Mary is taking us out of here. Be sure your safety lines are tight, because it's going to be rough. We're going to drop out of the clouds on the other side of the destroyers and sweep across the formation. Be ready with the bombs."

Samuel gave Jacob and Alice a two-fingered salute before he vanished below decks again.

Alice glanced up as she prepped another bomb. "How much time do you think we'll have to fire on each ship?"

"Not much, I'd guess. We need to reload faster. Let's open the bombs up so they're ready to go." Jacob cracked the last layer of bombs open so they were ready to receive a Burner or a Banger. Then they'd only have to close the top, latch it, and fire it. It wasn't much, but every second counted.

Jacob felt like his stomach had crawled up into his throat when the Skysworn dove out of the clouds. He clicked a Banger, locked it into a bomb, and took aim. There was a calamity off the starboard side, like two mountains colliding. The sound was awful, like the collapse of the cliffside base in Dauschen.

"Oh gods," Alice said.

Jacob fired. He didn't want to get caught with a live bomb in the breach, though he supposed he wouldn't have to worry about it for long if one of the things went off. Once the bomb was on its way, he followed Alice's gaze.

He blinked, trying to understand what the tower of smoke and fire floating in the air was. Two of the destroyers were nose-down, falling out of the sky. He couldn't understand how it had happened until he saw the blown-out smokestack in a brief clearance of fire and chaos. The wounded destroyer had crashed into another, and they were both going down.

Alice snatched up another bomb, locked it, and fired. Jacob did the same as Mary strafed the Skysworn across the loosely formed line of destroyers. It took almost two full minutes before they ran out of the bombs in the crate. The cannons still fired from below decks, but they weren't able to do much more than cause small leaks in the gas chambers.

There was a distant, thunderous boom. Jacob watched in awe as a series of fiery streaks lanced through the falling destroyers. The ships detonated. There was no other word for it. Whatever those lights had breached brought a fireball to life that could have swallowed a city. A charred rain of death sprayed out below, peppering the desert floor.

"Hold on!" Alice said as she threw her cannon to the deck and hunkered down against the railing.

Jacob did the same, and not a moment too soon. Mary punched the thrusters, and the Skysworn screamed to life, leaving behind two downed destroyers and a field of damaged warships.

The wind was beyond loud. Jacob and Alice held their hands over their ears while the sky screamed at them, smashing them into the railing. When the thrusters cut out, Jacob and Alice both rolled forward until their safety lines caught and wrenched them backwards by their vests.

The empty bomb crate spun toward Jacob's head, and he threw his hand out to stop it. The wood cracked against his palm and splinters cut through his flesh. Alice caught both their cannons before they slid past.

Jacob scrambled back to the railing and looked out. The Porcupines loomed nearby, casting long shadows and shaking the skies with their cannon fire. Ballern's fleet scattered, but not without purpose. They stayed in pairs, two going low and two going high. Each Porcupine would be faced with four destroyers until Warship Two caught up. At least it wasn't five.

"Let's get back to the cabin!" Alice shouted over the skull-rattling cannon fire.

Jacob nodded, retracted his foot plates, and scooped up the empty crate. Alice grabbed the cannons when an explosion off the starboard side rocked the Skysworn. Jacob stumbled but kept his feet. They followed the safety lines along the edge of the ship as far as they could. Ten feet from the cabin, Jacob unhooked the safety lines and they ran for the hatch.

Alice leaned on the lever and fell through the doorway.

"Get inside!" Mary screamed.

Jacob helped pull Alice in. She slammed the hatch behind them and tossed the cannons into the cabinet behind the jump seats. Jacob shoved the crate onto a shelf with a barred restraint, and then grabbed a seat beside Alice.

"The destroyers have a weakness at the base of the portside cannons," Alice said.

"By the observation deck," Jacob said.

"Good to know," Mary said. "I'll pass it on. Harness, now! Gunners, Smith, we're making the jump."

"Ready!" Drakkar and Smith shouted across the tinny horn, their voices distorted by a horrible whistling bleat.

Samuel didn't answer.

Jacob's eyes flicked from Mary to the horns, and over to Alice. "Samuel?"

Mary glanced back at Jacob. He clicked his harness into place after Alice, and Mary slammed the floor lever to the side and forward. The Skysworn's thrusters fired, and the turbines screamed, slamming them into their seats.

"It is holding," Smith said. "The patch is good."

"Get to Samuel," Mary said, her voice quiet. "Just ... just get to Samuel."

"On my way."

"What happened?" Jacob asked. He wanted to help, but he didn't even know what was wrong. "What happened to Samuel?"

"We got clipped by one of the destroyers. Samuel's pod was damaged by small arms fire and partially blown out."

"It hit him?" Alice said, her voice rising as her hand almost crushed Jacob's.

"No," Mary said. "It was just close enough to do damage."

"Mary," Smith said. "I am in the second gun pod. He is alive, but not unharmed."

"How bad?"

"I am not sure. There is a wound on the head, and he is not responsive. I will get him bandaged and then I will know more."

"How can I help?" Drakkar's voice was faint over the horn, made even harder to hear by the rushing wind. He must have left his own gun pod to help Smith with Samuel.

"Grab his feet. I need to get him to the workshop. Mary, we are sealing the horn and the pod. Give us one minute, and you can increase altitude as needed."

"Understood," Mary said.

The whistling cut off when something clanged across the horn.

Mary glanced back. "We have word from Dauschen. I'll explain on the way."

Charles was gone. Jacob stared at the floor. Charles was gone. They couldn't lose Samuel. They couldn't. He ground his teeth and remembered who was truly at fault.

The Butcher. None of this would have happened if it weren't for the Butcher. His parents would still have their home in the Lowlands. Dauschen would be thriving and the worst thing he'd have to fear would be getting caught pickpocketing … and Charles would still be alive.

Jacob's hands curled into fists and his arms shook. Tears pricked at his eyes while rage churned in his gut. It was a bizarre feeling, those simultaneous, opposing emotions. Charles had once told him the biggest trick in war was keeping people motivated. If Jacob had any more motivation, he'd explode. It was time to return to Ancora and unleash that motivation on the Butcher.

CHAPTER TWENTY-FOUR

G LADYS STARED AT Cage across the fire in the pit at the center of the canvas tent. Cage didn't have much of an army assembled, but it was better than nothing. Among the citizens of Dauschen were descendants of Midstream; Steamsworn and tinkers and brawlers. If what Cage said was true, they'd need every last man and woman, for all of their worst fears had already come to pass.

Gladys glanced at George, and then back to Cage. "It can't be that bad."

Cage nodded once. "I'm afraid it is. The Butcher all but owns Parliament. They're loyal to Fel. And Fel has allied itself with Ballern."

George tapped the hilt of his sword on the stone floor. "They mean to wipe out the Northlands, or enslave them."

"I think their goals are broader," Cage said. "It seems more likely they're after the entire continent."

"What would they gain by coming here?"

"We don't know much of the lands across the sea, only that Ballern has attacked Belldorn with relative consistency."

George blew out a breath and leaned back in a rickety old chair.

Gladys watched the two men casually discuss the rise and fall of what was essentially an empire. How did they stand against that? One warship, the Skysworn, and one broken detachment of soldiers? That was not what won wars.

The legend of Gareth Cave, the saga of the Butcher, what else could that monster bring about in their world? What else could they do but try?

"He has been stopped before, by politicians and farmers," George said. "No negotiations will stop that madman now."

Gladys knew how they handled mad beasts in Midstream. They slaughtered them. She looked up at George. "We cut off the head."

A slow grin spread across his face. "It will not be a safe journey, Princess. We will lose the lives of our allies and our friends, and in the end we may yet fail."

The story of Charles's final, fatal act of defiance came screaming back into Gladys's mind. Alice slaying a warlord, Smith cutting down half a dozen men with a chaingun, Drakkar forgiving the old tinker for the slaughter at Midstream. Those were her friends now too. She'd prove the blood of Midstream still ran strong.

Gladys pulled the top of her shirt down far enough to reveal the metal plate bolted across her chest. It was an old wound, and a rough mend, but it bonded her to a group of warriors like no other. She held out her fist.

George eyed it and then wrapped his fingers around it.

Gladys almost snarled as the words left her lips …

"Find me in that Steamsworn grave."

✧　✧　✧

MARY DIDN'T SLOW the Skysworn until Dauschen rose up against the evening sun. A column of smoke turned to shadows against the burning sky.

"Look at it," Alice whispered.

"I've never seen one outside of Bollwerk," Mary said. She took a deep breath and wore a sad smile.

Bollwerk's warship hovered near the destroyed base of Dauschen, near the last stand of Charles von Atlier. The smoke lessened, but an eerie glow still lit the chasm of the fallen cliffside, bathing the underside of the warship's cannons in fiery light.

Not long ago, Jacob would have seen that monstrosity as the most terrifying machine ever to take to the skies, but now ... now he'd seen Ballern's destroyers and Belldorn's Porcupines. He'd seen what death looked like in the skies, and one warship would never be able to face Ballern's strength alone.

"Go," Mary said when the Skysworn settled into an even flight. "I'll find the tents George was talking about."

Jacob threw off his harness and slipped through the door to the cabin with Alice. A short jog took them to the hatch that led below decks, and the yellowish lantern light guided them to Smith's lab.

Smith glanced up and released Samuel's arm when Jacob and Alice entered. He'd wrapped the Spider Knight's left forearm in a bandage up to the elbow. Another bandage circled Samuel's head, holding a bloody, square piece of gauze over his temple.

Drakkar pulled a saturated bandage off Samuel's leg, quickly replacing it with another wrap.

"He is awake," Smith said.

Relief flooded Jacob when Samuel's eyes flashed open and then narrowed. "Gods but that's a headache." The Spider Knight raised his right arm and prodded the bandage on his head. "I better not have a bunch of biomech implants."

Smith smiled and cocked an eyebrow at Jacob. "Biomechanics aren't so bad, eh, kid?"

Jacob rapped his knuckles on his leg. "Nope."

"Whatever," Samuel said. "Last thing Bessie's going to want when I get back is to be carrying around more weight. Damn Jumper is temperamental enough as it is."

"How is he?" Alice asked.

"Better than I expected when I found him," Smith said. "The head wound bled a great deal. I feared the worst when I saw it."

"Can he come with us? To Ancora?"

Smith hesitated.

Samuel twisted his neck to look at Jacob. "Us?"

"We're going to kill the Butcher." The words were so easy to say, though Jacob knew the act would be much more difficult to pull off.

"You're just a *kid*," Samuel said as he struggled to sit up. "Dammit, Smith, unbuckle me."

The tinker clicked the release on the harness and Samuel sat up, pausing only to wince.

"You can't go after the Butcher."

"You can come with us, or not, but I'm going. He's going to die, or I am."

Drakkar turned to Samuel. "We should go with him."

"No," Samuel said, "we should tie him up in a cellar until his common sense comes back. He can't win this."

Drakkar frowned slightly. "He is consumed with passion, and it will burn him alive or lead him to a great victory. If I can help, I will stand at his side. The Butcher has reigned in Ancora long enough."

Drakkar glanced at Jacob and then met Samuel's eyes. "I once mistook Charles for being no better than the Butcher. His creations left my city in ruins, trampled my brothers and sisters and led to the fall of Midstream."

"That wasn't Charles!" Jacob shouted, grabbing Drakkar by the cloak. Alice pulled on his arm, trying to drag him away from the Cave Guardian. Jacob couldn't let go, not yet. "He didn't kill those people. He would have traded places with them in a heartbeat."

Drakkar wrapped his hands around Jacob's and met his eyes. The Cave Guardian's eyes were red, and moisture gathered at the corners. "I know, Jacob. I was wrong … I was wrong."

Jacob couldn't stop the tears from running down his face when Drakkar's words all but pierced his heart. That wasn't what he wanted to feel. He wanted to feel the rage, not the pain. He wanted the hatred to fuel him in a mad, violent quest to destroy the Butcher. But if he'd learned anything from Charles, he knew he needed a plan, and he needed his friends. He fell back into Alice's arms.

"Nothing can save him now," Samuel said.

Jacob didn't know if he meant Charles or the Butcher, but it didn't matter. They were both dead.

✧   ✧   ✧

MARY STARED AT Jacob when they returned to the pilot's cabin. She offered a lone nod. She didn't speak, but she didn't need to; he knew she'd heard everything over the horn.

Samuel grunted and flopped onto one of the jump seats.

Smith leaned against the dashboard below the windscreen, arms folded.

"Drop us on the other side of the city," Samuel said. "There are a few small railcars there that we can ride to Ancora."

"That is madness," Drakkar said. "Railcars? What can you hope to do against the walls of Ancora?"

Jacob knew, and his eyes widened at his understanding of Samuel's suggestion. "Ride the railcars into the catacombs. You could sneak a small force through the old tunnels. Most of Ancora doesn't know they're there."

"The military knows," Alice said.

"It's a risk," Samuel said. "But the catacombs lead through the Highlands and up into Parliament."

"And what of the enemy soldiers left behind in Dauschen?" Drakkar's question was quiet.

"We destroy the bridge," Jacob said. "If they follow, they'll either die on the tracks or be forced back to Dauschen."

"We used all the bombs," Alice said.

Jacob shook his head. "No we didn't. We still have the impact fuses."

Smith stood up. "That could work. They do not *have* to be triggered by an impact. A Burner will work just as well, and once it is triggered on the bridge ..."

Mary shifted the wheel and the Skysworn began to drift to the east. "Are they hot enough to melt that old trestle?"

"It's reinforced with wood," Samuel said. "It'll burn. No doubt about it."

She pointed to the shadowed block of canvas below them. "There are the tents. Get down and find George and Gladys. Find out what kind of allies we have here."

Smith turned to the windscreen and leaned on the dashboard. "Looks like there has already been a fight. Some of the tents are down."

"Get ready," Mary said. "We'll be ready to drop in less than a minute."

Jacob walked to the hatch and threw the lever. He glanced back at Samuel. "Why don't you wait here? I'll get the landing lines, and once we find Gladys and George, we can come back for you."

Samuel leaned back into the jump seat and sighed. "Fine by me."

Mary glanced back at Samuel and then turned back to the windscreen. "Smith, Drakkar, are you staying?"

"No," Drakkar said. "There is more danger on the ground than in the sky. We will meet with this Cage and judge him for ourselves."

Alice slid around Jacob and pushed her way out of the hatch. Jacob grabbed Charles's air cannon off the rack by the door and followed.

"I'll get the other side," Alice said.

Jacob nodded and walked over to the spooled landing line closest to the pilot's cabin. He swung it up and over the railing and pulled the release. The spool unwound slowly at first and then picked up speed as the steel anchor whistled through the air.

Smith stepped up beside Jacob and grabbed the spool with a gloved hand. "Slowly. There could be people down there. We are not in the desert this evening."

Jacob jerked away with the realization of what he'd done. He spun away from Smith and looked across the deck at Alice. She let the rope out slowly, keeping one hand on the spool while she watched the anchor lower.

"She is a smart one," Smith said. The tinker smiled when Jacob turned around.

"I know."

Smith glanced over the edge of the Skysworn, tugged on the spool, and nodded. "It is down. Drakkar!"

The Cave Guardian exited the pilot's cabin and joined them by the landing line. "Is it time?"

Smith threw the lock on the spool. "Yes."

"I'll go down with Alice," Jacob said, turning away as Smith handed Drakkar a belayer.

"Stay close," Drakkar said. "There are Carrion Worms below."

Jacob hesitated and turned back to the guardian. "What?"

"They are dead, but the carcasses are around the felled tent. Be wary, and be ready."

Jacob jogged over to Alice. She handed him a belayer and then latched her own onto the landing line.

"What was Drakkar saying?"

Jacob glanced up at her and frowned. "Carrion Worms. They're dead, but they're down there."

Alice leaned over the edge and took a deep breath. "At least they're dead. See you at the bottom." She swung her legs over the edge of the Skysworn and jumped.

Jacob slid his own belayer over the rough rope of the landing line and hurdled the railing. Alice could take care of herself, but he didn't want her to be on the ground with Carrion Worms by herself. The damage just one of those things could do …

A chilly gust of wind pulled at his vest and he shivered. The cold made the cap in his leg ache, but he tuned it out.

Jacob pulled the brake on his belayer as he reached the bottom, making sure not to drop onto Alice. He released the brake once he found her. She'd already disengaged and was waiting off to the side of the landing line. His boots hit the trampled grass between the tents a moment before Drakkar's boots slammed into the stone pathway to the south.

It was only then Jacob noticed the heavy nail glove on Alice's right hand.

Smith touched down behind Drakkar and yelled back up to the Skysworn. "Down!" The anchor nearest them began rising into the air.

"Where do we start?" Jacob asked.

Smith squinted and looked around the Square. He pointed off to a far tent that still stood, and another closer by.

"The tent with the old Bollwerk flag," Jacob said. He gave the dead Carrion Worm a wide berth, passing it on the edge of the walkway. Wide, flat stones formed the path. He tried to concentrate on the difference between those and the cobblestones of Ancora instead of the rancid stench rising from the Carrion Worm's corpse.

Even after they'd passed it, the pungent smell of rot was almost thick enough to chew on.

Drakkar and Smith remained silent for most of the walk. Jacob glanced back at them, surprised to find Drakkar with two drawn blades and Smith with a wrist-mounted bolt gun at the ready.

Alice stopped before the first of the tents. Smoke rose from the rudimentary chimney. Voices sounded behind the closed canvas flaps.

Jacob reached out and grabbed the rough fabric.

"Wait," Smith said. "George!"

CHAPTER TWENTY-FIVE

T HE VOICES INSIDE the tent fell silent. Jacob heard a scrabbling sound and then rapid footsteps across a hard floor. The tent flap flew backwards, the coarse canvas ripping out of his hand as it revealed the warm lantern light inside, and the girl with a smile larger—but somehow colder—than any he'd seen on her before.

"Alice!" Gladys said before she threw her arms around her.

Both flaps folded back inside the tent. George stood within, beside another man, who Jacob didn't recognize. The man smiled and extended his hand, exchanging grips with Jacob and Smith in turn. The only thing remarkable about him was his lack of anything remarkable. It made Jacob uneasy, and he couldn't take his eyes off the medium-skinned, wide-eyed man.

"Welcome to the resistance. I am Cage."

"I've heard stories told of you in Cave," Drakkar said.

"I am Bollwerk's best." Cage's voice didn't take on the low tones of a braggart. He sounded more like Miss Penny, stating a simple fact.

Drakkar crossed his arms. "You fought against Rana in Midstream not so long ago, and yet he still lived to kidnap Gladys."

Cage frowned and shifted to look at Gladys. She'd only just pulled away from Alice. "Is that true?"

Gladys hesitated and then nodded. "He's dead now."

Alice shifted her feet, and her discomfort was obvious.

"My thanks to you. Please, join us by the fire. We have much to discuss." Cage moved with an easy grace. In every sparring lesson Jacob had ever had, be it with Charles or Samuel or even his dad, they'd told him to watch for men like Cage. Watch for them, and stay the hell out of their way.

Two dozen people huddled around the fire pit at the center of the tent. Men and women alike, some injured, some old, some so young that Jacob thought of them as children, not more than twelve or thirteen years old if he had to guess.

There was a burst of static from Smith's collar. Jacob turned to look at the tinker as he fumbled at the transmitter. Smith rolled a small dial to turn up the volume.

Mary's voice sounded faint and tinny. "Smith, respond. I lost sight of you at the tent."

Smith looked around the tent and clicked his transmitter. "We are in good company. Hold your position, and we will know more shortly."

"You're breaking up ..." Another burst of static came from Smith's collar. "Holding position until further ..."

"It's the wires," Cage said as he pointed up at the tent. "We're shielded here, mostly. Our transmitter is in another tent, though it's powered down. Fel seems to have learned to sweep for the signals. They took down our broadcasting safe houses in the span of a few hours after the base fell.

"Come, join our discussion, please." Cage ushered them closer to the fire pit.

Jacob almost felt like he already knew everyone there. That's what it was like to have a common cause.

Cage opened his arms and spread them wide. "Welcome to the resistance."

✧   ✧   ✧

THERE WERE BRIEF introductions, but they were almost all of Jacob and his allies. Most of the men and women around the fire stayed silent, save Cage. He had obviously taken on the role of leader, and it was doubtful anyone could challenge him for it.

Samuel laid out his idea about taking the railcars to Ancora. Cage watched as the Spider Knight used a piece of burnt wood to draw the plan out across the pale stone floor.

"It could work," Cage said with a nod.

"What kind of weapons do you have? And do you have enough?" Samuel looked around the tent. "This is not enough soldiers to fight an army."

Someone on the opposite side of the fire pit whispered, "Do we trust them?"

Cage glanced at Jacob and Smith and Gladys in turn. "I don't see any real choice. Dauschen's part in this is done. The base is destroyed and most of the soldiers have moved on to Ancora. You can stay in Dauschen and wait for the Butcher to return, but if it's my time to die, I'd rather spend it fighting against a madman."

Jacob crossed his legs and leaned forward. "The Butcher is not a madman."

Angry murmurs rose around the fire pit. Protests and accusations and suspicions that made Jacob's skin crawl. From the sound of it, some of these people actually thought *he* worked for the Butcher. The man who helped destroy his home, his city, his family!

"Stop it!" Jacob snarled. "We're from the Lowlands in Ancora! Do you understand what that means? Do you! They sent an army of Red Death through the walls of Ancora. I don't even know how many people they killed, but I saw the dead and the Carrion Worms that claimed them.

"Bodies piled to the second and third stories of what buildings weren't crushed in the waves. The base?" Jacob pointed out toward where he thought the smoking ruin was still burning. "The soldiers that we buried out there? The Lowlands were twenty times that size, or more. All that remained when we left was death. But it was not the act of a madman. It was a calculated attack. Read *The Dead Scourge* if you want to know more about what drives the Butcher. Archibald knew him, and so did Charles."

"You understand now?" Cage asked, his gaze focused on a group of men and women at the back of the gathering. "These are not the Butcher's pawns here to lead us into a trap. These are allies, even the Princess of Midstream, here to bury him."

A small frown crossed Jacob's face. He hadn't realized Cage was setting him up, prodding him in just the right way to make him convince these people to join them. Cage was too smart for his own good. Jacob exchanged a glance with Smith. The tinker gave a minuscule shrug.

A sad old man stood up and stepped into the edge of the light. "You've made your point. We will fight with the resistance. For my son, and his mother, I will join you."

"For my little girl," a woman said as she joined the old man.

More and more people stood up, and a few raised their fists in a Steamsworn salute.

"For my wife, who the Butcher hung from the walls."

"For Rebecca!"

"For my brothers."

"For the Steamsworn."

"For the Northlands."

The pledges and declarations continued for a solid minute before Cage raised his arms in a call for silence. In the empty air that followed, he said only, "We may not fight for you, but we will fight with you."

Jacob inclined his head. "I can ask no more."

Cage took a deep breath and turned to George. "Do you know where the gates to the old cemetery are? Near the hot springs?"

"I do," Samuel said.

"Good. Meet us there. We'll have to tear down the old wall between the stations." Cage turned to one of the older men beside the fire pit. "Gather the others. We make for the underground. And Ancora."

✧   ✧   ✧

JACOB CLENCHED HIS hands on the Skysworn's railing and watched the tent city below them come to life. "Look at them all."

Alice joined him and leaned into his arm. "It's more than I would have thought."

He nodded slowly. The resistance was larger than Jacob thought possible too. A line of men and women half a mile long began the march across Dauschen, weaving through the tents and out into the cobblestone streets. What would take those on foot almost an hour to traverse would be covered by the Skysworn in minutes.

"Alice!"

Jacob and Alice both turned toward the voice. Smith stood at the hatch to the pilot's cabin. He motioned for them to come closer. When they were only a few steps away, he said, "Samuel is discussing the layout of the old station."

Alice grabbed Jacob's arm and led him past Smith. Inside, Samuel leaned against the dashboard in front of Mary, pointing toward a mountain peak.

"It's at the base of that mountain. Can't miss the graveyard. It's all white stone."

Smith stepped past Gladys and George and leaned against the wall beside Drakkar. "Tell us."

"The station," Samuel said, looking around the group. "Okay. Cage was right when he said it was closed off. They boarded it up years ago, after they opened the new station above ground. Back when the trade routes really began to solidify with Ancora and Cave."

Alice frowned. "If the tracks lead to the new station, how do we get the railcars onto them?"

"There's a switch at the trestle. Fel's soldiers would've had to use it to get the personnel carriers onto the tracks too, so I'm sure it's still functional."

"What do you mean by boarded up?" Smith asked.

"Last time I was there, it was just wood. They hadn't completely sealed it, so we'll need to watch for bugs, but there should be a barrier about fourteen feet high."

"Solid?"

Samuel shrugged. "Solid enough, but we can cut the supports out without too much effort."

"What kind of railcars are down there?" George asked. "I have no desire to pump a manual engine all the way from here to Ancora."

Samuel huffed out a laugh. "No, they're all steam powered. It's the old brass carriers they used to use for civilians."

"Those will not be fast," Smith said.

"Faster than walking."

"That is little consolation when we need to get to Ancora at speed."

Mary glanced back at Smith. "I'm going to take the Skysworn into the mountains behind Ancora. If something goes wrong, or you need a quick escape, I'll be close."

"You could stay here and support Warship One," Smith said.

Mary shook her head. "There's nothing I can do that ship can't do for itself. The infantry has already swept Dauschen and removed any soldiers wearing Fel's colors. Whatever forces remain are hidden and aren't a threat."

Smith tugged on the glove covering his forearm beneath the bolt gun. "I would not be so sure after that display with Ballern's fleet."

Mary offered a small smile. "I'd need gunners for that, and the only men I trust will be below ground in Ancora."

"Has Archibald contacted you?"

"No," Mary said. "All of our channels are static. We're on our own for now."

Smith drummed his fingers on his leg.

Mary locked her gaze on him. "They're fine."

Jacob stared at Smith's gloves for a moment and then glanced at Alice. She was already wearing a heavy nail glove, the same glove she'd used to kill Rana. Her hand flexed, stretching the leather and webbing where she'd tightened it around her knuckles.

He pulled the locker open behind the jump seats. Inside were three more bolt guns, including the one he'd modified. Jacob unlocked the clamp on the hanger and slid the brass and leather construction out of storage.

"Don't forget the bolts," Samuel said.

The bolt gun itself held a full belt of ammunition, but that would only buy him twelve shots. Jacob pulled open the crate at the bottom of the locker and took two of the tightly-rolled belts for himself before tossing another pair to Smith.

Smith nodded and tucked them into a wide pocket on his dark leather pants. "Two more, if you would."

Jacob complied. There were at least six more belts in the bottom of the locker, but there were two more bolt guns as well. "Should we leave the rest?"

"How many?" Smith asked.

Jacob bent down to dig through the crate. There were two more in the corners, and another pair that had fallen out of the crate. "Looks like ten belts and two guns."

"I only need one gun," Mary said. "Leave me four belts and I'm good."

Smith looked at Mary and turned back to Jacob. "Leave her six. We will take an extra gun and the rest of the belts. George, are you armed?"

"Of course," the guard said. "As is the Princess."

"With more than blades?"

George brushed his leather cloak to the side to reveal a multi-gun holster that made Jacob curse.

"How many *is* that?" Jacob asked.

"Six for an easy draw and two for a cross-body draw."

"Right," Smith said. "Samuel? I know you are familiar with bolt guns. The Spider Knight's train against them."

Samuel hesitated and then nodded. "How did you know that?"

"Spies," Smith said. "It is how we know most of what we know." He tossed the tangle of leather and brass to Samuel.

Samuel caught it easily.

"Will it fit over your vambrace?" Smith asked.

Samuel tapped the silver plate across his forearm and nodded. He slid the straps over his knuckles and flexed his wrist, making sure the barrels cleared his hand.

"Been shot in the finger before?" Mary asked.

Samuel gave her half a smile. "No, but I saw it once. Nasty business." He finished strapping the buckles down and released the safety. The cylinder expanded, giving him just a bit more clearance. Samuel spun the barrels and made a fist. "Looks good." He pushed in on the central barrel, and the entire cylinder collapsed up against his wrist. The safety held it in check after that.

Mary stood up and leaned toward the windscreen. "We're here."

CHAPTER TWENTY-SIX

I F THERE WAS one thing Jacob was sure of, it was that jumping out of an airship would never get old. His boots cracked against the stone walkway before he snapped the belayer off the landing line. Alice landed moments later. She hadn't left much room for error.

Drakkar came down behind her, his cloak snapping in the mountain breeze, and almost disappearing before the gray stonework of the cemetery gates. "You are getting fast."

"At falling?" Alice asked. "I've always been fast at that."

Drakkar released a quiet laugh.

"How long until Cage and the others get here?" Jacob asked.

"Fifteen or twenty minutes," Samuel said. "Mary took it slow, but we still beat them here by quite a bit. That gives us time to find the old entrance."

"Is it actually in the cemetery?" Alice asked. Smith landed on the stone beside Drakkar.

Samuel nodded. "This wasn't always a cemetery. Before they built the base on the cliffside, most of the barracks were here. After the Deadlands War, things changed."

Smith stepped to the old rusted gate. "A mild way of putting it." He ran his fingers across the chain.

"I don't suppose you have a lockpick?" Samuel asked. "I guess we could scale it."

Smith threw one of the levers beneath his sleeve, reached out, and tore the chain from the gate. "I am never without a lockpick." The iron links clattered onto the stone when Smith let go.

Samuel stepped past the tinker and said, "I guess not."

"We will wait here," George said from behind them.

"No," Gladys said. "I want to see the station."

"We will, Princess, but here we may see things Mary cannot—our enemies hidden in the shadows or windows. Things that could keep our friends safe."

Gladys frowned, but George had clearly won her over with that logic. "Fine, fine. I'll setup over there by the reflecting pool."

Jacob followed her gaze and found a small rectangular pool set into the cemetery grounds. Above it stood a wide marble platform with benches and railings carved from a dark stone. The Midstream cloaks would almost vanish against that background.

"An excellent vantage point, Princess. I will watch from the east. Be wary, and watch for Cage."

Jacob followed behind Smith as everyone crossed the cemetery gates. Alice stayed close, and if Jacob was being honest, that made him happy.

"How far into the grounds is it?" Drakkar asked.

"It's below the old iron tower." Samuel said, pointing to the north-east.

"The bell tower?" Drakkar asked.

"Yes."

The sun was almost gone by the time they reached the old bell tower. Something ran past them in the low shrubs, chittering and clacking as it went. Jacob shivered in the shadowed darkness of the cemetery.

"Okay, it's a little creepy here."

"Not as bad as the catacombs in Ancora," Alice said.

"Not yet," Samuel said.

"You've never been in the catacombs," Alice said.

"I was down there with you and Charles and Jacob, if my memory isn't shot.

"Those weren't the catacombs," Alice said. "That was the old station and the old tunnels. You didn't see the dead."

Jacob's mind flashed back to that darkness, the whispers and scuttling things that passed them unseen, and the voice of the Butcher. The man who'd caused so much pain, so much death, and he'd been so close.

"We should have killed him then," Jacob whispered.

"What?" Alice asked. "You mean the Butcher in the catacombs? We didn't even know it was him. Besides, we didn't have any weapons."

Samuel muttered and walked around the bell tower for the second time. "I know it's here, dammit. We used the old station for a training exercise. Captain got us all excited like we were taking leave in Dauschen, but it was just more training."

"Do you need a lantern?" Smith asked, interrupting the Spider Knight's complaints.

"No, no, it's right here," he said as he traced a square with his arms. "This is the door, but I can't find the catch to release it." He pressed on a series of bricks that formed the pattern of a bell on the side of the tower. "I thought it was in one of these old bricks …" Samuel banged his fist on the mosaic and something clicked.

Samuel leaned onto the brick just to the left of the middle, and it sank slightly into the wall. Something loud and metallic slid and clanged inside the tower. Samuel pushed on the door, and the hinges squealed as the darkness inside came up to meet them. A small trail of ancient cobwebs fluttered out into the night on the stale air, thick as a rope.

"We're going into *that?*" Jacob asked, staring into an abyss.

"Please," Alice said. "It can't be any worse than the Widow Makers beneath Ancora.

"She's not wrong about that," Samuel said. The Spider Knight reached out and grabbed the web. "It's still tacky, but it's a fairly old web." He clicked the igniter on a lantern and lit the interior of the bell tower. "Oh, those are Jumper webs." He pointed to a cluster of looping webs that were almost as beautiful as they were terrifying. "Look at the curves and the thick tunnels of silk."

"Is that supposed to make us feel better?" Drakkar asked, clearly not excited at the prospect of navigating the old webs.

"You don't have many Jumpers around Cave, do you?"

The guardian shook his head.

"Jumpers avoid Widow Makers. If you have Jumpers, you don't have Widow Makers. It's a very good sign."

Drakkar took a deep breath. "So be it. Lanterns out?"

"Only shielded lanterns," Samuel said as he patted the thick glass globe on his own light. "You hit a dry web with an open flame, and we won't have to worry about what's waiting down below."

Samuel swept his light around the tower and stepped onto the staircase. "There's enough silk in here to braid a thousand belts, Smith."

The tinker reached out and snagged the silk that rose and fell slightly in the breeze. "It is aged well enough to be woven. If we survive this battle, I may have to return. This would be costly material in Bollwerk."

Samuel nodded and started down the tight spiral that vanished beneath the old stone floor. "I haven't seen any spiders, but keep your guard up. I know those are Jumper webs, but the lack of spiders is somewhat worrisome."

"Somewhat worrisome?" Jacob muttered as he stepped into the shadowy bell tower. The wind whistled through the small windows near the top of the belfry, almost an echo of the hinges that squeaked behind him.

Samuel's light began to fade down the stone staircase. Alice slid around Jacob and hurried down the steps to catch up to the others. Something brushed against Jacob's neck. He shivered and hurried down the stairs to catch Alice.

"It was only a web," Drakkar said from behind him.

Jacob kept one hand on the wall of the staircase, and the other on Alice's shoulder. She reached up intermittently to squeeze his fingers. This was not a place either of them wanted to be. The room opened wide near the end of the staircase, the stone spiral looked like a cylinder behind them, draped with spider silk. The dead air left the old silk to fall like curtains, lifeless and unmoving.

Something whispered at the back of Jacob's mind, an awful memory of Widow Makers dropping from shadowed heights in the caverns beneath Ancora. Adrenaline spiked and he shivered as his heart slammed against his ribcage. It was too dark, too quiet, too small, something terrible was going to happen.

"Spiders," Alice whispered.

Every fiber of Jacob's being told him to run, but there was nowhere to go.

Alice grabbed his wrist and pointed to a bulky shadow tucked behind the edge of the staircase.

"Looks like," Samuel said. He pushed his way into the darkness, clearing the webs as he made his way around the bottom of the stairs. His lantern caught on two carcasses as he reached the far side of the room. The Spider Knight pushed on one of the legs and it shattered.

"They've been dead for months. I doubt we'll see any Carrion Worms." He rubbed his fingers together and frowned.

"What's wrong?" Jacob asked.

Samuel glanced up. "It's nothing."

Samuel sighed. "I just hope nothing's happened to Bessie. With what we heard about the Lowlands ... I just hope she's okay."

The Spider Knight frowned and held his lantern up. The light flowed over three iron doors, each set an equal distance from the other. "What?"

Jacob glanced behind him. Drakkar watched the staircase.

"What is it?" Smith asked.

"I don't remember there being three doors."

"How long since you have been here?" Smith asked.

"Three years? Maybe four?"

"A man can forget things in a few years." Smith reached out and yanked on the nearest handle. "This one is locked."

Samuel tried the far door. It moved slightly before the deadbolt caught and clanged against the iron frame. He moved to the center door. The hinges screamed, shedding rust and debris from years of slumber. "I guess we'll go this way."

"What is behind the other doors?" Drakkar asked. He stepped off the bottom of the staircase, joining the rest of the group.

"Stop stop stop," Jacob hissed, throwing his hands out to the sides. "Did you hear that?"

Everyone fell silent, straining to hear. It came again. A quiet exhalation and then the scrabbling of a hundred legs.

"We're not alone," Samuel said. "The sooner we get out of here the better." He stepped around Smith and slipped into the corridor behind the middle door. Jacob followed the dim glow of Samuel's lantern up ahead while Drakkar brought up the rear.

The path took a sharp turn to the right, and it felt like they were walking on a downward slope. Jacob felt some minor relief when the corridor stayed clear of webs. Immaculate, if dusty, tiled floors led them forward, and old brass railings made for firm handholds in the walls.

The hall opened into a wide trapezoid shape, and Samuel slowed his pace. "This is it. This I remember. The left gate used to be the exit ramp, but it was collapsed last time I was here. The right will take us to the old platform."

A hinge cracked open on the rusted iron gate.

"Careful," Smith said. He reached out and shook the floor-to-ceiling construct. "This is ready to fall. He held the gate open while the others walked through.

Jacob squinted into the darkness beyond Samuel's lantern. Jacob couldn't see any more webs nearby, so he clicked the igniter on his lantern and hooked it onto his vest.

"Gods …" Drakkar said. "What happened here?"

There were railcars, no one could argue with that, but something had thrown two of the cars off the track and smashed them into another train.

Smith held up his lantern and ran it over the iron and steel carnage laid out in front of them. "Over there, in the corner. Looks like two cars are still seated on the track."

"Samuel," Alice said, "that wall looks like it's twenty feet tall and reinforced with almost as much iron as wood."

"Yeah, I noticed that." The Spider Knight blew out a breath and cursed.

"Let us take a closer look," Smith said. "Look along the top. The wall is already twisted. I do not think it will take much to knock it down."

"To knock it down without damaging the tracks will be the true test," Drakkar said.

Smith glanced up at the ceiling and then clicked the transmitter on his collar. "Mary, do you read?"

A tinny, static-laced response came back. "I can barely hear you."

"Do not let Cage enter the bell tower. There are bugs in the tunnels."

"Understood. Alternatives?"

"If we are able to drop the wall, you can setup the landing lines to use for rappelling."

"I'll get George to help. Watch yourself."

"What now?" Samuel asked.

"Now?" Smith said as he turned to the Spider Knight. "Now we need bombs."

CHAPTER TWENTY-SEVEN

J ACOB FROWNED AT the boiler on the fourth intact railcar they'd passed. A large hole marred the side of it, wide enough to stick his arm through. He glanced up at Alice and shook his head. "This one's hopeless. We don't have anything to patch that."

"What about switching it out with another one?" Her voice echoed around the station, mixing with the distant voices of the others.

"It'd work, sure, but I'd guess those boilers weigh about seven hundred pounds dry."

Alice glanced over at the wall. "Smith might be able to move it."

"Maybe. Let's check the last two. I don't want to bother him while he's setting those charges. One bad angle and we'll be walking to Ancora. At least we found a couple fuel bars in this one." He let the foot-long bars of slow-burning fuel clatter onto the deck.

Alice held out her hand while Jacob dusted his palms off. He grabbed her hand, and she used the leverage to help hoist him out of the engine room.

"That's a tiny space for an engine," Alice said.

Jacob looked back into the hole in the floor. "More like an engine closet."

Alice let out a tiny laugh. "Come on. One of these things has to be working."

They made their way down the dusty tracks until the next car loomed up beside them. Jacob let Alice climb up the ladder first and tried not to stare. He shook his head and tried to focus on the task at hand. It wasn't the first time the thought of her in that white shift had snuck back into his thoughts.

Alice pulled up the iron access panel near the front of the railcar. "Jacob, this one looks good."

He stepped up beside her and followed the lantern light around its path inside. "It looks really good. Let me hop down and take a look. We have two more to check after this."

"Give me some good news for a change, huh?"

Jacob looked up at Alice and smiled.

IN THE END, they had two working cars, plenty of fuel to make it to Ancora, and not nearly enough space to carry all of the resistance in one trip. Jacob said as much once Smith finished tinkering with the bombs.

Smith turned to him and crossed his arms. "None of that will matter if this wall does not come down right. Cage is waiting in the cemetery. Gladys and George are ready to drop the lines. It is time to find out how much of a hole we must dig ourselves out of."

Everyone but Smith made their way back to the rusted gate near the platform's entrance. The tinker stood silhouetted by the lantern he wore. There was a burst of light, and then Smith ran toward them. The old fuse was supposed to give them thirty seconds. Any less, and Smith risked being killed in the blast.

Jacob counted the seconds off in his head. Smith was almost to them at twenty, and then the world turned to fire and shrapnel with the blast.

Smith stopped running and turned back toward the wall. The mass of metal and wood creaked. Jacob couldn't make anything out through the cloud of smoke, but apparently Smith could.

Smith pumped his arm and shouted. "We got it!"

The smoke and debris filling the air moved in great whorls, displaced by the wall as it fell forward. The metal struck the ground, setting off the secondary bomb. Jacob winced away from the boom and the sudden slab of airborne wood and iron. It didn't fly far, but it didn't need to. Five feet to the side, the tracks were no longer blocked.

Smith started into the thinning cloud of smoke and dust. "So long as we missed the tracks, we are ready to go."

Something screeched and echoed above them. A great thunder crossed the ceiling of the old station, and Jacob stared up into the darkness.

Samuel looked up. "Smith?" When Smith didn't respond, Samuel turned to the rest of the group.

Alice hopped down the short flight of steps and made her way toward Smith as Jacob followed close behind.

They hadn't gone more than a dozen steps when Drakkar said, "Whatever it is, it's getting louder." Jacob didn't stop to listen, but between the crunch of his boots in the gravelly debris, he could still hear the screeches, and the thunder of more footfalls than he cared to count.

"Let's just get out of here," Alice said.

"I believe I can help with that," Smith said as he walked back toward them through the thinning cloud. "We may scrape up the edge of the railcar a bit on the way out, but the tracks are clear enough. We just need to load up the railcars."

The closer they came to the blast site, the more Jacob's nostrils burned with the sharp scent of gunpowder and explosives. More light shone on the station now that the wall was gone. It took a minute before Jacob realized it was the last bit of sunlight.

"It's gone," Alice said.

"You are actually standing on it," Smith said as he tapped his foot.

Alice glanced down and then behind her. Jacob did the same. They'd been walking on the fallen wall for several feet. It was covered with enough dirt and rock that he hadn't realized it was the wall. The largest iron supports had fallen a good five feet away from the track, leaving a few upright braces where the bolts had torn away. It was far enough from the rail to let the engine pass, but Smith was right. They were going to scrape the hell out of the wider cars.

Alice slid her foot along the rail beside the fallen wall. "You don't think they'll derail, do you?"

"The cars?" Smith asked. He shook his head. "It will be a bumpy start, but we should get by just fine. These old cars were built to last, and it will take a great deal more than a broken wall to stop them."

Something thumped, echoing out from the halls that led back to the staircase. Silence ran through the group as they all turned toward the sound. It came again, and then again, like stone smashing into stone.

"I will check on the noise," Drakkar said. He walked toward the platform and hopped up the stairs.

"Jacob," Smith said, "we need to start these engines. The old pumps should still work. Now hurry." He pointed to the wall.

Jacob squinted and then nodded. They were simple hand pumps, but if the gearing on the sides weren't frozen, it wouldn't take long to fill the boilers.

"Come on," Alice said, hopping up onto the nearest engine. She started twisting the brass valve to open the reservoir at the top of the boiler.

Jacob jogged to the nearest pump. He didn't even try to turn it on. Something had frayed the hose, and they didn't have anything to patch it with. The second pump, farther away from the blast that brought down the wall, had a hose that looked intact. He grabbed the nozzle and started pulling it toward Alice. The wheel supporting the coil of rope squeaked and rattled and finally froze with the nozzle only a foot away from the car.

"Dammit," Jacob muttered. He jogged back to the pump and tried to shift the rusted wheel. When straining with every fiber of his being didn't budge the coil, he picked up a length of bent iron rod and cracked it over the mount.

"Is it stuck?" Smith asked from the pump closest to the front car.

"No, I just wanted to hit something." Jacob raised the rod again and swung it into the side of the mount.

"I would expect that kind of sophisticated repair from a Spider Knight," Smith said.

"What was that?' Samuel asked, shouting back from the station's exit. Jacob wondered what the Spider Knight was doing there until a section of track shifted and creaked. He'd found the switch for the rails.

Jacob slid the pipe into the spokes of the wheel and levered it against his biomech leg. The entire coil assembly shook and broke free when he leaned into it.

Alice had the nozzle clamped onto the reservoir by the time Jacob turned to tell her it was loose. "Start her up!"

Jacob nodded and grabbed the pump handle. It shifted far easier than the coil of hose had, and he was relieved at the wheeze that ran through the system. It was pulling air, and if it could pull air …

The wheeze choked off, replaced by the fattening of the hose as water shot up through the pump. Water leaked from the connector, but not enough to stop them from filling the reservoirs.

"Working?" Smith asked.

"Yes. Bad gasket, I think, but it's filling."

"Here too. Go ahead and light the fuel. Once we have a little pressure, we can make sure these old engines are still rail worthy."

Jacob walked around the front of the railcar and crouched down. He shone a lantern up underneath the deck and along the tracks.

"Is it leaking?" Alice asked.

He shook his head and hopped up on the railcar beside her. "Not yet."

"I went ahead and set some of the fuel bars in the rack. Do you have a Burner?"

Jacob nodded and fished around one of his larger vest pockets near his waist. He handed Alice one of the small Burners. She pulled the iron rack out from beneath the boiler, clicked the Burner, and dropped it between two of the fuel bars.

"Whoa," she said, jumping away from the burst of heat and flame. "That went up a little faster than I expected." She reached the edge of the rack with her toe and forced it beneath the boiler.

Another rumble and crack echoed from the corridor behind them. Jacob turned around in time to see Drakkar come running back into the station, his cloak rising in the breeze behind him.

"Scythe Beetles!"

Jacob swung the air cannon off his back and racked the slide.

"Jacob, Alice!" Samuel's voice rang with authority. "Fall back with Smith. If you need to use the cannon, use it at the last second. You don't want to injure a Scythe Beetle. You want to kill it."

Drakkar's arm snapped out to the side, and his sword unfolded with a rapid series of clicks.

There was a calamity behind the Cave Guardian, and it grew louder with every second. Jacob and Alice scrambled off the railcar. Jacob paused and then ran to the pump to turn it off. The last thing they needed was wet fuel bars.

Alice made it to Smith ten steps before Jacob did. Samuel and Drakkar set up a loose line between the railcar and a steeper section of the shattered wall.

Smith spoke into his transmitter. "Mary! Get the chaingun down here *now!*"

Her static-laced reply came back in an incoherent burst.

"Chaingun! Now!"

Mary cursed and began shouting orders before she stopped transmitting.

Drakkar had the best view of the corridor, and everyone tensed when he said, "Here they come."

The iron gate in the stone hall collapsed at the first impact. The metal rattled and screeched as it was twisted and trampled. The creatures were not very fast, but once they were moving, nothing seemed to stop them.

They ran on three-toed claws, the spikes on their legs tearing through stone and rending metal as they crashed onto the platform. Jacob watched in awe and horror as the front most beetle paused, and its back split open. A pair of leathery wings extended from beneath the carapace and gleamed in the rising moonlight.

"Gods, they are flyers," Drakkar said. "Stay close to the cars or the wall. Do not let them catch you in the open." Even as he spoke, Drakkar shifted his position nearer the railcars.

More of the beetles surged around the first, chittering and roaring and climbing the far wall as they went. They were outnumbered three to one by the time the beetles stopped pouring from the corridor.

In another time, another place, Jacob would have thought them beautiful with their iridescent shells and delicate legs, but now he could only stare at the long, menacing horn that arced forward to a deadly point, measuring some two thirds of its body length.

The first beetle lunged. It looked as though Drakkar planned to meet it with his sword, but he dove to the side at the last moment. The scythe came down in a quick overhead strike that shaved off a three-foot section of the fallen wall. The beetle released a thunderous chitter and swept its head at Drakkar.

This time Drakkar did raise his sword, not to block the sideways blow, but to deflect enough that he could slide beneath it. He struck out with his sword, and the blade bounced off the Scythe Beetle's thick carapace, where its horn met its head. "Watch the ceiling!"

Samuel looked up in time to see another beetle release its grip on the stone above. It was silent as it fell, but Drakkar had provided all the warning the Spider Knight needed. The bolt gun on his wrist spun as he released the safety and fired when he bent his wrist. Four bolts cracked through the underbelly of the creature before Samuel dove to the side, grunting as he tripped and fell onto the wall.

The beetle smashed into the ground, blocking Jacob's view of Samuel. He thought the Spider Knight had gotten out of the way, but he couldn't be sure. The beetle didn't move. The underbelly had to be their weakest point, but how in the world could they get to that if the bugs didn't expose it?

The first beetle slammed its Scythe into the floor, narrowly missing Drakkar, who now took refuge beneath the edge of the fallen wall. The Cave Guardian couldn't see the other beetle stomping up the wall toward his position. If it reached him, it would flatten him.

"Drakkar!" Alice shouted. "Get out of there!"

Jacob ran forward and raised the air cannon. The beetle was only a few steps away from the edge of the wall, and Drakkar wasn't moving fast enough. He pulled the trigger, and the air cannon boomed in the cavernous station, echoing across the walls and ceiling.

The beetle screeched and opened its wings before lunging forward. The air cannon had shattered half the thing's armored head. It stumbled and collapsed. Something hit Jacob from the side. He didn't understand what had happened, only that the station floor was below him, and then above him, and then he slammed into something cold and hard and it stole the breath from his lungs.

Jacob tried to scream Alice's name as he slowly dragged himself back to his feet, but it was all he could do to gasp for air. He'd lost his grip on the air cannon, and it lay in the gravel some five feet away.

The Scythe Beetle raised its horn to strike Alice down. Smith joined Jacob's scream as he ran at the creature, but Alice was faster. She slid to the left, avoiding a blow that could have shattered a boulder, and then she punched the Scythe Beetle where its horn met its head.

The heavy nail glove fired an anchor through the beast, and the horn shattered. Alice started to turn when the creature flailed backwards and got itself stuck on one of the destroyed railcars.

Jacob was almost back to his feet when she leapt up onto the beetle's soft underbelly and began punching its eyes. Every strike fired another anchoring bolt into the thing's head until the glove clicked empty. Alice rolled off as two more beetles closed in on her, and she ran flat out toward Smith, joining Drakkar's retreat. Jacob dove for the air cannon and started pumping it again.

Alice raised her arm and pointed to the station's exit. "Get down!"

Jacob chanced a peek over his shoulder. The gun pod drifted into sight as Mary steered the Skysworn ever lower. Jacob turned back to Alice and immediately wished he hadn't. The Scythe Beetles were closing in on them, gleaming and roaring, raising their horns in anticipation of the kill.

He turned to run. There was nothing else they could do. He saw George behind the chaingun as the barrels spun up. There was no way George had the clearance he needed to sweep the station without killing half the people inside. Before Jacob was sure what had happened, Alice tackled him, throwing them both against the dirt before she rolled up underneath a fallen slab of wood.

George painted the station in lead and flame. Gunfire tore through the line of beetles behind Jacob and Alice. White and yellow pus-like fluids exploded from shattered carapaces and the beetles screamed along with the people.

CHAPTER TWENTY-EIGHT

J ACOB ROLLED OUT of their shelter first. Smith panted, leaning against the wall by the broken shell of a Scythe Beetle. Drakkar shook on his hands and knees and took a deep breath before trying to stand up. Alice crawled out and stood up beside Jacob.

Gore dripped from her right arm. It was a foul, sticky mess, but Jacob held on to her anyway.

"Samuel?" Alice's call echoed through the smoke.

"Yeah … I'm here."

An awful knot of dread untied itself in Jacob's gut. It was a knot he was getting too familiar with, and he hated it. "Where are you?" He still couldn't see Samuel.

One of the Scythe Beetles wobbled, and Samuel slid out from under its broken wing.

"Eww," Alice said.

"Not my blood," Samuel said with a grin. "Well, the blood is, but not the nasty bits."

Jacob stared at the Spider Knight. He was covered from head to toe in the exploded innards of a Scythe Beetle.

"Gods, man," Smith said. "Come over by the pumps. We will get you washed down. Mary will never let you on board the Skysworn again with a stench like that."

"We're taking the train," Samuel said.

"Not with us," Alice said. "Not smelling like that. Gag."

It hadn't really hit Jacob before, but as the adrenaline subsided, the sheer stench of the exploded bugs grew overwhelming. They made for the pumps while the Skysworn dropped its landing lines onto the edge of the station behind them.

"I hate caves," Jacob muttered.

"Will the water be okay on the nail glove?" Alice asked.

Jacob nodded. "It's bronze and brass for the most part. The water won't be great on the leather, but one wash won't hurt it. Just be sure to oil it later."

Alice didn't need to hear any more. She almost dove into the stream of water when Smith cracked one of the pumps open. The tinker throttled his biomechanics, and the gears on the pump whined before breaking free. Alice grimaced and scrubbed at her arm, shivering in the blast of cold well water.

Cage and his people began dropping onto the platform by the time Samuel finished washing off. It took him a while to scrape out the joints of his armor.

"You look like a drowned man," Cage said. He stopped more than arm's length from the Spider Knight, far enough that Samuel would have to put some effort into slapping him.

"Hilarious," Samuel muttered, looping his vambrace back into the latches at his shoulder.

"How many are functional?" Cage asked, his eyes roving across the ruined railcars and the fallen wall.

Smith released the pump arm and adjusted his biomechanics. "Two engines and a flatbed … if we are lucky."

"You're alive. I'd say you've some measure of luck left." Cage frowned and scratched the back of his neck. "We have nearly two hundred fighters. How many can we fit on the car?"

"If it works, perhaps twenty-five." Smith hopped up on the engine closest to the exit. "It is an old design where the steam vents out the sides of the car. We can stand eight people around the engines."

"We'll have to travel in groups," Cage said, and his displeasure was plain to see. "I have no desire to split my people up. Six trips … I suppose it could be worse."

"We'll go first," Jacob said. "Alice and I know the catacombs. We can make sure the path is clear, scout ahead before you get there."

Cage rubbed his chin and glanced at Smith.

"He's right," Samuel said. "Jacob and Alice know the underground as well as any of us."

Cage turned from Samuel back to Smith.

Smith pressed his transmitter and continued talking to Cage. "We can shorten the rail time by using the Skysworn as a relay. If Mary drops off groups of forty midway between Dauschen and Ancora, we have a much better chance of entering the catacombs undetected."

Mary's voice crackled to life. "You have a better chance going in with a small group instead of two hundred."

"We need them," Samuel said. "If anything goes wrong, we'd be over-run in an instant without them."

"No plan is without its risks," Drakkar said. "We may be overrun with or without them."

"I'll do it," Mary said. "It's not a bad plan. Lead with scouts, check the station, and I'll send the rest of the cars in with your signal."

"Understood," Smith said. He turned a valve on the railcar's engine, pulled one of the levers down, and a burst of steam shot out the side vents. Smith released the brake, and the railcar slowly began moving forward before he locked it down again.

"Not so out of luck," Cage said.

Smith gave him a nod.

Jacob hopped up onto the other engine and raised his voice. "After we check the underground station, I want to go to the old lab in the observatory. We can make it there and back before the railcars finish a second run."

"Why?" Smith asked.

"Charles liked his secrets too." Jacob turned the valve, mimicking what Smith had done. He flinched back, surprised at how hot it was. With the help of his sleeves, he managed to get the valve turned and the brake released. The gauges showed a constant pressure, but the cars didn't move.

"Open the valve more," Smith said. "Bring the pressure up to the red. Once she moves, we can pull it back."

Jacob spun the valve open, the needle shot into the red, and the engine lurched forward. His heart leapt at the sudden movement and he scrambled to make adjustments. Jacob quickly closed the valve and slammed the brake back in place.

"I think it works," Alice said.

Jacob flashed her a grin. "You might be right."

"Night is on us," Cage said. "If it takes two hours to reach Ancora from here on the rails, it will be past midnight by the time all our forces reunite."

"That's the best time," Samuel said. "The night patrols have always been lighter. I doubt they've stepped them up since the Fall." He curled his hands in to a fist. "Now that there are fewer people to protect."

Samuel's words weren't anything Jacob hadn't thought himself, but he almost flinched hearing them aloud. What was left of the Lowlands now?

"You know the city better than most," Cage said. "I'll be interested to hear the results of your scouting. My men can take over if you fail."

Smith eyed Cage for a moment before nodding. "Samuel, Drakkar, Alice, Jacob, with me."

"They will not be your only companions while you scout."

Jacob turned toward the voice. George walked up the rails with Gladys at his side.

"Thank the gods you're okay," Gladys said, sliding her arms around Alice before squeezing Jacob's hand. "Those beetles ... That was awful. I'd rather face Tail Swords."

"Me too," Alice said.

Cage ran his hands through his hair. "It's almost too simple. Walking in through an abandoned tunnel, straight into Parliament?"

Smith adjusted a series of small valves on the engine. "No plan ever survived a war. Complex plans have more room for disaster." He clicked the transmitter on his collar. "Mary, we are ready." Smith looked up from the engine. "Well, friends, I believe the time has come."

✧   ✧   ✧

THE RAILCAR SQUEALED and creaked for the first mile outside of the underground base, sending the two chainguns rolling across the deck. Jacob set his feet against the guns to still them. He worried they'd never be able to sneak into Ancora with all that racket, but the axles quieted more with each mile. The air outside was fresh, much more than that in the abandoned station had been, though he thought it was funny he hadn't realized how stale the air was at the time.

"I haven't been on a rail since I was ten," Alice said. "Back when they used to run the shuttle between Ancora and Cave."

"Six years for me, I think. My dad took us on a ride to Dauschen and back to celebrate his new job in the mines."

The railcar thumped and squeaked. Samuel and Smith discussed whether or not they should slow it down, but let it be in the end.

"I've never been on one," Gladys said. "I like it though. It's ... peaceful." She leaned against George.

Drakkar shifted on the wooden bed of the railcar. Every time the engine rattled across a rough spot in the tracks, it seemed like a new splinter cracked up from the floor."

Samuel spun something between his hands, silver and almost glowing in the moonlight.

"Is that your whistle?" Jacob asked.

The Spider Knight froze and looked up. "Bessie's whistle." He held the oblong instrument out before sliding it back into his pocket.

They traveled in silence for a while, leaning into each other when the curves were severe enough to push them around the car. They'd been on a slight incline, and now the track flowed out onto a long, curving trestle.

Smith leaned forward and began closing one of the valves. "Up ahead. Turn off the lights and keep as silent as you can."

Jacob's boot scraped against the wood of the railcar as he jumped to his feet, wobbling slightly the few steps it took to reach Smith. Alice stayed beside him.

The lights of the Highlands stretched across the wall far above them. In the shadow of the moonlight, the city threatened anyone who dared to approach. Jacob had never seen his home like that. He'd never thought of it as a fortress, but that's exactly what it was. He hoped that unwelcoming vision was keeping his family safe.

"No lights in the station," Smith said.

"They opened the entire wall," Samuel said. "That's madness, or it's a trap."

"What about the invaders?" Jacob asked.

"Invaders?" George stood up at the word.

"The bugs."

The railcar closed on Ancora faster than Jacob had expected. It wasn't another ten minutes before Smith all but shut down the engine. He clicked the transmitter on his collar and almost whispered. "Mary, we are at the station. No lights, but they opened it wide. Could be a trap, could be nothing. We will contact you again."

"Understood," came back faint and quiet.

"Look at that," Alice said. "They opened the entire wall up." She pointed off to the side of the mountain. "Is that the path we took with Charles?"

Jacob nodded, remembering the hellish journey it took to even *get* to that trail. "We can take the mountain path back to the old lift by the observatory," Jacob said. "I need to stock up on Burners and Bangers. Charles kept a stash hidden in the floor, and there's no way they found it, if they even went looking."

He could see by the look on Samuel's face that the Spider Knight wasn't happy about the idea. "Fine, but make it quick. We'll be in the station. We need a while to setup the chainguns in the catacombs anyway." Samuel paused, and then said, "Keep your leg covered. I don't know if they're looking for Biomechs, but they might be."

Jacob ran the layout of the catacombs through his mind. He thought there were at least two prime spots to set up an ambush. "Stay to the right in the catacombs. You'll have shadows and an obscured view from the hallway."

Samuel nodded.

Alice grabbed Jacob's forearm. "I'm coming with you."

Jacob didn't want her to come. He didn't want her in more danger than she needed to be in, and he had no idea what was waiting at the lab. But she was quick, sharp, and good at killing things.

"Me too," Gladys said.

"No," George said, placing a hand on the Princess's shoulder. "They are going in silently. The more people that are with them, the more likely they are to be caught. Leave this to the Ancorans and help us inside the station."

Gladys didn't argue. She only gave Alice and Jacob a look of longing as they hopped off the railcar at the mountain path and waved as it vanished into the abandoned station.

"Jacob."

He turned to Alice in the dim light.

"We're ending this."

CHAPTER TWENTY-NINE

"I DON'T LIKE this," Jacob said, his voice barely above a whisper as they made their way farther down the mountain trail.

"What?" Alice asked.

"Every time I take a step, I'm afraid someone's going to hear. Some guard's going to pop out and catch us."

"Why would they have guards out here? The invaders are a bigger threat than any person could ever be."

It hadn't been ten minutes, and they were already passing the pool of water where Jacob had escaped the raging underground river. Alice was right, and he knew it, but something still felt wrong. The full scope of that gut feeling waited around the next bend.

Alice gasped, and Jacob froze. The winds shifted, no longer blowing at their backs, and a putrid stench threatened to overwhelm them. Jacob pulled the edge of his leather vest up over his nose, but he still gagged.

There were bodies, of men, and beasts, and women, and Red Death. The path stood half blocked by fallen stones—massive square stones that should have formed the walls of the Lowlands, but instead lay fractured and broken where they'd slid to a stop.

Jacob expected to see Carrion Worms, and he did, but they were all dead; crushed by stones or skewered by spears and halberds. He tried to look up the cliffside, stepping to the edge of the path to see if any of the wall remained above, but the angle was too sharp.

"Let's see if the lift is still there," Alice said. "If it's not, we go back, if it is …"

Jacob nodded. "We go up."

They didn't speak of the broken, decayed dead at their feet. They didn't mention the horrible cracking sounds the dead and dried carcasses made when there was no way around but over. Jacob cringed when a bone snapped under his foot, but he didn't look. He didn't want to know.

He slipped toward the end, and when he caught a glimpse of the body at his feet, he almost screamed. The face he couldn't recognize, but the tiny metal brace attached to the child's arm was unmistakable. He frowned, and breathed, and stumbled away from that ruined child, far enough to vomit over the edge of the trail.

"Jacob," Alice hissed. "Jacob, what is it?"

He glanced back when her arm clamped down on his shoulder.

"I … I knew him. I made his arm … in the hospital … I just …" He cursed and snarled and stormed off. They were almost to the lift.

Alice caught up with him and squeezed his arm. "That's why we're here. Don't forget it. We have to stop these people, Jacob."

"I know."

"Then keep your head. We won't do anyone any good if we get caught." Alice stopped and looked up. "Isn't this it?"

A groove cut through the side of the mountain and seemed to stretch into the night sky. "It should be, but I don't …" Jacob stepped in where he expected to find the lift, and something rustled under his foot. After a moment's hesitation, he reached out and touched what he expected to be earth or bodies. Instead he found fabric.

"Something's here. Grab that edge."

Alice did, and they pulled. A cloth tarp slid away, revealing the lift beneath. "Who hid it?" Alice asked.

Jacob shrugged. "I don't know. Let's just get to the top." He stepped to the back of the lift. "Stay close. Whoever hid it removed the railing."

Alice sidled up beside him. Jacob put his arm around her before he hit the button. The lift jerked to life and sped them toward the top of the cliffside in almost complete silence. Jacob pulled Alice closer, breathing in the familiar scent of her hair before the lift crested the wall.

"Shit." Alice said everything Jacob needed to say.

The observatory still stood, an odd-shaped cone at the edge of a ravaged city. The ruins of the Lowlands hid in the moonlight, and some part of Jacob stayed thankful for it. He pulled Alice by the hand, hugging the right side of the observatory, pausing only to listen for voices, or footsteps, or any hint of life.

The nearest row of homes still stood, though one roof had collapsed and slid into the street. Ashes and debris formed the next block. Burned and leveled, homes seemed little more than grave markers left to rot beneath the night sky.

Jacob turned his attention back to the observatory. What had happened in the Lowlands, they couldn't know, but what they could do now ... He peeled back the loose bit of paneling he knew so well and pulled Alice into the shadows of Charles's old lab.

Alice wrapped her arms around him. He wasn't sure if he was shaking, or Alice was shaking, or the observatory was about to fall down around them.

Jacob took two deep breaths and squeezed her tight. The Lowlands were gone. That much ... that much was true, but Alice was still here. *He* was still here. That meant Lowlanders weren't gone yet. He pushed her head back with his hands. Her tears glistened in the thin stream of moonlight that crept in through a sliver in the observatory's roof.

Her kiss was as soft as it was surprising.

"Alice?" he said when she pulled away.

"Shut up," she said, pressing her finger to his lips.

He kissed her back, and hard. Her lips were warm, and right, and his heart hammered away in his chest. She leaned into him, her breath warm on his face, and he pressed back. She broke away, wrapping her arms around his waist when he tightened his own arms around her shoulders.

"We should hurry," Alice said. "We need to get back to the station."

"Right ... right." Jacob fumbled at his pocket and pulled out the reflector for his lantern. He clipped it onto the mount and clicked the igniter. They both winced at the sudden burst of light. Jacob crawled beneath the old shelves. He felt sick as he looked at Charles's workbench. Almost nothing remained. Someone had taken every project the old man had in progress, and gods only knew where they were now.

Alice stepped around him and glanced up at the shelves. "There's more left than I would have expected."

Jacob looked up at the crates and barrels. Most of it was heavy supplies they didn't much have a use for. "Check the fourth crate down. Charles kept the belts we'd been using for the nail guns in there."

The glint of the yellow lantern flame on polished metal caught Jacob's eye. The old arm brace he'd accidentally used to punch a hole in the wall sat discarded on the floor beside the bench. Charles hadn't even seemed mad when he'd done it. Jacob smiled as he picked up the abandoned project, but that smile fell as he remembered Charles's last words. He set the brace on the workbench.

A crate squeaked behind him when Alice tugged it out into the light. He heard metal shifting behind the wood as she dug through the old box.

Jacob bent down to the leg of the workbench. Still bolted to the floor, and it didn't show signs of anyone trying to unbolt it. Jacob flipped the false corner of one of the legs off and pressed the button beneath. A series of pops and clicks chased the top of the workbench. Jacob lifted the edge to reveal the old tinker's most dangerous inventions, most precious metals, and his proudest contraptions.

He took the powders and springs and clips that he'd need to build more Bangers and Burners. Some of the white powder Charles used to make Flashers rested in the corner of the bench. Jacob took it all, stuffing his backpack as full as it would go.

In the bottom, beneath the last handful of preassembled igniters, he found one of the little flywheels mounted into a base. Charles had been working on the design when Jacob had spied on him what seemed like just a couple weeks before. The little light had made the old tinker so happy, even if it had only burned for a few moments.

Jacob slid the rounded slab of wood into one of the last pockets on his backpack and tucked the flywheel into a pocket on his thigh. He grunted as he picked up the pack and slid it over his shoulders. Jacob closed the hidden door and started to walk away.

The brace caught his eye, gleaming on the workbench. Jacob picked it up and slid it over his arm. It flexed easily, and the padding for the shoulder mount felt good beneath the backpack's strap. Maybe he could use it for something. Something to remember Charles by.

"Two more belts," Alice said. She held up a long pair of belts studded with anchoring bolts before sliding them into her own backpack.

"That's great. Did you see any shells for the Burners?"

"Better," Alice said, sliding two tin boxes across the floor.

Jacob leaned down and opened them both. He stared at the mountain of Bangers and Burners hiding inside. "How did they miss these? They clearly raided the lab." He rummaged through the boxes. There had to be three dozen of each, or more. "This is great, Alice."

He glanced up when she didn't say anything more. "Alice?"

"You take one step and I'll turn your brain to paste."

Jacob froze. Alice was gone. Where was she? Was she safe? Did they have her? Who the hell was so ready to kill him?

Something else clicked in the shadows of the observatory. "Drop it." That low and deadly voice belonged to Alice.

Metal rang as it hit the floor and bounced. Jacob turned around. A small crossbow—that's what had been aimed at his head. He looked up at its wielder. "Reggie!"

A confused look passed over the boy's face. "Jacob? I thought ... we all thought you were dead."

Reggie didn't look like the boy he'd played Cork with at the fair. They'd laughed together, played together, and won more strawberries than anyone could have hoped to eat by themselves. Then the walls came down.

Reggie looked thin, and his pale color spoke more of illness and isolation. A scar puckered along his left cheek, and Reggie raised his hand to cover it while Jacob stared.

"What happened?" Jacob asked.

Reggie dropped his hand. "What happened to *you?*"

Jacob hurried through their tale. He left out some details, but he told Reggie of everything from the Tree Killer to Gareth Cave, from Fel to the Butcher's brother to the loss of Charles in Dauschen. It still hurt, talking about the old man like that, and it still boiled his blood.

"You really have a biomech leg?"

Jacob glanced at Alice. She shrugged. He pulled up the cuff of his denim pants and showed Reggie the plates that now formed his leg.

"Wow," Reggie said, keeping his eyes on the biomechanics. "Does that mean you're going to go crazy?"

Jacob shook his head. "Biomechanics aren't like that anymore. What happened here?"

"Half of Parliament's dead," Reggie said, meeting Jacob's eyes. "The Smith sentenced the Lowlands to death."

"What do you mean?" Alice asked.

Reggie raised his eyes and almost snarled. "They're executing anyone known to be from the Lowlands. They knocked down part of the wall, been throwing people off the cliff for weeks now. Bat's hiding as many as he can, but once they find one of his hiding places, they're sure to find the rest."

"We need to tell Bollwerk's Speaker," Jacob said. "We can't let that continue."

"We're gathering an army in the old underground station," Alice said. "It's not a lot, but it's something. We need a bigger army."

"Bigger?" Reggie asked.

"No we don't," Jacob said. He slapped Reggie's shoulder. "We need bombs and brains and men on the inside."

"Anything I can do," Reggie said.

"What do you know of the underground?"

"Rumors, mostly," Reggie said. "I've never been there myself."

"You know the old lift out back?"

"Yes, we've been using it to take refugees to Cave. I know there are guards in the Highlands that know of it, but no one has shut it down. I don't think all of the guardsmen support what's happened to the Lowlands."

"A lot of them are from the Lowlands," Jacob said.

Alice filled a small leather sack with Burners and Bangers. "That's one of the things we're counting on. Once the resistance strikes, we hope the guards and the Spider Knights will join us." She held the bag out to Reggie.

"Some of them won't." He looked into the leather sack and nodded. "The joy on their faces when they throw people from the wall ..." Reggie shivered. "Just know some of them will never help you."

Jacob squeezed his forehead. "If anyone wants to join us, take the lift to the old mountain path. They've opened the wall to the old station, so you can get there without much trouble. It's ... it's through the outer wall though. So be ready for that."

"I'll see who wants to join. I have a few groups who work behind the Highland walls."

"Like Bat?" Alice asked.

Reggie nodded. "Yes. They may be willing to help. If you need to relay a message, go through Bat. He's the brain of the resistance in Ancora."

"Have you seen my parents?" Jacob asked, not sure if Reggie knew who his parents were.

"I never met them," Reggie said. "I'm sorry, but I wouldn't know if I saw them."

Jacob knew the answer would come eventually. He had to be patient, and he had to keep that small hope alive, a hope that faded with every new bit of horror he learned about his city.

"Did any of Archibald's spies survive?" Jacob asked. "Any of their equipment?"

Reggie raised his eyebrows slightly. "He told you about the spies here?"

Alice nodded. "We spent a lot of time with him in Bollwerk."

Reggie shook his head. He looked out at the sky through the crack in the dome overhead. "Now everything's gone to hell." He turned back to them after a moment. "None of them survived. None of the spies, I mean. The Smith knew more than he should have. The spies were rounded up and executed within a day."

"What about their radios?" Alice asked.

"The transmitters? They were taken into Parliament along with everything else they found in the spies' homes. I can only guess they wanted the technology for themselves."

"No," Jacob said. "They wanted to spy on Archibald's network. If they had it turned on, they would have heard his attempts to contact the spies here. If they found the right frequencies, they may know a lot more than we think."

"Maybe," Alice said. "I don't think they know we're coming in through the old station though. It wouldn't be left wide open like that."

"Still, we better get back."

Reggie held out his hand. "I'm glad you brought the resistance."

"I'm glad you're here to join it." Jacob clasped Reggie's hand. Reggie did the same with Alice.

"I'll see you behind the walls."

CHAPTER THIRTY

S AMUEL TIGHTENED THE base of the tripod onto one of the chainguns and stepped back. "We shouldn't have let them go alone."

"I should have gone with them," Gladys said.

"Quiet, Princess," George said.

Gladys crossed her arms. "My complaining is no louder than Smith hammering those spikes into the ground."

Smith smiled and lined up the last of the bolts. He brought a hammer down and the strike echoed through the catacombs.

"One hit?" Samuel said. "You drove that into the stone in one hit?"

Smith patted the biomechanics in his shoulder. "I can do some work on you if you would like."

Samuel frowned. "No, I'm good. I'll just spend five minutes doing what takes you one tap." It may have taken him five times as long to drive the anchors, but when he pushed on the tripod, it didn't move a hair.

"Drakkar should be back in minutes with Cage and the others. The relay of resistance fighters should not take more than two hours, assuming everything goes smoothly."

Samuel glanced at Smith. "When was the last time *anything* went smoothly?"

The tinker swiveled the chaingun and chuckled. "You are not wrong, Samuel. You are not wrong. Alright, these mounts look good."

"Jacob's suggestion for their placement was well designed," George said.

"I would have set the chainguns to defend the tracks. I would have been wrong. We could have been flanked on all four sides. I was not aware of the hidden passages and the old tunnels."

George turned back toward the corridor that led to the station. "By design, I think. They have multiple escape routes and multiple attack points. If it was not for the cancer behind their walls, Ancora could have stood for millennia."

Samuel swung his chaingun in a half circle. The belt slid smoothly and allowed a full range of motion. "I doubt that, George. Their aerial defenses have always been weak. One of Bollwerk's warships could level this city with little problem."

"Perhaps," George said, "but the windstreams that lead to the city are dangerous and chaotic. There is only one safe path through the mountains. Most others are almost certain death."

Samuel looked up. "How do you know that?"

"The Royal Family in Midstream helped Archibald design … contingency plans for all the cities of the Northlands."

"Those were different times," Gladys said.

"Yet here we are, beneath the streets of Ancora, ready to infiltrate Parliament and remove as many traitors as we can."

Silence fell over the group at those words. George spoke the truth, and they all knew it. Samuel exchanged a look with Smith.

The tinker blew out a breath and tested the quick-release lever below the chaingun. It popped off the tripod effortlessly. "We should be set."

"I'm worried about Jacob," Samuel said.

Gladys crossed her arms and narrowed her eyes. "What do you mean?"

"He's just a kid," Samuel said. He tried the quick release on his own tripod. It clicked and did nothing. Samuel slammed his fist against it and cursed.

George put a hand on his shoulder. "He is not a child any longer. You do not see what he has seen, lose what he has lost, and remain a child. Have faith. He may be troubled, but we must show him our trust if we are to earn his."

"He trusts me," Samuel said. "I've known him too long for him not too. I've saved him more than once, from himself more often than not."

"He will be a Steamsworn unlike any before him," George said. "Born of Ancora and forged in the Skeleton. Even Mary likes him."

Smith crouched down beside Samuel and wiggled the release lever. "That is an odd sight, Mary liking someone."

"I wouldn't trust people either," Gladys said. "Not after what she's been through."

"What happened to her?" Samuel asked.

"That is not our story to tell," George said with a small smile. "Perhaps she will tell you of her less … law-abiding days if we survive this."

A quiet hiss and a clank sounded through the corridor.

Gladys turned back toward the hall that led to the station. "What was that?"

Samuel tried the quick release again once Smith finished tinkering with it. The chaingun popped right off, and snapped back on just as easily. "I'd guess that's Drakkar and Cage, back with our reinforcements."

"Then it's time?" Gladys asked.

"Yeah," Samuel said. "Then it's time."

✧　✧　✧

Jacob and Alice rounded the bend on the mountain path in time to see the last of the railcars vanish into the station.

Alice whispered, "Do you think that's the first load?"

Jacob nodded. "No way they've made more than one trip yet." Something chittered in the distance. Jacob and Alice froze. It started softly and then rose into a stuttering screech.

"Where is it?"

"Down the mountain. It's ... I think it's pretty far away. Let's get inside and tell the others."

Hiking up the path proved more difficult with loaded backpacks, but that wasn't what really made Jacob nervous. Crossing back over to the station with the extra weight on their backs ... he dreaded it. Rocks shifted above them and he checked the bolt gun on his wrist and the air cannon for what had to be the third time.

Alice hurried forward to the edge of the open station with Jacob close behind. Once there had been a door from the path into the underground, but bolts and rust sealed it now. Alice didn't so much as speak before she hopped from the edge of the path to the tracks. She made it look easy, belying the fact a missed jump was a two-hundred-foot drop to certain death.

Jacob took a deep breath and adjusted his pack. He followed her jump, bouncing one foot off the rails and hurling himself into the dim light of the underground station. He stumbled a few steps and blew out his breath, unable to contain the relief of not having to jump over another abyss with the heavy packs.

"Good thing Samuel didn't have to jump it," Alice said.

Jacob adjusted his backpack as Alice led the way across the tracks.

The station felt different from below. Jacob ran his fingers along the smooth stone walls of the channel below the bridges. Darkness lived below those arches, though it may have been the contrast of the lanterns flickering in the distance. A dozen voices whispered above them, and the effect unnerved him. When they'd first come in from that basement in Ancora, the entire room had been darkness and silence.

Alice hopped up on the back of the flat railcar. She turned and took Jacob's hand, helping him up the short step with his heavier pack. Jacob shrugged his shoulders to adjust his backpack and then led the way to the stairs. The others would be waiting in the catacombs.

People were seated at the tables in front of the little bookstore where they'd found *The Dead Scourge*. Jacob thought back to that night spent with Alice exploring the catacombs. As frightening as it had been, now he realized it was the first time Alice had been more to him than just another friend.

"Jacob!"

He tried to follow the voice, but the echo in the station made it hard.

"Jacob!"

Alice elbowed him and nodded toward the entrance to the fallen door near the catacombs. Drakkar stood up and gave them a short wave.

"I expected you to be with the others, my friend." Drakkar placed a hand on Jacob's shoulder when they walked close enough. He tapped the strap of Jacob's backpack a few times. "You have a heavy load there."

"Some Burners and Bangers that were left over in the lab," Alice said. "Are you driving the railcars back for the next trip?"

Drakkar shook his head. "Two of Cage's men used to work the rails. They will be running the rest of the transports."

"Come on." Jacob grunted and shifted his backpack. "Let's put these bags down somewhere."

"Smith and the others are in the catacombs. Come, I will show you."

They followed the curving path into the catacombs. It didn't seem quite as dark or menacing as the last time they'd been there, but the whispering voices didn't help. A pale yellow light illuminated most of the corridor, brightening as they approached its source. Around the next turn, before he saw his friends, he paused at the sweeping room of stone vaults and crypts.

"Jacob and Alice are back!"

He turned to find Gladys standing beside Samuel. Smith adjusted a chaingun mounted to a tripod while George muttered something about angles and herding.

"Find anything good?" Samuel asked.

Jacob let his backpack slowly slide from his shoulders, wincing as his muscles tried to bounce back without the heavy load. "A few things."

"Where should we stash everything?" Alice asked.

Smith looked around the room. "I would say here. This is our base of operations."

"Out in the open?"

Smith glanced down at one of the crypts beside the chaingun. "Here." He pulled out one of the wide drawers set into the stone slab.

"That's a memorial case," Alice said with a frown. "I don't know if we should ..."

"They will not mind," Smith said. "Everyone here is quite dead." He slid the contents of the drawer to one side. "It is a heavy enough surface to use as a bench if we need it as well."

Jacob dragged his backpack around the crypt and looked in the drawer. There were a few ancient photographs inside, yellowed and stained with age. A small book and a handful of medals were piled in the corner.

"Keep some Bangers and Burners for yourself. We can toss the other supplies in the corner."

"I'm taking the extra bolts with me," Alice said. She fished the leather belts out and threw them over her shoulder.

"Mary sent these with Drakkar," Smith said. He pushed a small crate closer to Jacob with his toes. "There are only eight left."

Jacob lifted the edge of the crate up. Inside were the bombs with impact fuses. "I don't think we should use those underground."

"Nothing like a cave-in to start the day right," Samuel said. "Toss me a few of those Burners. They'll come in handy if we cross the Spider

Knights. I don't care how well trained a mount is, spiders hate fire."

Jacob laid everything out inside the drawer except for the Bangers and Burners. Those he set on top of the crypt and opened. Jacob made sure Alice had her pockets full before filling his own and passing them to Samuel.

"Distribute those to the resistance along with some of the bombs," Smith said. "Be sure they understand the damage those can do. I do not want innocents to die here."

"Then you should not be fighting a war," Drakkar said. The Cave Guardian snapped the blade of his sword out and inspected the cutting edge before folding it up once again.

Jacob looked at Smith and Alice before focusing on George. "The Lowlands are gone. Most of the homes were torn apart by invaders or burned to the ground by Parliament. Bat is sheltering some of the surviving Lowlanders, but the Butcher means to kill them." He slowly closed his hands into fists. What if his parents weren't among the refugees under Bat's protection? What if they were at the bottom of that cliff?

"I meant no disrespect, Ancoran," George said.

Jacob liked that. He liked being called an Ancoran. Not a boy, not a kid, but an Ancoran. A Lowlander. "None taken." He glanced up when the lantern light shifted and caught on the mummies mounted to the wall. Not so long ago the mummies made his skin crawl. Now … now they seemed peaceful.

Someone laughed in the shadows of the corridor, a quiet, dark sound. Cage walked into the dim lantern light and smiled. "People die all the time. It's just the way of the world, but please, tell me more about these bombs."

"Samuel will show you all you need to know." Smith slid the drawer in the crypt closed. "If things fall apart, this is where we regroup. Come back through the catacombs in Parliament, or back through the hatch in the Highlands."

"Tell me more about the hatch," Cage said. "The ceilings here are far too high to reach.

"It's above the stairs," Samuel said. "Comes out in a cellar. Above ground, it's along the western wall, inside the Highlands but outside the Castle."

"It's not too far from Bat's," Jacob said.

"True," Samuel said, "but I don't think Cage cares about that."

"He might. Bat is hiding refugees from Parliament. Reggie, one of our friends from before the Fall, said Bat's the brains of the resistance behind the walls."

"That's who we need," Cage said.

Samuel took a deep breath. "He's my uncle."

Cage glanced at Samuel. "If he's leading the resistance here, we need him. Come with me. He'll be more likely to trust me if you're my escort."

Smith shook his head. "He cannot. Samuel is a deserter in the eyes of the knights. He abandoned his post after the Fall. They will be looking for him here."

Cage scoffed. "You give these fools too much credit. With everything that's happening here, they won't be concerned with a deserter."

Drakkar picked up one of Charles's bombs and slowly spun the steel orb in his hands.

Jacob tossed him a Burner. "Don't forget that. You'll want to be sure everything dies."

Drakkar let a slow smile crawl over his face. "I will at that, my friend. I will at that."

Smith stuck a handful of Burners into his own pocket and took a deep breath. "I will scout ahead with Jacob and Alice. George, you have a mind for maps?"

George nodded.

"Good. You and Gladys come with us. Drakkar, Samuel, help Cage and the resistance get organized. Samuel, you said you know the layout of the Highlands as well as anyone here. Give them their targets and get a message to Bat. If he is as good as you say, we will need his help getting the refugees to safety."

The Spider Knight frowned and then gave one sharp nod. "Consider it done."

Smith ran his hands through his hair and closed his eyes. "So it begins."

CHAPTER THIRTY-ONE

JACOB AND ALICE led the others down into the catacombs, along the corridor lined with the thirty-foot-tall burial wall.

Smith held his lantern high and blew out a slow breath. "In all my years, I have never seen anything like this."

"This is a place of kings," George said. "It is said the founders of the Northlands were buried beneath Ancora. I didn't realize the stories were so literal."

Smith ran his hand over one of the smaller wooden coffins. "Look at the detail on these. These people were masters of their craft."

They reached a curve in the wall that Jacob remembered quite clearly. The corridor narrowed, and the coffins grew closer together.

"How much farther?" asked a small voice.

Jacob wasn't sure, but he thought the voice belonged to Gladys. "Not too long. We'll be at the old coffins soon enough, and then the lake."

"How did you find your way through here?" Smith asked. "I have seen at least five other tunnels already."

"We stuck to the wall and followed it all the way down," Alice said.

Gladys rubbed her arms. "It's cold."

Jacob looked over his shoulder in time to see George wrapping a cloak around her shoulders. The Royal Guard said, "There was a time we said the cold spots were ghosts in the mines. I could almost believe it in this place."

Alice shivered beside Jacob, and he didn't think the cold had anything to do with it.

"Look at these coffins," Smith said. "They are ancient."

Something clanged in the distance, and everyone froze.

"Lights," George whispered. "Lower your lights."

Alice looked over her shoulder. "Was that behind us?"

"I don't think so," Jacob said.

George scooted deeper into the group so he could speak without raising his voice. "No. It was in front of us. I'm sure of it."

"Either way, we're not turning back now." Jacob snuffed his lantern. "Wait here." No one said a word as he walked into the darkness up ahead. He kept one hand on the wall of coffins until it solidified and became solid stone once more, and then nothing.

He crouched at the edge of the wall and leaned out just far enough to see an infinite darkness, and a tiny golden glow far down the next corridor. He clicked the igniter on his lantern and waved it back and forth. The shielded lights of Gladys and Smith bounced down the path toward him.

"The lake's here," Jacob said, pointing to the glassy, unmoving surface and the pillar-like columns formed from stalactites and stalagmites.

"This is a place of peace," Gladys said.

Alice's voice whispered through the shadows. "It will be after we end the bloodshed. This is the Butcher's home, and he has sullied it long enough." She stepped up beside Jacob and then pulled on his arm.

The lake seemed lower now, leaving plenty of space beside the wall to walk side by side. Jacob focused on the glow in the corridor ahead. It grew as they crossed the lake, and by the time they slipped into the next corridor, another clang sounded, freezing everyone in their tracks.

Laughter followed the clang this time. Who could be laughing after everything that had happened here? They'd murdered hundreds of people in Ancora alone. The death toll in Dauschen …

A hand clamped down on his shoulder. Jacob turned to attack, but then he found Smith staring at him. Jacob flinched, and frowned, and tried to understand what had just happened.

"You are shaking."

He looked up at the tinker. "What?"

"You are shaking," Smith said again. "Are you well?"

"I'm fine. I just … I don't like that laughter. They've set out to exterminate the Lowlands, and I …"

"And they've done a good job," Alice said. "It's what people do after a successful mission. They celebrate."

"They die," Jacob snapped. The words felt foreign on his lips, but some acts deserved no redemption.

"Keep your head, kid," Smith said. "We need you thinking straight if we want to get out of this alive."

Jacob took a deep breath and started forward. All the lanterns were out now, and the only light flickered through the bars of the window up ahead. A few more steps and Jacob settled in beside Alice, looking at the room where they'd watched the Butcher and Benedict.

"This is it."

Smith slid past Alice and ran his fingers around the bars on the window. "It will not be quiet, but I can break this out of the wall easily enough. We are below Parliament here?"

"I think so," Jacob said.

Alice slid to the other side of the window. "We have to be. Charles said the catacombs were built below the Castle wall. We're well past that. There's nothing else this could be."

A series of heavy bootfalls echoed up from the halls on the other side of the bars.

"Back!" Smith hissed.

Jacob threw himself to the other side of the window, settling into the shadows beside Alice. He caught a glimpse of Gladys and George vanishing into the darkness, and then one of the doors slammed open. Two men walked in, one carrying a helmet under his arm.

"I don't know … I kind of wish the old pub, Randy's Roof Jack, was still open in the Lowlands."

"The owners were Lowlands sympathizers. We burned it down."

"Did we?"

"Yeah, we locked the staff in."

"Right, that was where they came running out like a shooting gallery." The man laughed. "The extra pay was great."

Rage. There is a simple anger in everyday frustrations, and then there is a rage that moves flesh of its own accord. Jacob's lips quivered as he adjusted the biomech in his leg. He swung into the light and shouted.

"Hey!"

A pale knight looked up. "What the fu—"

The pistons in Jacob's leg slammed together as he kicked the bars into the cellar with the force of a train. Stone shattered as the bars exploded out of the wall. The first soldier's helmet collapsed, and blood sprayed across his comrade's face.

Jacob was in the room before they finished falling to the ground. The safety was off his bolt gun and he had his arm wedged into the other man's neck.

"Now, you son of a bitch. Where's the Butcher? Where's Newton Burns?"

The man tried to scream beneath the weight of his dead comrade and the iron bars, but Jacob just leaned into his jaw.

"You scream and I kill you now. *Where is he?*"

Jacob let the pressure off the man's jaw enough that he could speak. "Throne room, he never leaves the throne room."

"Where is it?"

"Through that door. The lift is at the other end of the hallway, third floor. Please, I have a family."

"So did Randy."

Jacob clenched his fist and the bolt gun rammed a shaft through the soldier's forehead. The man's jaw moved twice before his eyes rolled back into his head. "We know where he is. Now we just have to get there." Jacob turned back to the window.

"Kid ... fucking hell, kid." Smith hopped down out of the window.

"They don't get to live, Smith."

"George, help me move the bodies. If no one has come yet, we may be in the clear." Smith turned back to Jacob. "You *cannot* do something so reckless. You put us all at risk with that. Charles taught you better."

The fire in Jacob's gut flickered and died. He'd put their entire mission at risk, and he'd put his friends at risk. If they'd been caught, or killed, no one else could reach the Butcher.

"There's a lot of blood in here already," George said. "I don't think a little extra is going to be noticed." He grabbed one of the corpses and pushed it up into the window. Gladys and Alice dragged it back into the shadows while Smith grabbed the other.

Jacob looked around at the gore-splattered room. They'd killed a lot of people here. The shackles on the wall ... the spiked chair ... "They torture people here."

"Yes," Smith said. Once the bodies were hidden, the tinker turned his attention to the bars. He engaged his biomechanics and straightened the bars as best he could before wiping off the blood and setting them back in the window frame. "It's not perfect, but I doubt they check this too often." He pulled the bars back down.

Jacob climbed back up into the window.

Alice pulled him close and wrapped her arms around him before kissing his cheek. "I would have done it if I could have."

He sighed at the realization Alice wasn't disgusted by him, but he feared what that meant for both of them.

Smith climbed up into the corridor, dragging the bars with him. He leaned the straightened iron back into the window and turned to George. "What now?"

"Finish the sweep," George said. "We need to know where the corridor ends. We get above ground and get a message to Mary. With any luck they'll have reached Bat and the resistance behind the walls. Then we fight."

CHAPTER THIRTY-TWO

S AMUEL GLANCED AT Cage in the lantern light. He wasn't sure what to make of the spy. One of Archibald's best? What did that mean? It meant Cage could lie better than anyone in the Northlands, and how did you trust someone with that kind of skill?

"What?" Cage asked. He shifted and sat down on a barrel near the cellar stairs.

"Nothing. Just trying to remember the quickest way to Bat's from here."

Cage nodded.

"It isn't the fastest, but it may be best if we stay on the outskirts near the wall."

"I don't know about that. If they're keeping prisoners, they may be watching the walls more than usual."

Samuel didn't like it, but Cage had a good point. "Then we go left when we get out of the cellar, cut through the heart of the district. Drakkar?"

The Cave Guardian crossed his arms and stepped away from a rack full of linens. "Your people can handle the defense of the underground station?"

"Samuel gave us all the details we needed," Cage said. "They'll stay out of the Widow Maker lair, and seal it off in the meantime." He paused. "I trust them with my life."

Apparently that was enough for Drakkar. "Then we go."

Samuel took a deep breath and walked up the cellar stairs, framed by dark stonework. He half expected to find a halberd pointed at his throat, but no one was there when the doors cracked open and the moonlight streamed into his eyes.

"Clear." He gestured for the others to follow. He walked to the corner and looked down the street. Where once there would have been nothing but silence and shadows in the night, now there were drunken patrons stumbling from one bar to the next. Hooded figures exchanged small packages and coin purses on dim street corners, away from the brilliant lights of the Highlands.

"Gods, it looks more like the worst slum in the Lowlands." He glanced back at Drakkar. "I don't think anyone will take issue if you keep your hood up."

"I agree," Drakkar said. "I believe I may have been concerned at nothing."

Samuel tuned out his surroundings as best he could, but the Highlands around the fourth watchtower had always been an elegant place. Now the streets were overflowing with garbage, and a sharp, pervasive stench of sewage and rot assaulted his senses.

A shattered guitar sat broken in the gutter of the street corner. Blood stained the pale wood and a crushed copper mug beside it. Samuel slowed when he recognized the old musician's mug, and then he locked himself down, turning off any emotion that could be seen as weakness. This was no longer the city he knew. This was a city that would prey on the weak and eat them alive.

He kept his eyes straight ahead. Knowing Drakkar had his back gave him an easy confidence. Cave Guardians were well known for their stealth and ferocity in battle. Drakkar was no different. Cage was still a question.

Samuel led them around the corner. The dull thud and muffled screams of someone being beaten echoed out from a shadowed doorway. Samuel stopped and looked at the man holding someone down, another man raining punches. He caught snippets of their conversation.

"Stealing bread, maggot ..."

"... off the cliff ... knights won't stand for it."

Samuel started toward the men when Cage's hand flashed out and stopped him. "We have a mission."

Samuel needn't have worried. When Cage turned his attention away from the conflict, Drakkar stepped into the shadows. He struck twice with his folded sword, bloodying the first man's face and rendering him unconscious. Drakkar let him collapse to the stone walk while he raised his boot and delivered a sharp blow to the second man. A hollow thump sounded when the man's head rebounded off the iron-barred door.

Drakkar bent down and scooped up a smaller form, and Samuel wanted to run the two men through when he saw a kid in the Cave Guardian's arms. He couldn't have been more than fourteen, sixteen at the most. Close to Jacob and Alice's age, swollen and bloody and bruised.

"We take him with us," Drakkar said. "I cannot abide abandoning him."

Cage cursed and let his hand slide from Samuel's arm. "You risk too much." He looked between Samuel and Drakkar and cursed again. "Hurry."

The rest of the walk did nothing to raise Samuel's spirits. "How can we ever bring the city back from this?"

"Reconstruction takes time," Drakkar said. "The real damage is inside the leadership."

Samuel led them around another corner, and Bat's home loomed into view. "What ..." The two sliding doors that led to the workbench were covered in a series of bars. Samuel didn't see any method to open them.

"Some of the best locks money can buy," Cage said. He ran his hand along one of the dark bars. "These would take hours to crack."

Samuel retraced his steps and went to the front door. He knocked, and a small thunder of rapid footsteps sounded inside the home. After a while, the locks began to click open and the door swung inward.

It hadn't been all that long since he'd seen Bat, but his uncle looked thin, and dark circles beneath his eyes told a story of exhaustion that was unmistakable.

"Samuel?" Bat's eyes flashed around their group and then the street behind them. "Get inside. Now."

They shuffled through the door and Bat slammed it behind them. He locked the deadbolts, turned around, and threw his arms around Samuel. The familiar strength felt like it might crush the armor hidden beneath Samuel's cloak. "I'd heard from Archibald's men that you were still alive, but it's been so long since we heard from him."

"Are we safe to talk here?" Samuel whispered, returning Bat's hug.

"Yes, we're well insulated." He turned to Drakkar. "And Bobby, where did you find him? Here, put him on the couch. I have medical supplies."

"Not that bad," the bruised and battered form muttered from Drakkar's arms.

"Bobby," Bat said when Drakkar stepped away. "Bobby, what happened?"

Bobby squinted at Bat and the others. "Went by the bakery to pick up the day-old bread. Some of the knights walked in and saw me with the bread. Baker had to tell them I was a thief. Not his fault."

"Get some rest, Bobby. I'll let Reggie know you're here. You're safe now."

"Some guys helped me. One of them looked like Samuel. Funny, huh?"

Bat glanced up at Samuel. "Yes, Bobby. Very funny." He stepped away and said, "Come with me."

They walked down the hallway that led to Bat's workshop. Beyond the iron-barred door, three people huddled together. Two of them wore clothes spotted with dirt and blood. The third looked clean, and she wrapped a bandage around a man's forehead.

"Bobby's on the couch. They grabbed him on a bread run. He'd likely be dead if not for these three."

The woman looked up, and Samuel almost froze. Alice's mother met his eyes.

"Samuel!" She almost jumped out of her seat to embrace the Spider Knight. "Thank the gods you're all right."

"Alice will be so relieved." If Alice's mother survived, maybe Jacob's parents did too. Maybe more of his Lowland friends did as well.

She smiled. "Bat, I'll see to Bobby as soon as I'm done here." She turned her attention back to Samuel. "Reggie said he'd seen Alice. Where is she?"

"She stayed with Jacob," Samuel said. "Those two rarely separate without a good reason. After seeing what happened in Ancora, I'm glad she was with us as it was. Are Jacob's parents still here?"

Bat shook his head. "After one of the raids, they decided to make a run for Cave. A lot of refugees tried. Some of them made it, but many didn't. I don't know if they did."

"I am glad your friends and family are well," Cage said, "but we need information, and time is of the essence."

"Who are you?" Bat asked.

"I am Cage, and I serve Bollwerk."

"My name is Drakkar. I am a guardian from the city of Cave."

Bat extended his hand and shook Drakkar's. "It's an honor, guardian."

Drakkar nodded.

Bat exhaled loudly through his nose and eyed Cage. "So be it. What do you need to know?"

"Do you have fighters?" Cage asked. "In your refugees?"

"A few, yes," Bat said. Samuel had known his uncle long enough to know the man was lying through his teeth. They either had more fighters than he was letting on, or they had none.

"We need their help," Samuel said. "Our people are going to strike at Parliament from the inside. We need chaos in the Highlands to keep the knights divided. The attack will be a good time for the refugees to escape if you can get them to the lift by the old observatory. It's … There are a lot of bodies down there too. Be sure they're prepared for the sight."

"There is no one left in Ancora with a weak stomach."

"Where was the resistance?" Cage asked.

Bat slowly turned to Cage. "We fought back a great deal. The Butcher slaughtered the Lowland soldiers like so much livestock. That's when he turned the cannons against the city and burned it to the ground. You don't understand what's been lost here, Cage. They've set men along the walls with orders to kill anything that moves outside the perimeter. Our refugees can't even leave the city."

Three even knocks sounded from the wall. Bat frowned and turned away from Cage. He slid a framed painting of an armored tinker toward the ground, and something clicked in the wall. The paneling beside the workbench slid open and revealed a veritable army of men and women hidden away inside.

"You heard everything?" Bat asked.

The man in front nodded. He was young, emaciated, but a fire burned in his blue eyes that sent goosebumps down Samuel's arms.

"You're Jacob's friends," the man said.

Samuel nodded. The man's voice wasn't as deep as Samuel expected, and only then did he realize the person before him was barely old enough to be called a man.

"My name is Reggie." He traded grips with Samuel and nodded to Drakkar. "We'll do more than provide a distraction. We owe the Butcher his weight in blood."

Samuel looked into Bat's secret room. There were at least two dozen refugees hidden away there. Bat's stash of bizarre guns and cannons hung from the far wall like a backdrop. The refugees didn't look defeated. They looked determined, and that surprised the hell out of Samuel. How did you watch your city burn around you and still summon the strength to band together?

"I must see to my brother."

Samuel stood to the side and let Reggie pass.

"Reggie and Bobby have more or less taken over the resistance inside the walls," Bat said. "I help keep everyone fed, and hidden—"

"And armed," a voice said from inside the room.

"—but they help pick the targets, and protect those who wish to run. We have two more safe houses hidden inside the Highlands and a few pockets of survivors out there in the Lowlands. They're all fighters."

Samuel looked up at Drakkar, and the guardian bared his teeth in a vicious smile. Samuel knew exactly what he meant. This was what they needed. These were the people they needed. Once they understood the plot to bring down the Butcher, there'd be no stopping them.

Samuel stepped into the dark room and slid into one of the empty chairs. "I'd like to tell you a story about the Butcher, and how we are going to take him down."

CHAPTER THIRTY-THREE

J ACOB COULDN'T BE sure how much longer they walked through the catacombs. It's hard to keep track of time in the darkness, and every minute stretches infinitely long when every sound could spell your death. Jacob hadn't really expected the catacombs to lead anywhere else, but now they stood in front of an old iron door, rusted through by an unknowable stretch of years.

"Where does it go?" Alice asked.

"It may be from the old city," George said. He ran his hand over the lock. "It's rusted out." He pried at something inside the door, grimacing in the lantern light until something popped.

The door wasn't as loud as Jacob expected, but it sure wasn't quiet either. He cringed at the short squeal of the hinges. The echo died away, and once more they were left in silence but for the distant scampering of some unknown creature.

Smith held his lantern up. "The corridor appears empty as far as I can see."

Alice slipped past Smith. "What are we waiting for? Let's find out where it goes."

"Alice, wait," Smith said in a harsh whisper.

Jacob smiled as Alice's lantern bobbed down the hallway, and then it came to an abrupt stop. She held her light high and motioned for them to follow. When they were almost to her, Alice's light vanished down another hallway.

Jacob heard Smith curse under his breath, but they followed. Gladys stayed close to George, and Smith led them all after Alice. The lantern waited on the floor when they reached the other end of the hall, and Alice was gone.

Jacob's heart pounded in his chest. Smith had been right. They should have stayed together. They should have—

"Pssst."

Jacob turned his head from one side to the other. He saw nothing but shadows and dark stone turned golden in the lantern lights.

"Up here."

He turned his face up, and Alice was hanging out of the ceiling, a huge grin splitting her pale face. "How did you get up there?" he asked.

She brushed her hair back. "Jump. It's a low ceiling."

"What can you see up there?" Smith asked.

"Well … I left my lantern down there, so not much."

Gladys scooped up the little light and passed it up to Alice. She vanished into the hole in the ceiling. The lantern light dimmed and brightened as Alice inspected the floor above them. It wasn't long before she appeared in the hole again.

"There's a barred window at the end," she said quietly. "Looks like some narrow spiral stairs on the other side."

"One of the watchtowers?" Smith said.

George let out a low laugh. "We're inside the wall. It's perfect."

Smith glanced at him and then turned back to Alice. "Okay, we are coming up."

Alice backed away.

"Princess?" Smith asked. "Would you like a hand?"

Gladys scoffed at the tinker, measured the distance with her eye, and jumped up to the square hole above them. Her cloak disappeared into the shadows, and George followed her up.

"After you," Smith said.

Jacob reached up toward the hold, but couldn't quite reach. He tried to jump, but the biomech in his leg kept him off balance, and he missed the grab. "Dammit."

"Push off harder with your right leg," Smith said. "You have more weight on that leg now."

Jacob crouched down, and then he leapt. His body still tilted, but he was more centered, and his palms caught the rough, gritty edge of the opening. Someone grabbed his wrists as he started pulling himself up. Alice's face greeted him in the golden light.

Smith grunted and pulled himself up the instant Jacob's feet cleared the second floor.

George stood by the barred window. The rest of the room looked much like the first floor. The stone may have been paler, but the surface remained masked by the lantern light. Smith joined George and crouched down below the bars.

"This is a very old door," Smith said, his voice barely above a whisper.

"A door?" Gladys asked.

Smith nodded. "The old builders used to cut them in at an angle. From the staircase, I doubt you can tell there is a doorway here. Look at the angle of the frame. We can open the door into the stairwell, but it would be impossible to push the door open. The stones block it."

"Oh ..." Gladys said. "And if they don't have a handle on the other side?"

"Exactly, Princess," George said.

"Have you heard anything?" Smith asked.

Alice walked closer and whispered. "When I first came up, I thought I heard voices. I haven't heard anything else since."

"Change of guard?" George asked.

"Possibly," Smith said with a nod. "It would buy us a short time to contact Mary if this is a watchtower."

George pushed down on the gleaming metal handle set into the stone and leaned on the door. It seemed impossible for a forgotten, entirely unmaintained mechanism to work in absolute silence, but it did.

"Built to last," Smith said, echoing Jacob's own thoughts.

George turned to Gladys. "Stay inside the room. If anyone walks by who isn't us, kill them."

"I'll stay," Alice said. "I'll stay with Gladys."

George nodded and then slipped into the stairwell. Smith followed, and Jacob stayed on their heels. He caught a glimpse of Alice as she closed the door, sealing the hidden room once more.

They stuck to the edge of the staircase, following the spiral ever upward. It seemed like half an hour had passed by the time the hatch came into view.

Smith kept his arm held high, with the safety off his bolt gun. A normal man would have been exhausted by the time they reached the top of the tower, but Smith's biomechanics gave him an advantage. The tinker held his arm up, calling for a stop.

George slid around him, leaning to the left and right, trying to get a view into the tower. He turned back and put his hand over his eyes and pointed left. Once they started, there was no turning back.

George vanished through the hatch, and voices sounded in the tower. Smith leapt through the hole, and Jacob followed. He turned to find George with his arm around one man, and a crossbow aimed at the pair.

Smith shouted, drawing the bowman's attention an instant before he hit him like a charging Walker. The man screamed as he fell out of the tower, vanishing into the darkness outside the wall. George jerked the other knight's head to the side, and then there was only silence.

"Make the call," George said. "We need to be elsewhere."

Smith clicked his transmitter. "Skysworn, we are in the walls, come in."

Something grunted in the stairwell below them before it gasped. A horrific gurgling sound mixed with the grunts, and then silence returned.

"Make ready," Smith said.

Jacob slid around behind the hatch, ready to strike at whatever, or whoever, showed their face.

"Jacob? Smith?"

Jacob lowered his air cannon and peeked over the hatch cover. "Alice?"

"Clear?"

"Yeah, come up."

Gladys appeared first, a long streak of blood glistening in the moonlight. Alice followed, the side of her face splattered in gore.

Jacob's heart leapt and he stepped closer. "Are you okay?"

She nodded. "It's not our blood."

Jacob took in a deep breath through his nose and blew it out through his mouth. The pungent scent of rot and blood and decay filtered up from somewhere below. It was far from the crisp Ancoran air he remembered.

He leaned on the railing. It must have been an awful way to die. Jacob looked over the edge of the watchtower, into the infinite black abyss. He turned away from the edge. Alice rubbed her arms and leaned against Gladys. George stayed on the other side of the hatch, watching the stairwell from the shadows.

Smith clicked the transmitter on his collar. His breath formed a small cloud when he spoke. "Skysworn, we are in the walls, come in."

Jacob waited, hoping to hear Smith's receiver crackle to life. This was the tinker's third, or maybe even fourth, attempt to contact Mary. Jacob shivered in the cold breeze. The watchtower didn't seem much higher than the wall, but it must have been high enough to catch an occasional gust from the windstreams. "Why isn't she answering?"

A moment later the speaker barked in the silent night. "Position?"

Smith leaned over the watchtower's railing and stared up at the night sky. "Northeast corner of the house."

"Is there another tower to your north?" Mary asked.

"No," Smith said.

"You're near the seat. Two buildings over on the north side is your target. The last load is on the rails."

"Understood."

"The knight reached his goal. I received confirmation of fifty guests."

Smith glanced around the group. "We could not ask much more than that." The tinker clicked his transmitter. "Let the guests know dinner is in half an hour."

"I'll prepare the hall," Mary said.

Smith's speaker fell silent once more. "You heard the lady. Our target is close by."

Jacob turned his attention back to the city far below. "We're by the throne room?"

"She's right," Alice said. "Look, that's the old stained glass window over there." Alice stood hip to hip with him and leaned on the watchtower's railing. Jacob wrapped his fingers into hers and squeezed. His palm stuck to hers, mired in drying blood, and she squeezed back. Alice looked at him and said, "What are we waiting for?"

"They'll have guards at the gates, no doubt," George said. "We exit the watchtower and stay along the wall. Look for a servant's entrance along the western edge of the Castle. I like the shadows there."

"How can you be sure?" Jacob asked.

"Contingency plans," George said with a small smile.

Smith tapped his fingers on the edge of the watchtower. "Be quiet.

Use silent weapons. We get to the throne room and remove the Butcher."

Alice tugged on Jacob's arm and pulled him toward the hatch. "This ends tonight."

No one protested, and the entire group followed Alice onto the staircase. Just above the hidden door, a knight stared at the ceiling. His throat showed three separate cuts, and blood pooled around his body. An anchoring bolt stuck through his chest plate.

George shuffled past Jacob and Alice, paused, and then continued down the stairwell. His voice stayed at a whisper. "I'd say we should hide the body, but with that much blood it's pointless."

"Agreed," Smith said.

The air warmed as they descended the stairs. The lower they got, the more Jacob strained to hear around the next bend, wondering if they were about to be discovered. Something scraped and shuffled nearby, and he froze. It sounded again, but it seemed farther away. Farther was better, and he crept down past Alice, trailing behind Gladys and George.

George held up his hand at the bottom of the stairs. An open doorway stood between them and the outside world, but what caused the pounding in Jacob's chest were the two guards to either side of the door.

George pointed to Gladys as she walked out the door.

Jacob wanted to scream, to stop her, but by the time he realized what was happening, the first guard shouted, "Halt!" He stepped quickly after Gladys, abandoning his post.

George moved like a Tail Sword. He swept up behind the nearest guard and something crunched in the man's neck. The sound wasn't loud, but the falling armor drew the attention of the first guard.

Gladys's blade cut a smooth line through his neck. The only sounds he made were the thrashing of his armor and an awful gurgle. George dragged both men into the shadows of the stairwell.

Alice tightened her heavy nail glove while Gladys wiped her blade off on the knight's cloak.

Smith looked at each of them in turn. "Everyone in this city is our enemy until we know different. If you hesitate, you die. Now move."

They slipped around the watchtower and disappeared into the shadows, moving silently toward the western edge of the Castle.

CHAPTER THIRTY-FOUR

"YOU HEARD THE lady!" Samuel said. "Our people are already inside the walls. Let's make damn sure they have all the time they need to kill the Butcher. March! And don't be shy about it!"

Some fifty men and women shouted their support. The time for silence had passed, and their boots fell heavy in the passage beneath Bat's home. Samuel couldn't believe what Bat had carved out beneath the streets. He'd dug a byway that led underground to a network of tunnels connecting his safe houses. It was a testament to his ingenuity, and his dedication to Ancora's people.

Drakkar interrupted Samuel's thoughts. "We need to create more of a distraction than stomping our boots beneath the streets."

Samuel patted his pocket, and a small stash of Burners clinked together. He looked up at Drakkar and smiled. "I have some ideas."

Samuel took a deep breath and shouted, "So I heard the miner's song!" Two more voices echoed him.

"Tell me of that miner's tune!"

A dozen took up the chorus, and then the entire line began to sing.

Well he sat and sang inside that mine
That mine that claimed his brother
He sat and sang inside that mine
That mine that claimed his mother
No mine can come to take his son

No man survives that story

A butcher's tale is not the end

For us there is another

The song didn't speak of the Butcher—he knew it was far too old for that—but today it did. Today it was a righteous anthem.

✧   ✧   ✧

JACOB FELT A moment of rising panic when they first reached the side of the Castle. There wasn't a door to be seen until they walked farther back, deep into the shadowed corner. The iron door sat tucked behind a stone turret, almost invisible in the dim moonlight.

George and Smith had a lantern out at the door. Small and shielded, but it still felt like they were all but asking to be captured.

"I should be able to pick it," Smith whispered. "It will take some time."

"I'll hold the lantern," George said. "Gladys, watch the back wall. Signal if you see guards. Jacob, Alice, keep your eyes forward."

A burst of light cast the turret into a silhouette. Jacob tried his best not to flinch, sure they'd been discovered, but then something boomed in the distance. A fireball half the size of the Skysworn billowed into the air, and then another.

"Samuel ..." Smith pushed George to the side. "Enough, this is our distraction." Something hissed in his shoulders. The short scream of metal died away in the boom of another Firebomb, and the door fell. Smith slid the broken door into the bushes and vanished into the Castle.

Jacob followed Alice into the short corridor. A pile of half-folded linens sat off to their left, and a room filled with steam and shouts waited at the other end of the hall. Smith slipped into a shadowy doorway. Jacob turned the corner, expecting to find a closet of some sort, but it was another corridor. He hurried beside Alice, as silent as he could be.

A glance backwards showed him Gladys and George, quiet enough to be ghosts. The corridor ended in a dining hall grander than anything Jacob could believe, every plate framed by golden dinnerware. Jeweled goblets sat beside napkins made of finer material than most Ancoran's clothes.

Smith led them to a back corner, drenched in darkness. Near the head of the table sat a small goblet engraved with NVB. Jacob snatched it up and dropped it into his pocket. If they survived this, he'd melt it down and make something of it, a memorial for Charles.

They crouched in a small circle beside a curio that stood over ten feet in height. Smith looked at each of them in turn. "I do not know the fastest way to the throne room."

"Multiple exits," George said, "We cannot stay together and keep eyes on them all."

"Then we split up," Gladys said. "We'll cover more ground that way."

Something boomed in the distance, and people screamed somewhere else inside the Castle. The echo of armored boots stomped through the corridors and faded with the shouts and orders belted out by nearby knights.

George glanced up and smiled.

"There'll be more guards," Alice whispered. "Just because a few are being drawn off doesn't mean there aren't enough left to put us in a world of shit."

Smith reached out and squeezed her shoulder. "Keep to the shadows. You find a lone soldier, you kill them. If there is a group of guards, we attack as a group."

"Signal?" George asked.

Smith looked around the room. "There, horns." He pointed to a wide cluster of brass pipes. "They will be in every room. Hit the entire assembly with three rapid taps and we will regroup here as fast as we can."

"We will take the far end of the hall there," George said, pointing at the far door.

"Jacob, Alice, check the hall behind Gladys and George. We do not want them to get flanked. I am going back through the corridor. There is almost certainly a path to the throne room from the kitchens." Smith placed one hand on Alice's shoulder and the other on Jacob's. "Be careful. If you need to run, run. Do not engage if you do not have to." He gave them a sharp nod, stood, and left.

George jumped to his feet and ran across the hall. Gladys followed close behind. They paused at the far door, and then they were gone.

Jacob and Alice were left there in the darkened room, staring at each other.

"If we don't …" Alice said. "If we don't make it out of this. I want you to know you mean a lot to me."

"You too," Jacob said. Those words weren't enough. They weren't what he wanted to say. He stared into her eyes, but the words wouldn't come.

They made for the same door Gladys and George had gone through. Jacob stood in the shadow of the doorway, looking south through the hall while Alice looked north. She nodded, and he stepped out into the hall. The wooden floor creaked, and he sped his pace to get away from the awful sound, his heart pounding.

Jacob took a sharp right into a dimly lit hallway. A thin rug ran the length of the corridor, flanked by useless tables and more paintings than any wall could ever need. He adjusted the brace on his arm and then cursed.

"What?" Alice whispered.

"Brace is getting in the way of the bolt gun." He untied it as quickly as he could and moved it to his other arm.

"Here," Alice said. She looped the trigger over his fingers and grabbed the leather straps to tie the bolt gun down, stealing glances down the hall. She patted his arm when she finished.

Jacob nodded and continued down the hall. They made it to the end before he heard voices. Alice pulled on his backpack and almost threw him into the dim corner of a recessed doorway.

"I'm telling you I heard something," a voice said from the opposite hall.

"No one's in the dining wing. We're locked down."

The voices began to fade. "You think any of those people are stupid enough to steal from him? I imagine …"

Mumbling followed the footsteps of the speakers, and that became all they could hear.

Jacob held up a finger, asking Alice to stay put. He peeked around the corner and then shifted to the other side of the door before motioning for Alice to follow.

Alice took the lead, sprinting up a short flight of stone stairs on nothing but her toes. Jacob followed, albeit less quietly. More voices sounded above them, and the pair hurried into the next corridor.

Where the last hall had been bathed in artwork, here they were closed in by ancient weapons and broken swords. Some flickered in the lamplight beside stone and bronze plaques. Others seemed to be covered in ancient gore, rusted and unclean.

Footsteps echoed behind them and stopped. Jacob didn't take a chance at looking back. He grabbed Alice around the waist and pulled her through an open door. Heavy boot steps came closer, and Jacob readied himself for the kill, holding the bolt gun level with where a man's head would appear.

The heavy steps stopped in front of the door again before fading as they walked away. He felt the breath leave Alice's lungs. They didn't speak, only snuck into the hall once more and continued toward the next. Something boomed in the distance, and orange flames lit the stained glass in the southern wall.

"Stained glass …"

They were close. Very close to the throne room. He thought the throne room was right behind the stained glass, but here was the glass, and there wasn't a room in sight. They were at the edge of a wide hall.

Alice nodded toward the end of the hall and whispered. "Guards up there, it has to be something."

"No way we can get by them."

She tugged on his arm and led him into the last room in the corridor. "These old buildings always have extra doors. They'd never build something for Parliament without an escape." She walked over to the back of the room.

"Now!" A voice shouted from outside the room.

The door opened fast. Faster than Jacob could move. Alice's bolt took the first man through the temple, and he collapsed. The other man wasn't ready, and Jacob flexed his wrist, sending a flurry of bolts into the soldier's face and bouncing more projectiles off the stone wall behind the man. Jacob's senses came back long enough for his brain to remind him to let off the trigger, and the bolt gun snapped to a halt.

Alice grabbed the first soldier's feet and started dragging him back into the room. "Get the other one."

Jacob slid his hands under the man's arms and started to lift him. The soldier jerked, and blood poured from his mouth. Jacob cringed, but he kept pulling on the soldier until he was fully inside their hiding place.

"Close the door and go," Alice said.

"We can't just kick in the main door. They'll have more guards."

"They have to have a side entrance for the kitchen staff," Alice said.

"Where?"

"It has to be in the last hall before we get to the entryway."

Jacob pulled on Alice's arm, and they dashed down the hall. It was only a matter of time before someone found the bodies, or the blood. The corridor came up quick, and Jacob slipped into the shadows as fast as he could, Alice pressed up beside him.

She leaned forward and squinted into the dim light from the hanging lanterns and nodded.

Jacob crept forward. He shivered at every creak in the floor, every faint breeze that could be a soldier's breath. Deeper into the shadows, the voices grew louder, and then Alice pulled on his backpack.

She pointed into a pitch-black recess in the wall. A golden bar of light peeked through at the bottom of the door. With his ear nearly touching the ironwood, the voices became clear, distinct.

"Benedict, I will not send out the city knights. The uprising is well in hand, and they will hold position here until it's over."

Benedict made an exasperated noise. "You murdered their *King*, Newton. And then you exterminated half the city. Of *course* they will come for you in force."

"One must remove the disease before it corrupts the body, and the Lowlands had been ill for far too long."

"You could have exiled them."

"Exiled people can *fight*, Benedict."

"You're a fool, Newton. You made one mistake this night, for you *did* send out the city knights."

"What?" the Butcher snapped.

"I handed down the orders when the first bombs struck. It's just me and your personal guard now."

"You ungrateful worm!"

The Butcher roared and something heavy slammed against stone on the other side of the door. A boom echoed through the halls of the Castle when another bomb detonated outside its walls.

Alice tugged on Jacob's sleeve. She pointed back to the hall and then pointed at his chest and to the door. She made a fist and acted like she was pounding on the door, and then she was gone.

He understood what she was doing. She'd pound on the entrance to the throne room, and that would be the distraction he'd need to slip inside. He pulled the air cannon off his back. He'd primed it earlier.

Three heavy knocks echoed around the hall and through the door, and then again.

Jacob grabbed the door handle and his breath grew heavy. Three more knocks. He clicked the latch before the knocking stopped, and then he threw the door open.

CHAPTER THIRTY-FIVE

THE COLD METAL leeched the heat from Samuel's fingers. He watched the pair of Spider Knights running along the roofs of the ravaged Lowlands, and raised the whistle to his lips. Three notes in a rising crescendo, and three notes descending. A quick arpeggio caused one of the spiders to freeze, and Samuel smiled.

He repeated the tune again, and the spider reared back, sending her knight flailing into the air. His armored form slammed into the tiled roof and he scrabbled to catch a handhold on the slope. The spider charged, leaping from roof to roof until she finally rocketed toward the ground, sending up a cloud of dust and stone.

Bessie almost ran Samuel down when she reached him, smashing her face into the Spider Knight's chest and unleashing a high-pitched chitter. She turned around and lowered herself to the ground. Samuel hopped into the saddle. It wasn't a good saddle for Bessie. It cut into two of her legs a bit, and that wouldn't do for a long ride. He'd have to get her patched up after the battle.

"Halt!"

There was no mistaking that voice. It was enough to make Samuel nervous, but he'd also been hoping for it.

"Who are you? So bold as to assault a Spider Knight?"

Samuel urged Bessie to turn around, and she did, moving in that all-too-familiar stutter-step motion. He scratched the finer hair behind her eyes before coaxing the halberd free of its saddle sheath. Samuel hefted it in his grasp. It felt good. It felt right.

"Hello, Captain."

The look on his Captain's face was the best thing he'd seen all day. "Samuel? I thought … we all thought you were dead."

Samuel shook his head. "Do you stand with the Butcher?"

The Captain's face fell. "I didn't believe that rumor when I first heard, but now … That madman murdered our King."

"It's worse than you know. He's allied with Fel and Ballern."

"Ballern?"

Samuel nodded. "Bollwerk and Belldorn are engaged with Fel and Ballern as we speak. Archibald freed Dauschen. Charles died fighting the Butcher's schemes. Did you know that?"

"No. I'm sorry. I know he … I'm sorry to hear that."

"Will you fight with the resistance?" Samuel asked.

"I'd be better off ordering the Spider Knights to throw themselves from the walls, and then joining them. The Butcher has a detachment of almost fifty knights loyal to him."

"Mercenaries?"

The Captain let out a humorless laugh. "You're sharp kid. I'll give you that." He looked up at the moonlit sky and took a deep breath. "I don't know if we can win."

"Win or not, we're not running from this fight. Look behind you."

The Captain slowly turned his mount.

The resistance stood behind him, covered in old, rusted armor and wielding every weapon Bat had been able to scrape together. Some bore only swords, while others held crossbows or bolt guns, and a few had small air cannons.

One boy stood at the front of the line of resistance fighters in the alley. His name was Reggie. Samuel didn't know him, not really, but the boy had no love for the Butcher and some kindred friendship with Jacob.

"Cage, the leader of Dauschen's resistance, should be on the other side of the city by now," Samuel said as he watched the Captain. "Once he gives us the signal, Drakkar—a Cave Guardian no less—is in position to blow the gates."

"What signal?"

"You'll know it when you see it."

The captain eyed Samuel for a moment before nodding. He pulled a bronze whistle out from a deep pouch hanging on the outside of his silver-armored thigh.

"Are you calling them to join us, or to fight us?"

The captain gave Samuel a stern look. "Did you know they killed my boy?"

"What?" Samuel hissed. "Why are you still here?"

"He wasn't my only family. I have no loyalty to these people. None of the Spider Knights are happy with what's happened here, Samuel. I'm calling them to choose for themselves." He blew on the whistle, three notes repeated in the same pattern. The same phrase echoed out over the Lowlands from half a dozen different positions, and the captain nodded.

"Who did Bessie throw off?" Samuel asked.

"One of the mercenaries," the Captain said. "Sadly, my halberd fell on top of him when I was trying to help him up."

Samuel nodded. "I wondered what took you so long to follow Bessie."

"Alright," the Captain said. "I'll circle back to the other Spider Knights. I doubt they'll come into the open here, but you'll have allies, Samuel, I've no doubt of that. We'll watch for the gates to fall, and those that wish to will join you on the inside." He gave Samuel a sharp nod and then urged his Jumper to the west.

"That was the Captain of the Spider Knights," Reggie said. "He's going to help?"

"Yes," Samuel said. "There's no stopping us now."

Reggie's posture straightened slightly. Samuel was glad the presence of the Captain filled the kid with more confidence, but Samuel knew there were no guarantees. Spider Knights weren't the immortal warriors so many seemed to think they were, but he choked that down. There was no reason to remind these people what was at stake, or how likely they were to die.

The earth shook and the sky turned orange. A fireball the size of a watchtower billowed up from behind the wall. The sound was a boom like that of a thousand cannon shots.

"That's it," Samuel shouted. "We move!"

The resistance started toward the wall in a loose march. They hadn't gone far when another blast tore through the chilly night air. The western gate squealed as it tore from the wall, slamming into Lowland ruins outside.

"For Ancora!" Reggie shouted as he ran past Samuel.

Goosebumps and adrenaline rushed through Samuel's body, and he urged Bessie to speed, passing the resistance and all their battle cries. Two shadows shot through the gates ahead of him. Two Spider Knights. The Captain worked fast.

Samuel's strategy had seemed half insane when he'd first said it aloud, but it was working. The knights tried to run back to the gate from wherever they'd been posted. No one expected the voices they'd heard from below the streets to come in through the front door.

Samuel's halberd took the first knight in the chest, punching clean through the mercenary's leather armor. Stealing a knight's helmet and greaves … it made him sick to see the cannibalized armor of his brethren draped across mercenaries. The blade drew blood and viscera when he ripped it from the man's chest.

In the distance another boom rattled the city and sent flames and debris rocketing into the air. More mercenaries poured into the square.

When they saw what was storming through the gates—Spider Knights and resistance fighters from the very people they'd been abusing—many fled.

Drakkar sprinted past Bessie from wherever he'd triggered the charges, his sword snapping violently out to the side in audible clicks. A mercenary met him head-on, dressed head to toe like a city knight. He even moved like a city knight. It was then that Samuel realized not all of the mercenaries were mercenaries. Some were knights, bought in whole by a madman.

"We've come for the Butcher!" someone shouted behind Samuel. "Join us!"

Another explosion rattled his senses. Samuel hoped Cage had stuck with the plan and only targeted the military installations. It would be a hard thing to convince a people to ally with them if they destroyed their homes and families.

"Protect the people!" Samuel shouted. He'd seen what soldiers could become in the heat of battle.

One of the more lightly armored mercenaries managed to close in on Bessie. He lunged at the spider, but she reared away from the sword and brought her fangs down into the man's neck. He'd be dead in moments. Samuel didn't wait. He slammed his halberd through the mercenary's skull with a crack.

Drakkar whirled and met another sword strike from his opponent. The rebound left the woman exposed, and he ran her through, taking her in the heart. The mercenary had a look of confusion on her face before she collapsed and Drakkar moved to the next target.

Samuel caught a glimpse of Cage and his men across the square. Cage moved like death. He fought in broad, graceful strokes that left nothing but corpses behind. The rest of his men cleaned up the mess.

"Samuel!"

He brought his attention back to the crowd in front of him in time to see the spear hurtling toward his chest. He braced for the impact, but it never came. Bessie's leg shot up into the air and took the blow. Samuel barely locked in his grip before the spider screamed and charged the man who'd injured her. Spear or no spear, she ran him down.

The knight tried to run, diving into a small alley, but Bessie crouched and then exploded forward. Samuel could do nothing but hold on to the saddle with all his might, bracing the halberd between his chest and the spider. Samuel grunted as the brutal impact slammed his face into Bessie's saddle. The spider screamed as she bit through the knight's armor over and over and over. When she pulled away, only a bloody mangle of metal remained.

Samuel patted her head and urged her out of the alley. It was too tight a space for her to be effective. The spear in her leg shattered against the stone wall. Enough of it remained to staunch the bleeding, but it was going to need attention soon.

Samuel turned and stared in awe and horror at the scene laid out before them. Reggie stood at the edge of the alley, firing crossbow bolts at a squadron of knights. The armored men shuffled forward in a tight, shielded formation. Samuel knew it as one of Fel's formations.

The knights cut down fleeing citizens and resistance fighters alike. A bloody trail of dead piled up along their path. They held one Spider Knight at bay until Drakkar's cloaked form dashed out of another alley and shouted, "Fall back!"

The Spider Knight didn't so much as hesitate, and when the mount spun in his direction, Samuel realized it was the captain. They'd already swept back around to rejoin the resistance.

Drakkar's cloak billowed out and he raised his arms. He slammed a glowing ball into a larger shell and roared, "A gift from Charles von Atlier for the kingdom of Fel!"

The ball vanished into the cluster of knights. They couldn't have known what it was. They didn't even try to run. The concussion shook Samuel's head and sent four of the knights into the air. The white-hot fireball consumed the rest in screams and terror cut short by a pillar of flame.

When the worst of the fire receded, Drakkar walked into the charred ruin of bodies. Anything that moved, he ran through with his sword. That's when Samuel noticed the people standing in doorways and peeking out of windows behind drawn shades.

A woman inched her way out of the shadows of one of the hospitals. Samuel watched her and those around her. No one seemed to be fighting anymore. The mercenaries had all run or lay dead on the ground. They were likely regrouping, but for now at least twelve of them were finished.

"What can we do to help?"

Samuel frowned. "What?"

She wore a dress that had once been white, but now it shone with rusted stains. She straightened her back and repeated herself. "What can we do to help?"

Samuel hadn't expected that. He didn't think the Highlanders would join their cause. He thought they would have stayed inside and waited for the danger to pass, let the poor and less fortunate die in their stead. But this woman, and the man walking up behind her, and the stodgy old banker making his way out into the streets ...

"Help the wounded," Samuel said. "If you have weapons, keep them at the ready. The Butcher's mercenaries could be back at any time, and if they find you helping the enemy, they won't take kindly to it."

Samuel urged Bessie forward and glanced back to Reggie and the other resistance fighters. He raised his fist into the air and shouted, "To the Castle!"

CHAPTER THIRTY-SIX

J ACOB HAD BEEN ready to take on half a squadron of guards with the air cannon and bolt gun. Only one man sat in the throne room, on a golden seat raised on a low podium. He was older than Jacob expected, muscled and fit, but nearly as old as Charles had been, his hair streaked with blacks and grays. The man wore a breathing apparatus, all polished bronze and silver.

Benedict's body lay broken on the floor.

Jacob leveled the air cannon. "Newton. Victor. Burns."

The Butcher's eyes were cold, and his face stone, staring down the barrel of Jacob's cannon without flinching. "Who are you?"

"Jacob Anders. You wanted my hands."

The man let out a slow laugh. He lifted the breathing mask as his face curled up into an awful smirk. "Atlier's apprentice. You brought the base down in Dauschen. I have followed your story on Archibald's transmissions. I was much like you in my youth, but you are on the wrong side. I wish to raise Ancora from the plague of invaders and rid it of its weaknesses."

"Ancora defined by its people, and you're destroying it," Jacob said as he paced slowly to the front of the throne, carefully avoiding Benedict's body.

"Ancora is a city full of burdensome halfwits."

"So you'll kill them and bring new blood," Jacob said, keeping the air cannon leveled at the Butcher's head. "Why help Ballern?" It had been eating him up inside, not having an answer, not having a clue why this man would rain hell down on every city in the Northlands. "I understand Fel. It's ruled by your brother."

The Butcher narrowed his eyes. "Mordair is ambitious, visionary. I only want Ancora, and the answers it holds." The Butcher leaned back in the throne so the sweep of the ornate back looked like a crown. "You are picking the losing side. Not even my death can stop what is in motion, and your resistance will not live to face it."

"Your guards outside are long dead, if that's what you're stalling for."

The Butcher twitched. He hadn't known his guards were dead. Jacob could see it on his face. "My brother will shatter Bollwerk and burn Belldorn to the ground, as they should have in the Deadlands War."

Jacob narrowed his eyes. "You're still carrying a grudge?" He watched the Butcher's hand inch ever lower over the side of the throne. Jacob had little doubt there was a weapon there.

"Their payment was hard to resist as well. Ancora needs a firm hand."

"Money. You already had everything you could want."

"Some payments must be in blood." The Butcher's hand flexed around a knob.

Jacob pulled the trigger. The air cannon boomed and echoed in the cavernous throne room. The man's fingers collapsed into broken, mangled strips of meat. The Butcher screamed and clutched his hand. His gaze flashed back to Jacob, eyes wide as he must have realized he'd underestimated the boy from the Lowlands.

"Stop! I'm the only one who can save your allies in the catacombs." His voice broke as he winced and held his hand. "Even as we speak, my stablemasters are preparing to release a horde of Red Death onto them."

Jacob stepped closer, rounding the throne beside the Butcher. "Charles couldn't finish his mission, but he didn't fight alone. I'd like to resolve his biggest regret." Jacob heard the doors fly open and slam against the wall behind him. It was either Alice, or he was already dead.

"Jacob!" Samuel said.

He heard Drakkar shouting to Smith before Alice said, "Finish it."

"Charles was a fool," the Butcher said, his voice cracking and trembling behind the pain of his wound.

Jacob stepped forward and slammed the butt of the air cannon into the man's face. When the Butcher's head rebounded off the throne, Jacob met it with the metal brace on his right arm and a snarl. "Charles built this arm, Newton, and he'd be proud to know it was your end."

Jacob clicked the igniter on a Burner and slid it into the bracket at his elbow. His arm began to shake and the Burner smoked.

The Butcher lunged forward, a short dagger glinting in his good hand.

Jacob knocked the blade away with the air cannon, twisted at his hips, and screamed as he punched the Butcher in the chest. The gears in the brace let go, firing steam and smoke and fire into the air. The Butcher's ribcage collapsed with a horrific crunch. The dagger clattered to the floor as the man's body slammed back into the throne. Gurgling, choking gags echoed around the room before he slumped to the side. Jacob grabbed the Butcher's collar and threw him onto the polished stone floor.

The body came to a stop at Alice's feet. She glanced at the face and slowly turned away.

Jacob's mother had once told him there was no joy in revenge, no joy in the act of bringing another wrong into the world. He understood what she meant. Jacob didn't feel joy, but he felt justified in bringing an end to Newton Victor Burns.

Samuel and Drakkar stared at the ruin Jacob had wrought upon the Butcher. The guardian was somber, but the Spider Knight smacked Jacob on the back and said, "Nicely done, tinker."

Jacob looked to Samuel. "The catacombs."

"What?" Drakkar asked.

"It's a trap," Jacob said. "There's an ambush waiting."

"Son of a bitch." Samuel pushed down on the helmet covering his head and cursed again. "We tore the gates down. They could get up into the city … They'll kill everything."

Jacob looked at the Butcher of Gareth Cave. His actions had birthed the Steamsworn and helped bring a new order to Bollwerk. With his final days, he'd brought war upon the Northlands. Jacob bent down and slid the ring from the man's hand, an extravagant thing carved with NVB.

"Jacob."

He turned and looked at Alice.

"We have to go."

Jacob looked back at the Butcher once more. He'd killed the man. He should have felt remorse, or joy, or something, but all that was left was an empty hole. Jacob stuffed the Butcher's ring into a pocket on his chest.

Alice turned to leave, and then she stopped, turned, and spat on the Butcher's corpse.

Smith shouted from the doorway. "Alice! Jacob! Move!"

They ran.

✧   ✧   ✧

MARY STARED AT the glowing horizon. She knew that light wasn't natural. She knew those were the very fires Smith had told her of. Taking the Skysworn into battle by herself would be madness, but she'd never been one to linger against the wall.

She glanced at the speakers beside her transmitter. The Butcher was dead, but her friends weren't out of the woods yet. What if they still had knights arming the ballistae? They could shoot her down with ease. She didn't have the same maneuverability here that she'd had in the open against Ballern's ships. Mary cursed and the Skysworn lurched forward. Madness or not, she wasn't sitting idly by.

Mary glanced at the transmitter beside her. She cursed and pressed the button. "Warship One, this is the Skysworn, come in."

✦   ✦   ✦

JACOB AND ALICE hurtled into the streets behind Smith and the others. Gladys and George waited by a gutter full of bodies, and Jacob almost screamed. The mercenaries were still fighting. The resistance was giving as good as they got, but it left almost two dozen dead strewn across the courtyard.

Jacob stormed forward and screamed, "Stop! The Butcher is dead!" He raised the ring he'd taken from Newton's hand. "Your contract is done!"

Even the men close enough to hear him didn't listen. No one listened. Blood and viscera flashed in the moonlight, and the keening screams of the dying filled the night.

"I don't think the Butcher held their contract," Samuel said. He grabbed Jacob's shoulder and pushed him forward. "You'll only get yourself killed. Now run! Get to the catacombs."

"I thought they only had fifty mercenaries," Smith said as he picked up a steady pace beside them.

"They had more," Drakkar said. "and it is horrible."

A towering form limped across the street in front of them. The sword in his hand caught the streetlight first, and then his bloodied face came into view.

"Bartholomew!" Samuel shouted, his voice rising into a near scream. "Bat, no!"

Bat went down onto a knee, and one of the knights ran out of the alley behind him with a bloody sword. The knight bled from a head wound but charged at the larger man regardless.

Samuel ran at the knight, but it was a smaller form that reached the man first.

Gladys's first blade sank into the man's thigh. The next cut his hamstrings and took him to the ground. She brought both blades into the fallen man's neck and then tore them out through the front of his throat. Blood fountained onto her chest. She booted the knight in the head for good measure as she stood up.

"Well done," George said. Gladys slowly backed into the group again.

Samuel was already at Bat's side. Bat wasn't moving.

"Bat, Bat, can you hear me?"

"Yes … I can hear you." Bat smiled and raised a shaky arm to pat Samuel's thigh. "They are underground. More than we thought … too many."

The awful truth of what Bat said sank in. Jacob looked up at Smith. "The knights, the knights loyal to the Butcher—"

"Shit." Smith bit off the word. "Those were not the men on the railcars. We have been baited from the start."

Bat's voice grew weaker. "Cage … sent him to the station … get there … trust him …" A horrible rattle sounded in Bat's chest, and then he fell silent.

Smith pressed his fingers against Bat's neck and shook his head.

Samuel's breath came rapidly and he closed his eyes. Gladys moved herself underneath his shoulder and prodded the Spider Knight to his feet.

"He wouldn't want you to die out here," she whispered. "Help us fight."

Samuel shook, and then he screamed. The cry wasn't like anything Jacob had heard before. Samuel's wail pulled at his very bones, and all he wanted to do was help the pain go away. Instead he left it to Gladys and Alice.

Three men charged out of the alley. They weren't dressed like knights. They dressed like Highlanders. Their long bows and the dark metal of their cannons marked them as something else. The rest of the fighting drifted to the eastern edge of the courtyard.

Samuel drew his sword and stalked toward them.

"Samuel, no," Alice said. "You're in no shape."

Samuel let out a scream that caused the veins in his forehead to throb and the muscles in his neck to bulge. "I will kill you *all!*"

They laughed and raised their weapons. Jacob and Smith did the same, but before either pulled the trigger, a screeching Jumper slammed into the trio. Bessie raised her head and struck over and over, her legs pinning two down while she bit the third. The men screamed, their confidence broken and terror overtaking them in full.

When the last of them stopped moving, Bessie leapt to Samuel's side. He climbed into the Jumper's saddle. "Go. I'll meet you in the station. Burn my uncle for me. I don't want the Carrion Worms to take him."

"Samuel …" Alice watched the Spider Knight jump away with the same worry that Jacob felt.

Drakkar watched Samuel vanish over a rooftop, and then he turned to Smith. The Cave Guardian pulled a pouch out of his pocket and sprinkled its contents over Bat. "Rest well, friend. You have given this city hope in its darkest hour."

Drakkar clicked the igniter on a Burner and dropped it onto Bat's chest. The flames burst ten feet into the air, hot enough to burn Jacob's arm almost ten feet away. "Now we end this."

No one argued with the guardian.

CHAPTER THIRTY-SEVEN

"IT MAY NOT be the fastest," Smith said, "but I believe it is the best. We will reach the chainguns before we reach the station. We need better weapons to face a larger force."

"The door into the wall is locked," George said, gesturing to the stone barrier. "We *can't*."

Smith reached into his jerkin and clicked a lever down on either shoulder. The pistons and gears began to click in the tinker's biomechanics. "I can."

Smith braced himself on the stone steps and grabbed onto the iron bars. "Get above me." Everyone walked up the stairs when shouts sounded below.

"We don't have time for this," George said. "We have mercenaries coming up the tower."

Smith grimaced and pulled. Something screeched inside the hidden hall, and then something crumbled and snapped. The stone door came away in Smith's grasp as two men with spears rounded the corner.

"Halt!"

Smith didn't hesitate; he threw the stone door down the staircase. It crashed and flipped and shattered as it rained doom on everyone below.

"Oh, *gods!*" Alice put her hand over her mouth.

The mercenaries didn't have time to so much as scream. The door crushed them in an instant.

Smith adjusted his biomechanics and then clicked his lantern on.

"Move!"

Drakkar flowed into the cavern behind him, followed by Jacob and the others.

"They could follow us through the catacombs," Drakkar said.

Smith shook his head and stepped around the hole in the floor. "It is done."

Smith dropped through the floor and grunted when he hit the bottom. His lantern light circled the lower floor before he said, "It is clear. Come."

They gathered at the other end of the hall, beyond the rusted iron door George thought might be from the old city. Smith wrenched it shut. He pulled a length of spider silk cable out of his pocket and tied the door into its own frame. The tinker gave it a few sharp tugs and nodded.

"If they decide to follow, this will slow them down."

With everyone's lanterns on, it was a much easier thing to navigate the old corridors and halls of the underground. The dark passageways echoed with their footfalls, the need for stealth minimized by their need to reach the catacombs.

"Watch yourself," Smith said.

Alice shifted up against the right edge of the corridor. Jacob wondered why until the crushed helmet of one of the men he'd killed flashed in the lantern light.

They skirted the bodies and slowed to snuff their lanterns when they reached the lights. Drakkar inched forward and looked into the room where Jacob had killed those two men. Jacob's hand moved to absently rub at his biomechanics. Drakkar motioned them on.

Darkness accompanied them for a short time. When the corridor began to curve, Drakkar relit his lantern. More lanterns followed. The underground lake spread out on their right, which meant they'd be back at the burial wall in moments.

Light flickered in the distance when they turned into the burial corridor. The ancient, crumbling wood coffins sat more defined by a quartet of lantern light. Long-buried shoes poked from the ruined end of one—rotted through except for some copper bands—while a burst of dirty red hair showed from another. Jacob shivered. Somehow the long dead seemed far more unsettling than those so recently dead.

The voices rose and fell in whispers.

"Allies?" Gladys asked.

"Likely," George said. "If there was fighting, we'd hear it. If it was an ambush, we'd hear nothing."

Smith picked up the pace, breaking into a slow jog as he turned his lantern up. The rest of the group followed. The shadowed passages that trailed off their path were still dark as pitch. Jacob felt like there were a million eyes watching him from that darkness, but he let it slide off. Sometimes you needed to trust your gut, and other times you needed to keep some common sense about you.

The faster pace brought them back to the open cavern faster than Jacob thought possible. He looked up at the mummified dead set into their stone displays. With more light in the room, they were less terrifying, and more disturbing, all at once. One of the figures wore a cloak of dust and bones and held a scythe across his chest.

"It's like the old stories," Alice said, walking closer to Jacob.

He nodded. Childhood stories they'd been told around campfires, meant to be scary but not be actual horrors, came flooding back to him. Cloaked figures with wide, glowing scythes, come to harvest the children of another nation. It rang awfully true to the Fall of Ancora and the return of Ballern. Jacob frowned and looked away.

"Here we are," Smith said, settling in behind one of the chainguns. He checked the ammo belt and spun the barrels. "Everything looks good." He tied a makeshift strap of spider silk leather onto the chaingun, pulled the quick release lever, and hung the massive weapon from his shoulder. Smith bounced it in his grip twice and nodded.

Alice opened the stone drawer of Bangers and Burners. They all grabbed a few extra until only the building blocks remained.

The voices outside began to rise.

"Come," George said. "Let's find Cage and see what we can do to help.

Smith hurried to the other chaingun and looked it over. "This one is ready to go as well."

The second chaingun had a direct line of sight into the station's cavern. Jacob turned toward the tracks and froze. The station seemed alive. People surged in every direction, distributing weapons and pointing and yelling. It was chaos given life.

Smith jogged into it without hesitation. Jacob eyed the first knight they saw with suspicion. George grabbed the man's arm and spun him around. It was the knight from the watchtower ... the knight Charles had shown his Steamsworn medal to before they'd tested the glider. The man's eyes trailed past George and landed on Jacob.

Jacob lifted the hem of his pants. This was not a man from which to hide what he was. The knight's eyes flashed wide and he held out his fist. Jacob reached past George and wrapped his hand around the knight's.

"Brother. I am sorry to learn of Charles's passing. Do you trust these people?"

"Yes," Jacob said, though he didn't know if *everyone* here was an ally.

"Good, that's good."

"Where is Cage?" George asked.

The knight turned and pointed toward the other side of the station. "Cage is by the other end of the tracks. They've heard shouts and gunfire lower in the cave system. We're not sure what's happening."

"Thank you," Jacob said, stepping towards the tracks.

"Fight well, Steamsworn," the knight said. "This is not the end for Ancora."

Jacob slammed his hand onto the knight's shoulder and nodded. They all jogged across the station, dodging knights carrying crates and resistance fighters hauling bundles of swords and food and water.

Cage stood on the lower tracks, by the giant carcass of a long dead invader. Alice leapt off the edge and landed beside him. Jacob followed.

Smith and the others lowered themselves down with a bit more patience.

Cage glanced at them and then resumed talking to another man. "I know that's what you *think* you heard, but this city is not sitting on a nest of Widow Makers."

"Umm," Jacob said. "Actually it is."

Cage stopped talking and blinked. "What?"

"They're a few levels down," Alice said, "They almost killed us when we escaped."

"I *told* you," the other man almost snarled. "Someone in that cavern screamed, 'Widow Makers,' and then there was nothing but gunfire."

Cage nodded. "Take a scouting party into the first level. See if you can find anything, but do not engage unless your lives are in danger."

The other man nodded and left.

Cage squeezed the bridge of his nose. "The other mercenaries and soldiers are coming up the mountain path, and we can only assume up through the caverns. They've set up defenses in the Lowlands to prevent a retreat. Good news, I need good news."

"We're here to help?" Alice said.

Cage smiled and a small laugh escaped his lips. "Ah, thanks, kid."

"We can retreat through the catacombs if we need to," Jacob said. "There's another hatch at the top of the stairs we can climb through, but you can't move people quickly. It's only one ladder."

A teeth-grinding screech echoed up through the cavern beyond the bars. A thousand more creatures took up the call, and Jacob covered his ears.

Cage stared into the darkness before turning back to Jacob's group. "I have scouts saying that these bastards are marching with Red Death. Can someone explain that? Red Death hordes kill anything that isn't a Red Death."

"They are likely using the technology of Charles von Atlier to control them," Smith said.

"Like the transmitters used to bring the Fall?" Cage nodded.

"That is our theory," Smith said. "Yes."

Cage cursed. "I thought my scouts had lost their damn mind."

A series of screams went up where the tracks exited the station. Jacob turned to see a lone Jumper. He breathed a sigh of relief when he saw it was Bessie, with Samuel still riding on her back.

"We will help defend the entrance from the mountain," Smith said. "It would seem our most vulnerable spot."

Cage looked at his hand and then held out his fist.

Smith wrapped his hand around it and nodded. "Fight well."

Alice pulled on Jacob's arm, leading him through the thinner crowd on the tracks until they could walk up the marble stairs. Bessie skittered from one side to the next.

"She's nervous," Alice said.

"Samuel!" Jacob shouted. "Here!"

The Spider Knight gave Bessie two quick taps on the head. She covered the distance to Alice and Jacob in one mighty, furry-legged leap, slamming into the stone walkway beside them.

Samuel looked frantic. "They're coming from the upper paths *and* the lower paths. I don't know how they got onto the upper paths. I didn't think there were any access points left."

"Where does it lead?" Smith asked as he joined them on the platform.

"Here," Samuel said. "They'll all meet here. The side of the mountain is black with Red Death, Smith." He leaned forward in the saddle and spoke quietly. "We don't have enough bullets and bolts to kill them all."

"How long do we have?" George asked.

"Minutes," Samuel said. "At most. The lower group is rounding the last bend on the mountain path."

Jacob looked out across the platform. These were desperate people, and desperate people were the best fighters in the world. Their travels since the Fall had reinforced that knowledge, but these people were hopelessly outmatched. A horde of Red Death? An army of Fel soldiers fighting for Ballern?

Alice grabbed his head and pulled his eyes down to hers. "It's okay. Whatever happens, it's okay."

He tried to take a few deep breaths, but they were shaky and shallow.

Alice kissed him, deep and hard. "It's okay."

He stared at her, in that final chaos that would either spell their end or the beginning of a painful reconstruction, and knew she was right. They'd done everything they could. All they had to do now was see it through.

Smith tossed Samuel two of the Firebombs. "Go make some noise."

Samuel nodded and spun Bessie around. She launched them both out onto the tracks and then bounced up and over the entrance to the station.

CHAPTER THIRTY-EIGHT

"CHECK YOUR AMMO," Smith said. "Be ready to make for the catacombs. We will stay at the edge of the station for now, but the moment we start to be overrun, make for the catacombs and the second chaingun."

Alice started checking the belts strapped to her chest, filled with anchors and bolts. Jacob checked the clip for the air cannon. Ten rounds filled the clip, and he had a half dozen more clips in his backpack. After that he'd be left firing rocks.

The Red Death screeched again, and this time Jacob knew they were close. This could be the Fall all over again. Only underground, with nowhere to run.

"Keep your heads up!" Cage shouted. "If we lose the station, nothing will stop those things from reaching the Highlands. Ancora will be lost."

Two massive booms sounded outside the station. Barely a minute passed before Bessie came bouncing back into the station.

"How many?" George asked.

"The blast may have sent a hundred Red Death and soldiers off the mountainside. I don't suppose we have about fifty more of those bombs?"

George shook his head.

Samuel raised his voice so everyone in the vicinity could hear. "The soldiers above us are setting up rappelling lines. If they stick to Fel tactics, they'll try sniping us from the top edge of the station. Be ready to shoot them down." Blood dripped from a gash in the armor on his left shoulder.

"How bad?" Alice asked.

"How bad what?" Samuel glanced at his shoulder and cursed. "Didn't even feel it. Must not be too bad." He rooted through his saddlebag and pulled out a swath of white linen. Samuel stuffed it into the break in his armor and nodded.

Jacob couldn't stop the frisson of terror that lanced through his body when a series of high-pitched shrieks echoed up from the tunnel behind the bars. He'd heard it before, and it meant only death.

"Widow Makers," Gladys said. "Nothing else makes that sound."

"Nothing I've met before," Samuel said.

"Here they come!" Smith shouted. "Ready!"

The Red Death poured onto the tracks first. They weren't smart enough to realize that's where everyone was aiming. Cannon fire and bolts and Smith's chaingun shattered the first wave of Red Death. Dead and broken carapaces slid to a stop inside the station. Minutes passed before Jacob realized where things were about to go wrong.

"It's full!" he shouted over Smith's chaingun. "They can walk right onto the plat—"

The next wave scampered over the corpses of their fellow invaders, and swung right, mauling and dismembering their defenses on the opposite platform. Jacob physically flinched at the explosion of blood and carnage that tore their allies' lives away.

The Spider Knight beside him fell into a heap. Jacob looked down at the man's face. Samuel's Captain … a round hole leaked blood from his cheek, and the back of his helmet was distorted. Where was his mount? What had happened? What had shot him?

Jacob's eyes snapped up. "Sharpshooters!"

Smith's chaingun elevated before the tinker even had time to aim.

Bullets ricocheted off the stone before cutting into a half dozen sharp-shooters. Flesh and ropes separated in the hail of gunfire. The living ones retreated above the breach, but Jacob knew they'd be back.

Something slammed against the far gate. The gate that protected them from the things below.

Smith shouted over the chaos. "If it falls, you run. If it falls, *you run!*"

A shadow moved above the tracks outside of the cave, too graceful to be an invader, and far too large to be a railcar.

"What is that?" Jacob asked.

"Mary ..." Smith said, his voice not much more than a whisper. "What are you doing?"

The shadow of the Skysworn vanished a moment later, devoured by something wider, and longer, something that shouldn't be there.

Jacob shivered and pointed. "It's one of Belldorn's warships!"

He hadn't finished speaking before fire and sparks streaked from the cannons mounted all across the Porcupine. The earth shook as the shells detonated, bathing the side of the mountain in fire.

Jacob ran to the edge of station and joined a small cluster of soldiers at the tracks. His jaw slackened at the wall of Red Death still surging up the mountainside. Craters from the cannon fire showed remnants of a hundred dead beetles, but for every pile of dead, there seemed a thousand more of the skull-like glowing eyes. The chainguns opened fire, strafing the wall and sending fountains of gore up all across the mountainside.

The Skysworn's lone chaingun joined that percussive cacophony of destruction, tearing through hundreds of Red Death and—if the rain of blood and viscera said anything—the remaining sharpshooters at the station's entrance. No matter how many died, the horde didn't stop.

The screams began. Screeches of warning, hysterical shouts, and the terrible clicking chatter of a thousand Red Death surging through the caves below Ancora.

"Fall back!" Cage's voice carried above the shouts and gunfire that turned the world to chaos. "To the catacombs!"

Jacob didn't look back. The noise was all he needed to know. He ran, crossing the bridge as fast as his feet would carry him. The scream of failing metal sounded behind him, and he didn't have to see it. The gates had failed. Metal slammed against stone in a thunderous calamity, and the very air shook with the sound.

Jacob risked a look back over his shoulder and slid to a stop. Gladys was back there. She was limping and had George's arm around her shoulders, helping him move through the throng of panicked men and women. The Red Death flowed from the shattered gate, piling one atop the other, screeching as they went, and the Widow Makers took to the ceilings.

Men from Fel swung into the station with the horde. Some were trampled by their own supposed allies, but others ran freely among the Red Death, untouched and nearly impossible to track.

"Above you!" Jacob screamed. He raised the air cannon and fired. One of the Widow Makers went to pieces, raining down onto the Red Death and dying resistance below. The horde trampled two dozen people in a heartbeat.

A shock of red hair ran past him. Alice sprinted to Gladys and George, taking George's weight from the other side. Jacob couldn't hear what they were saying, but it looked like George was yelling for them to leave him behind.

One of the Fel soldiers leapt out of the tide of Red Death, running at Alice, running at his friends.

"Alice!" he screamed and pointed. He didn't have a clear shot. He'd hit George or Alice or Gladys.

Alice dropped George's arm and spun. The soldier hesitated, and Alice uppercut him through the lower jaw. The anchoring bolt fired into his brain, sending a spray of blood from his mouth. Alice didn't stop to watch him die. She was back with George and Gladys a moment later. The soldier's corpse vanished into the crush of invaders.

Jacob pulled a Firebomb and a Burner out of the pouch at his waist. He clicked the igniter, closed the outer shell, and hurled it as far as he could. It bounced off a Red Death and then vanished into the horde by the gate.

The explosion rocked the entire station. Dust and loose rock fell from the ceiling, peppering invaders and allies alike. The tunnel channeled the blast, tearing apart forty feet worth of Red Death in either direction.

"Go!" Jacob screamed when Alice and the others reached him. He raised the air cannon and fired again, and again. The relentless pop of a chaingun tore through the air, laying waste to the first line of Red Death and strafing the ceiling. Widow Makers fell into the horde to be trampled and consumed by the beetles.

Jacob backed quickly, bumping into allies and tripping over the dead. The sharpshooters had taken out more people than he'd realized. Knights and resistance fighters alike were discarded and trampled in a grotesque mixture of blood and bodies and death.

The walls of the catacombs closed in around him as he backed into the corridor. Smith stood at the entrance, strafing where he could.

A blood-soaked Cage came running at them at full speed, flanked by Drakkar. The left side of Cage's helmet was a ruin of mangled metal. The blood running down his neck said the wound beneath wasn't superficial.

"Use the bombs!" Cage shouted. "We have four ways out of here. There's still a chance. Bring it down!"

"Fall back!" Smith said. "Drakkar, the bombs are in my backpack! Use a Banger!"

The Cave Guardian didn't hesitate. He pushed on Smith's back, located the bombs, and pulled them out in three quick motions. Jacob handed Drakkar three Bangers, one for each of the monstrous bombs.

"Last three!" Smith shouted. "Make them count!" He stepped forward and strafed the horde, leaving enough room for Drakkar to step forward and hurl the bombs.

Jacob watched the bombs arc through the air. If the tunnels fell on top of them, that was the end. No one could survive a cave-in like that. One sailed to the front of station, the second closer to the breach into the lower tunnels, and the last shattered a window on the old bookstore.

Smith's chaingun clicked when his last belt fell empty, and he grabbed Drakkar, pulling everyone back behind the mounted chaingun. It was only then that Jacob realized some of the steam and smoke he thought rose from the chaingun actually rose from Smith's biomechanics. The tinker grunted and cursed as he disengaged the biomech boosts he must have been running since the battle started.

Jacob pumped the air cannon and blasted the nearest invaders.

Alice already had her fingers wrapped around the trigger when Smith stumbled past, and the chaingun roared to life, cutting through the first of the invaders to reach the catacombs. She couldn't stabilize the fire the way Smith had with his biomechanics, but the wild shots still cut a deadly path.

Jacob stared and shot into that writhing sea of death. Nothing but darkness and bursts of fire greeted his eyes in the wait for the bombs. He didn't think the delay had ever seemed so long. When Red Death and Widow Makers began to crush themselves, pushing into the catacombs, the bombs detonated.

CHAPTER THIRTY-NINE

MARY STARED OUT of the Skysworn's windscreen. The mountainside smoked where the entrance to the underground station once stood. Now, for all she knew, her friends were lost and buried.

She glanced at the floating fortress beside her. A Porcupine warship in Ancora ... how? Why?

The speaker beside her crackled to life. "Skysworn, this is Archibald, come in."

Mary blinked and stared at her transmitter. She clicked the button. "Archibald?"

"Yes. I apologize for the radio silence. It was necessary."

"What about Bollwerk?"

"The city still stands, guarded by Warship Two and a Porcupine. Your bombing run slowed Ballern's fleet and evened the engagement. We cut them down, thanks to your discovery of a weakness. Speaking of which, the Master at Arms of this fine warship would like to ask about those bombs. Another time, though, another time. We had to dock Warship Two for repairs, but it should be back in the skies before long."

Bollwerk survived the attack after all. She'd been worried that no place would go unscathed in this mad conflict. Mary's gaze roved across the cratered mountain. A few surviving Red Death skittered aimlessly inside the debris. The horde itself lay mangled and shattered across the earth, except for what had made it inside.

"Archibald?"

A burst of static preceded his response. "Yes?"

"Smith and the others were in the station when it collapsed." Saying the words gave them truth, and the thought of Smith lost in that ruin cut her to the bone.

"There are miles of tunnels beneath Ancora," Archibald said. "Charles ..." Archibald laughed and sighed. "Charles used to say if you straightened out the tunnels beneath Ancora, they'd stretch all the way to Belldorn."

"They knew about the tunnels," Mary said. "They were planning to reach Parliament through them."

"Do not lose hope. If the entire station is gone, they'll be forced to climb up through Parliament, or one of the old watchtowers. Either path will bring them into the courtyard in front of the Castle."

Mary let the Skysworn drift higher, until she could see over the wall. There were still soldiers sprawled across the courtyard. Men still fought and bled and died. If Smith and the others had survived the collapse ... what if they weren't in good enough shape to fight again? A cluster of men dressed in knight-like armor stood at one end of the courtyard. The dead citizens around their feet told Mary all she needed to know.

Mary clicked her transmitter. "Then we clear a path."

Archibald released a cold, terrifying laugh. "Allow my new friends to assist you."

The Porcupine rose beside the Skysworn.

✧   ✧   ✧

JACOB'S FATHER HAD once told him what a mine collapse felt like. The thunder, and darkness, and hopeless terror that rose up while the world swallowed you.

The bombs added their own instruments to the chaotic symphony of stampeding invaders and the cannon fire of a warship outside. The first shattered hundreds of Red Death, causing the press of beetles and Widow Makers in the catacombs to slide back out into the station, the pressure behind them no longer there.

It cleared the tunnel enough that Jacob and the others could see into the station when the second bomb exploded. A short burst of flame and light showed the shattering of a thousand carapaces as it shook the earth beneath their feet and ripped through the bridges above the tracks.

The last blew out the face of the bookstore, and though Jacob couldn't see it from that angle, he knew where the glass and brick came from. More bugs broke apart into a mass of gooey black pieces. The dying glow of their red eyes made a terrifying spectacle.

The shaking didn't stop. It rose into a frantic shiver as the mountain shifted. Stone and rock and steel fell from the cavern ceiling, crushing Red Death and sending Widow Makers to the tracks in pops of gore. Cannon fire echoed from outside the station, and the reports still shook the air, but the shaking beneath their feet was something more. The mountain roared as larger and larger pieces fell into the remnants of the old station. A boulder the size of a house gave way, bringing mud and water with it.

"Yes!" someone shouted from the catacombs behind Jacob.

Jacob glanced at Alice when she let off the chaingun. The worry etched across her brows only confirmed what he thought. There was nothing good about that at all.

"Fall back!" Smith shouted. "It is caving in!" The tinker threw his own chaingun onto the ground and picked up Alice's instead.

Jacob wrapped his fingers into Alice's and forced their way into the throng of men and women and children behind them.

"Follow me!" Jacob shouted. "I'll lead you out."

The earth shook again. One glance back toward the station showed him only darkness and a rough stone wall where the entrance to the catacombs once stood. Smith's discarded chaingun lay crushed on one end, entombed beneath a massive stone.

Jacob's heart leapt until he found the tinker on the edge of the cave by one of the mummies, staring wide-eyed at the fallen cavern. Everyone froze as the thundering collapse continued and dust rose up in heavy clouds around the blocked entrance.

Alice slid her arms around Jacob and shivered. "Where are the others?"

He didn't know. He'd lost track of Samuel and Bessie, and Gladys and George. Drakkar stood beside Smith. He held a lantern and led the tinker through the shouting masses until they reached Jacob.

"Lead them back to the interrogation room," Drakkar said. "We can get back to the surface through there."

"Have you seen Samuel?" Alice asked. "Or Gladys or George? I haven't seen Gladys since we came back to the catacombs."

Drakkar took a deep breath and shouted, "Silence!"

The entire room quieted.

"Princess, are you here?"

A shuffling at the far end of the room, by the wall of dead nobles, ended in a girl climbing up onto one of the crypts. Gladys, bloodied but alive, waved.

"Is George with you?" Drakkar shouted. "Is he well?"

"Yes, and mostly."

Drakkar nodded.

Something shifted above them and caught Jacob's eye. "Bessie?" The Jumper hung from the ceiling. Her saddle was empty save for a splash of blood. Jacob's voice rose and panic turned his stomach. "Samuel?"

An old man with a bandage wrapped around his upper arm looked up. "You looking for the knight that rides that?"

"Her," Jacob said. "Bessie's a her."

The old man nodded. "He's over in that makeshift hospital they set up down the hall. Took a nasty blow to his left arm. Should live though, long as it doesn't get infected."

"Where at?" Jacob asked. He pushed forward as fast as he could, dragging Alice with him.

When they were closer, the bandaged man pointed deeper into the catacombs. "Second or third hall on the left. Leads to a ... well, I think it's the room they used to prep these mummies."

"Thank you," Jacob said with a frown. "Can you start taking these people down to the lake?"

"The lake, young sir?"

Farther into the catacombs, past the halls, you'll find a lake. It's near the exit. I'll lead you there, but I need to check on my friend."

The old man smiled and nodded. "I would be glad to be of some use, young sir." His voice took on an authority that surprised Jacob. The frail old man was not what he seemed. "Attention, all. Take those who cannot travel into the hospital. The rest with me. We make for the underground lake and wait for our young master."

He turned back to Jacob and whispered. "Now go. I'll keep an eye on your other friends for you."

Jacob stumbled forward. "Who are you?"

"A friend of Charles von Atlier, Jacob. Let us leave it at that."

There were a dozen more questions he wanted to shout at the man, but Samuel was the priority. Once they'd seen Samuel, they could leave, and hopefully take the Spider Knight with them.

Jacob thought the crowds might thin somewhat in the burial hall, but he was wrong. The crowds of wounded, screaming, terrified people seemed to grow closer, stealing the very air from his lungs. Alice dragged him forward when his pace slowed, until one of the tunnels on the left showed a light in the distance. She darted into the passageway, her hand wrapped firmly in Jacob's.

Shouts echoed in the passageway behind them. Jacob glanced back and saw the line beginning to drift past the hall, toward the lake. Jacob and Alice rounded the corner into a surprisingly large room, fitted with a few small cots. Most of the wounded were on the floor, and Jacob grimaced at the small pile of dead stacked unceremoniously in the corner.

"Samuel ..." Alice's voice drew Jacob's gaze to the floor not far away.

A blanket covered the Spider Knight's left arm, forming a makeshift bandage, but the blood soaking through told the worst of the story. Samuel's eyes flashed open and he sat up before his face crumbled in agony. After a few deep breaths, he looked up at Alice and then Jacob.

"What are you two doing here? There's still a battle going on."

Jacob shook his head. "We collapsed the station. We don't ... we don't know what's going on out there now."

Alice crouched down and put her hands on Samuel's ankle. "We're taking the survivors out through Parliament."

Samuel nodded. "My left arm's useless, but I can walk. I'll help clear out the hospital."

"There are more coming," Alice said.

Samuel sighed. "I'll wait with them. Have you seen Bessie?"

Alice nodded quickly. "She's hanging out on the ceiling."

Samuel smiled and blew a quick puff of air out through his nose. "Crazy girl. Here ..." He handed Alice a pouch with white powder inside. "She has a leg wound, and that saddle's cutting into her other legs. Pat the wounds down with this. It'll stop the bleeding. The nurse here used it on my arm."

A short brunette nurse nodded. "I did at that. Kept saying he had to save it for his spider. Damned fool knight."

"No arguments here," Alice said.

The nurse smiled. "You two go with the others. I see they're moving."

"Go," Samuel said. "We'll catch up." He raised his right fist and Jacob wrapped his fingers over it. Alice did the same. "Now go."

They scooted back toward the burial hall as fast as they could.

Alice glanced toward the front room where they'd stood with Smith and the others. "There's no way we're getting back to Bessie through this."

"Don't need to," Jacob said. He slid the Spider Knight Whistle out of a pants pocket as they started down the hall. Jacob played Bessie's song, and several of the people around them gave him a nasty look at the sudden explosion of sound.

Alice glanced at the ceiling. "She'll fit, but it's going to be tight for a while."

"We'll be to the lake soon enough," Jacob said. "She'll have room there." He glanced back toward the opposite end of the hall when someone shouted. He couldn't see anything, but he was hopeful that meant Bessie was on her way.

The spider caught up to them a few minutes later, following along the ceiling. She reached down with her forelegs and pulled at Alice's hair. Alice patted the spider's foot and smiled. Bessie kept pace with them the rest of the way, until they finally entered the deep chamber with the underground lake.

Bessie skittered onto the wall and stayed beside Alice until they reached the other end of the room. Jacob patted his thigh, and the spider jumped down to a small clearing.

Alice pulled open the little leather pouch filled with white powder. "Where's the old man?"

Jacob looked around. "I don't know. Let's get Bessie patched up and get out of this place. They're still fighting on the surface."

Alice took a handful and treated a split in one of Bessie's legs. "Looks like a spear or something." She hissed out a breath. "Looks bad, but the bleeding's stopping."

Jacob treated the wounds where the saddle had cut into the spider's legs.

"What are you kids doing with that spider? We need to get out of here!"

"We're done," Jacob said, unable to find the source of the voice. "This spider is one of our friends. Her knight helped save you today. Don't forget that."

"Bessie," Alice said. "Wait here for Samuel."

Jacob didn't know if the spider really understood what Alice was saying, but Bessie bounced up and down a few times and then sprang up onto the wall. Jacob unhooked the lantern from his vest and started into the dimly lit path up ahead. It narrowed enough that only three smaller people could stand shoulder to shoulder.

He glanced at Alice. "It's going to take forever to get these people back to the courtyard."

Alice leaned closer. "Then we better get started."

Jacob stopped in front of the broken grate and stared down at the bloodied floor inside. He kicked the bars out of the wall, and they fell to the stone below in a ringing clatter of iron and rock.

CHAPTER FORTY

JACOB STARED INTO the lock on the heavy door and sighed. This was their only option since Smith had barricaded their previous exit. "I'm no good at picking a lock this complex, Alice. Anyone else?"

The room was filled with people, and more were climbing in through the broken window by the minute.

"Break it down," Alice said.

"What?"

She gestured to his leg.

Jacob frowned, shrugged, and pulled the cuff of his pants up high enough to reach the levers. He pulled one up until it clicked and fell to the opposite side before doing the same with the lever by his built-in tourniquet.

A shaky voice said, "You're a Mech? He's a Mech!"

Jacob glanced back. It was younger woman, not much older than Alice. She backed away from him, clawing past men and women alike as a round of shouts began to grow. Jacob looked back down at his leg and sighed.

"Yes, I'm an Ancoran, I'm a Biomech, and I'm fighting to save this city."

Alice backed away from the door, and Jacob stepped into his kick. The door didn't give by very much, but the frame cracked. More mutters went up behind him, but he blocked them out, focused, and slammed his foot into the iron handle.

The bowed metal collapsed, and the ironwood frame shattered, letting the door fly open to slam against the stone wall behind it.

"Stairs?" Alice asked, sticking her head through the doorway.

Jacob stepped through and looked up. "Spiral stairs, like the watchtower we used before."

"If it's a watchtower, it's a way out," Alice said.

Jacob nodded and turned to the group. "Be ready for anything. Keep your weapons up if you still have them."

Someone muttered something about shooting the Mech. Jacob planned to ignore it, but Alice … Alice stepped into the small room and punched someone hard enough to put them on the floor.

"There's half a dozen Biomechs fighting for you," Alice spat, leaning over a bloodied man lying on the stones. "You threaten my friends again, and I won't have the safety engaged." She tugged on her heavy nail glove and stormed up the stairs.

Jacob followed, glancing between the shocked look on the man's face, and Alice's backside. Someone helped the man up, and the group surged around him, following Jacob and Alice up the stairs.

"You could have killed him," Jacob said as he hurried up a few steps to catch Alice.

She didn't respond.

Jacob shook his head. The footsteps of dozens of people echoed around them in the stone stairwell. Hushed voices and thinly veiled accusations joined the echoes. Jacob tuned it out. They were alive, and they were moving.

"You know they'll talk," Alice said. "Everyone's going to know about you."

"It's just a leg, Alice." He reached up and awkwardly squeezed her shoulder. "It's just a leg."

She turned her head and gave him a small smile. The lantern light cast her eyes into a half shadow that made them seem infinite. The light changed, and the illusion left as quickly as it had appeared.

They continued up the stairs in silence until they reached a landing set with an iron-barred door. Alice tried the handle.

She glanced at Jacob. "It's unlocked."

He took a deep breath. "Let's see what we can." He pulled the air cannon off his back and racked the cold brass slide. Jacob turned to the staircase behind them and said, "Be ready. We don't know what's waiting."

Alice pushed the door open, and they swarmed into the moonlit courtyard.

"Oh gods," Alice said, her voice cracking.

The center of the courtyard lay filled with the dead. There were Lowland refugees and Highland nobles alike. They'd fought, and died, together. To the north, beside the Castle, a small group of armed citizens gathered, yet another mixture of Lowlands and Highlands wielding everything from walking sticks to gilded crossbows. Far to the east, almost to the opposite wall, a cadre of knights and mercenaries formed ranks.

Jacob watched in awe and horror as that mass of silver and bronze began marching toward them. It wouldn't be another minute before they were in range of the crossbows and small arms.

Someone fired from the enemy line, and a bolt landed not five feet from them. Jacob raised the air cannon. The boom drowned out the shouts of the people around him, and one of the mercenaries stumbled to the side.

A metallic voice sounded behind them. "Fire."

Jacob turned to see a Porcupine cresting the wall—becoming a hellish fireball as its mortars roared to life. The mercenaries finally understood. Some tried to run. Some screamed, and some fell to their knees. The whistling of the mortars cut off on impact.

Mushrooms of flame and earth and stone erupted into the air. Soldiers died in the span of a heartbeat. The far watchtower began to crumble. By the time the second wave of mortars hit, the battle was already over.

Disbelief warred with joy and relief and rage inside Jacob's chest. Tears ran down his cheeks, and he saw the same on Alice's face. Alice. She was still here. He was still here. Jacob raised the air cannon to the heavens and screamed.

Alice's shouts joined his own, and the cries spread down their line. The Butcher was dead, and Ancora's people still lived. And there, in that ruin of flesh and stone and fire, they were one people.

JACOB WATCHED THE Porcupine circle and finally descend into the courtyard. It hovered, not twenty feet off the ground, when a large section of the steel hull hissed and lowered between two of the front cannons. Soldiers garbed in armor with a midnight blue sheen marched out of the light of the airship's hold, and almost vanished in the darkness of the courtyard.

They lined up, row after row, forming ranks that passed the front gates of the Castle. A few squads peeled away and disappeared into the streets and towers of Ancora. Jacob stepped closer when a lone figure appeared at the top of the ramp.

"Is that …" Alice's hand reached out and squeezed Jacob's briefly.

"I think so. Come on." He walked at the line of soldiers until the nearest raised his hand.

"Halt!"

"Archibald," Jacob said.

The Speaker of Bollwerk wore a flowing royal-blue cape as he descended from the warship. He was imposing, awe inspiring, and a total stranger. Every bootfall sent a ringing echo across the courtyard before the smoldering ruin of the watchtower. The lines of soldiers who answered to the Speaker of Bollwerk lent a feeling of true power to his presence.

"It's like it's not even him," Jacob whispered.

"Power is an illusion."

Jacob jerked in surprise. When he turned around, Drakkar was smiling at him.

The Cave Guardian kept his voice quiet. "No person is much greater or lesser than any other, but those with an army command the illusion."

Jacob stared at Drakkar. It was easy to forget that the quiet man was a scholar and a fighter.

"Stand down, Captain." Archibald's voice drew the attention of all who were around him. "Jacob, Alice, Drakkar, all of you." He motioned for the group to join him.

Someone patted Jacob's shoulder, and he glanced back to find Mary smiling beside Smith and Cage.

The crowds huddled along the wall crept closer, and Archibald clicked a button on his collar.

"Ancorans." Archibald's voice boomed from the hold of the Porcupine, tinny and filled with static, but it demanded attention. "My name is Archibald Jones, and I am the Speaker of Bollwerk."

There were shouts of absolute rage sent up by some of the older men and women in the courtyard, but others called for calm. A wave of voices circled the area, and Archibald waited for the outburst to die down before he spoke again.

"I know," he said. "I know we have a ... colorful history. There are things we must never forget from the Deadlands War, but we must set them aside if we are to survive what awaits us all. You know now your city smith was the Butcher, Newton Burns. What you may not be aware of is the fact he did not act alone.

"I say to you this: none of us will survive a combined assault from Ballern and Fel if we let old biases divide us. We have had decades of peace and prosperous trade. We have come to depend on each other for foods and goods and medicines, and we are all stronger for it.

"Belldorn sent two of her mighty warships to protect Bollwerk. With their assistance," Archibald said as he placed a hand on Mary's shoulder, "we fought off a fleet of Ballern's destroyers. I sent our warships to free Dauchen from Fel's grasp, and Dauschen sent its men here to free you." Archibald squeezed Cage's shoulder before he stepped forward and settled his hands on the shoulders of Jacob and Alice. "And you, Ancorans, have fought from the beginning."

Archibald paused, and barely a whisper rose. "We have all suffered loss." He raised his arms to the south. "Our cities. Our friends. Our family. But we must persist, for if the rumors are true—and I assure you we *will* discover the truth—Ballern has three dozen more destroyers."

Whispers and cries went up around the courtyard. Declarations of an inevitable fate for the Northlands, the end of Ancora, and the failure of the trade alliance.

Jacob's gaze followed the ring of bystanders. He saw fear and resignation, and it felt as though the light of Ancora had gone out. It was an awful thing. Jacob laced his fingers through Alice's and squeezed.

Archibald studied the crowd, looking for something, or someone. "Princess," he said as he held out his hand and gestured to the watchtower.

Jacob turned and almost cried when he saw Samuel standing beside Bessie with a very bandaged George, and Gladys.

She walked forward with George. Gladys had cleaned some of the blood from her face since last Jacob had seen her, but it was still obvious, and her chest was stained red.

Gladys stopped beside Alice and laced their fingers together. Archibald held out his hand. Gladys took it with her free hand and joined him in the center of the guards.

"This, my friends, is Gladys, Princess of Midstream. You all know the story of that lost city, crushed by rampaging Mechs, only to be terrorized by warlords and plagued by the fears many of our cities harbored for their differences."

Gladys looked sad, and Jacob wanted to hug her and remind her that he and Alice didn't feel that way. George seemed downright normal next to Drakkar, and hell, they even liked Drakkar quite a lot. Jacob glanced up at the Cave Guardian beside him, a man who had fought for a city full of people who feared him.

"The last of Midstream's royalty now lives within the walls of Bollwerk." The boom of Archibald's amplified voice drew all the attention of the courtyard back to him. "It is my intention to help them rebuild, and become stronger."

Gladys no longer looked sad. She looked stunned.

"The reconstruction efforts are already under way in Dauschen," Archibald said. "In time, their medicines will flow freely between the cities once more."

The crowd grew louder, talking amongst themselves.

Archibald raised his voice. "Ballern would make ashes of us all. Our peoples would be lost to history. The Northlands *must* stand together!" Archibald's calm, placid tone cracked, and a passion appeared that Jacob hadn't seen in the man before. "We must drive back out any aggressors! We'll need Cave," he said, landing a heavy hand on Drakkar's shoulder, "and Belldorn, and Ancora, and *all* of the Northlands to stand as one. If we do not, our very country will be lost to Ballern's warmongers.

Small cheers and a round of shouts started around the courtyard. A few dissenters cast an understandable doubt on Archibald's claims.

"Know this ..." His voice fell to almost a whisper, and then the passion returned.

"I will not leave Ancora in ruins. I will help my friends rebuild and raise the walls once more. Your gates will be restored. The Lowlands will be rebuilt, and with our armies at each other's sides, Ballern will fall!

"So I ask you, people of Ancora, will you stand with me? Will you fight to restore your home?"

Goosebumps marched down Jacob's arms as more people shouted, coming forward to pledge their support of Archibald and his mad plan. And there, in the middle of it all, stood a Spider Knight and his mount. Samuel slid the halberd from Bessie's saddle and took a knee, his bandaged arm showing signs of fresh blood.

The Spider Knight took a deep breath and shouted, "Aye! My blade is yours!"

Half the courtyard echoed Samuel, and Archibald visibly relaxed. Gladys cried beside the man, and he placed a hand on her shoulder.

"This will not be an easy journey, my friends, but we will have a better world when it is done. The gates will be rebuilt. You will all be safe inside the Highlands this night. These fine soldiers from Belldorn will help support the remaining Spider Knights and the few knights left behind still loyal to Ancora."

"Thank you." A rumble of agreement rounded the courtyard.

"It is the least I can do," Archibald said. "Gather what leaders you trust. There is a great deal of planning ahead."

He clicked the button on his collar, and the static-laden buzz from the Porcupine died away.

"You're going to rebuild Midstream?" Gladys asked, her voice shaking and cracked.

"Yes. It should have been done half a century ago. I am sorry I allowed the warlords to rule the deserts, Princess."

Gladys curtsied and took a hesitant step toward Archibald. When he opened his arms, she launched herself at him. Archibald looked up at Drakkar. His gaze trailed to Samuel and Alice, and the injured George being helped forward by Smith. Finally he turned to Jacob.

"Charles would be proud."

CHAPTER FORTY-ONE

THE PORCUPINE WAS a monstrous ship. Every corridor seemed as wide as the Skysworn, and every room they passed large enough to fit twenty soldiers. Archibald led them through the heart of the warship, and Jacob wanted to stop and study the mass of gauges and levers and valves clustered around the largest boiler he'd ever seen.

Smith paused and whistled. "Archibald, where are you taking us? I would rather like to stop and speak with the engineers in this place."

The Speaker glanced over his shoulder. "You'll have time, Smith. For now, come with me. It's important."

No one spoke for some time. Jacob kept his fingers laced together with Alice's. Samuel stayed behind to be looked at by some of Archibald's medics, and George.

"Here," Archibald said, pushing through a thin bronze door.

The room beyond bathed them in a dim golden light. Jacob let go of Alice's hand and followed her into that shadowed space before freezing in his tracks. On the far wall stood a Steamsworn fist the equal of Gareth Cave.

"Gods ..." Smith said. "From Belldorn?"

Archibald nodded. "I was surprised myself. The tinkers you met? They'd been carrying the mantle of the Steamsworn for decades. Taught by Targrove."

Jacob looked up at Smith, and the man's eyes were red.

Smith rubbed at his face. "I did not know. No one ever told us, or I would have stayed. I could have helped them with so much …"

"You can help them now," Archibald said. "You and your new apprentice." He nodded at Jacob. "If you're planning to take him on, of course."

Smith smiled and laughed with tears leaking from the corners of his eyes. "Gods yes. A proper trade … an alliance with Belldorn, and a Steamsworn apprentice. I would be honored."

"He's not Steamsworn yet," Archibald said as he stepped away from the fist. "But this is as good as any cave for that old oath. Do you know the oath, Jacob?"

Jacob nodded. "I do. Alice does too."

"I'm not a Biomech," Alice said.

Gladys stepped up beside her. "Doesn't matter. You don't have to be a Biomech to take the oath." She pulled her hair up into a bun and looked down, exposing the nape of her neck. A Steamsworn fist stood etched into her skin, a tattoo that would stay with her to the grave and beyond.

"I have not sworn in an oath taker in some fifteen years," Archibald said. "There comes a time when you don't want to set foot into Gareth Cave ever again. But here, inside one of the warships of Belldorn, welcoming new Steamsworn to the fold feels right, like a new beginning. If you would join us, take the oath."

Jacob looked at Alice. His question didn't need to be said aloud. She nodded. Jacob took a deep breath and stepped toward the Steamsworn fist. He'd read *The Dead Scourge* enough to memorize half the book, and the oath was something he'd never forget. He started with the first word, and Alice joined.

Through the black we ride once more
Within the flames our fortune's told
The gates of Hell lie broken wide

Within the steam, no hold abides

Feared and cast upon the stones
We fight to save the sacred lives
When all is done and all are safe
Find me in that Steamsworn grave

Archibald nodded. "Welcome to the Steamsworn."

Tears rolled down Jacob's cheek at the end. Alice sniffed and wiped her eyes. He put his arm around her shoulders and squeezed. Maybe it was the honor of joining the Steamsworn, or knowing that Charles and Smith and so many others had taken that same oath, or the tears in his eyes, but the fist seemed to glow brighter.

"There is a power vacuum now," Archibald said. "With the Butcher and most of Parliament dead, there will be more than one person who tries to take control of the reconstruction. Ballern will send its spies to infiltrate our alliance."

"More fighting," Jacob said once the words sank in.

Archibald nodded. "It's likely. I won't lie to you. It's going to be a long and trying time. This city is going to need people who are loyal to it. More loyal to it than any paid politician could ever be. The Northlands' alliances will take work as well. We have a great deal of history to overcome."

"A small task for the Steamsworn," Drakkar said. He slapped Jacob and Alice on the back in turn.

A heavy hand slammed down on Jacob's shoulder, and he turned to find Smith. "I can stay in Ancora for a time. Help with the reconstruction while we start your apprenticeship."

"Oh really?" a voice said from the hall behind them.

"Mary!" Alice said before hopping toward the airship captain and crushing her in a hug.

"You found a place to land?" Archibald asked.

She nodded and said, "Once the courtyard cleared out a bit. We'll need a proper airship dock here if I'm going to ferry you and the kids all over the Northlands, Smith."

"And in Midstream." Gladys gave Archibald a beaming smile.

"Yes," Archibald said with a smile. "You'll need airship docks too, Princess."

"We need to go to Cave," Jacob said. "My parents might still be there."

"I would be honored to help you look," Drakkar said.

Archibald extended his fist to Jacob. "Then we part ways as allies, and friends."

Jacob wrapped his fingers around Archibald's hand. The Speaker nodded, turned to Alice, and extended his fist again.

"At journey's end, come find me in Bollwerk. We have a great deal of planning to do." Archibald traded grips with Smith and Drakkar, and hugged a surprised-looking Mary. "Farewell, friends."

He walked out of the room and disappeared down a dim hallway. Smith led the rest of them back the way they'd come. Eventually the hold opened wide before them.

"What now?" Alice asked.

Jacob laced his fingers into hers. "Another journey."

Alice looked to the south. The flames were almost high enough to mimic a sunrise in the early morning.

They left the Castle behind.

ABOUT THE AUTHOR

Eric is a former bookseller, guitarist, and comic seller currently living in Saint Louis, Missouri. A lifelong enthusiast of books, music, toys, and games, he discovered a love for the written word after being dragged to the library by his parents at a young age. When he is not writing, you can usually find him reading, gaming, or buried beneath a small avalanche of Transformers. For more about Eric, see www.ericrasher.com.

57591177R00202

Made in the USA
San Bernardino, CA
20 November 2017